A voice behind Tim hissed, "Shut up!" He began turning, but the voice came again. "You don't move . . . ! You don't move . . . !" Tim recognized the voice, and his heart sank. The voice said, "Lose the gun now!"

Tim tossed his Model 10 in Pyne's direction, where it landed amidst a pile of pine needles.

Emerging from the darkness behind him, he saw a glistening bald pate, and rows of gold necklaces. Ronny. Behind Ronny came another large, dark-haired man he did not know. Both had pistols pointed at him.

Ronny said, "Mr. Pyne, I was just comin' out with my friend Mecro when I seen what was goin' on. Why don't we do this guy and get outta here—the cops're comin'."

Pyne grinned hysterically. Waving his pistol at Tim, he said, "So, Mr. Reardon, I win in the end. You have cost me much, and you will die painfully."

Tim stared hard into his eyes. Somehow, he would kill Michael Pyne. In preparation, he tensed his legs for the leap.

"No, I will give this pleasure to Mecro."

Mecro stepped before Tim and placed his pistol against Tim's crotch. Tim tensed for a last desperate lunge at Pyne. . . .

Also by T. Michael Booth:

PARATROOPER: The Life of General James M. Gavin (co-author)

RETRIBUTION

T. Michael Booth

BALLANTINE BOOKS • NEW YORK

Map designed by Diana Goodwin

 Published in the United States of America by Ballantine Books, a division of Random House, Inc., New York, and simultaneously in Canada by Random House of Canada Limited, Toronto.

Library of Congress Catalog Card Number: 93-90711

ISBN 0-345-37867-9

Manufactured in the United States of America

First Edition: March 1994

10 9 8 7 6 5 4 3 2 1

To
Jackie, A. J., Joe, and Andrea.
Thank you for your patience.

AUTHOR'S NOTE

Bringing the characters and events of this novel to life took a great deal of research, and I am indebted to several people. Blair Wellman embodies Andrea as much as anyone alive, and her help was invaluable. Dr. Joseph C. Booth made it all possible. And the following all contributed: Jim Stehn, Kris and Kim Valente, Melissa Morse, Michael Moore, Jennifer Fernandez, Jeff Doctoroff, Lisa Williams, Gail Ross, Duncan Spencer, Elizabeth Outka, Tony Pulcinella, Ken Goff, and especially Robin Moore, who gave me the encouragement to keep on going while teaching me how to survive the frustration all writers endure. My deepest thank you to all of you.

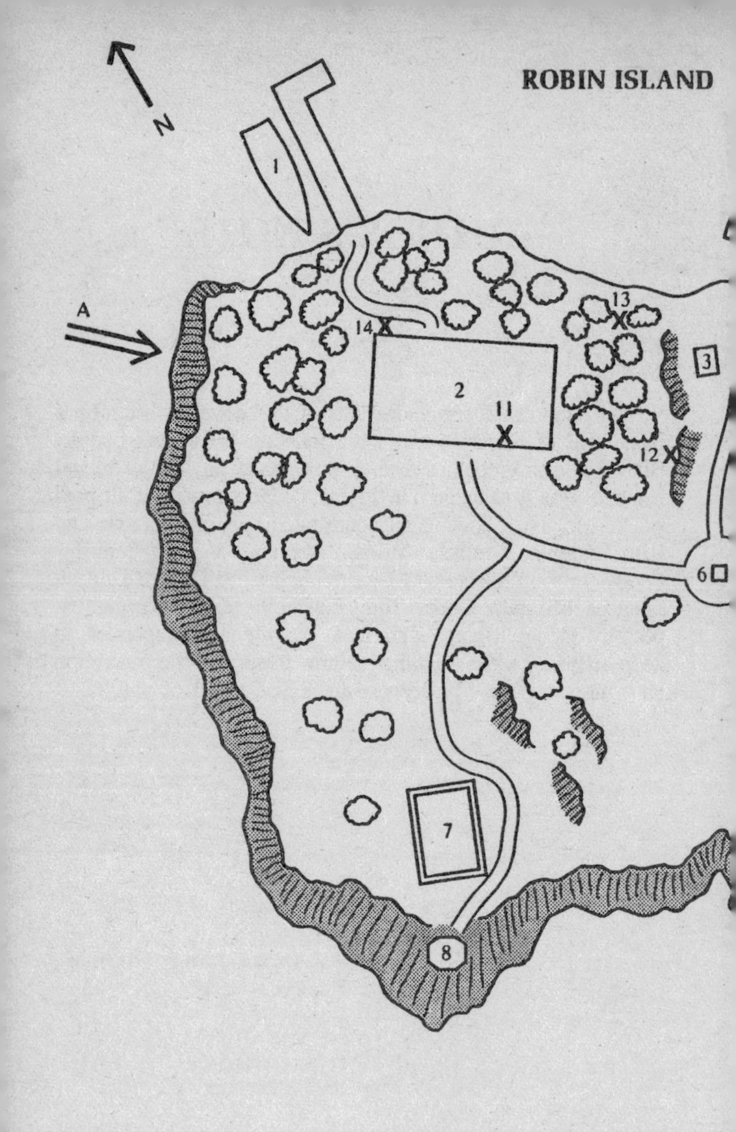
ROBIN ISLAND
N
A
1
2
3
6
7
8
11
12
13
14

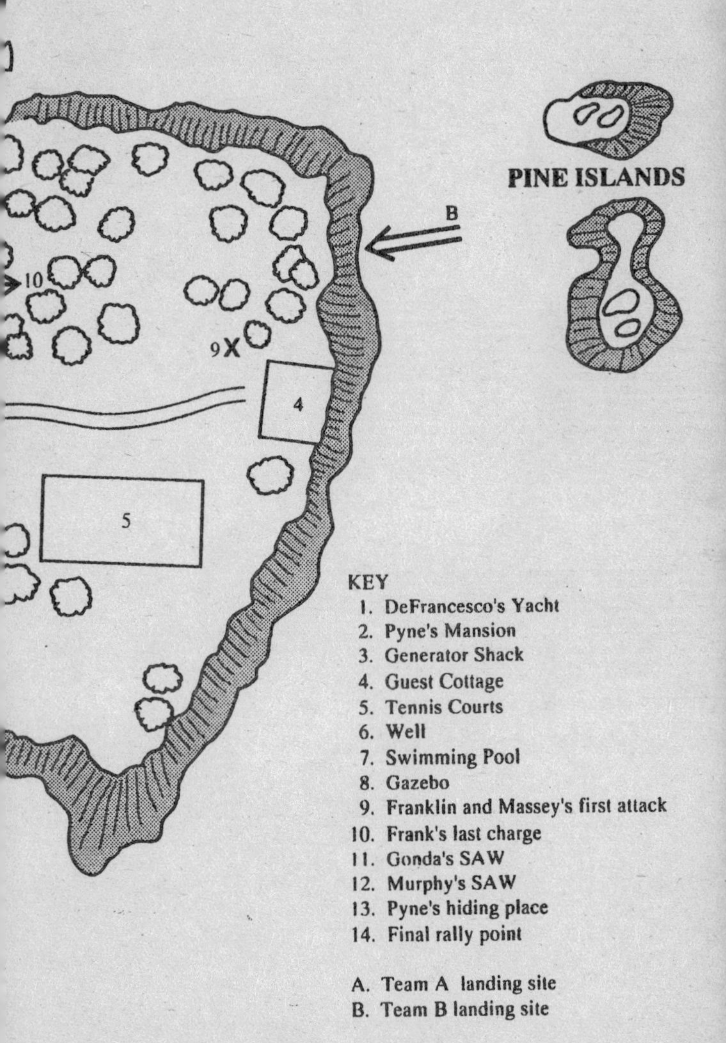

KEY
1. DeFrancesco's Yacht
2. Pyne's Mansion
3. Generator Shack
4. Guest Cottage
5. Tennis Courts
6. Well
7. Swimming Pool
8. Gazebo
9. Franklin and Massey's first attack
10. Frank's last charge
11. Gonda's SAW
12. Murphy's SAW
13. Pyne's hiding place
14. Final rally point

A. Team A landing site
B. Team B landing site

PROLOGUE

7 P.M., Friday, March 17, 1989—New Haven, Connecticut

A custodian at Hill Place High School for nearly twenty years, Emma Jones sloshed her way down Shelton Avenue and pondered once again how much she hated rainy days and pep rallies. She felt certain that the throbbing ache surging up her spine was the result of the awful mess the kids had left behind in the gym and the terrible weather. The pain also reminded her that she was overweight and working entirely too hard for a person past fifty.

As she approached the front gate of her seedy apartment building on Shelton Avenue, Emma remained alert. A longtime Shelton Avenue resident, she knew that vigilance meant survival in this neighborhood, where robberies and shootings were the rule, not the exception. Without this alertness, her talent for noticing the out-of-place, the bodies might have sat until morning.

As she neared her front door, she saw a car parked by her sidewalk; at first it looked much like any other car in the neighborhood, old and needing fresh paint; but as she opened her front gate, she paused. She saw bullet holes in the rain-streaked glass of the passenger window, and something more. Leaving her gate ajar, she cautiously moved closer, one foot following the other, her eyes transfixed on a ghostly blur behind the glass. From just inches away, the blur became a man's face, a face with a small, nearly bloodless hole in its forehead. A second man slumped against the steering wheel. His dead eyes were still wide open, and mangled flesh hung where his left cheek should have been. Clutched in the passenger's right hand was a gold detective's badge.

BOOK ONE

THE TARGET

Where youth grows pale, and spectre thin, and dies.

—John Keats

CHAPTER ONE

8 P.M. Friday, March 17, 1989—New Haven, Connecticut

Detective Sergeant Anthony J. Pulcinella had endured a dismally long day, and he considered it as he drove up Winchester Avenue. As usual, the phone had rung when he had least wanted it to; the desk sergeant had made it clear that once again the detective would not enjoy a quiet evening with his family. The night shift again had more killings than detectives, and the lieutenant had told him to take this one.

Now he struggled to see out the window of his old Plymouth and noted once again that he needed to replace his wipers. He sighed as they fought a losing conflict with the downpour and wondered why people couldn't wait for good weather to kill one another. He hoped the body would at least be inside. He was soon disappointed.

His destination was a crack house in the worst neighborhood in town: a sea of damaged and burned-out buildings where more windows were made of plywood than of glass. He surveyed the front of the gabled house from his car—even for this neighborhood, it was an eyesore. Long abandoned, its soot-stained brick front and ramshackle, collapsing front porch seemed grotesque from the flashing blue and white lights of the patrol cars in front of it.

He paused before opening the car door. Something seemed different—wrong. Shootings and drug deaths happened often in this neighborhood, and few of them received TV news coverage. Yet, there on the overgrown lawn, Pulcinella saw a mad tangle of reporters, cameras, wire, and sound trucks. And amidst it all milled far too many uniforms for a routine death. He popped a piece of hard candy in his mouth and found its sweet taste nearly as reassuring as the cigarettes he had given up some years before. Sighing, he gave the door handle a vigorous push. As usual, the car door creaked and sagged as he opened it, and he had to simultaneously lift and push to slam it closed.

Pulcinella opened his umbrella quickly and ran over the muddy lawn, through the reporters, and past the police cordon with his gold badge extended until he reached the alley beside the house, where a female body lay. The investigation would, in fact, not be indoors.

Police lights flooded the alley with harsh glare, and in their center lay a body surrounded by two uniforms, some coroner's office people, a man Pulcinella recognized from forensics, and two old friends, narcotics detectives Art Foster and Ralph Brown. As Tony approached, Brown, the garrulous one, called, "Hey, Tony! What's this? I didn't know you worked past five."

"Yeah, I know. You people in Vice are the only ones with a job in this city." As the men about the body laughed, Tony eased his way past Brown, stopped, and looked down at the girl. No matter how many times he looked at victims, he still dreaded it—and this one was particularly bad. A now impossibly contorted young woman, teenaged by the look of her, lay amidst a sea of vomit and soggy cigarette butts. Her bulging blue eyes still stared skyward, making her look quizzical. Her makeup had formed haphazard patterns on her badly bruised face. She was naked from the waist down, and her tattered blouse hung open, exposing bloodily mangled breasts. Her pubic hair was soaked with too much blood for the heavy rain to wash away. Without looking up Tony asked, "Everything's been left just like it was found?"

Brown answered, "Yeah, we knew you'd want it that way."

"How 'bout inside the house?"

"Same thing. But so far we ain't found anything in there 'cept the kid's pocketbook and the rest of her clothes. Forensics are working it now. There wasn't much use of their wasting time out here. The rain would've washed anything useful away a long time ago."

Tony nodded and knelt next to the body. Brown helped him

roll her over. Seeing nothing obviously useful, he motioned for the coroner's people to take her away, stood, and let his eyes wander the alley. He saw little there: nothing but overflowing garbage cans, trash bags, and a rusty bicycle frame.

He popped another piece of candy into his mouth and looked back at the body one last time as they slipped it into the bag.

Brown put his hand on Tony's sleeve. "Let's get out of the water and into the house so we can talk."

Tony nodded, and they walked up an overgrown path to the crumbling front porch. Once under shelter, he folded his umbrella and surveyed the reporters out front. He hated dealing with the press.

Turning to Brown, he had to look up. Someday, he mused, there would be a cop on the force shorter than himself. He envied both Brown and Foster their height. Tall cops had presence. Short ones were never taken seriously. Brown was about six foot two, white, with a substantial belly that protruded from his jean jacket. Foster was an inch taller than Brown, black, and a former college football player who could end most conflicts with a stare. Brown did all the talking, and Foster did all the thinking. Together, they were the best vice team in the city.

Brown spoke first. "Tony, you're homicide. They just called us in since it happened at a crack house. This baby's all yours. We're just here to help. OK?"

Tony nodded. He had other things on his mind. Motioning toward the sound trucks in front of the house he asked, "Anybody know why we got all these people here tonight?"

Brown replied, "Yeah, kid's name was Heather Reardon—some kinda special yuppie kid from Branford. You know, the homecoming queen for Branford High School this year, A student, cheerleader. General all-American girl type . . ."

Looking out at the press again, Tony finished the explanation for him. "Oh I see, 'Branford Homecoming Queen Dead in Crack House.' "

Tony turned to Foster. "What you think, Art?"

Foster nodded. "I think we got trouble. Little white angel raped, beaten, and dead in a black neighborhood she ain't got no business being in. This thing ain't gonna die anytime soon."

Tony nodded. "Yeah, except we don't know she was raped

yet. Let's be careful what we say until the coroner's report's ready. You find anything inside?"

"Yeah," Brown responded, "whatever they did to her, they did it there." He motioned toward the front door. "Lots of blood on the floor."

Tony started towards the house. Brown caught his sleeve from behind. "Hey, Pooch! You hear about the Crown Street guys?"

Tony stopped and peered back over his shoulder at Brown. "No, should I know about something?"

"Yeah, somebody wasted two vice guys over on Shelton."

Closing his eyes and exhaling a long breath, he asked, "Who got it?"

"Ferucci and Mongelo."

"Shit! I went to the academy with Ferucci. His wife's gonna fall apart. Christ! What a night!"

Pulcinella opened the front door and headed in. Behind him, he heard Brown echoing, "Yeah, a hell of a fucking night."

6:22 P.M., March 18, 1989—Bad Toelz, West Germany

Staff Sergeant Timothy Reardon stood perplexed before the post commander's office door on an army base known as Flint Kaserne. The young Green Beret wondered why Colonel Dwyer had called for him on a Saturday evening when he should be off duty downtown, admiring young German ladies. He shook his head. He had just three months of military service remaining and had hoped to get out and finish his education at a college in Connecticut this fall with a minimum of fuss. He also hated reporting to the colonel in jeans and a turtleneck, but the duty officer had told him to forget about changing. Tim took a deep breath, threw back his shoulders, straightened his twenty-seven-year-old frame to its full six feet, and rapped his knuckles on the door crisply, as a professional soldier is expected to do.

The colonel called for him to come in. Tim opened the door and felt even more disconcerted as he entered, drew himself to attention, and saluted. Standing and flanking Dwyer, seated behind his desk, were Tim's battalion commander; his battalion command sergeant major; and his team sergeant, Master Sergeant Carl Langdon—sure signs that this was serious. All, he noticed, wore off-duty civilian attire.

His diminutive form accentuated by his massive desk, Dwyer was short, grizzled, and fast approaching fifty. Yet, to Tim's ear, the old soldier's deep voice and slow Southern drawl made him seem much larger than he was.

Tim decided his best course was to be as militarily correct as possible. Trying for a confident demeanor, he said as he saluted, "Sir, Sergeant Reardon reports."

Dwyer looked embarrassed, returned the salute, and said, "At ease, Tim, please take a chair. In fact, everyone sit down."

Tim noticed that the colonel was avoiding his gaze. The old man seemed damned uncomfortable. Dwyer said, "Relax, Tim. I know what this must look like, but you're not in trouble."

Tim nodded in response.

Dwyer continued, "Sergeant, as you know, as the post commander, I try to get acquainted with as many people who live in our community as possible, and one of the first names I learned when I arrived here was yours. Your performance over the last eight years has been outstanding, and the work you have done here in youth activities—coaching, chaperoning—and just being there for the children of our community has been extraordinary. That's what makes what I have to tell you even more difficult." Like a man doing something distasteful, he took a deep breath before continuing. "The Red Cross contacted us today with bad news. It seems that your sister, Heather, with whom I am told you were close . . . died yesterday in Connecticut." He shuffled a paper on his desk.

Tim slumped in his chair. For a moment, his mind ceased working and his body felt numb. Then he realized that Dwyer was continuing. With effort, he tried listening. "At this time, we do not have many details, but we are informed she died violently and that the death may have been drug-related. I have already spoken with your chain of command, and they concur with me that if you need leave to go home and sort things out, it is no problem. As you know, Sergeant, it is within army policy to grant emergency leave for . . ." he cleared his throat as he searched for the right words, "for problems with immediate family members. I like to think of us here in Bad Toelz as kind of a family, and if you need anything, just let us know. The paperwork is already here, and we can have you on a plane tonight. Just sign your DA-31 leave form and we'll get you to the airport in Munich."

Tim barely heard the second half of the colonel's speech. When it ended, the room remained silent for some moments until he realized they expected a reply. "Uh, thank you, sir. I think that would be good. I'll go and pack my stuff."

"Fine, Sergeant. Be back here in a half hour and I'll have the duty officer dispatch a driver to take you to the airport. I can't get you onto a military hop this fast, so you'll have to pay for a commercial flight. Do you have enough?"

"Yes, sir, I'll be fine."

"Then good luck to you, son, and I wish I had better news. You know if there is anything else we can do, don't hesitate to ask. I understand the girl was only seventeen. I'm sorry . . . We're all sorry."

"Thank you, sir."

Tim stood stiffly, saluted out of habit, and left the office feeling far older than his twenty-seven years.

On the way to the airport the driver, unaware of the news Tim had just received, kept up an incessant stream of small talk. Lost in his own thoughts, Tim only half listened.

With the driver's help, he was seated on a sparsely patronized Lufthansa flight to New York by nine P.M., German time. On the near-empty plane, he found the privacy he needed to try to absorb the news.

My God, he thought, she can't be gone! Images of Heather from the past invaded his mind. The night they had lost their parents flashed into focus with vivid intensity. He had been a senior in high school, and Heather had been only eight years old then. He saw with strange clarity the sad face of the social worker who had returned from the Christmas party instead of Mom and Dad. She had told them that their parents had been killed in an automobile accident. Heather had cried for days.

Their mother's sister Marian was the only relative they had had, and she hadn't wanted them. Oh, she had taken them in—appearances were very important to Marian—but Heather and he had always known that they were not wanted. Living with Marian was rough on Heather, especially after Tim left for the army. But he had given her as much time and attention as he could. No matter where he was, he had always responded to her weekly letters, and he had flown her out to visit him at his various postings. It had been a strain financially, but she was the only real family he'd had.

Both of them were farm kids, born in Vermont. Tim had only spent six months in Branford, but that was long enough to convince him that he hated the suburbs. With Marian drunk most nights, his Branford memories were the worst of his life. Heather, though, had been far younger than Tim. She had adapted, and for the most part, had managed to raise herself—and she had done a terrific job. This spring, she'd been about to graduate at the top of her class. She had had a bright future. How could she be dead? Drugs! The colonel had said drugs had killed her! No! He knew Heather, and she took no drugs. Whatever they said, whatever had happened, he would never believe she had overdosed.

For the first time since Tim had lost his parents, he felt tears running down his cheeks. He reached above his head and turned off the reading light. Darkness comforted him. It was a hiding place, a place for gathering his resolve. He was going to find out what had happened to Heather.

March 18, 1989—Thimble Islands, off Branford, Connecticut

The Thimble Islands lie in a chain off the central Connecticut coastline. Once a haven for pirates and smugglers, today they are, for the most part, a playground for a few very wealthy individuals. Robin Island is the largest of the chain to remain under individual ownership.

This morning, the owner of Robin Island, Michael F. Pyne, stood with his attorney in an old but well-maintained gazebo on a small spur jutting from the base of a hill on which his eighteen-bedroom English country house stood.

The storm that had lashed New Haven the previous evening was still working its fury upon the Thimbles, so Pyne's view of the waves lashing the brown rocks below was spectacular. Rough seas had held the launch from its morning run to the town dock, so the helicopter had flown to the shore. It returned with the day's mail, the newspapers, and his attorney, George Rembard.

Rembard and Pyne were both thin and Princeton-educated, but their similarities stopped there. Pyne was short and the lawyer towered over him. Pyne had thick, immaculately groomed black hair that no amount of wind and rain could ruffle. Gray streaked Rembard's thinning blond hair, and the wind played havoc with it.

On this particular day, there was much for Pyne and Rembard to discuss. In spite of his public image as a fantastically successful investment banker, Michael Pyne was not in banking at all. He had once been a junior clerk on Wall Street, but he had failed at the job. However, with a powerful instinct for self-preservation and a keen eye for a fast buck, he had used his Wall Street connections to his advantage; during the cocaine boom of the early 1980s he had become a major player in the illicit drug trade. The drug business had provided the power and notoriety Pyne had always yearned for, and now he controlled one of the largest direct Colombian cocaine pipelines to the Northeast.

Rembard began, "Mike, I'm afraid this I.R.S. investigation is the real thing. I'm not sure how much they can prove, but there is no doubt they at least know your business. It is going to be rough in front of that grand jury."

"George, you are supposed to be the best. Why should I worry about the I.R.S.? That's why I hired you."

Rembard fidgeted. "This 'war on drugs' thing is getting big with the public and the media. There's a lot of pressure on the Feds to do something." To highlight his point, he waved the morning paper. "And publicity like this doesn't help!"

"Publicity like what?"

Rembard handed him the paper. The headline was dramatic: "Branford Homecoming Queen Dead in Crack House." Pyne scanned the article briefly. "What does this have to do with me? I don't make the drug problem. I just run a business."

"The point, Mike, is that the drugs are hot. What I am trying to tell you is that this tax thing may grow into something a lot bigger than you expect."

"Look, I'm not responsible for every goofy teenager who wants to screw her head up. And as for the taxes, I've got plenty of legitimate investments. If you can't handle this, then I'll have to find someone who can."

March 19, 1989

Tim arrived in New York shortly after midnight. It took him little time to retrieve his baggage and rent an inexpensive Dodge for the drive to Connecticut. Traffic proved light, and he pulled into Marian's driveway just after 1:30 A.M.

As he crunched his way up the white gravel walk to the front door, he thought of the Marian he remembered, the cold woman who had grown rich through marriage and divorce, who had wanted neither him nor his sister. But the weeping woman who greeted him at the door was not what he expected. She looked decimated.

She hugged Tim before he could set down his bags, at the same time using him for support. He helped her to the living room. She had the bleary-eyed look of someone who had been drinking and crying too much. Her once epic beauty was finally fading—she had gained weight, and new lines were everywhere. When she spoke, Tim felt some of his old animosity dying. Her son Larry, who worked at a gas station and smoked marijuana incessantly, had become her greatest failure; but as she talked about Heather, Tim could tell that her admiration and love for the girl had been her recompense for her failure with Larry. She went on long into the night while Tim listened. It was after 3 A.M. when he finally lay down in the guest bedroom.

CHAPTER TWO

Sunday, March 19, 1989—Branford, Connecticut

Detective Sergeant Anthony Pulcinella had been on the force for nearly fifteen years, and though he had always been overworked, it seemed to be getting worse every year. If anyone had cared enough to ask him, he would have told them that his case load was too heavy, that the city should hire more cops, and that he was tired of busting lowlifes who were guilty several times over but hardly ever went to jail. These were the reasons, he decided, he was working on Sunday instead of spending it with his family. Sighing, he scanned his file-littered desk. Each folder called for his attention, but one bothered him far more than the others, and he picked that one out from the stack and opened it.

Pulcinella hated unsolved cases, but the Heather Reardon case made no sense at all. He reached for the candy dish on his desk. It was empty. He would have to remember to pick up more. Disappointed, he turned his eyes to the pages before him and studied them again.

Soon, he gave up on the reading. He had already been through it several times and knew he would find nothing. He decided to speak to the girl's stepmother one last time. Perhaps there was a lead there he had missed in his initial questioning. He stood, shrugged on his sportcoat, and headed for the personal-effects cage. Returning the girl's effects would be the perfect pretext for a visit to Branford.

Pulcinella knew Branford well. It was one of several suburbs along the shoreline that, in contrast to New Haven, were predominantly white and shamelessly prosperous. Still, within Branford there was a definite social order, and where one lived in the town spoke to where one was situated within the order. Generally, a good indicator of the wealth of any given Branford resident was the distance that person had to travel from their house to reach the beach. In this regard, Marian Daniels could not have been better situated. Her small, well-kept red ranch was one short block from the water.

With the brown manila folder full of Heather Reardon's possessions in his hand, he knocked on the front door and waited. Seconds later Marian Daniels, drawn and wearing a red dressing gown, opened the door. Seeing him brought surprise to her face.

Pulcinella said, "Good morning, ma'am. I hope I haven't come too early. I was hoping you would have a few minutes to discuss your stepdaughter's case."

She nodded slowly. "Please come in, Sergeant."

She led the way to the living room. Her son Larry was seated in a recliner wearing old blue jeans and a black heavy metal T-shirt. He had tangled shoulder-length black hair and an adolescent stubble on his chin. He was watching a rock video on television, and if he noticed the arrival of company, he didn't show it.

Marian stopped next to her son and asked, "Larry, please turn that thing off. We have a visitor."

Annoyed, he seized the remote control on the arm of his chair and clicked the television off, then he jumped to his feet and sauntered for the hallway leading from the living room.

Pulcinella said, "Son, if you would be willing to stay for a few minutes, I'd appreciate it."

Larry continued his way toward the hallway as if he hadn't heard the policeman, so Marian spoke up. "Larry! Detective Pulcinella was talking to you!"

Head down, he turned and walked back to the couch where he flopped into the cushions and studied his shoes intently. Marian took her seat in the recliner, and Pulcinella sat in a wingback next to the recliner with its back to the door.

Marian asked, "May I offer you a cup of coffee, Sergeant?"

Pulcinella responded with what he hoped was his warmest smile, "No, thank you, ma'am, I'm kind of coffeed out this morning."

Marian nodded and sat waiting expectantly. Larry continued studying his shoes. While Tony pulled his notebook from an inner pocket, he wondered how long the kid would be able to keep up his deliberate nonchalance.

Tony began, "Ma'am, as you know, I'm the investigating officer on this case, and in situations such as this, I find it is usually best if I speak with people relevant to the case at least twice. People often remember things better once they've had a day to think on them. . . ." Pulcinella let his voice trail off. He felt someone's presence next to his chair. Looking up, he found a powerfully built young man, around six feet tall with short brown hair and determined blue eyes, standing patiently and quietly next to him. The man wore an open gray wool double-breasted overcoat, a black turtleneck, blue jeans, and running shoes. Pulcinella saw powerful abdominal muscles under the shirt, and the face looked vaguely familiar, but he couldn't immediately place it. That bothered him. He was proud of his memory for faces, and he was certain that if he had seen this one before, he should have remembered it. The eyes were unforgettable. Simultaneously placid and serious, they were large and bright with intensity. Pulcinella could not fathom why, but as he looked into them an image of a wolf crossed his mind. Shaking the sensation off, he sat up in his wingback and asked, "Yes?"

"Are you Detective Pulcinella?"

Tony nodded, "Yeah."

The man extended his hand. He seemed to be smiling, yet Pulcinella saw no warmth on his features. "Detective, my name is Tim Reardon, and I was told you are working on Heather Reardon's case. I'm her brother. If you don't mind, I'd like to sit in."

"Certainly, glad to have you."

Reardon thanked him and sat on the opposite end of the couch from Larry. As he sat, Tony remembered where he had seen the face before. His photo had been in Heather's wallet.

"Detective, I've been out of the country for a while . . . ."

Pulcinella interjected, "Yeah, I interviewed Mrs. Daniels earlier. She said you are in the army stationed in Germany. Is that correct?"

"Yes, it is. Then you must also know that Marian is my

adopted mother, but Heather and I were blood brother and sister and we were very close."

Pulcinella nodded. "I understand," he encouraged. He wondered where Reardon was going with this. He was not sure why, but he felt nervous. Maybe it was because he was short and the soldier was tall, or maybe it was because the soldier had taken control of the conversation. Pulcinella didn't like that, but he decided he would go along with it for now and see where it went.

Reardon continued talking while removing his overcoat and draping it over the back of the sofa. "To tell the truth, Detective, I really cannot understand how she ended up where she did. I guess I just wanted to ask you what you know. First of all, are you sure she wasn't killed?"

Tony leaned back on his wingback and looked about the living room. It was an attractive room: large, airy, tastefully done in pastel blues, and illuminated by brass lighting fixtures. He reached for the candy he usually had in his pocket and remembered that he had forgotten to pick some up. Looking back at Tim he said, "As for your first question, you probably know a lot more about what kind of person she was than I do—though I'm getting some ideas. As to the second . . ." He paused, unsure over whether or not to take a chance. He decided to move on slowly and see how it went. "I see no reason why we can't tell you what we do know. Though I ask your cooperation in keeping it quiet."

Marian said, "Certainly. I would like very much to know how things are going."

Reardon said, "Thank you, Detective. I appreciate this."

Larry had not lost interest in his shoes.

Pulcinella nodded. "OK, we do know that on the day she died she was dropped off at the Mill Mall by Mrs. Daniels," he motioned with his pen in Marian's direction, "to do some shopping around three o'clock in the afternoon. That was the last time you saw her alive?"

Marian closed her eyes and nodded. It was obviously painful for her to hear it once more, but Pulcinella had business to conduct, so he continued, "Next, Mrs. Daniels, you said that you were supposed to pick Heather up at about 5:30 P.M., but you were half an hour late due to heavy traffic. A man at a flower stand remembered seeing Heather waiting out in front of the mall around five-thirty. He doesn't remember how or when she left. He said that it was busy at the time and a lot of people were going in and out. The next time we know anyone saw Heather, she was dead. We got an anonymous call about the body shortly before eight. We still haven't been able to establish what happened between five-thirty and eight."

Marian remained motionless. Larry stood and left the room. Reardon leaned forward in his chair. His face was an opaque mask. "Could you tell me how she died?"

Tony hesitated. He hadn't wanted to go into this. He said quietly, "It wasn't pleasant."

Reardon nodded. "That's OK."

The detective studied his notebook momentarily. He wanted to do this gently, but no matter how they were presented, the facts were brutal. "OK, you understand that the press has been jumping down our throats on this one. For that reason, we have been reluctant to release details until the investigation is complete. Therefore, I'm gonna have to ask you once again to keep all of this quiet."

"I understand. I won't do anything to hinder the investigation, and I am certain Mrs. Daniels will not either." Marian nodded to indicate she would cooperate.

"Fine," Tony said, "as long as you understand. She died of a heroin overdose in an alley next to a crack house on Winchester Avenue. Well, the heroin actually killed her, but before she died, she was raped and someone attacked her with a knife. The evidence indicates that she was bound while this occurred. The damage was severe enough that had she survived, she would have required extensive surgery. Given this evidence, we believe she was deliberately tortured."

Pulcinella paused for a few seconds to let it all sink in and to study Reardon. There was no doubt about it, this man was hard. Tears traveled silently down Marian's cheeks, but Reardon, with his face expressionless, stared out the window. In a low voice he asked, "About the drugs, do you think Heather used drugs regularly? I mean, did she inject the heroin herself?" His voice betrayed him, Tony decided. Reardon was hurting.

Gently, Pulcinella responded, "No, Mr. Reardon, blood screening revealed that she was totally clean—except for the heroin that killed her. She was definitely a cigarette smoker, but there was no pot or alcohol in her blood, and there were no needle marks anywhere on her body except for the one that proved lethal. The quality and concentration of the heroin leaves little doubt that someone intended for her to die. No one could've lived with what they put in her veins. Mr. Reardon, your sister was raped, tortured, and murdered—and right now I have no idea who did it or why."

Reardon's eyes met his. "Do you have any idea how she got to that crack house?"

"None."

"Why do you think you found her outside instead of inside?"

"We think they untied her after they hit her with the needle. She was probably incoherent when she stumbled outside. The coroner speculates that there was a sudden exhilaration before her heart burst and she convulsed to death in the alley."

Reardon remained silent. Pulcinella had seen this before. It was time to take it easy on the guy. "Perhaps you would like to have her personal effects? We're through with them."

Reardon nodded, "Yes, thank you."

Tony took the manila envelope off his lap and removed two clear plastic evidence bags. They contained some cash, a watch, a half-smoked pack of cigarettes, a lighter, some makeup, some old receipts, her class ring, and a wallet with two pictures. Tim and Marian examined the pictures. The soldier held up the first so Pulcinella could see it. It was a photo of a kind-looking middle-aged couple. He said, "They were our parents."

Tony pointed at the second photo of a young Heather and a high-school boy in a football uniform. "Let me guess. You're the ball player."

Tim looked at him. "I guess I haven't changed much."

"Your basic features haven't. Well, that's about everything. You can keep the bags. I'm really sorry about your loss."

Marian was sobbing intensely, and Reardon moved to her side and placed his arm around her shoulder. He said, "I was in Europe in the army. . . . God, I'd give anything to have been with her that night. Maybe you wouldn't be dropping off her stuff right now. . . ."

Tony felt for both of them. Scenes like this never got better, no matter how often he saw them. "Don't put all this on yourselves. There are some bad people out there. We can't protect our kids from everything. I know, I've got three of them myself. Go to her funeral tomorrow. Mourn her, but don't blame yourselves. Whoever did this—I'll find them, even if it takes ten years."

Reardon smiled politely and raised his eyebrows. "Ten years, Detective?"

The wolf had returned to his eyes. Pulcinella said, "Whatever it takes."

Reardon looked down at Marian as if to end the conversation. "Thank you, Detective."

Pulcinella had a hunch that this soldier had no intention of sitting and waiting. "Listen to me, kid. Let us handle this. It's what we're paid for. I did you a favor telling you what's going on because I'm soft-hearted. You fool around in this, you'll either end up dead or in jail. Besides, you ought to think about one thing: whoever hit her with the heroin had to be a dealer to get hold of stuff that potent. These are bad people. Stay home and out of trouble. We'll get the bastards."

The soldier smiled his odd smile again while he turned the evidence bags over in his free hand softly and slowly. "Sure, Detective. I don't want to make things worse. Just keep me posted on what's going on, huh? You can reach me here. . . . Please let me show you out."

Pulcinella did not believe what Tim Reardon had just said, but he tried to act like he did as he walked to the front door with the soldier behind him. He paused with his hand on the knob and said, "Good luck, soldier, and take care. . . . Oh, I used to be in the army. What unit ya with?"

Reardon shook his head. "Doesn't matter. I'm a cook. You know how it is. You do your time and get out. Thanks, I appreciate all you've done."

Tony twisted the knob and under his breath he muttered, "Glad to be of service, kid."

Outside, Pulcinella wondered what Reardon really did in the army—whatever it was, he wasn't a cook. He decided to send for a copy of Reardon's service record, and he put in the paperwork as soon as he returned to the station. According to the clerk, it wouldn't be in until the next day. It was hard to get such things on Sundays.

Satisfied that he had done all he could for the present, the detective headed home to shine up his dress uniform. He had a wake to attend that evening for the two vice cops from Crown Street.

CHAPTER THREE

March 19, 1989—Thimble Islands, Connecticut

Michael Pyne was not pleased. His relations with the Cartel were strong, and for many years they had been mutually beneficial. In fact, they were so strong that Pyne had been able to operate independently throughout New England. Now there was a new element waiting for him in his office, an element that meant problems: the syndicate. That was why he found himself standing on the wrong side of his own desk while a tall, dark-haired man with a New York accent named Salvatore Nicotra sat in Pyne's own chair. Nicotra, comfortably attired in slacks and a sweater, showed no sign of moving from behind the desk, and Pyne knew better than to ask him to do so. For a moment, he felt like a naughty child who had reported to the principal—only this man was far more dangerous than any grammar-school principal.

Deliberately cautious and with exaggerated politeness Pyne said, "This is a surprise. Had we known a representative from Don DeFrancesco was going to visit, we would have planned some entertainment."

"I'm not here to be amused. I'm here for business."

"Is there a problem?"

"You think I came out here for my health?" He paused. His relentless black eyes bored into Pyne. "Yes, my friend, there are problems. My boss, he's not happy—you know that?"

Pyne felt his calm cracking. His cheeks felt hot, and a shake ran through his hands. He blurted, "Hey! For years I have had good relations with you people. We have respected your business in every way. Don Colasanto promised us . . ."

Suddenly sitting upright, the New Yorker hissed, "That was then! This is now. Don Colasanto is six feet under. And he's there because he was getting soft in business with people like you. The man you got to worry about is Don DeFrancesco. We're gonna be nice for now. We got nothing against business. We *do* got something against you doing business on our turf without tribute. You got that?"

"You know my friend in Colombia might be disturbed by your interference."

The man from New York smiled and leaned forward over the desk. Pyne saw no humor behind the smile. "Ah, your friend in Colombia, Quintero." He stood up suddenly and his fist crashed onto the desk. "You threaten us? Who the fuck are you?"

Pyne found himself backing. "No! It's not a threat! I'm just trying to point out that our business has . . . other considerations. You must realize I have problems too."

"Only problem you got that matters right now is the DeFrancesco family. You got that?"

Pyne nodded.

Nicotra continued, "This shit's gotta change. The Colombians, they're smart. They know enough not to fuck with business here without a little courtesy to those who make most things possible. Quintero, he don't care about you. He gets paid the same one way or another. Now get this. Right now you got no approval playing on our turf—that is, unless you buy a ticket."

"How much is a ticket?"

"Thirty percent, and you better get our approval anytime you want to expand."

Nicotra smiled once again, and his voice softened. "Michael, you work with us, you got no problems. You're happy, we're happy. Hell, whole fucking world's happy. You want to do your own thing, you're shut down. It's as simple as that."

Pyne knew better than to argue now. "OK, you got your thirty percent."

Nicotra's smile broadened. "Now you're making sense.

We'll send people over in the morning to work it out. Don DeFrancesco expects you to make a courtesy call and will ignore the insult you have offered by not making one since he took control of the family last month. Michael, you're lucky. I think he likes you. You got one hell of a business here." Without waiting for a reply, he eased smoothly towards the door with the grace of a professional athlete and paused before it. "Michael, don't fuck this up. The Don is a nice guy as long as he's treated right. I hope you smart enough to treat him right."

With that Nicotra was out the door. Pyne pulled a bottle of very expensive Scotch from a nearby drawer and took a long drink. After the burning subsided, he thought of how much he hated those people.

CHAPTER FOUR

Monday, March 20, 1989—Branford

Andrea Volente hated funerals, but this morning while stopping home to drop off her mother's dresses from the cleaners, her younger sister Lisa had demanded a favor, and given the circumstances, Andrea could not refuse her. Lisa had been a cheerleader on the same squad with Heather Reardon, and she was devastated by her close friend's death. She simply insisted that Andrea go or she would not, as she said, "make it." Andrea was reluctant—she sold real estate for a living and had a busy day planned—but one look at her sister's hollow face told her that she could not refuse. She phoned her boss, and as usual, he was understanding. She had the morning off.

Next came the wardrobe problem. The funeral was at ten. It was already 8:45, and she was dressed in a bright green skirt and jacket—fine for business but not for a funeral. She would have to change, but all of her clothes were in her brownstone in New Haven. Fortunately, Lisa had dressed already, so they hustled out to Andrea's bright red Firebird, and with a fresh cigarette dangling from her lips she squealed off to New Haven.

On the way from Branford to her brownstone near Yale, Andrea broke most of the traffic laws that mattered, and they made record time. Leaving Lisa in the car, she ran upstairs. After rummaging through her closet, she picked out a dark gray, full-length suit with a white blouse and matching wide-brimmed hat. Once changed, she lit another cigarette, touched up her makeup, and stood before her full-length mirror to check her handiwork. While adjusting the hat to the right angle, she put the cigarette in her mouth and inhaled a puff of mentholated smoke deep into her lungs. Momentarily, she wondered how many cigarettes she had already smoked that morning and realized that she had no idea.

Andrea examined what she saw in the mirror. Since she had graduated high school eight years before, she had not put a pound on anywhere along her five-foot-ten-inch frame—unlike many of her friends who had already run to fat. And the outfit flattered her. Cascading in discrete folds, her dress highlighted her slim hips, and its wide belt accentuated her narrow waist. Her bright green eyes glowed beneath the dark wide-brimmed hat. And the white blouse contrasted perfectly with her waist-length dark hair. She mused once again that maybe she was too tall to sell real estate since some men found her size threatening, but she was practical about it. Without the height, she never could have modeled while she was in junior college or before she entered real estate; without the work, she could not have afforded to go to school. Satisfied, she ran down the stairs looking for Lisa.

She was not in the car or the living room. Perplexed, Andrea called out, "Hey Li! Where'd you disappear to?"

A voice came from the bathroom. "I'll be out in just a minute."

Impatient, Andrea paced and smoked. Finally, Lisa emerged from the bathroom, and Andrea took a minute to inspect her. No one who didn't know them would ever guess they were sisters. To her eye Lisa was very pretty, but also very different.

Blond without the help of a bottle, brown-eyed, well-endowed, and about three inches shorter than Andrea, her sister was developing into a real knockout. She also looked a little better now than she had on the way over.

Andrea remarked, "Li, are you gonna be all right? I don't want to have to carry you to this thing this morning."

Lisa smiled a little and she embraced her sister. "I'm OK, Andie. It's great to have you in my corner."

Andrea gave her a tight squeeze, then pushed her away and urged, "C'mon, girl, if we don't hurry we'll never make it."

Lisa waved a wisp of Andrea's smoke away from her face and remarked, "I wish you'd stop smoking those things. You know they're going to kill you someday."

Andrea shook her head playfully. "No, they won't. You will if you don't stop nagging me and let us get out of here. Now hang in there. If you keep a positive attitude, you'll be fine."

"Sure, Sis," she said as they hustled out the door to the Firebird.

Andrea arrived with Lisa just in time for the church service, which she found unremarkable aside from the opulence Marian had lavished upon it. The generic sermon did little to remind her of the bright young girl she remembered. She was grateful when it ended and she and her sister gathered outside with the rest of the mourners for the silent procession to the burial plot on a small rise behind the church.

During the slow march, she at first marveled at how perfect the weather was. The sky was very blue. The wind was light, and the trees surrounding the freshly opened hole were just beginning to show their first buds of spring. As they neared the burial plot, she became aware of Lisa sobbing beside her, and as she reached out to put her arm about her shoulders, she suddenly had a thought that sent a cold sensation through her body: how would she feel if it were Lisa they were there to bury instead of Heather?

Finally, they reached the plot, and in an effort to shrug off her momentary dark thoughts, Andrea turned her attention to the mourners about the grave—particularly Heather's family. Marian was impeccable in her mourning clothes, her dress a simple but opulent black satin affair that hid her slackening waistline well.

Larry, whom Andrea knew well from high school, stood to Marian's right. If he had intended to look bad, she mused, he had succeeded admirably. His suit hung off his emaciated frame in folds; it was old, black, and badly in need of a cleaning. She suspected his shoes hadn't seen polish since their manufacture. His tangled hair looked unbrushed, and he was unshaven. She shook her head in disgust and let her eyes settle upon the other member of the family.

He was in uniform, at Marian's other side. Andrea did not recognize him, but she liked what she saw. She asked Lisa who it was and discovered that he was Heather's natural brother, Tim. She found his striking form a strong contrast to Larry's. His strong face was carefully shaven, and his hair appeared fresh from the barber's razor. Andrea's father had been a World War II paratrooper; since he had had no sons, he had raised her as one, so she instantly recognized Heather's brother's silver parachutist wings glistening above his three rows of ribbons in the sunlight. And his feet were shod in black paratrooper's boots made conspicuous with the gleaming care they had received. Atop his head was the distinctive Green Beret she recalled hearing Heather brag about on certain occasions.

She forced her eyes elsewhere and studied the crowd as the ceremony droned on. But she soon found herself staring at Heather's brother. The anguish in his eyes was tangible, yet he seemed so steady. In spite of the solemnity of the occasion, she couldn't remember when she had found a man this compellingly attractive before. Inwardly embarrassed, she caught herself speculating what his broad-shouldered body might look like out of uniform.

The service ended with a final word from the minister. Andrea looked on quietly as the casket was slowly lowered into the ground. The onlookers who had flowers shuffled forward and dropped them into the freshly occupied grave, and within minutes she was assisting a very distraught Lisa toward her car. Still, as she helped her sister into her car, Andrea paused and looked back over the field they had just traversed. All but a few people had already driven or walked away, but Tim was still there, standing alone amidst the freshly dug earth and flowers above the open grave. A wind that still carried some of winter's chill came up suddenly and ruffled the tails of his uniform coat, but he remained unmoving. She wondered what he was thinking on his solitary watch.

CHAPTER FIVE

Monday, March 20, 1989—Branford

After the funeral ended and the family made ready to leave for home, Tim explained that he needed time to clear his head, so he would walk back and rejoin them at the house. Marian nodded her understanding, gave him a tearful kiss, and left for her car. Yet Tim did not depart immediately. Instead, he remained standing at the foot of the open grave wrapped in the morning breeze, bouquet in hand.

If he had felt pain before, the sight of Heather's closed casket squatting alone and silent in the open hole paralyzed him. Eyes that had functioned just minutes before suddenly stopped seeing and muscles that had served him a lifetime turned to stone. As if a giant hand had seized him, he was transported from the grave to another place; and where he had once seen the desolate casket, haunting images of his Heather flashed through his mind in a vivid whirl. Knowing he was alone, he let the tears come, wet, silent, and desolate, streaming down his cheeks.

He remembered one of their long camping trips with their father. There was Heather again dancing along the mountain trail with a handful of wild flowers and a face bright with the pleasure of life. He had helped her carve her first hiking stick that day, then that night in the flickering orange light of the campfire she had asked him, "Timmy, when I grow up can we climb even bigger mountains together?" He had promised her that they would.

Then came the image of her tears the night the policeman and the social worker had come to tell them their Mom and Dad would never come home again. He remembered another promise he had made her then. He had told her that no matter what happened, he would take care of her. She had hugged him tight and said that she knew that.

More images came of the intervening years: her visits to the places where he was stationed, her pride and excitement when he had graduated from Special Forces School, her cheerful letters when he was in Beirut all those long, lonely months, and finally, her jubilant phone call this past autumn when she had told him the school had selected her as homecoming queen.

Then his mind came to Colonel Dwyer with his somber face and oversized desk. Suddenly, the images disappeared, and once again he saw the casket stretched before him. All his life, he had been Tim Reardon: steady, tough, decisive, and ready for just about anything. This time, it was different, for Tim found himself lost. This time, there was no enemy he could strike—had there been, he would have been superbly equipped to handle it. Instead, he knew only pain and an awful frustration.

Suddenly, he felt the bite of the brisk breeze, and he shivered against the cold. From some remote place inside him a voice spoke the words his sanity needed. Looking down at the casket, he said, "I'm sorry for the broken promise, Heather. I hope somehow you can forgive me, Sis. But there is one promise I can make to you now—and this one will be kept. The people who did this to you will be found and brought to justice, no matter what it takes."

As if in slow motion, he raised his arm and allowed the bouquet to fall into the grave. The wind caught it as soon as it left his fingers and it spiraled downward gently to come to a rest in the center of the casket. Silently, Tim turned and walked slowly toward Marian's house.

Upon entering the house, he found that there had been a reception in the living room after the funeral, but it had ended, and the caterer was cleaning the aftermath. Larry had disappeared to wherever it was he usually went, and only Marian remained seated in a recliner with a gin in her hand.

Tim said, "Marian, I'm sorry I wasn't here to see everybody, but I really don't know any of these people. . . . I would have felt awkward."

Marian nodded. "I understand."

Tim was about to start towards his room when she looked up and said, "Tim, I think I know what you're feeling, and you're wrong. It's not your fault. I don't think anyone could have stopped what happened. Sometimes fate is stronger than human intention."

"I know. I just . . . Heather was the only real family I had. . . ."

She nodded. "I understand. I know how close you two were. How long are you planning to stay?"

"Well, right now I'm not sure, but no more than three or four more days. I'm getting out of the army in three months, and I want to save some of this leave time so I can sell it back to the government for some money when I get out."

Marian looked surprised. "Tim, I thought you were a soldier for life."

"No, it was fun while it lasted, and I definitely don't regret it, but hell—being in Special Forces is a hard row to hoe. You know, gone nine months out of twelve, always humping a rucksack—it's no way to spend twenty years. Someday I'd like to have a family, and maybe a house somewhere while I'm still young enough to enjoy it."

"Have you made specific plans?" she asked.

Tim smiled. "Maybe. I've taken some classes for an associate in management studies. The University of Connecticut has some good business programs, so for now it looks like I'll be there in the fall to get my B.A. Meanwhile, I'll need some kind of job to keep me going this summer. Since I'm already here it makes sense to kind of sniff around for one in New Haven now."

"Tim, you know I'll help you any way I can."

Tim nodded. "Thanks, I'll remember. Watch out, I may take you up on it."

Marian stood and reached for him. He held her. She said, "You know, I really did learn to care for that girl."

Releasing her, he whispered, "I know."

Silently Marian headed for her room. Tim watched the last of the caterers go, then the house fell into a quiet he found intolerable. This had been Heather's house, and alone in the living room, he felt her all about him. Partially because it was habit, but mostly because he wanted to do something, he changed into sweats and went out and ran a few miles. The run was good. Instead of thinking about Heather he concentrated on the pace and stretching to the limit. The rhythm of his arms and legs working in unison gave his mind a chance to rest. He ran long, and he ran brutally fast. But it was over entirely too soon.

The shower felt wonderful after the run, but as he toweled off, his eyes lit upon a plate on the bathroom wall. It was pink with bright flowers, and it had the word Heather in cursive scrawl across it. He had made it for her in high school. Now the images of his sister returned. He shook his head to clear it, left the bathroom, put on blue jeans and a T-shirt, and turned on the TV for escape. It didn't work. The longer he sat, the more the house seemed to close in, and he saw Heather in everything. Finally, at about 6:30, he gave up. After changing into one of his turtlenecks and his long gray overcoat, he got in his rental car and, lacking specific plans, he drove aimlessly around Branford. Mostly, he just smoked and pondered the day's events and the girl they were centered on.

Once out of the Short Beach area, he ended up on the wide portion of Route 1 where all the shopping centers and car dealerships were. There was little of interest there, so he headed for Main Street, a typical dying downtown area with a nice green and some classic New England–style wooden churches. Darkness fell, so he turned on his headlights. Soon he was past the small downtown and back out on Route 1. This portion was far less gaudy, so he felt more comfortable with it. Off in the distance to his right, he saw a little bar called My Dad's that bore a close resemblance to some of the small bars he had used to frequent in Massachusetts when he was stationed there. He decided to stop and parked his rental near the front door. After turning off the engine, he paused momentarily to rethink whether or not he really wanted to go in, and he let his eyes scan the building. It was a low-slung affair with neon beer signs in the windows and a wood shingle facade that looked far more welcoming than Marian's sad red ranch. Locking the car behind him, he went inside.

As soon as he stepped in the door, he knew he'd found the right place. The interior was not brightly lit but not too dark, and rock and roll of moderate volume came from a stereo behind the bar. A dart board hung in one corner next to an electronic bowling machine; the bar was a square affair that afforded him both a comfortable corner and a fine view of the dart game—which seemed to involve about half of the patrons, the other half being locked in debate over whether or not the Knicks could go all the way. Tim decided that the people in My Dad's that night were typical of those found in neighborhood bars everywhere. Everyone knew everyone else, so naturally, a stranger entering the establishment inevitably attracted attention, and Tim could feel a discreet surveillance as he sat in his corner seat at the bar; but the regulars seemed cordial nonetheless.

The woman behind the bar was pretty, blond, and had a nice smile. Her name was Candy, and she served up Tim's Southern Comfort on the rocks in seconds. He drank it fast, and within a half hour, he had just as swiftly dispatched three more.

Andrea Volente arrived at My Dad's at 7:45 in a white button-up blouse and blue jeans with her customary cigarette. My Dad's was her father's bar; and despite her own busy real estate schedule, she tended bar two nights a week.

As she entered, several people sent smiles her way and said, "Hi, Andie." The men were particularly polite, viewing Andrea as long sought-after, but never captured. She had a reputation for always remaining polite but ultimately uncooperative. One large, red-bearded man in a plaid shirt with massive arms and a generous stomach straining over his belt didn't offer her greetings—though she saw him turn away as she entered. Holding a beer bottle in his hand, he acted mesmerized by the dart game.

Once behind the bar, she placed one hand on her hip, motioned with her cigarette towards the red-bearded customer and quietly asked, "Candy, why did you serve Tully MacDonald?"

"I'm sorry, Andie. I know your dad said not to, but he's never been any problem for me, and how do you say 'no' to a guy that big?"

"He threatened you?"

"No, he just ordered a beer, and I served it."

"Well, if he never caused you a problem, that's because you're day shift, and he isn't plastered yet. Aside from insulting and chasing off customers, that idiot's the one who smashed the jukebox last month. You want to see how to *not* serve him? Watch me."

Spinning toward MacDonald, who remained with his back to her, Andrea turned the stereo down and shouted, "You got five minutes to drink up and hit the road, Tully, or I'm calling the cops! You're not served here, and you know it."

MacDonald turned his six-foot-two-inch bulk to face her and retorted, "Yeah, yeah, who gives a fuck?"

"Five minutes, Tully. Then we'll see who gives a fuck!"

Andrea turned back to Candy and found her hurriedly ringing out the cash register. Andrea asked, "Any other problems?"

Candy shrugged. "Naw, it's been quiet tonight—well, there is one thing. You see that guy in the corner?" Andrea glanced over and, to her surprise, saw Tim Reardon. Candy continued, "Well, he's on his fourth Southern Comfort in an hour, and I think he drove. You might want to cut him off soon."

"No problem, I think I can handle this one."

"OK, Andie, you're the boss's daughter. Good night."

Andrea lit a fresh cigarette as Candy left and studied the man who had captured her interest that morning. She made her way to the corner of the bar, where he sat next to a cashew machine. She flashed her best smile, leaned against the bar, and said, "Hi Tim, are you trying to run us out of Southern Comfort?"

Surprised, he looked up from the counter top he had been studying and asked, "How do you know my name?"

Andie took a drag of her cigarette and said, "My little sister Lisa was Heather's best friend, and she told me about you. I saw you at the funeral today."

"I'm sorry, there were a lot of people there. I can't remember that many faces."

"That's OK."

Tim frowned. "I, well, I'm afraid you have the advantage over me."

"Oh, my name is Andrea Volente—most people just call me Andie."

"Good ta meet ya, Andie." He lifted his glass in a toasting motion and took a sip.

She frowned. She wanted to tell him that the stuff he was drinking wouldn't solve any problems, but she thought better of it. It might be true, but it sounded too much like a tired cliché. "You planning to be in town long?"

"No, just a couple of days. I have to get back to Germany."

"Tim, I know you are probably tired of hearing this, but I would really like to say it, and it is from the heart. I am sorry about what happened to Heather. Every time I think about it, I realize that the funeral could have just as easily been for my sister as it was for yours."

He nodded and looked down at his drink. The silence held for a long minute until Tully MacDonald sat down on the stool next to Tim.

Tim Reardon had heard MacDonald approaching, and sensing trouble, he had moved his hands away from his glass and tensed his feet on the bar rail. He had heard the way the red-bearded man had spoken to the nice, pretty bartender, and he was ready for a confrontation, but none came. MacDonald sat quietly, put his beer bottle down, and stared at it.

Tim measured him. MacDonald had a weightlifter's developed upper body, but his soft stomach would make him easy. He would just have to stay away from the power of those big arms.

Andrea said, "Glad you could join us, Tully, but you have two minutes to get out the door."

MacDonald's head snapped up, he lurched against the bar, and kicked the stool behind him. It flew several feet back and crashed against the wall. Tim slipped from his stool and faced MacDonald.

Ignoring the Green Beret, Tully stepped towards Andrea and rasped, "You might have a cute ass, but you're a stupid bitch. You think I'm gonna go if I don't want to? Who the fuck you think you are?"

Tim interjected, "You're a fat, stupid bastard, aren't you?"

With surprise on his face, Tully turned and faced Tim.

MacDonald asked, "What the fuck you say?"

Tim responded, "I said that you're a fat, stupid bastard—"

Tim heard the roar and saw a big right hand headed towards

his face, and he responded even faster. Ducking left and crossing his hands above him, he slipped the punch, seized MacDonald's hand and spun it hard against its natural rotation.

The big man's face crashed forward into the bar as Tim held his arm locked in a tight wrist lock. Tully jerked violently, but Tim threw a hard kick into his solar plexus.

Tully grunted as his breath left him, and Tim felt the arm he still controlled go limp. He spun the wrist in the other direction and bent the arm behind the big man's back. Then he quickly turned Tully around and drove him toward the door. Tim hit the latch with his foot, piled the still gasping MacDonald through the doorway, and left him sprawling in the dirt outside. Softly, he said, "The next time you're asked to leave, maybe you'll be nicer about it."

Tim heard a noise behind him, and, still balanced on the balls of his feet, spun to meet whatever might be there.

He saw Andrea, her green eyes flashing, her feet shoulder-width apart, holding a baseball bat. She said quietly, "Tim, we can handle our own problems here."

"I'm sorry, I just, well, I had to go to the bathroom, and he was in my way."

Andrea tossed her long hair. "Looked more like male macho shit to me."

"OK, so my testosterone was high, and the bonding thing wasn't working out."

She laughed, and Tim heard gravel scraping behind him. He turned and saw Tully scrambling for the parking lot. From behind, he heard Andrea shout, "Maybe you want to try coming in again, Tully?"

MacDonald didn't slack his stride, so she continued, "Remember, next time it'll be the cops!"

Tim faced her once again, motioned at the bat and asked, "You going to use that thing on me?"

She laughed. "The night isn't over yet."

"Well, I know I've got to go now too, but could I go inside and get my jacket?"

Lowering her bat and turning towards the door, she responded, "Oh, shut up, come inside, and let me buy you a drink."

He did.

Tim was suddenly popular—drinks lined the counter before

him, and patrons who hated MacDonald clustered about him. Soon, the alcohol and the banter of his fellow customers had pushed thoughts of Heather out of his mind. Though he said little, his companions entertained him with several Tully MacDonald stories as he drank and smoked relentlessly while he watched Andrea work behind the bar.

Andrea was busy, so their conversation was limited. But whenever they did talk, he found it went easily. Finally, around 11:30, all but two of the regular patrons had departed, and she pulled her stool behind the bar across from him.

"Tim, my father was a paratrooper in World War II, and I've heard about Green Berets all my life, but I've never met one before."

"We're not exactly like the movies."

She smiled. "Tell that to Tully MacDonald."

He returned her smile, looked into her eyes, and mumbled, "Yeah, well, we practice and work out a lot."

She kept her gaze locked in his, and he decided her face—large, green eyes, high cheekbones, and angular chin—was the most beautiful he had ever seen. Below her lips, he noticed a small V-shaped scar, but he liked it. Without it, she might have been so perfect as to be generic; but the flaw made her unique. He realized he was staring, fumbled for something to say, and came out with, "Andrea, you make a good drink."

She laughed the same little laugh he had heard several times earlier and responded, "Tim, I didn't make the Southern Comfort; I just poured it."

"Yeah, but you did it so well."

"The secret's in the wrist. I gather you're not a beer drinker."

"You gathered wrong. I love a good beer, but I've grown accustomed to German beer. There are no substitutes for it here."

She continued, "I've never been to Germany, but I've heard a lot of people say the same thing. . . ."

A patron at the opposite end of the bar called her name, and she excused herself.

When she returned she found his large blue eyes locked on hers, and his stare made her feel uncomfortable. While she had left him alone, the smile she had seen in them had left and been replaced with the pain she had seen earlier. But behind the pain, she still saw the pride and strength she concluded made him what he was.

He said, "Andie, I am not really sure what I'm doing, but I just want to know about Heather. What hurts the most is that no one seems to have any idea why it happened or who the hell did it. Somebody's got to answer for this."

"What do you mean 'know'?"

"I mean there is more to this than some girl just dying on a street. Who are the people involved? How does something like this happen?"

Andrea remained silent a minute. She wasn't sure she should do this, but what could it hurt? "OK Tim, maybe I can help you. My sister knew Heather about as well as anyone did. This morning she was pretty broken up. You should probably talk to Lisa. . . ."

As if shot with electricity, he sat up straight. "Arrange it. Arrange a meeting between me and Lisa."

"I don't know, Tim . . ."

"Just do it, please. I have to know who she was."

Those compelling blue eyes bored into hers once again. She felt nervous, looked away, and reached for a cigarette. A lighter clicked. She dipped her cigarette toward the flame he held, and the taste of the tobacco reassured her. "Thank you," she said. Suddenly, she had an idea. She began to understand. "You feel guilty, don't you."

He looked away, his face tense. In a low voice he began, "I don't really know what I feel. Right now, I just know that the only way I can put Heather to rest is if I find out what happened." He grabbed his glass with force, raised it, and drained it as if it were beer. He set it back on the bar and said, "Andrea, maybe I shouldn't say this, but damn, the government spent a lot of money teaching me how to take care of myself. Well, Heather was my sister, and I bet I could find those bastards. And I will find them if the police don't do it soon. I at least owe her that."

Andrea paused, then replied, "Tell you what, be at a place called Captain Jack's tomorrow at 11:30 A.M. I'll have Lisa there. If anything changes, I'll call you."

"Thank you, Andie, I owe you. Let me give you my number."

"That won't be necessary, Lisa has it—she was Heather's friend."

"Yeah, that's right." He picked up his empty glass. "Can I have one more?"

Andrea decided to shut him off while there was still something left to shut off. "Tim, I know you've had a bad time, but don't you think maybe it's time to call it a night?"

"Yeah, what the hell, any more and I'll be sleeping in the toilet." Resolutely, he stood up and pulled out his car keys.

"Oh, no," Andrea said, "there's no way I'm going to let you drive home tonight. You're riding with me. Give me five minutes to ring out the register, and we're out of here."

A small grin flashed across his face and he shrugged. "Lady, I can tell when it's time to surrender."

They said little during the ride to Marian's house. She was tired, and he was obviously very drunk. Silences between newly acquainted companions are usually awkward, but not this time. She kept thinking of the strength and vulnerability she had seen in his eyes, and she felt very safe in the darkness.

She pulled her red Firebird up Baltman Place slowly; and when she came to a stop at the end of Marian's driveway, she turned off the lights and engine. She didn't know quite what to say and sensed that he didn't either. After a moment, Tim thanked her and opened the door. She put her hand on his arm. Through the open door she heard the sound of the wind rustling barren tree branches, and she saw the sky filled with stars. In a voice just above a whisper, she said, "Tim, I can only imagine what you must be feeling. There aren't many people in the world I call close, just my family, I guess. Today, at the funeral, I thought about it, and I realized that above everything else—even though I'm so busy with my career—I count on them. I couldn't imagine what I'd do if I lost my sister like you did yours. I hope someday you will be able to remember Branford for something besides what you lost here."

He took a deep breath and let it out slowly. "It'll take a while. Andrea, I know you had to think about it before you offered to introduce me to Lisa, and I appreciate it. I want you to know that if there is ever anything you need, I will be there for you too. Words are cheap, but I mean that." He got up, closed the door, and walked unsteadily toward the dark house. She wished she hadn't let him go.

9:22 P.M.—New Haven

Tony Pulcinella was working late once again, more out of frustration than hope. Six active case folders sat stacked neatly in his out box. He and his men had solved all of them and arrests had been made, but there was one folder in the middle of his blotter, a folder that continued to trouble him. It was the Heather Reardon file, and it was no closer to being solved than when he had first begun the investigation.

He and his men had done all of the leg work directly by the book. They had searched thc mall for anyonc who knew anything. They had canvassed the neighborhood where she had died. Still, they had found no new information. After checking her school records and interviewing those who had known her, he was even more frustrated. In every way, he was convinced, Heather Reardon had been one of those rarest of things for this day and age: a truly decent kid. She belonged at a prom, not in a casket.

To cheer himself up, he decided to consider the positive side of things. The investigation was still ongoing, so answers might yet be found. They were checking the whereabouts of known sex offenders, and with some luck, that might turn up some potential candidates. Meanwhile, Brown and Foster were still probing for anything they could get from local drug dealers. So far, they had found nothing, but they might get a break.

He looked at his watch. Realizing that if he did not leave soon he would miss his kids before they went to bed, he reached for the two envelopes remaining in his in box. He would have liked to have forgotten them, but he believed in clearing his desk before he left at night. The first envelope contained an old file from a dead case. He filed it, then opened the second. In it was the service record of Tim Reardon.

Leaning back in his swivel chair once again, he skimmed the early routine portions such as his dates of service, place of entry into service, and family background; but the second half made him sit up straight and reach for a candy.

One thing was definite—Tim Reardon was no cook. He had graduated from Airborne, Sniper, Ranger, and Special Forces

Schools. He was trained in communications and electronic surveillance, light and heavy weapons, and demolitions. According to a pamphlet on Special Forces included with the file, the guy was expert with most of the world's small arms, could tap a phone with ease from materials he could buy on the open market, and could make any type of explosive or detonating device he needed.

An abundance of commendations followed the list of schools and stations, and open records indicated distinguished service in both Lebanon and Central America—and a note indicated that there was even more information in classified files.

Tony's mind worked furiously. Was the warrior he had met on the pages of this service record one who would take the loss of his sister passively? Searching for answers, he turned his attention to Reardon's evaluation reports. They were all written by supervisors who obviously liked the man they were evaluating, and they discussed such things as his bravery in Lebanon, his coolness under pressure, his conscientiousness; however, one captain wrote something Pulcinella decided was a good summary of all of Reardon's evaluations. It read:

> Above all else, what separates Sergeant Reardon from his peers is his single-minded determination. Once this N.C.O. is given a mission, and he has resolved himself to its completion, the steadfast dedication this serviceman displays in the fulfillment of that mission, coupled with his many talents, gives him the capability of achieving what many others might deem impossible. Sergeant Reardon is a man difficult to deny, in uniform or out of it. He always accomplishes his goals.

Pulcinella got Marian's phone number and dialed it.

Reardon wasn't home, so the detective left a message to have the soldier call him as soon as Marian saw him. As Pulcinella set the file down on his desk, he asked himself, "What mission is Tim Reardon on now?"

CHAPTER SIX

Tuesday, March 21, 1989—East Haven, Connecticut

Most military men are habitually early, and Tim was no exception. By 11:00 A.M., in spite of a powerful headache, the man with the reputation for relentlessly finishing what he started had already run five miles, showered, shaved, picked up his rental car, and chosen to ignore a message from Marian to call Detective Pulcinella. By 11:15 he was at Captain Jack's, awaiting the arrival of Andrea and her sister. After choosing a corner chair from which he could see all comers, he surveyed the restaurant, a stereotypical Connecticut seafood place done in light blue and pink pastels.

He ordered a soft drink, and was glad when he saw Andrea's hot red Firebird pulling in to the parking lot. An attractive young girl with blond hair emerged from the passenger side. As soon as the girl was safely clear, Andrea squealed off as if late for something, and Tim found himself feeling disappointed. He wanted to see the tall, green-eyed woman again.

The girl Andrea had dropped off entered the bar area wearing blue jeans and a red blouse, and she carried a designer shoulder bag. The set of her head and the way she glanced about gave Tim the impression that she was either very nervous or very disoriented. To help her locate him, he stood. Their eyes met, and she approached. Tim held out his hand. "Lisa, right?"

"Hi, Tim, uh . . . I remember you from the funeral." He noted that she averted her gaze. Perhaps some polite conversation would set her at ease before he began his questions. "How are you?"

"Pretty good." Tim offered a chair, she sat, and a waitress wearing a pink skirt and blue blouse that matched the decor arrived.

He said, "I'm hungry. How about you? Want some lunch?"

She shook her head. "No, thanks, maybe just a soda."

He ordered a turkey club for himself and soda for her. As the waitress departed, he commented, "I was hoping your sister would join us for lunch. Do you think she'll come back?"

Lisa smiled. "Andie? No way. Unless you make an appointment three weeks in advance, you have to go to My Dad's to see her. She's gotta be the busiest woman in New Haven. I mean, my sister is *always* working. I don't think she knows the meaning of the word tired. Believe me, if you knew Andie well, you'd realize that there are three things she always has plenty of: energy, smiles, and men wanting to date her."

Tim was disappointed. He belonged to the third category.

The banter had seemed to relax her somewhat—though she would not meet his eyes. She asked, "My sister told me you had some questions about Heather? So what do you want to know?" Her demeanor was sullen, yet her question was direct. Tim wondered what Andrea had done to get her there.

Tim let Lisa's question remain suspended for a moment while he considered how best to begin. Obviously uncomfortable, she toyed with the strap on her shoulder bag. Finally, he began: "I don't know what Andrea told you, but I'm interested in learning about Heather. The past few years, I didn't see too much of her, so I was hoping to hear someone who knew her well describe what kind of girl she was. Andrea said you were one of her best friends, and Heather mentioned you in her letters. If you can, would you tell me about the girl you knew? Please don't hold anything back. I need to know everything."

Tim watched her face carefully. Like many kids her age, she was made up to look far older than she was; but the nervous way she fidgeted in her chair and fingered her shoulder bag strap belied the image she was trying to create. "Well, we were friends, I guess—you know, we used to hang out together. We were also on the same cheerleading squad."

In reply, Tim put on his most encouraging smile.

She stared down at the table, her fidgeting stopped, and he

saw hesitation in her face. Finally, her eyes became distant and she said, "Well . . . she was just a good friend . . . you know?"

Friendly encouragement wasn't getting him anywhere, so he decided to try a more direct question. He would see how truthful the girl was willing to be. "Lisa, did Heather do drugs—any kind of drugs?"

"No, she was absolutely clean. There was no way she did drugs."

"Did she smoke?"

"You mean cigarettes?"

"Yes."

"No way." She now stared past his head out the window.

"That's strange," he said slowly, "when she visited me in Germany last year, she was smoking pretty heavily. Then, when I got her personal effects from the police, there was a half pack of her favorite brand in her purse. As her best friend, I would have thought you'd have known she was a smoker."

Her fidgeting intensified. "OK, so maybe she did smoke."

"Why didn't you tell me that?"

Lisa was defensive. "She, well, she was kind of secretive about her smoking. I sort of want people to remember her in the best way."

"Lisa, I appreciate that, but I was the only real family Heather had. She told me about things as they happened." Almost absently, he continued, "For instance, two years ago, she told me in a letter that she had started smoking." He sighed. "Now, it would be a big help if you would be totally straight with me. Did Heather do illegal drugs?"

"No! I swear she didn't."

"Any idea why she was in New Haven that night?"

"No."

Tim looked at the hand that had been playing with the strap. The fidgeting had stopped, but she now squeezed it hard enough for her knuckles to turn white. He decided she was lying. It was time to go farther. "Who sells the drugs in Branford?"

She started in her chair. At first, Tim thought the question had caught her off guard. Then he realized her attention had gone somewhere else. He followed her eyes. A tall, swarthy man in a black jumpsuit standing by the bar was waving to Lisa. He had a light, slender build, a shaved head, a thin mustache, and dark eyes. He had several large gold chains around his neck, and he gave his fellow patrons exaggerated greetings while making himself at home.

Lisa was already out of her chair. She glanced nervously at the man, then turned back and smiled for the first time. "Look, Tim, I have to go. You take care, huh—I hope I helped." She began backing away, but he grabbed her wrist.

He repeated his question. "Lisa, do you know who sells the drugs in Branford?"

She fought against his grip and her face grew hostile. She shook her head. "No, I'm not into that kind of thing, and you're hurting me. My mom is supposed to pick me up in front of the grocery store across the street, and I'm already late. Now would you let me go!"

Tim didn't believe her. He smiled politely and relaxed his grip. "Sorry, thanks for everything, Lisa."

His eyes followed her as she made her way to the door. She had wanted the gesture she made to the man with all the gold necklaces to be discreet, but Tim had missed none of it—nor did he miss the man's casual answering nod. The man stood, said something to the bartender, and headed for the exit.

Though his sandwich had still not arrived, Tim sensed something important was about to happen, so he hustled to the bar and passed a ten to the bartender. He said, "I'm sorry, I forgot about an appointment. Thank the waitress for me and give her what's left."

The bartender nodded. "Sure, buddy."

Tim gestured towards the stool the tall swarthy man had just vacated and said, "Tell, uh, what's his name, uh . . ."

"Ronny," the bartender offered.

Tim smiled, "Yeah, that's right, Ronny. Anyway, tell him I'll catch him later, huh. My name's Jim."

The bartender was about to reply, but Tim was already gone.

Once outside, Tim, on light feet, moved quickly down the gravel path leading to the parking lot. He saw Ronny and Lisa standing near a small Mercedes with their backs to him. Confident that he had gone unnoticed, Tim slipped between a parked car and a pickup truck just a few feet from them.

As Tim watched, Ronny, holding a wad of bills, leaned against the side of the car and began counting.

Lisa got on tiptoes to give him a kiss on the cheek, then began walking towards a stand of trees near the entrance to the parking lot. Once she had departed, Ronny pocketed the money and headed back in the direction of the gravel walk Tim had just traveled.

Seeing him approaching, Tim quickly slid under the pickup and lay still as Ronny's feet slowly passed by. He remained motionless until he heard the footsteps disappear and the hydraulically operated front door of Captain Jack's hiss closed.

Rising as swiftly as he had gotten down, Tim scanned the direction he had last seen Lisa heading in, and he saw a red blouse just disappearing into the trees. As efficiently as he could, Tim did something he knew how to do well—he followed her.

Within seconds, he reached the woodline. Once there, he was concealed—though his close-up view revealed to him that the stand of trees the girl had entered was only about fifty feet wide, nothing more than a separator between the restaurant and the highway that ran past a shopping plaza located opposite. She had followed a well-traveled trail. Fortunately, the foliage was thin, so Tim had no trouble following her red blouse. She had left the path. Paralleling her along the edge of the parking lot, he watched as, after glancing in all directions, she sat down with her back to a large oak and took something from her shoulder bag. Moving silently, Tim closed to within a few feet of the girl in a very short time. To his great satisfaction, there was a small bush with a hollow behind it where he could remain prone and watch her.

One of Lisa's hands held a glass vial containing a crystalline substance. The vial had a tube jutting out from one side. Her other hand held a lighter. After heating the pipe, she took a great drag of smoke deep into her lungs and held it there. Soon, she closed her eyes, laid her hands in her lap, and leaned her head back against the tree trunk.

CHAPTER SEVEN

Tuesday, March 21, 1989—Branford

As he watched the girl recline against the tree, Tim felt confused. Heather had died with heroin in her veins, and now her best friend was smoking crack. He felt himself smile bitterly. Now he knew something, and he planned to know more soon. Now who to follow, Ronny or Lisa? To go after Ronny might be dangerous, and he might also turn out to be the wrong guy to follow. No, he was going to stick with the girl. Lisa was a kid, and he read her as a weak person. Once he had gotten what he needed, he would tell Andrea about her little sister's problem. Then, the girl might be saved before she joined Heather in the cemetery.

Armed now with a plan, Tim eased himself into a crouch. Given her condition, it was easy for him to sneak up on the girl. Kneeling beside her, he picked up her shoulder bag and found three more unused vials, along with some cocaine in powdered form. Keeping her bag in one hand, he placed his other on her upper arm and squeezed. Her eyes opened but remained glazed.

"Lisa," he said.

Her pupils slowly focused on his face. When they did, alarm replaced euphoria and she jumped to her feet.

He held the vial and the lighter where she could see them and dropped them into her designer bag. The shake of her hands told him that she was frightened in spite of the high. He smiled and said, "Come with me, Lisa."

She nodded dumbly and followed. He kept possession of her

bag while they went to the parking lot and he opened the door of his rental car for her. She got in without resistance, and he joined her, being careful to place her bag between himself and the driver's door. He knew that as long as he had the drugs, he had Lisa.

Casually, as if he had ample time for what he was doing, he started the car, put it in gear, and drove away from Captain Jack's.

As they left the parking lot she asked, in a voice much like a little girl's, "Where are we going?"

Tim smiled but did not answer for a time. He wanted to keep her nervous, and he knew that his smiling silence would achieve this aim. A red light came up, and he stopped for it. When it turned green, he swung the car left and headed for the shoreline. Her voice an octave higher, Lisa repeated her question.

In as gentle a tone as he could manage, Tim asked, "Lisa, why were you buying coke from Ronny?"

"I've had a bad couple of days. I just want to get a little high. I'm not hurting anybody."

"You don't see giving your money to a snake like that as doing anything wrong?" Tim had slowed and now cruised on quiet residential side streets.

"I just get high once in a while . . . and you don't really know him. He's always good to me. He's just in business like anyone else."

"But he does sell crack?"

"And liquor stores sell whiskey," she chided.

"Did he sell drugs to Heather?"

"No, I told you, she didn't do drugs. . . . She was always trying to get me to stop."

"Lisa, you've got a problem, a cocaine problem. And you're lying to me."

From the corner of his eye he saw her sullen face turn away toward her window. He came to a stop sign back on the main street and spotted Captain Jack's in the distance. He turned that way, then pulled into the shopping center parking lot and turned off the motor.

Twisted in the seat facing her, he continued, "Now, you say you were Heather's best friend. What I'm trying to do is find out who killed Heather. I would think you would be anxious to help me do that. I know you're not telling me everything you know, and the reason you aren't is that white stuff in your pocketbook." He sighed, placed both hands on the steering wheel, and looked straight ahead. In a low voice he continued, "Tell you what. You have twenty-four hours to change your mind and help me out. If you don't, I'm taking the stuff in your shoulder bag to the police and telling them all about you and your little problem—not to mention your friend Ronny. I assume you have my phone number. It's the same as Heather's used to be." With his handkerchief, he removed the cocaine and crack from her bag, then returned the bag to her. "Good-bye, Lisa."

Her eyes finally turned. First they looked at the handkerchief, then they rose and met his. The fear was gone. In its place, Tim saw a blankness. She looked away. Slowly, she began easing her door open, then she paused. Staring at a woman taking a baby out of a car, she spoke in a voice like a child's. "I really did like Heather. Drugs made her nervous, so we weren't as close as we used to be. I wish I could give you the name of whoever killed her—I really wish I could. Just believe me when I say that it wasn't Ronny. I know he wouldn't hurt someone like that."

Before Tim could reply, she was out of the car and scurrying for the market. As soon as she was out of sight, he also got out of the car. Walking to a storm drain, he dropped the handkerchief and its contents into it and returned to the rented Plymouth. Once there, he wondered if he had made a serious mistake with Lisa. Would she help him? Could he help her?

7:00—Branford

It was dark when Ronny parked his Mercedes in front of his condo that night, but he didn't think about it because he had had a very good day selling cocaine.

He was surprised when he found Lisa waiting by his door. Once inside, she gave him a hug, and he felt her body shaking. "What's the matter, Li?" he asked.

"Oh, Ronny, things are bad. You don't know how bad."

Smiling, he guided her to a very plush sofa, lit a gas fire in a brightly colored metal fireplace, and turned his stereo on low.

Satisfied with the atmosphere, he sat next to Lisa and said, "Now you tell Ronny all your troubles."

"First can I get a whiff?"

"Sure," he smiled, producing a vial and a spoon for her convenience. He loved the feeling of power the powder gave him.

After a long snort, Lisa started talking, and as she did, Ronny's mood darkened. Her story began with Heather. On the day Heather died, Lisa had borrowed her mother's car, ostensibly to drop off some friends at the mall. In reality, the reason she had wanted the car was far more basic: she had run out of coke and could not reach Ronny. Fortunately, she still knew their connection in New Haven, and she had planned to score some there. Then, she had pulled away from the entrance to the mall, but Heather had seen her car, and waved to her to stop. She had told Lisa that she was late for a hair appointment in Branford and asked if she could have a ride. Lisa had given her the ride but decided to stop in New Haven for the cocaine anyway. Heather had always been naive, so Lisa told her that she was stopping in New Haven to run an errand for her mom, and her friend had asked no questions.

The deal had gone fine at first. She had told Heather to wait in the car while she went in the house. Their friends had great quality stuff and the high was just getting good when she heard a knock on the door. She answered it and found Heather there. Angry at the interruption, she told her to go back and wait in the car while she took care of things. Heather had shrugged and walked back down the steps. Meanwhile, Lisa had taken another minute to enjoy the feeling, taken one last toot, then had gone out. That was when things had gone bad. She'd found the car door open, and had seen two men rounding the corner with Heather struggling between them. Scared, she had panicked and run straight to her mom's car. Instead of following Heather, she had driven back home. That night she had seen the story about her friend on the news. Naturally, she had wanted to tell the police what she had seen, but how could she? If she did, then their friends would all get busted—something she knew she couldn't let happen.

Ronny asked her what the men who had taken Heather away looked like.

She told him that it had been too dark and rainy to get a good view, but one of them had been a huge man with a bad limp. Alarm bells went off inside Ronny. He knew a man like that, a man who was capable of doing what had been done to Heather.

Ronny refocused on Lisa. She was going on to her next problem—as he heard more, he paid more attention, because it directly affected his business.

She spoke of what Tim Reardon had done at Captain Jack's and what he had threatened.

Angry, Ronny raged, "You mean he got the whole load?! You fuckin' idiot. I let you work the high school because I thought I could trust you. Now you let me down. I'm really disappointed, Lisa."

She started crying. "Ronny, after what happened to Heather, I just haven't been thinking. . . . You've been wonderful. . . . I'm really sorry. You know that."

He pulled her head against his chest and stroked her hair. "Look, honey, let me check this out. Don't worry your pretty person about any of this shit. You did right comin' to Ronny."

Her tears came faster, and her body shook. "Ronny, what happened to Heather . . . it was horrible. I mean the paper said that she was raped and beaten so bad she didn't even look like herself! Sometimes I feel like it was my fault. If only I could've found you that afternoon!"

He pulled her head even tighter to his chest and said, "You got to get that crazy shit out of your mind. You didn't do nothin'. Ain't your fault she ran into some bad people."

"What am I going to do about Heather's brother, the soldier?"

"Don't you worry about him. I'll handle that. You just go home now—and don't fuckin' call him! He won't bother you. I'll make sure. . . . Here." He handed her a fresh vial. "That's 'cause you've been so good and told me everything."

After Lisa left, Ronny poured himself some rum and thought hard. He had several problems and he needed to find some quick solutions. The first threat was the fuckin' soldier. How the hell did the bastard know who he was? And who the fuck was he to mess with one of his shipments—even if it was just a small load for the school? This son of a bitch had to be stopped and *now*. Picking up the phone, he dialed some people he knew in New York and made arrangements. Ronny instructed them that he wanted this soldier "severely discouraged." When he hung up, he felt better. After they pushed his head in, the soldier would be a lot less enthusiastic about his questions. Next he wondered what to do about what Lisa had seen in New Haven. That one was heavy. He would have to give it further thought.

March 22, 1989—Short Beach

The weather was poor when Tim awoke the next morning. He had planned to rake Marian's lawn, but because of the heavy rain and high wind, it appeared he wouldn't get to it. At first he thought about skipping his early morning run as well, but he reconsidered. A run in the rain might help make up for the nearly sleepless night he had spent wondering what Lisa would do and what he could do if she didn't contact him. He had tried to call Andrea at My Dad's after he dropped off Lisa, but she wasn't there and whoever was working would not give him her phone number. Today, he would make a concerted effort to find her. She had to be told about her sister. His optimism grew. He would find Andrea, and together they would work it out.

Clad in an old pair of green sweats, he started down Baltman Place. At the end of the street he turned right and headed for the coast road. The thick sheets of rain water felt cold, and the puddles were deep, but he compensated for the discomfort by running faster earlier. Soon his muscles warmed up and he began feeling good. As usual, he kept his concentration almost entirely on running at his optimum pace. Everything else in the world could wait. He turned left onto the coast road. Soon he reached a long, deserted straightaway where the road narrowed and ran over some of Branford's familiar brown weather-beaten rocks. He liked this part of the run best. Here, the highway became more causeway than road and virtually hung out over the ocean. On clear days, he loved the scenery.

Tim did not see the anonymous brown Ford sedan when he left the house, but then he had not been looking for it. Because the two men in the car had been told by his cousin Larry which way Tim usually ran, they had carefully parked on an adjacent side street the Green Beret did not take. From where they sat they had a great view of Marian's house.

The driver, a former professional boxer known as "Ice," was short, thin, well-muscled, and spent most of his time collecting protection money from selected small businesses. As for his boxing career, the scar tissue on his face reflected more than adequately his lack of talent in the ring. Nevertheless, those who had run afoul of him had learned that his size was no reflection of how hard he could hit. The other man was also in the collection business. Named George, he possessed all the size Ice did not—though he was considerably slower. If George lacked the professional training of his companion, he was no less effective. Natural size, strength, and a proclivity for nastiness made him one of the best strong arms in the business. Both knew Ronny, but not that well, so their price for the morning's labors was high—besides, their instructions were that the soldier be "severely discouraged," and they charged a great deal for killing someone.

At least the job looked easy. The rain worked for them by offering a twofold advantage: it kept pedestrians off the street, and other drivers were preoccupied with just keeping their cars on the road. Ice and George would be able to perform their work unnoticed, as they preferred. As soon as the target turned off Baltman, Ice put the car in gear, and they followed him.

Running hard, Tim had the hood of his sweatshirt up and his face down; the farther he ran, the more he enjoyed the rhythmic sound of the falling rain. When he reached the causeway, he had the additional pleasure of the sound of the waves crashing against the rocks below and the taste of salt spray on the wind. Then he noticed a new sound growing, a car approaching from the rear. Knowing that visibility was limited, he slowed and started turning to make sure the car saw him. It was nearly too late. Snarls from a revving engine filled his ears, and the corner of his eye picked up the hurtling shape. To save himself, he tried to jump off the road towards the rocks below, but the car was too near. The right front fender caught his hips hard and painfully; then his airborne body glanced off the hood and the outside corner of the rain-slicked windshield. From there, shocked and disoriented, Tim spun over the top of the wooden guard rail and into the frigid waters ten feet below.

When Tim's body hit the cold water, the shock felt like a kick to his abdomen. Breathless, he sank fast; his brain commanded him to fight for life and get to the surface, but his shocked body refused to respond at first, and he felt his air leaving him. Finally, he oriented himself to the light above him, and he used his last ounce of energy for a desperate thrust. It worked. He moved upward and it got lighter quickly. Dizziness filled his brain, then, like a shot, powerful legs propelled him through the surface, and he filled his grateful lungs with air.

Even with the fog of rain and surf about him, he could see the rocks of the causeway just feet away, and he made for and reached them quickly.

He found a tenuous foothold and two handholds. Waves broke against him, but he felt well-enough situated to be able to hang on—at least for now. He took physical inventory. He could breathe, but only with difficulty and terrible pain. Most disconcerting of all, he found his left arm only functioned reluctantly. At least the pain hadn't fully set in yet. That, he knew, would come later—along with time to locate exactly what was wrong. No question, he was hurt—but not that badly.

Now he reviewed his situation. He knew he could not survive long in the frigid water, the rock he held was slick, and the swirling seawater breaking against him sometimes submerged him completely. But he didn't know if the people who had done this to him would check to see the results of their handiwork. His view of the road was limited because at this point there was a near vertical pitch to the highway. Nevertheless, he could see the guard rail, so he concentrated on that. For now he figured he could do little more than react to whatever might come; so he would hang on for a few minutes and await developments.

Minutes passed, but he saw no car, nothing but the pouring rain and the crashing waves.

Now his extremities felt numb, and the weakness of hypothermia tugged at his energy reserves. He knew he had to move to live. Part swimming and part hugging the rocks, he made his way slowly toward a wooded area in the direction of Marian's house. The distance, he calculated, was about a hundred yards. Fighting the swirling water beating his body against the rocks and keeping his attention focused on the road where the car might be waiting, he ignored his injured arm and fought for every yard.

After what seemed an interminable amount of time, he made it to a small beach where he lay exhausted in the surf hoping he was partially concealed. Here, his years of conditioning paid dividends, because he felt his strength and breath begin to return quickly. A wooded area lay only twenty feet in front of him; still, he was cautious. Cold and wet was better than dead; so, patiently waiting, he fought the breakers while he scanned the shore. He saw no one, so he took a chance and, with what was more a stagger than a run, charged for the safety of the trees.

Once there, he paused again to see if he had attracted any interest. Satisfied he had caught no one's attention, he started making his way back to Marian's house. The cold had weakened him nearly to the point of incoherence, but years of training and experience facing hardship took over, and he kept his mind to the task at hand. He avoided the roads and sidewalks. They were now danger areas, and he did not even know what make of automobile the enemy drove. He had to mistrust them all. He bet that they would have Marian's house under surveillance, so to be safe, as soon as he had it in sight, he kept close to neighboring buildings and hedges and slowly circled the area. He saw nothing suspicious. Optimistic that he might be safe, he vaulted over a side hedge and entered by the back door. He braced himself, but no bullets flew behind him.

Tim need not have worried. By the time he reached the house, his assailants were already on I-95 bound for New York. The rain caused even more traffic delays than usual. They arrived at the city late and nearly missed one of their collections. That afternoon Ice telephoned Ronny.

Ronny asked, "You did it?"

"Yeah, the soldier won't bother you no more. He's shark bait."

"What?"

"I said we did him good."

"You mean dead?"

"We didn't stick around to be sure, but it wouldn't surprise me. Consider him 'severely discouraged.' "

"You shithead, I didn't want the fucker dead—just bruised.

Don't you think that two dead bodies from the same family in the same week might attract some fucking curiosity?"

"Hey, we don't know nothing about that. We just know what you told us. Don't matter anyway. Body's in the ocean, so nobody'll find it."

"They better not."

"Hey, we did the job. Just send us the fucking money, or we come back for it in person."

"You'll get your goddamn money." Ronny hung up the phone and fell back into his plush couch. The last thing he wanted was the extra attention two dead Reardons would bring to Branford.

CHAPTER EIGHT

Wednesday, March 22, 1989—Branford

Once indoors, Tim first checked the house. Marian was sleeping. The night before she had been drinking again and had taken tranquilizers—she would be out for some hours yet. He checked his watch. It was only 9 A.M., and he had left the house shortly after eight. It had all happened in less than an hour—albeit a long hour.

For the moment, he seemed to be safe, but for added security, he grabbed a knife from the kitchen before heading for the large pink bathroom. Once naked, he stood before a full-length mirror attached to the back of the door. His body was a mess, with severe bruises on his chest, legs, and arms. Close inspection revealed that his arm was probably not broken; however, the shoulder was definitely separated. It had happened once before and he recognized the sensation. Pain would nag him for a couple of weeks, but it would heal; and in spite of the pain, it could still be used if necessary. His physical condition was the first good news of the morning. It hurt, but he knew it wasn't serious.

He showered quickly, using the hot water to cure his hypothermia. Drying himself, he felt the stiffness and pain increasing, but he still felt better than he had, and with his head now clearer, he assessed his situation as he dressed and packed.

Somebody wanted him dead, and while he didn't know who that somebody was, they knew both his identity and where he was staying. That meant there was only one course of action open. To stay in Marian's house meant death, so he had to get out quickly. Then an idea cut through his thoughts with force: death! Though he was not positive of it, he was fairly sure that whoever had tried to run him down thought they had killed him. If they believed him to be dead, he would have the advantage. With this in mind, he stopped packing and replaced his things where they had been. If death gave him an advantage, dead he was—at least for a while.

The next problem concerned how he could find whoever had driven the car. Here, he decided, his answer (or at least his starting point for finding it) was obvious: Lisa. His sister's old address book was still in her room, and from it he got Lisa's address and phone number.

Now he had a starting place. He was on their turf, he didn't know all the players, he was in bad physical shape, and he had no weapon but a knife; but Tim Reardon cracked his first smile of the day. If the game was to be a violent one, he believed he would win it; and in the process, he reasoned, he might just find the answers he sought. Grabbing only what he could carry and wear, he stepped out into the rain. He could call a taxi when he reached a pay telephone. Then he could rent a new car. Throughout his walk to the phone he remained alert, but the smile never left his lips. The man known for finishing whatever he started now had a mission, one he relished pursuing.

Meriden, Connecticut

Tim remembered a string of inexpensive motels on Route 66 in Meriden from a trip he had long ago taken with his parents to see a Yale football game. They were very private, and only twenty minutes north of New Haven on I-91; he selected a small establishment known as the Woodsman Motel. It was typical of thousands of similar motels which can be found throughout America: low-slung, long, and family-owned. On the way, he began plotting his next moves. By the time he had checked in, the plan was formed.

The room was small but comfortable, and it had a telephone. But because he did not trust the bored manager who manned the switchboard, he decided he would go to a nearby gas station and make his calls from a pay phone.

Once he was settled, he drove his new rental, a beautifully anonymous Chevrolet Cavalier, back to Branford. Parking it down the street from Lisa's house, he waited. It was just before two in the afternoon.

The wait was not a long one. Lisa returned home from school on a school bus slightly after three, and minutes after that, she pulled out in what Tim guessed to be her mother's car and headed for town. Following her proved easy. Traffic remained light and the kid was not suspicious at all. But before long, Tim was. She made three stops. The first two were to shopping centers, where she parked some distance from the cars clustered close to the entrances. At each one, kids either drove or walked up to her car. Then he saw a ritual repeated several times. The kids gave her money and she passed something back to them.

But it was her third stop that interested Tim the most. After conducting some brisk business in the shopping centers, she drove to a residential area. Following her there was more difficult because traffic was lighter, but Tim managed it nonetheless. When she finally came to a stop, it was at a condominium complex. He pulled into an adjacent parking lot and watched her carefully as she left her car, strode purposefully up to number seventeen and rang the bell. Ronny answered the door, and that confirmed Tim's suspicion.

He had been right about Lisa from the start. She was not just a user, she was a dealer who worked for Ronny. She did know something about Heather. He could feel it.

As to why men had tried to kill him, Tim could only form a supposition, but he was confident that it was fairly accurate. After he had talked to her, she had gone to Ronny. Ronny had seen him as a threat to his business and called a hit. It was that simple, and at the same time, that complicated. Tim now knew that he had a real problem. People like Ronny survive in a tough world on their mystique as much as their money and intimidation. Without that air of invincibility they work so hard to create, the Ronnys of the world would not be able to function. No, he decided, Ronny would not give up trying to kill him. Tim would have to bring that idea to an end himself. Suddenly, he smiled. He had a plan. It was still rough, but he would refine it during dinner. With luck, his problems and his questions would all be solved tomorrow.

He had dinner at a Chinese restaurant in Meriden. After eating, he went to a gas station to use the telephone. His first call was to a number at Fort Devens in Massachusetts.

Tenth Special Forces Group consists largely of three battalions and assorted support elements. The headquarters and two battalions are located in Fort Devens, and the forward, or 1st battalion, is located in Bad Toelz, West Germany. Each battalion contains fifteen to eighteen A-Teams of twelve men each that are the actual striking elements of Special Forces. Their leadership consists of one captain, who is the team leader; a warrant officer, who is the team executive officer; and a master sergeant, known in slang as "the team sergeant" but officially titled "the operations sergeant." Because this man has usually been in S.F. longer than anyone else on the detachment, the experience level and competency of the team sergeant has incalculable impact on the character, quality, and proficiency level of the detachment itself. Below this group, and on fairly equal footing, even though they are designated as "senior" or "junior," are two medics, two demolitions men, two weapons specialists, two radio operators, and one intelligence man. The reason there are two of everything is so that if any one member is killed, another can step in to fill his place; additionally, having two men with the same skill means that the detachment can be divided to perform two missions simultaneously. To further promote versatility, most S.F. soldiers are cross-trained to perform more than simply their own specialty. In theory, one twelve-man detachment may be inserted and operate anywhere in the world without support because each man can live off the land, use any weapon, speak the local language, and make supplies such as demolitions on his own. In practice, teams vary in abilities and character just as the individuals who comprise them do, and it is impossible for everyone to stay proficient at everything—though they do try.

Because Special Forces must fulfill missions around the globe, most of its soldiers develop a certain set of skills relevant to a particular area of the world in which they specialize. Consequently, once a man is assigned to a group (and there are three others besides 10th Group), he tends to stay there for a very long time. However, because the army loves to move its soldiers about, each soldier does rotate periodically. The movement usually occurs between his forward, or overseas, battalion and his stateside unit. In the case of 10th Group, this means that most of the men stationed in Bad Toelz were once stationed at Fort Devens and vice versa. Therefore, many know each other well, no matter where they might presently be stationed.

Tim telephoned a medic friend at Fort Devens named Fred MacIntyre. They had known each other a very long time, and had been on a detachment together. The phone rang twice, and then Fred picked up. "Hello."

"Hey, Fred, this is Tim Reardon."

"Timmy! How the hell are ya? You back from Toelz? Don't tell me you're calling from Germany?"

"Naw, I'm in the States on leave. How's it been with you?"

"You know, same old shit—just got back from winter-warfare training two days ago."

"Look, Fred, this isn't a social call. It's business. I got a problem, and I need help."

"Well, talk to me. If I got it, you got it. You know that."

Tim told him both his plan and his motives. When he finished, Fred remained silent for a moment. Then he said, "Man, this is some heavy shit. . . . What the hell, the guy sounds like a true blue asshole—let's do him. You send this girl my way, give me a time and a place, and I'll see she gets the stuff. Just be sure she don't know who I am. Give her a place to meet me and I'll be there in civvies. Tell her to look for an orange windbreaker with 'Florida' written across the back and front as a far-recognition signal. Then she should ask me if I've ever been to the Brauneck. I'll answer, 'Yes, and I loved it.' "

"Great, I'll call her, pass it on, and get back to you in about ten minutes. I'll also get a far-recognition signal for her. I owe you one, Fred."

"You don't owe me shit, asshole. Just make sure I don't have to go to your funeral. It ain't that I care about you so much. It's just that I hate shining up my dress uniform. Good luck."

"Thanks." Tim hung up and placed another call to an old girlfriend named Tina. She was a nurse at a hospital near Fort Devens—they had met on a range where she had been practicing her favorite hobby: pistol shooting. Though the relationship had eventually ended, they had remained friends. When he related what he needed her to do, she turned out to be more than willing—the chance to make a drug dealer uncomfortable appealed to her sense of adventure. Smiling, Tim hung up and called Fred back with the instructions. The plan was on.

CHAPTER NINE

March 23–24, 1989

At 8:30 P.M., Tim pulled a rented nondescript Plymouth Reliant K into the Branford Creek Plaza on Route 1 just outside of Branford. Fearing the Chevrolet might have been spotted, he had left it at the motel. Tina was expected at 9:00, but as usual, Tim liked to be early—besides, he'd finished with all his shopping and errands and felt anxious to get the mission under way. At 8:45 a new yellow Pontiac Grand Prix with Massachusetts plates and a gorgeous blonde pulled in and parked in front of the furniture store as Tim had instructed. Clad in a black sweater, black knit wool hat, and blue jeans, he walked over to the car. He saw her smiling as she watched him approach, and when she opened the door, she looked as good as ever, and even better, if possible. About five foot four in height, thin-faced, high-cheekboned, and extremely well-endowed, she had dressed and made herself up to advertise each attribute with deadly effect.

They embraced, and Tim felt pangs of memory stirring with the scent of her perfume. After some seconds, she extended her arms and surveyed him. With a sentimental smile she said, "Timmy, you look terrific. Why'd I ever let you get away?"

"That's easy, it's because we're both so damn stubborn that we fight more than we make love."

"Maybe, but it was terrific while it lasted."

"Yeah, it was—and you're still the craziest and most hard-headed woman I've ever know. If you weren't, you wouldn't be here."

Like a thoroughbred before a race, she smiled and tossed her hair. Tim remembered the gesture well. He said, "C'mon, we've got to talk about this thing and make sure we're both working off the same script or everything'll get screwed up. This one could be tricky. You as devious as ever?"

Her blue eyes glowed. "You bet."

She reached through the still-open door of her car and pulled out the package from Fred. "Here's the goody bag from your friend. He said it's all there."

"Good." Tim took the package and reviewed the plan with her once more. As usual, she was a quick study, and he had no doubt she would do well.

When he was satisfied she was ready, he got into the rental and drove off. She followed him in her Pontiac. Their destination was Captain Jack's.

He parked in the most remote corner of the parking lot. She parked near the entrance and casually sauntered over to the Reliant. He tossed her the keys. "He was in there at eight when I left. If he's not there now, tell the bartender he has something you're looking for and see if you can find out where he went, but when I left, he didn't look as though he was going anywhere for a while. Following the silly son of a bitch for the entire day was quite an education. He's a hell of an entrepreneur. You got the description straight?"

Tina smiled. "Don't worry, hon, if he's in there, I'll be out in half an hour with the man in tow." With a wave, she headed for the front door.

Tim remained in the car, climbed over the bench seat into the back, and began getting ready. The package from Fred contained three hypodermic syringes, several drugs, and a new double-edged fighting knife. Into the first syringe went fifty milligrams of sodium pentathol. The second required a bit more time because it contained a mixture: ten milligrams of Haldol, seventy-five milligrams of Demerol, and seventy-five milligrams of Vistaril—in medical circles, what he made was known as a "cocktail." The reason he needed two syringes was simple. The sodium pentathol knocked out the victim fast, and the cocktail kept him that way for about four hours. Next, Tim checked the knife. Not suspecting he might need it, he had left his fighting knife in Germany, so Fred had sent him this replacement, a Gerber Mark II; for his purposes it was far superior to Marian's borrowed kitchen knife. With a razor-sharp four-inch double-edged blade and a black metal handle, the Gerber was a superb weapon. He liked the way it gleamed in the semi-darkness of the back seat and the familiar feeling of its heft. It was one of many tools common to his trade, one with which he had a great deal of familiarity.

Satisfied, he watched the front door of the restaurant and prepared a blanket in the back seat that he could hide under. A familiar calmness settled over him, as it always did when he knew action was impending—he just hoped the shoulder would hold up.

Tina was good to her word, and within twenty minutes, she approached the car with a very pleased-looking Ronny following close behind. Under the blanket, Tim heard them pausing for a minute outside the driver's door. She giggled, and he moaned. Then the car doors banged shut and the engine roared to life. Slipping from under the blanket with an easy shrug, Tim grabbed Ronny about the throat in a smooth, powerful motion with his good arm just as the drug merchant reached for Tina. Right behind came his other arm with the knife. He felt agony in his shoulder, but he now had Ronny's head immobilized and his knife against the frozen drug dealer's jugular vein.

A small pistol magically appeared from Tina's purse and a metallic sound filled the car as she clicked the safety off. Tim said, "Put your hands on the dash, shithead." Ronny, his eyes fixed on Tina's gun, did as instructed.

"That's a good boy."

Tina grabbed the syringe on the back seat with her free hand, and with the proficiency of an experienced nurse she found a vein in Ronny's left arm and pushed the needle in. Within seconds, the drug merchant was drowsy and mumbling. A minute later, Tim felt him go completely limp. To be sure the dealer was not just acting, he held him for an additional minute, then said, "Cocktail." Tina hit their victim with the second needle, and Tim released his hold.

The next part of the operation was high-risk, but they had to chance it. After making sure that the parking lot was empty, they wrapped Ronny in the blanket and placed him in the trunk. When it was over, Tina looked at Tim. "He'll be gone at least four hours. . . . You won't kill him, will you?"

Tim smiled. "Much as I would like to, I'll fight the urge and leave it to some lucky guy in the future. But I can guarantee you one thing, it'll be a night this son of a bitch will remember."

"Tim, you were right about this guy: he is a slimeball. I've got to go home and take a shower to wash his odor off. Take care, animal."

"I really owe you for this one. Drive careful . . . and don't worry, nobody will ever know who you were."

"I'm not worried," she said, and kissed him on the cheek. "You know, for this one, dinner better be good, and there better be candles on the table."

He laughed. "You got something in mind for dessert?"

The toss of her hair and the smile indicated that she did, and with a wave she strode confidently toward her Pontiac. Tim slid into the Plymouth. Momentarily, he wondered whether or not he should have left her to begin with. Then he shook the thought from his mind and started the car. The body in the trunk gave him more serious things to contemplate.

They left the parking lot separately. She headed east for home. He headed north.

Three hours later, Tim was driving with his headlights off down a Vermont logging road that wound through tall trees and dense foliage. He knew the area from a field exercise staged there some years previously. Once he was a couple of hundred yards in the forest, he stopped the car, blackened his face with carbon paper, grabbed a small black backpack from the back seat, and opened the trunk. The snow on the ground was old, partially melted and then refrozen, and it crunched under his feet with each step. Ronny was still unconscious but breathing. He picked him up in a fireman's carry and moved into a small ravine just out of sight of the car. Once there he squatted, opened his pack and went to work. He finished in about ten minutes. Now all he had to do was wait for his enemy to wake up. He did not have long to wait—which was good, because it was very cold in the early morning hours in that forest.

Ronny woke up with his mind befuddled, but the powerful cold cut through the fog fast. Still groggy, he opened his eyes. Something was very wrong. He was completely naked, in impenetrable darkness, and he smelled what he thought were pine trees. Slowly, his mind began working. He saw images of a girl in a car with a gun. Then he remembered a knife at his throat. That was unnerving enough, but what he saw now was even more bizarre. Four ropes held his body to four trees in the spread-eagle position horizontal to and barely touching the frozen ground. His head throbbed, and he moaned in pain. He felt other ropes about his chest and waist that made it impossible for him to move anything but his head, and all he heard was the wind rustling through unseen dark branches. For a minute, he wondered if he was dead and this was hell.

Suddenly, a dark unrecognizable face loomed out of the blackness. It kept approaching until the piercing eyes behind the mask stared at him from only inches away. A wave of panic filled his mind. With difficulty, Ronny found his voice. "Who the fuck're you?"

No answer.

"Whoever the fuck you are, you fuckin' with the wrong man. I hope you know you dead already."

Still no answer—now the shadowy figure tickled his throat with a knife. He felt blood trickling down his neck from needlepoint cuts the blade made. Then a hand grabbed hold of his testicles and pulled them away from his body. In shock, he stopped breathing. He felt pain between his legs and warm liquid he knew to be his own blood trickling down his crotch. Stunned, he realized that the knife was cutting at his testicles. He screamed, and even to his own ears, it was completely unrecognizable as a human sound. He felt tears pouring down his cheeks, and his body began quaking.

From somewhere in the darkness a quiet, inhuman voice whispered, "Stop shaking! If you want a clean cut, stop shaking. Oh, go ahead, scream all you want. It probably hurts, and there's no one here to hear you anyway—except maybe the bears. But don't shake. Personally, Ronny, I have no idea if bears like to eat these things or not. Guess I'll see soon—bet you'll bleed to death before they get here, though."

The voice gave Ronny hope. Whatever was doing this to him was at least human, and humans could be bought. His words poured out like flooding waters, "Whatever you want, man—you got it. I can make you rich. . . ."

Someone laughed in the darkness. Were there more than one?

Still, there was hope! The cutting had stopped. "Please, please," he begged, "don't cut no more. Whoever the fuck you are, we can deal, man. I'll give you anything."

"Deal, Ronny?" That whisper again. "You've already dealt enough. You've dealt pain and personal destruction to children for years. That's why I'm here, asshole. A lot of people don't like you. I'm going to take care of it for them."

"Man, you fuckin' crazy? I ain't shit. Really, I'm just a small businessman. I ain't shit. You want the bad people, I tell you, man."

The whisper said, "I think you are a liar." Ronny felt the knife between his legs again.

Desperate, he cried, "No, man! Don't do it! I'm tellin' you straight. Anything you wanna know I tell you. I'll make you rich too." The knife wasn't moving, so he kept on talking. "The real man—he's Michael Pyne. He got a big house in the Thimble Islands. Yeah, Robin Island they call it. I been there, man. He's got more money in his office safe than the government! He's got boats! He's got everything! He runs it all, man! I mean, he's big!" He felt cutting again.

"Jesus Christ! No! What the fuck you want from me?"

The whisper said, "You're not talking fast enough. I want to know everything, and you are lying—and talking too slowly."

Now Ronny talked—as fast as his lips would move. There was little about the Connecticut drug scene he didn't know, and he told it all—names, places, and the fact that a large shipment was coming from New York the next day, along with where, when, and how. Finally, the whisper said, "Ronny, little Ronny, you just bought your balls."

The drug salesman's body relaxed.

"Don't get too happy, asshole. I said you could keep your balls—not your life."

Suddenly recognition hit Ronny's crazed brain. The eyes! He knew the eyes! He had seen them at Captain Jack's. The fuckin' soldier boy was back from the grave! Now he had a threat he could identify. Anger filled him. He cried, "I thought you were dead, asshole!"

Tim was off balance. He had not planned for this. How did the dealer recognize him? He let the drug merchant's words hang on the soft forest wind for a moment while his brain worked. His plan had been to warn Ronny off his trail as if he were protected by a rival drug organization. Now that the dealer had recognized him, it had to be abandoned. The only real option left seemed to be killing him—even then there was no guarantee one of Ronny's friends wouldn't keep up the chase. Still, no matter what he did, if he let the animal live through the night, he was sure to pursue—if he killed him, it might be over.

Ronny babbled again. "Soldier boy, I know you don't get paid shit in the army. I can make you rich, man. You stop this shit now and we're even, right? You were fuckin' with my business so I fucked with you. So now you fucked with me. It's over, OK?"

"No, it's not over. Why was Heather Reardon killed? You like your balls, you'll tell me."

The dealer's head fell back into the snow. "Look, man, I don't know why the fuck the kid was killed."

Tim placed the knife back in his crotch and began cutting. The dealer howled once more. "Christ! Please stop! OK, you check with Pyne's men. I think they got something to do with it."

Tim had had enough. The nearness of Ronny made him want to vomit, and at the same time he felt disgusted with what he himself was doing. He didn't mind fighting to defend his country, but this was different. This was torture. He had never done it before, and he didn't like it now that he was. His fingers tensed on the knife. If he was going to do it, it had to be now. He stopped. He hated Ronny. The world would be a better place without him, but he couldn't commit murder. Self-defense or war was one thing, but murder was Ronny's game, not his. He hissed in the darkness. "Shithead, it will never be even. But you better know one thing. If by some miracle you survive this night, you better leave me and mine alone, or I'll be back. And next time your balls'll be bear food."

Tim had the third and final syringe in his hand, and he injected it into Ronny's thigh. Ronny cried out, "Hey, man, what the fuck you doin' now?"

"Shithead, you know all the crap you've been getting rich over? Well it's only fitting you get the chance to use your product before you die. Don't worry about your body. The animals will probably munch on it for a while, but eventually somebody will find your bones . . . or maybe not. You'll like hell, asshole. Good-bye." Tim walked away and waited. He heard the dealer sobbing in the darkness. After a few seconds, the sobbing slowed, then stopped.

As soon as Ronny grew quiet, Tim ran back to where he lay unconscious, and quickly untied him. What he had in fact given him was another shot of sodium pentathol that would wear off in about fifteen minutes. Working quickly, he had him loose in seconds; then he ran back to his car, started it, and drove back down the trail in the direction he had come. His destination was the main highway headed south, and he reached it without incident.

On the way back to Branford he made one stop. At a rest area next to Interstate 91, he took Ronny's clothes—including his gold watch, chains, rings, and bracelets—from the trunk, stuffed them in a garbage bag, and put the bag in a green roadside trash can. He smiled to himself as he thought of the dealer waking up. And he was glad he had decided not to kill him. At least he wasn't a murderer. Besides, he had a new plan, and if it worked, it wouldn't be necessary to kill anyone.

CHAPTER TEN

Friday, March 24, 1989—New Haven

It was nearly nine A.M. when Tim reached Connecticut, so he drove directly to the rental-car place and returned the Plymouth. From there, he took a taxi to the motel in Meriden, checked out, and returned the rented Chevy. It was ten when the taxi brought him to Marian's house. He apologized for disappearing without warning, packed up his gear, and bid her good-bye. They both swore to get together again, but Tim really didn't believe it would happen. With all his gear packed in the original rental, he pointed the Dodge in the direction of New Haven. With luck, he thought, it would all soon be over.

Tim found the police station easily. And, having called Pulcinella from Marian's house, he also knew where he could find the detective. As soon as he entered the squadroom, he strode up directly behind Pulcinella and waited.

Pulcinella turned about in his gray swivel chair and with surprise on his face said, "Damn, this is the second time you've done that. I didn't see you come in, soldier."

Tim smiled. "Detective, I've got something I think you're really going to like. Is there someplace we can talk?"

He shrugged. "OK, let's go to the interrogation room. But I also have some questions for you, my young friend." As he got up from his chair, Tim was again surprised at how short the detective was. Momentarily, he wondered if the police force had some sort of height requirement, then decided that it didn't. Pulcinella grabbed several candies from his dish and offered one to Tim. He declined. The detective shrugged again, put one in his mouth, and led the way through the maze of desks to the interrogation room.

The interrogation room was of the type common to all police stations—off-white soundproof walls, a single table, four chairs, and no window. The detective waved Tim into a chair. "What's so important?"

Tim related what he had learned from Ronny. Pulcinella interrupted, "Where did you get all this stuff?"

"Does it really matter, Detective? The point is that I have it. All I want to do is make it useful."

"Look, these people aren't stupid. You should know that before you go any farther."

"Don't worry, Sergeant. I can handle myself."

"Yeah, and that's what I've been meaning to talk to you about." He took off a rumpled gray suit jacket he was wearing and slung it on the back of his chair. He sighed and looked down at the table. When he lowered his head, Tim saw that his graying short hair was thinning severely on the top. Finally, he raised his head again. The lines on his face looked deeper. "Mr. Reardon, I did a little research, and what I learned is that according to your service record, you are not a cook. What I would like to tell you is that if you try to use some of those skills you have been developing in the defense of your country to disrupt New Haven, I'll make sure you go to jail even faster than the dealers. Now, you want to continue our conversation?"

Tim considered what he was going to say carefully, then shrugged. "Detective, I have no plans on disturbing the natural order already in place here. What I would like is to see whoever killed my sister pay for it. What I have done is ask some questions that might help you, and as soon as I am done telling you what I know, I'm leaving the country."

Pulcinella nodded. "Fair enough."

Tim continued with his in-depth description of the Connecticut drug world.

The detective took some notes, and let Tim talk until it was all over. Then he leaned back in his chair and studied some of the holes in the soundproofing. "I appreciate you coming, and I really don't want to disappoint you, but we already know most of this. Pyne, for instance, we've known about him for years, and there is no doubt that he's the largest connection in New England. The problem is that we can't prove it. The Feds have got him up on some income-tax charges, but those might not stick. In the end, we just hope we've done somebody some good somewhere. What I am saying is that I appreciate your help, but it is probably good that you have decided to go back to the army and let us handle things. Kid, I know you're mad right now. After what happened to your sister I can understand that. The problem is that if you stay around here asking questions, bad things are going to happen. Now go home!"

"What about the shipment?"

"We'll follow up on the information. If it pans out, then we'll get them. How sure are you about the shipment?"

"Detective, if I say it's coming, then it is."

"OK, I believe you. We'll check it out. Now go home!"

"There is one more thing, Detective."

"Yeah?"

"I've got a name for you—someone who I think can help you find out who killed Heather, but I want one favor in return."

The detective's face remained impassive. "Yeah, what's the favor?"

Tim handed him a slip of paper. "On that paper, you will find my address and phone number in Germany. When you figure out who did it and make an arrest, call me."

"All right kid, you have my word on that."

"OK. There is a girl in Branford named Lisa Volente. She sells drugs at Branford High and used to be Heather's best friend. I think she knows what happened to Heather and why. Anyway, she can lead you to someone who does."

"I'll check the girl myself. Anything else?"

"Yeah, get 'em, Detective."

"Believe it or not, I want to solve this one as bad as you do."

Tim stood. As he did, he moved his shoulder and an electric jolt of pain reminded him of his error. He winced.

Pulcinella watched attentively. "Something wrong, kid? You look like something hurts."

"I tripped when I was jogging."

Branford

That evening a small sedan of Japanese manufacture pulled into a vacant lot along Route 1, and two of Pyne's men met it. Once the money and drugs had changed hands, the police moved in and made the largest drug haul in Branford history. Curious friends pummeled Pulcinella with questions on how he'd gotten his information. He smiled and remained mute.

Saturday, March 25, 1989—Branford

Ronny hadn't thought much about the information he had given Tim. He had been too angry. That morning had been the worst of his life. Naked and freezing, he had only procured clothing by convincing a farmer that he was the victim of an angry wife. Then he had hitchhiked home. It had taken until late that night; once he had made it, he had endured further suffering at the hands of his doctor in the form of five stitches on his privates. When it was all over, he made an irrevocable decision. That fucking soldier was dead. Exhausted, he had then slept the night through.

He woke up to a ringing phone. It was Lisa. Apparently, the soldier had gone to the cops, because the police were looking for her. She had run away as soon as her mother had told her about a detective calling, but, unable to find Ronny, she had had to hide with their friends in New Haven. Ronny told her to wait there, and said he would call her back later. He had some thinking to do.

Once showered, he made some toast and turned on the television. The news was on, and the lead story was the drug bust in Branford, the shipment he had told Reardon about. Angry, he threw his toast back on the plate. The fuckin' soldier had told the cops about more than just Lisa. Christ, Ronny thought, if anyone ever found out where the bastard got his information, he was finished. Nowhere on earth would be safe for him. Ronny's anger turned to fear.

He leapt to his feet and furiously paced the floor.

The problem now was damage control. Lisa was the only one who could link him to the soldier; it was remote but enough. He had to turn that around, and an hour later he had an idea about how. He made a call to his friends in New York and got exactly what he wanted. They were on their way.

In a second phone call, he told Lisa where he wanted her to meet him in New Haven. She sounded relieved and said she would be on the corner waiting.

When he pulled his Mercedes up to the corner, she was there as promised. He threw the door open, and she jumped in and threw her arms around him. As Ronny gently loosened her grip and she slipped lightly into her seat, he almost regretted that he was going to kill her.

"Ronny, thank God. I knew you'd help me." She reached across the center console of the Mercedes and gave him another hug.

Ronny smiled, put the car into gear, pulled away from the curb with his usual deliberateness, and headed into traffic.

"You gonna send me to New York or someplace, Ronny?"

"Yeah, something like that. I'm taking you to meet the people who're gonna take care of you now." He reached into his jacket pocket, pulled out a paper packet, and held it before her. "Look, I brought you some magic."

Like she was drowning and someone had thrown her a rope, she grabbed the drug with joyous intensity. Seconds later, much of what he had given her was up her nose, and Ronny saw her face relax.

Head leaning back onto the headrest, she settled into her seat. Dreamily, she looked at her protector and asked, "Where are we going?"

"We're going to a party, sweetheart. A party where you can have more whiff than you ever dreamed about. Then you're going away to where it's safe."

Back in the pleasure of her high, she remained quiet.

After a drive of less than five minutes, Ronny pulled his car into an isolated vacant lot. It was far too cold on this March day to have a party in a vacant lot; but in Lisa's state, Ronny doubted that this would ever occur to her.

At the far end of the vacant lot sat George and Ice's old Buick. Ronny pulled up next to them, and as he unlocked her door, Ice opened it. Ronny said, "Lisa, I would like you to meet a couple of friends of mine. They're going to move you somewhere safe just like I promised."

George grabbed her arm. She smiled, "Hey, dude, we gonna party?" Then Ronny saw the smile leave her face. Half out the door and standing uncertainly on one foot, she looked back at Ronny and said, "I don't know these people. Don't leave me here, Ronny!"

The drug dealer smiled and grabbed the arm that was still in the car. In seconds he had her sleeve rolled up. "Girl, you got one chance to stay alive: tell me the truth. Did you tell the soldier, Reardon, all about the drugs in Branford?"

Lisa stared. Fear filled her face. "You won't hurt me, Ronny?"

He tried to look sympathetic. He knew she lied easily, and he bet that she would do just that if she thought it would save her. "No, babe, if you tell me the truth, I'll protect you."

"Yes, I told him a few things."

Ronny's grin grew. "Baby, didn't your mother tell you not to listen to men like me?" Disbelief filled her eyes as the needle entered her arm. Reacting far too late, she tried to pull away. George made sure she couldn't.

The drug dealer studied her panicked face. "Ronny's had a bad couple of days. I think you know why. Thanks for some great fucks, but good-bye, Lisa." The silent men outside grabbed her and brought her staggering to their car.

Once she was safely unconscious and stowed in the back seat, Ice came over to the driver's side of the Mercedes. Ronny slid the electrically controlled window down silently. With a New York accent Ice said, "You were right. This kid's got something to do with the lost shipment. You sure you cleared this with Pyne?"

"Yeah, take care of it good, huh?"

Ice nodded. "You got it."

The window closed as softly as it had opened, and the Mercedes eased away. Ronny felt satisfied. Court had been held and the verdict was guilty. "Someone," he said to himself, "had to be convicted. Better you than me, Lisa." The thought made him laugh out loud.

It was a very bad week for Branford cheerleaders. The next morning Lisa's body was found in a stolen car in Branford Creek Plaza with a short, shaky suicide note Ice had written in such a way that it could have been anyone's writing on the seat next to her. If there was a bright spot in the affair, it was that her death was painless.

J.F.K. International Airport, New York

About the time Ronny took Lisa for her last trip, Tim sat in a departure lounge preparing to return to Germany. Lack of space on previous flights to Munich had forced him to spend the evening in a New York hotel. While waiting for the plane he read the paper. The drug bust in Branford had been spectacular, and overall, he was convinced he had accomplished a great deal. A major setback had been handed to the underworld; Ronny was probably too intimidated to be much of a problem; Tim's revenge had been swift and efficient, with a minimum of damage to himself or anyone else. It didn't make up for Heather, but it felt good nonetheless. He did not then know about Lisa.

CHAPTER ELEVEN

Sunday, March 26, 1989—Robin Island

The sun shone brightly as the launch carrying Ronny approached Mr. Pyne's small boat dock, but it did little to relieve Ronny's nervousness at being greeted by Pyne's massive enforcer, Julian Salka. Pyne liked maintaining his clean, sophisticated Ivy League facade, so Salka handled all the dirty business on the street. Salka had been a small-time thug before Pyne, but with his muscle and Pyne's connections and business smarts, the two had made it big. He was the only man Pyne really trusted.

Ronny put his hand out for the giant to shake. Salka ignored the gesture and instead nodded his head toward the mansion on the hill.

Ronny froze and stared at the enforcer's face. It was framed with thinning blond hair, and blue eyes stared back over the hooked nose, but it was Salka's body that was most striking. A devout weightlifter and a giant to start with, Salka had swollen his muscles to the point of the grotesque. Salka turned away and began whistling softly under his breath as he walked toward the mansion.

Ronny followed the smiling, whistling giant, and noticed once again Salka's slight limp. Some said he'd got it on the street; others claimed it was an old football injury. Ronny didn't know, but mused that anyone who didn't know the enforcer would have the impression that he was a man who enjoyed a good joke. And Ronny was sure that he did—as long as the joke had something to do with kicking a puppy or breaking bones. With that in mind, he could not help but feel, as he followed him up the path, that his contract had already been drawn up and the giant was just waiting to implement its terms. He would be very careful about what he said to Pyne that day.

Salka preceded Ronny into Pyne's office and stood next to his partner's oversized desk with his massive arms folded across his chest. Pyne himself sat behind the desk and remained that way until Ronny came to a stop before him. Then, with the banker's manner he favored, he stood, reached out for Ronny's hand with a warm smile, and asked, "Well, Mr. Milano, how can I help you? I trust your business is going well?"

"Uh, business is fine, Mr. Pyne. There is something else I . . . uh, know about. . . ."

Salka interjected, "Mr. Pyne is busy. Get to the point."

"Sorry, you know that shipment that got busted? Well, I know how it got busted."

"Yes?" Pyne leaned forward with interest, and encouragement spread across his face. Ronny began to relax.

"Yeah, well, see there was this high-school girl who sort of got around. . . . Anyway, I don't know how, but she found out about the shipment. I was sitting in Captain Jack's and she came over and hinted to me like she knew something special. I told her to keep her damn mouth shut. . . ."

Pyne interjected, "Who was the girl?"

"Uh, Lisa Volente. Anyway, there was this army guy who came back for his sister's funeral, Tim Reardon."

"Who was his sister?" Pyne asked patiently.

"Heather Reardon. She was also Lisa's best friend. You know, she was the kid the papers were harpin' on when she got herself killed in New Haven."

"We know who Heather was. Continue."

"This guy Reardon was running around town asking about our business, and the word was that him and this Lisa got together and then he went to the cops."

"Where are Lisa and Reardon?"

"Well, the soldier sorta disappeared. The girl—I thought you'd like it if it was handled, so I did her, then Ice and George from New York took care of the body. But she talked before she was offed."

Ronny thought he saw suspicion in Pyne's eyes. His question confirmed Ronny's fears. "Did anyone else hear what Lisa had to say?"

"Oh, yeah, George and Ice were right there. I got their number. You can call them if you want."

"Mr. Milano, I want to thank you for the information. Would you be so good as to wait outside for a moment while I confer with Mr. Salka on this matter."

"Yes, sir." Half backing and half walking, Ronny departed the office.

Salka eyed Pyne. "I think we better call the two shitheads in New York."

"Julian, I think you are correct." Pyne motioned towards the phone and Salka placed the call.

When he hung up he nodded towards his boss. "Looks like it all checks out."

"Do you think the soldier's life is worth fifty thousand?"

"Sounds fair to me. I'll put the word out. We'll find him." Salka frowned.

"What is it, Julian?"

"The Milano shithead. I don't like the way he thinks he can take care of our business. I'd have liked to talk to that kid myself. Don't look good we got somebody that stupid making decisions for us. Seems like this guy ought to become an example. He shoulda brought the girl here, and he knows it."

"My sentiments as well. Take care of him, Julian, only let him live. He does make us some decent money."

Salka departed with a smile. There was work to be done—his kind of work.

When Ronny Milano got home that afternoon, he could walk only with difficulty, and each breath caused pain. Nevertheless, he preferred hurt over dead, and the contract was out. That fucking soldier's days were numbered, and Pyne would never know who had really squealed on his shipment.

CHAPTER TWELVE

Tuesday, March 28, 1989—Branford

Larry had not planned to attend Lisa's funeral, but at the last moment, he changed his mind, donned his suit, and went anyway. He had gotten high with her several times and had kind of liked her. This time, he had been unable to procure any pot to smoke before the ceremony, so he was more or less clear-headed when he arrived. Immediately feeling uncomfortable, he stood next to someone he really did like: Ronny.

The similarities between Heather's and Lisa's services were undeniable—even to Larry. Each was buried in the same section of the cemetery, and each received more or less the same ceremony. The main difference was one of opulence. Lisa's parents did not have as much money to spend as Marian.

Because Larry was not high, this funeral got to him. For the first time, he wondered about the drug world. Previously, he had simply not seen anything wrong with what he was doing. And he still did not see anything bad about smoking pot—nor the people who sold it—but he was beginning to question the safety of harder drugs. His opinion of the people who sold drugs was about to change dramatically.

Larry had cooperated in setting up Tim in the attempted rundown (he had always hated Tim), but he had done so not knowing anyone would try to kill him. Ronny had claimed that the Green Beret had interfered with business, and he simply wanted to "talk to him and scare him off." As far as Larry knew, that is exactly what had happened, and he still looked upon the dealer as a friend who helped him stay high. Accordingly, he was neither surprised nor nervous when the drug merchant put his arm around his shoulders after the funeral.

To Larry, Ronny was a powerful man to be envied, so the gesture made him feel important. Looking appropriately solemn, Ronny looked down and said, "Hey, Larry, it's rough about what happened to the kid, huh?"

"Yeah, I guess it is."

"I got a surprise for ya. Why don't you follow me, and I'll show you something."

Larry smiled. He felt good that an important man like Ronny was taking some interest in him.

There were stores across the street from the cemetery, and Ronny led him to a small, quiet parking area behind them. As soon as they rounded the corner, three men, whom Larry immediately recognized, stood before them, and his excitement turned to fear. Dressed in black pants with a blue windbreaker stretched taut against his heavy muscles, Julian Salka stood, smiling and whistling an obscure tune. The men with Salka were named Mecro and Rick. Mecro was nearly as large as Salka and was said to be his weightlifting buddy, but unlike his boss, he had dark hair, little physical grace, and his dull eyes betrayed none of Salka's alertness. He wore a black overcoat. Rick was smaller than the two giants but known for his karate skills. He too wore an overcoat, but his was brown. Ronny said to Salka, "Here's the soldier's stepbrother just like you wanted." Then, turning his face towards Larry, he said, "If I were you, I'd tell them whatever they want to know. Goodbye, kid." Larry heard him running back the way they had come, and, with the sound of the disappearing footsteps, he suddenly realized this was serious trouble.

Salka leaned against the wall in front of Larry, and Mecro and Rick moved to his sides. Then the giant stopped whistling.

When Larry returned home, he found he could do little more than lie in bed. When he coughed, flecks of blood spotted his saliva, and any movement at all hurt.

Salka had been after information about Tim. He had told the giant he didn't know where Tim was, other than that he might be in Germany; but Salka hadn't believed him until he was in too much pain to stand. As he lay splayed in the filth of the alley, Salka's last words had burned into his brain. "Larry, your stepbrother's gonna be dead soon. Not you, not anybody else can change that. You got information, and you don't come to us first, you're dead too. Because we're nice guys, you get a grand you give us something we can use. Next time, maybe we're not so nice. You remember that."

For the first time in his life, he decided he was into something he could not handle. Fear and anger overcame him. He didn't just dislike Tim, he despised him. Tim was always the success story: so sure that he was right, so confident of his ability to master the world, the tough guy who could handle anything. Marian always told him he wasn't fit to clean Tim's shoes. But, in the final analysis, Tim was still family. It was one thing to help scare him off, but it was another to help them kill him. As much as he disliked his stepbrother, he hated Ronny and Salka even more. Ronny had set him up for the beating, and Salka had made him feel helpless. He had had enough. He was going to fight back. Larry's next action was by far the bravest and most unusual thing he had ever done. Later, he would always wonder why he'd done it at all.

Overcoming the pain, he picked up a sheet of paper and wrote a letter to Tim. The letter was brief, but in it, he described and apologized for how he had given Ronny information on when and where Tim jogged so the dealer could talk to him and "scare him off." Then Larry told Tim about Michael Pyne's contract, and that it had been put into effect because he had helped the police in the drug bust.

Feeling good about the letter, he hobbled out to the mailbox and placed it inside. The postman came around three, and the letter began its journey into the Military Postal Service and on to Europe.

CHAPTER THIRTEEN

Monday, April 1, 1989—New Haven

Andrea's condominium was a two-story townhouse adjacent to Yale in one of New Haven's better neighborhoods. It featured thick carpets and a tasteful modern motif, but, most importantly, to her it was a sanctuary from a cold business world. Today, though, was different. Her sanctuary was now a prison. Since Lisa's funeral the previous week, she had remained there, isolated in body and spirit. Ignoring food, work, and everything else she had once enjoyed, she now did little but smoke and watch old movies she had always loved, again and again, as if she would somehow find some lost clue to her sister's death from Bogart in *Casablanca.*

Her boss had given her the week to herself; but with an important client due, he had made certain she understood that her grace period would be over tomorrow at 9 A.M. And Andrea dreaded the idea of returning to work, for Lisa haunted her.

She could not believe the police report. Yes, there had been a suicide note in Lisa's car, but the suicide thing didn't make any sense. Lisa had been upset over Heather's death, but not so upset that she would have killed herself. Of that, Andrea was certain.

What disturbed Andrea even more was the news that her sister had been a serious drug addict. At first, she had rejected the idea, but the results of the autopsy had verified it. Lisa had done a lot of drugs. She thought of how her sister had so often admonished her for smoking. Lisa hadn't smoked cigarettes, just everything else available. Sitting on her couch, Andrea held her head in her hands and felt the wetness on her cheeks once again. She should have seen the signs: Lisa's unexplained absences, her wild mood swings, even the runny nose she kept charging off to colds. "My God," she asked herself, "how could I have missed it?" She had loved her sister. Now, she felt as responsible for the girl's death as the dealers who had supplied her. It was all because of her career, she reasoned; if only she had not been so intent on making money, she might have noticed her sister was dying. She might have been able to save her.

For days she had pondered the death. But the more she thought it over, the less sense it made. Yes, the veins in Lisa's nose had showed considerable cocaine damage, but there was only one needle mark discovered on her body. Did that mean her sister had suddenly developed a taste for massive doses of heroin? No, she decided, none of it was true. Someone had killed her. Unfortunately, neither the cops nor anyone else would listen. Restless to do something, she picked up her phone and dialed the number of the investigating detective. On the second ring a nasal female operator's voice came on the line. Finally, she got him.

He answered, "Brownley."

"Hi, this is Andrea Volente."

"Oh, yes, how are you, Miss Volente? I hope you and your family are doing better. How can I help?"

"Detective, I know you investigated thoroughly, but isn't there any possibility you may have overlooked something?"

"Miss, when we filed our report we informed you in clear terms exactly what our findings were. I know you have a difficult time accepting that your sister injected the drugs herself, but believe me, if we could find any proof at all of anything different, we would gladly follow it up. It just wasn't there."

Andrea's voice rose several octaves higher. "Lisa would *not* have committed suicide! Please listen to me! She didn't!"

She heard Brownley sigh. "I'm sorry, miss, but as near as we can tell, your sister was upset over the death of her friend. There was a suicide note next to her body. We have found no evidence to indicate it was anything other than what it seemed. I wish I could do more for you, but I can't. Look, there are other people in your position, and they have formed groups. If you would permit me, I will be happy to connect you with one such group in your area."

Her voice now back to normal but colder, Andrea responded, "No, Detective, that won't be necessary. I can see you've done your job already. You're right, I'll just have to accept it. Thank you."

"You sure you won't let me give you the number of that group? I've seen these things in action, and they really do help."

"No, thank you. That won't be necessary. Good night, Detective."

"Good night, miss."

She hung up.

Andrea had called Detective Brownley for reassurance, but his dry, self-assured, patronizing voice had only magnified her frustration. She jerked herself to her feet, and for several anxious minutes paced her living room. Grief had been consuming her all week, but now she felt something different; she felt anger stirring where the remorse had been. She turned on the television to watch another old movie, but found the news on and paused with a videotape of *It's a Wonderful Life* still in her hand. The smiling local anchor was just giving the introduction to one of the night's headline stories. The camera cut to courthouse steps, and the field reporter took over.

"Al, in a few seconds, alleged drug czar Michael Pyne will come down these steps after having the tax-evasion charges against him dropped. The grand jury did not hand down the expected indictment today. The prosecution's main evidence was connected with files seized by the Federal Bureau of Investigation during a sweep of Pyne's home off Branford, Connecticut; but the court ruled that the files were illegally seized, and the prosecution's case fell apart. Here comes Mr. Pyne now."

Amidst a sea of scurrying reporters, Michael Pyne emerged from the courthouse flanked by his bodyguards and a man the reporter introduced as Pyne's attorney, George Rembard. They paused on the steps, and the camera zoomed in on Rembard. "My client will not answer any questions; however, we have prepared a statement. Today justice was in one way served, but a far greater injustice will live on. My client is nothing but an honest businessman, as the grand jury has confirmed. But the slander that has been heaped upon Mr. Pyne since these proceedings began has been even crueler than the legal process itself. Mr. Pyne was not arrested on drug charges, yet the press and the government acted as though he was. Clearly, the damage done to Mr. Pyne's personal reputation will take years to repair. End of statement."

One aggressive reporter shouted out, "Hey, Michael, how do you feel about the verdict?"

The camera panned in on an elated Pyne holding clenched hands above his head. The press surged forward, he lowered his hands, and he and his entourage pushed their way through the tightly packed mob to their waiting limousines. The camera caught Pyne sliding into his car, then his chauffeur in full double-breasted livery shut the door.

Horror filled Andrea. She did not merely recognize Pyne; she had made the biggest sale of her career when she sold him his house in the Thimble Islands. Always ambitious, Andrea socialized with the "fast crowd" in Branford, a crowd where casual cocaine use was normal. She had known for a long time that Pyne was in the drug trade. Still, she had sold him the house. The big commission had made it easy for her to overlook the man's negative side. But now Lisa was dead, and Michael Pyne was alive and rich. In a rage she dropped the videocassette she still held, grabbed a dirty wine glass from the end table next to her, and threw it against the wall. Seconds later she was up and pacing once more. The grief, anger, and frustration were too much. Someone had murdered her sister, but no one seemed to understand that. Her parents were too grief-stricken for questions, and the police had deserted her. No one else she knew wanted to make even a half-hearted attempt at finding the truth. Aloud, she raged, "No! It will not end this way."

Suddenly, she reached her decision. She would find out what had happened to Lisa herself, and she believed she knew where to start.

She grabbed her car keys, coat, and shoulder bag, ran out her door, leapt into her car, and launched her Firebird toward Branford.

Shelton Avenue, New Haven

Andrea sat in her Firebird on Shelton Avenue in one of the worst neighborhoods in New Haven. She had suspected that Lisa's room might hold some answers, so she had started there. Since her father had gone to My Dad's and her mother to a friend's house, she had been able to conduct a thorough search in private. And it had paid a dividend: a scrap of paper with an address she had found in the pocket of a pair of Lisa's jeans, the address of the faded, brown, dilapidated house she now watched.

She knew her white skin would be conspicuous, so she had parked her car several doors down and across the street from the address on the slip of paper. Electing to remain in her car, she had sat for an hour watching the house, smoking, and wondering what she was doing.

She saw no one exit or enter the house, but the street was busy. A group of gang members sold drugs on the far corner; nearer, children, who should have been asleep hours ago, played on the sidewalk. But that was normal for Shelton Avenue, where crack was king.

She looked again at the house and considered her situation. One part of her, the part that had grown up a paratrooper's tomboyish daughter, said that being there made sense. The address was the only out-of-the-ordinary item in Lisa's effects. Somehow, she believed, this place must be a significant piece of the puzzle.

But her more cautious side told her she was crazy. Killings were common on Shelton Avenue. She was unarmed, conspicuous, and she had no idea what she was looking for—or what to do if she found it. She should probably let the whole thing die, or give the address to the detective and let him do something.

The determined side of her won, so she continued her surveillance. Finally a tall black man wearing gang colors broke away from his cronies at the corner, walked to the brown house, and entered it. Minutes later, he reemerged and walked past Andrea's car on the opposite side of the street.

Andrea felt disappointed. She had seen a gang member entering and leaving the house, but what did that mean, that he had killed Lisa? She lit a cigarette and exhaled the smoke toward a side window she had left slightly open for that purpose and returned her attention to the house. Then she heard the noise at the window.

When she turned, she saw the barrel of a pistol poking through the crack she had left. Behind it, she saw the man she had just seen leaving the brown house, and he was smiling.

"Look what I got. A pretty white girl's come visitin' the 'hood."

Andrea's keys were in the ignition, and she glanced at them; but as though he read her mind, he continued, "I'd foget them keys I was you. Face gonna look funny with a big hole in it. Now why not just come on out and join the party in the 'hood?"

Andrea hesitated.

"You dumb, bitch? That means open the door slowly."

Andrea opened the door, slid from the seat, and stood beside the rear fender. She noticed her hands shook, her legs felt unsteady.

The tall man had removed his pistol from the window but kept it pointed at Andrea's chest as he reached into the car and grabbed the shoulder bag she had left on the passenger seat. Deftly, he slid her wallet out with one hand and flipped it open.

"Woo, I got me a poor white girl here. You only got forty dollars cash?"

Andrea nodded.

"Then you must be down here to rip off the brothers."

"No, no, it's nothing like that."

"Then what you doin' sittin' here fo the last hour."

"I'm looking for someone. If you'll give me back my wallet, I'll show you."

He extracted her cash with two fingers and tossed Andrea the wallet. She fumbled to get it open and finally, with awkward fingers, found Lisa's picture and held it out for his inspection. "She's my sister. I was looking for information about her. I understand she used to come here . . . to meet friends."

He studied the photograph for a moment, then asked, "Where she now?"

Andrea heard him, but her eyes had fixed on the pistol barrel, and, though she tried, she could not speak.

"Bitch, you deaf?"

She realized she still held her cigarette and took a deep drag on it. Somewhat reassured, she said, "Uh, she died."

"Damn! Some white girl dies and right away, it's us caused it."

Andrea blurted, "No, it's not like that, really. I just want to ask people who knew her what they know."

"Woman, either you crazy or you stupid. 'Les you want to do business, you got no reason to be here. Know what they call me?"

"No."

"They call me the Axeman 'cause I don't take no shit offa nobody. I axe 'em. Tell you what, tonight your lucky night. Ain't nobody here know no bitch look like your sister, but you keep buggin' us, bad things gonna happen to you." He held up her forty dollars. "For that valuable information, and all my trouble, I'll just keep this, and you best get yo ass back to yo white yuppie fuckin' world and don't come back—less you gonna do some business or you want pain. Remember, I seen your license, so I got your address now, and I know what yo car look like. I see you, then I got to figure you fuckin' with me, and you gonna find out why they call me the Axeman."

Already scrambling for her shoulder bag, Andrea responded, "Thank you." She was in her car and starting it before he could respond. As she roared away from the curb, she saw the Axeman laughing in her rearview mirror.

Back in her condo, her hands still shaking, Andrea poured herself a glass of wine, then collapsed in her recliner. She felt physically and emotionally drained, but in spite of the Axeman, in spite of feeling foolish over her trip to Shelton Avenue, she also felt some satisfaction. The confrontation with the street thug had reinforced her suspicions. Someone on Shelton Avenue knew what had happened to Lisa.

Yet her problem remained. She was not a trained investigator, she could not sway the Branford police, and she feared the violence the Axeman represented. She gazed at a framed photo of Lisa on the coffee table and saw once again the sparkle in her eyes, the long, blond hair she had brushed so often, and her mischievous smile.

No, the Axeman didn't matter, or the Branford police. She would not rest until she knew the truth about her sister.

Then she thought of someone else who had lost a sister and she remembered his offer to help her if she ever needed it. If no one else cared or knew what to do, maybe Tim Reardon would. Just hours before, she had felt the situation had overwhelmed her. She needed control, and she believed Tim Reardon might help her get it.

She picked up the phone and dialed Marian Daniels.

"Hello."

"Hello, Marian? This is Andrea Volente—Lisa's sister."

"Oh Andrea, please—let me say how sorry I am. It was bad enough I lost mine. Now you've lost one of yours." Andrea noticed she sounded drunk.

"Thank you. Uh, I was hoping you could do me a favor."

"Well, if I can, I'll be happy to try."

"When Tim was here he did something for me. I wonder if you have his address—I would like to send him a thank-you note."

"Now, Tim, there's a good man. Why can't Larry follow his example instead of hanging around with bums?"

"Yes, he seemed like quite a guy. Do you have that address?"

"Oh, sure, here it is." Marian said the address slowly, like she was reading something unfamiliar. That finished, she spent another fifteen minutes going on about her wonderful Heather. When she finally hung up, Andrea breathed a sigh of relief, moved to her computer, and began typing.

Dear Tim,

We met two weeks ago at My Dad's bar in Branford. You also met my sister Lisa.

This letter might sound strange, but please bear with it. If you don't answer, I'll understand.

The thing is that something happened to Lisa. The police say it was suicide, but I think she was killed. Now everyone thinks I'm crazy.

Anyway, you once told me that if I needed you, I should call, and I had hoped that, after Heather, you might understand how I feel. Perhaps, with your background, you have some suggestions for me. I don't think I'm crazy, and someone should answer for Lisa.

I hope you are doing better now than when I last saw

you. After this I really can say I understand how you felt that night in Dad's. I want you to know that I enjoyed meeting you, and I think you are the only person in the world who can understand what I'm going through right now.

Friends,
Andrea

She mailed the letter via overnight mail on her way to work the next day. The clerk assured her that Tim would have it first thing on Tuesday morning.

BOOK TWO

THE TEAM

When bad men combine, the good must associate; else they will fall, one by one, an unpitied sacrifice in a contemptible struggle.

—EDMUND BURKE, Irish Statesman

CHAPTER FOURTEEN

Tuesday, April 4, 1989—Bad Toelz, West Germany

Bad Toelz, nestled along the Isar River Valley where the Alps rise abruptly from the Munich plain in southern Germany, is a traditional Bavarian community. In Roman times, it was thought that the water flowing beneath the town possessed magical curative properties. The belief persists today, so not only is the town beset year-round by tourists and skiers, it also attracts an inordinate number of Europeans looking for "a cure." Since visitors are a primary source of income for the community as a whole, the ancient storybook air of the town is carefully preserved by its residents.

Another significant source of income in Bad Toelz is located on its outskirts: the small American army base known as Flint Kaserne. Constructed in the 1930s as an academy for S.S. officers, the Kaserne is a collection of several buildings centered on an extremely large edifice known as Building One. Building One is not one but four long, narrow buildings each about five hundred yards long and four stories high. They are set in a square surrounding a large grassy quadrangle, connected on each corner by towering turrets, and accessed by large, graceful archways on three of four sides. In the summer, the snow-capped peaks and the deep greens of the mountains behind the base form a striking contrast to the white walls and red roofs of the Kaserne itself. Immediately after World War II, General George S. Patton, a man with a keen sense of history and the dramatic, was so taken by the facility's striking beauty that he chose it for his occupation headquarters.

Today, Flint Kaserne is well known throughout the U.S. Army in Europe for two principal reasons. Enlisted men think of it with trepidation because it is the home of the United States Army N.C.O. Academy in Europe, but to the High Command it is significant because the sole combat unit stationed there is a battalion of the 10th Special Forces Group—commonly known as the Green Berets.

Tim Reardon had been "on profile" (medically prohibited from certain activities) for a week because of his injured shoulder. Profiles are often given to Special Forces soldiers because the nature of their work causes injuries on a regular basis, but most doctors treating Green Berets are endlessly frustrated. Profiles are considered embarrassing by those who receive them and therefore are largely ignored. Tim was typical. Even now he stretched his medical limitations by accompanying his team on an all-day hike up a jagged mountain known as the Reichelkopf. The walk went faster than expected, mostly because of the grueling pace set by the team sergeant, so they made it back to the main gate of the Kaserne two hours early, shortly before three.

Tim gave a sigh of relief when the team finally reached the gate. His shoulder throbbed, he was caked with mud, and inwardly, he cursed his hard-headed decision to go on the march. Still, he felt determined not to show his discomfort to his friends, so once they passed through the gate, he completed the walk across the quadrangle at a brisk pace, and entered Building One as if he had enjoyed the exercise. Once in the hall, he and the others split up in several directions. Some of the men headed for the snack bar, but Tim was anxious to get his gear put away, so he headed for the team room, making one detour en route—doing what all GIs overseas do as often as possible, he checked his mailbox. To his surprise, he found an overnight letter from Andrea Volente, and a letter from his stepbrother Larry. Preferring to think about the pretty Andrea, his eager fingers ripped into the overnight envelope.

Seconds later, his mood changed from excitement to guilt. Another dead child. He thought, "My God! What have I done?"

Next, he opened Larry's letter. It was short but to the point, and if it was true, the nightmare was not over yet. But was Larry lying? As he always did, Tim immediately weighed the situation. If Larry was right, he had serious trouble. This couldn't wait. He had to know now. Deciding it was time to make a phone call, he took a detour to his room en route to joining his team.

Detective Pulcinella was just getting ready to leave his desk when, as usual, his phone rang. "Pulcinella."

"This is Tim Reardon. How are you, Detective?"

"Fine, but the question I have is: are *you* OK?"

"I don't know just yet. Depends on what you have to tell me."

"Where are you, kid? Sounds like an overseas connection."

"Yeah, I'm not in the States. Look, I don't know who to trust right now. I heard a rumor that some people are after me. Maybe you told these people who I am."

"Hey, soldier, first of all, the rumors you heard are the same ones I'm hearing. Pyne is offering fifty thousand dollars for you. And as far as who you can trust goes: I warned you about these people. They're not dumb, and they don't fool around. Somebody figured you out, but it wasn't me. You think I'd have made the bust if I was a bad cop?"

"So what am I supposed to do now?"

"Well, I don't think they can get to you in Europe, but I'd still watch myself. Next, I'd stay the hell out of Connecticut. You come back here, you'll end up in a morgue. If you do come back to the States, you need to go somewhere nobody knows you—and don't tell anybody around here where you've gone."

"Isn't there some kind of witness-protection program?"

"You don't qualify, kid."

"Is there any way I can fight it?"

"Fight it? Fight what? This isn't something legal to take to court. You're tried and convicted already and there is a contract out on your life. If you're thinking about doing battle with Pyne, forget that too. Unless you can find a way to make his whole organization disappear, the contract stays in effect. In time it'll calm down, but it'll never really go away. The only thing you got working for you is that Pyne is big in Connecticut, but he's not actually Mafia. That means he doesn't have much influence outside the state—except in Colombia.

Still, word of the fifty thousand is going to travel. You can bet on that."

"So what you're saying is that I have to hide for the rest of my life?"

"Basically, yes."

"And the police can't help me?"

"I already told you there's nothing we can do. I'm sorry, kid. You wanted to know what was going on, and I gave it to you straight. There it is."

"Thanks, Detective."

"Watch your back and good luck."

"Bye." The phone in Pulcinella's hand went dead.

Tim sat for some seconds, considering what Pulcinella had said. Then he shook his head. There was nothing he could do then, so he made his way out of Building One and down to his team room, located in Building Seventy-one.

Team rooms in Bad Toelz vary in configuration depending on the location of the detachment. Some are in Building One, and some are housed in Building Seventy-one. Building Seventy-one is a three-story white cement-and-wood structure constructed in standard Bavarian style with three entryways into three stairwells. One detachment is located on each side of each landing, and Tim's was on the first floor. Similar in layout to most of the other team rooms, it had an office for the team leader and team sergeant, a common area where they gave classes and held team meetings, a couple of side rooms, and an equipment room. He knew his team sergeant would want everything put away immediately, so he bypassed the other rooms and went straight for the equipment room to stow his rucksack.

There was a small bar in the common area with comfortable chairs; once Tim had finished stowing his equipment, he took a seat next to the bar and waited for the others. Reviewing his talk with Pulcinella, he surveyed his surroundings as if seeing them for the first time. The team had been there in various forms for many years, and over time, several enterprising detachment members had done a good job of making it a comfortable place to meet. The bar was of nicely varnished oak. The plaster walls were a tasteful blue color, and there was an old carpet that matched the walls to some extent. Furnishings, either donated or appropriated, included three bar stools, an old brown imitation leather couch, and a couple of easy chairs. Adorning the walls were various trophies stretching back for years, the people who had earned them long forgotten.

As he studied his surroundings, the other men gradually straggled in. As is usual for detachments in peacetime, some men were away in various schools or on detail for one thing or another, one was on leave, and one had the day off as a result of pulling Staff Duty N.C.O. the night before. This left only five members out of twelve actually present in the team room that night. The first man in was a short, powerfully built demo man named Al Tanner. Team Sergeant Carl Langdon—a tall, stocky, blue-eyed, blond-haired man who was as strong as he looked—was next to arrive, and he sat in one of the easy chairs with his customary smile.

Tim felt Carl's eyes on his face. He asked, "Hey, Tim, you doing OK?"

"Yeah, Top, I'm doing fine."

"Well, you know, after all you been through these past couple of weeks, we can't help but keep an eye on you."

Before Tim could respond, medic Tim Franklin (known as Frank to his friends) entered and asked, "Hey, Top, the bar open or what?"

Carl waved a hand. "Sure, and pour me one too."

With that, someone shouted from the depths of the equipment room, "I heard that, and you lazy bastards better not forget the old man in here!"

Before anyone could reply, the man behind the voice strode up and stood in the doorway. Chomping on a half-smoked cigar with his fighting knife still protruding from his boot, he was of average height, balding, powerfully built, and dressed in nothing but a sweat-soaked T-shirt and polka-dotted boxer shorts. The team burst into laughter.

Carl said, "Jesus Christ, Mac, you gonna get dressed or are you hopin' some sweet young thing will happen by and take you away from all this?"

"Hell, Carl, I thought I heard you say it was time to drink beer. Bein' a good soldier and all, I always follow orders, so here I am. Now where's my damn beer?"

Chuckling again, Carl motioned for Frank to get behind the

bar. "Frank, take care of the old fart before he takes off his underwear."

Frank popped the top off a beer bottle and tossed it to Mac, who caught it in mid-arc with one of his leathery hands and took a long pull. Tim found Mac a marvel. A highly decorated Vietnam veteran, he was the cagy old veteran every A-Team needed. His real name was Bob McCullum, and he was notorious as one of the most wily N.C.O.'s in the battalion, a prolific storyteller, and the best man Tim could think of to have around when everything went wrong. Mac, with his unfailing sense of humor, was a difficult man to unbalance. Satisfied now that he had his beer, he disappeared back into the equipment room.

In Mac's absence, Tim studied Frank as he continued to open beer for the rest of the team. Taller than Tim, but very slim and blond-haired, he was a kindly man who never seemed to get upset, a flawless soldier, one who accepted people for what they were, and totally devoted to his pretty wife Rhonda and his two daughters. Two of the more serious men on the team, Tim and Frank had become close while serving together, and Tim was often a guest at dinner for some of Rhonda's home cooking.

By the time Frank had distributed the beer, Mac was back. Frank yielded his place behind the bar to Mac. When talking over beer Mac always had a new story that he embellished well with exaggerated sweeping gestures. Often, his head would get set in a determined posture that defiantly decreed that he was giving the listener the true story and there was no argument about it.

At first the talk was of the day's march and the immediate future. Finally, Carl Langdon turned to Tim, who had remained quiet throughout, and asked. "So Tim, now you're sure you're getting out in June?"

Tim smiled. "Yeah, Top, I'm afraid it's written in the stars now."

"You know I'm required to give you a reenlistment speech, so this is it. They're paying a ten thousand dollar bonus to keep guys like you in—you know that?"

Tim nodded.

"In addition, and don't let this go to your head, you're a good soldier—the kind of guy they want to see stay in. On the other hand, you seem to have something decent laid on for when you get out. There's a lot of bullshit in the army, and I can see how a young guy could get tired of it. You got something going for you when you leave?"

"Don't worry, Top, I'm already set up for college at the University of Connecticut in the fall."

The team sergeant grinned. "What you mean is that before any of us know it, you'll be making a lot more than we ever will. Just remember, I'll need a job when I retire in five years."

Tim said, "Quit joking, you'll be corporate president a month after you get out."

Langdon laughed. "You mean I'll be sweeping the corporate president's office." The team chuckled with him. "Anyway, all I ask is that you don't get a 'short-timer's' attitude: just do your job the way you always have until you get out."

"C'mon, Carl, you know me better than that. I'll get it done."

Langdon said, "I never doubted it for a minute."

From behind the bar Mac chimed in, "Hell, what I really want to know—mostly because he ain't said shit about it—is how the hell he got himself run over by a damn car?"

The other men laughed, Tim's cheeks shaded a hue, and Frank chided, "Probably ran into a jealous husband."

Tim defended himself, "No, it was raining, so he couldn't see me. I had the hood on my sweats up, so I couldn't hear him. You know—shit happens."

Mac went on from behind the bar, "Sounds like bullshit to me. Who needs another beer?"

Everyone did. As Mac handed out another round, he looked at Tim and continued. "You know how this place is, there ain't many secrets about people's personal lives that stay secrets; so naturally we all heard some stuff about what happened in your family, Tim. Of course, everyone's dying to ask you about it, but so far they've all kept their mouths shut and so have you. Me being the crudest of the group, I've decided it's time we came right out with it. What I'm trying to say is that the rumors around this place have damn near everything in the world going on with you. Course all that don't mean shit, but if you ever want to talk to anybody about it, this bunch right here would be pleased to listen or do anything else we can to help. We know you've had it rough."

Tim felt a little embarrassed. "Mac, I appreciate what you're saying, but there isn't much to tell. My sister died of a drug overdose on a street in New Haven. She was a great kid, and we were close. The whole thing still doesn't make sense. . . . Seems like it just isn't safe to be a kid now."

Mac looked down at his beer and in a low voice began, "I know what you mean. We get all caught up in what we're doing, then something happens to remind us that there's some bad stuff happening back home. I don't know if you guys know it, but I had a big brother once. We grew up in Maine working on my Dad's fishing boat together. Anyway, in 'sixty-six he graduated high school and volunteered for Vietnam. The army being what it is, they obliged and sent him to 'Nam with the 101st Airborne that same year. I followed him over in 'sixty-seven. He was only two years older than me, and we were tight. He survived 'Nam and became a cop in Portland, Maine. Four years ago, a junkie shot him in the back of the head while he was trying to arrest some other asshole. I'm not going to say I know how you feel, but I just remember I had a hard time with it."

Frank added, "Tim, we're trying to tell you not to forget you've got friends if you need them."

On that note the conversation moved on to talk about some of the Kaserne commander's new training policies, and in another fifteen minutes Al pleaded that he wanted to make it to the mess hall before it closed at 6:00. Next, Carl said that he had to get home for dinner or his wife would kill him. Mac, however, was already started, and announced that he planned to drink some beer that night if anyone would care to accompany him to the Community Club. Tim and Frank were in the mood, so they turned off the lights and locked up the team room. Outside Tim watched the sun going down over the Alps as they walked up the hill that led to Building One and the club. The sun's rays shot out through clouds and momentarily, he thought of Heather and wished she could be with him to see it. Suddenly, he stopped and let his friends walk ahead. Pulcinella's words echoed through his mind. "Unless you can find a way to make the whole organization disappear, the contract stays in effect." There, he decided, was his answer. He knew hiding for the rest of his life was not an option he could live with. He would make other plans, starting tonight.

From up ahead, Mac's voice boomed, "Hey, Reardon, you gonna stand there, or do something productive like drink a beer?"

Taking off after his friends at a trot, Tim responded, "Hell, no, this is one beer I'm definitely not missing."

CHAPTER FIFTEEN

Tuesday, April 4, 1989—Bad Toelz

The Kaserne at Bad Toelz was too small to support both an enlisted and an officer's club. Instead, in the back corner of Building One's large quadrangle, it had the Community Club. As Tim and his friends entered the club, they looked for and found a secluded seat in the good-sized bar area next to a window. As with nearly everything else in the Kaserne, the motif was Bavarian.

Tim went to the long bar and bought a round. After bringing the beers, he began to talk. "Guys, a lot has gone down in the past couple of weeks, and I've gotten myself into some deep shit. But I've got an idea, and you, my friends, are my starting point. You're probably going to think I'm crazy, but hear me out on this."

Frank laughed, "Tim, we don't think you're crazy, we know it. But go ahead and spit it out anyway."

Tim grinned briefly, then continued, "There is a contract out on my life." He paused to let the words sink in.

Producing Larry's letter, he related what had happened in Connecticut. Mac read the letter and let out a low whistle. "Man! You are in a world of shit!"

"I know, but I'm not going to lie down. I've got something else in mind."

His friends nodded, so he elaborated, "We all agree that drug dealers are the lowest form of life on earth today. But what can we do about them? Imagine, if you will, a big-time dealer's mansion. Somewhere in that house there is a safe. Within that safe there is enough money to ensure the early retirement of any group of motivated Special Forces soldiers with enough balls to seize the opportunity. Meanwhile, I don't know what you think, but greasing some major drug types sounds to me like a public service, plus my problem can be solved in one night's work. Let me tell you, I've never met assholes as severe as these before, and nothing would make me happier than to prove to them that they're not untouchables. They can ignore the law all they want. Well, so can we—only we've been trained to do it a hell of a lot better than they can. Besides, I owe my sister something."

Mac ran his finger around the lip of his beer glass. "I've had the same idea for a long time, an' it sounds good in a bar, but it wouldn't be as easy as it sounds."

Frank said, "I don't know about the get-rich part, but I wouldn't mind doing the dealer. Tim, you did the right thing, going to the police. If more people had that kind of courage, these sons of bitches would be out of business. I, for one, am not going to watch you go down alone. Mac, you're the intel man, so what are the problems?"

Mac took out a fresh cigar, studied it, then lit it carefully. "Well, there're several. First, you would have to hand-pick the team carefully. Any security leak and you're finished—all it takes is one drunk in a bar going off at the mouth and you've got a mess. Next, you've got to find a target. Looks like Timmy already took care of that part. Also, if you're going to do this son of a bitch, the intel work has to be perfect. I mean you can't just walk in. You've got to know what the hell's inside before you go. And, if you want to make any money, you've got to find out when it'll really be there. Most likely the guy will always have some cash on hand, but you want to do him when he's got enough to make it worthwhile. I mean, we can get some people for this job just to do it, but we're gonna have to have enough money to make it possible, so we gotta be able to make back at least our expenses. Next, you've gotta accept one thing up front: you're going to have to waste everybody there. If you leave anybody alive, they'll spend the rest of their days looking for you. Now to the big problem: none of this is going to come cheaply. How do you finance the job?"

Mac's steel gray eyes glowed behind his cigar smoke. In a voice just above a whisper, he said, "This could be it. Ever since my brother died, I've wanted a payback. I'd do this for free, gladly, but the money makes it even better. There's a lot of guys out there—guys with talent—who would jump at the job just for the money and the chance to grease assholes like this Pyne fella. . . . You know, when the mission is over, we won't be able to spend the money and live in the fast lane. The man who does that gets himself caught. No, we'll have to give each guy a share, then he'll have to bury it. What it is then is a security blanket. It takes away all the daily pressures that make life suck. Anytime you've got an emergency, you've got the cash in the backyard. Sure, you can buy a new car—even make your payments with it—but you better have payments or the I.R.S. is gonna know something's up. Tim, I love it—I can't wait to meet this bastard Ronny. I've got something special for him. There's only one major problem. How we gonna get the funds together to start the mission?"

Frank now spoke. "I know where we can get the money. Mac, how much do we need?"

"Yeah, right. Shit—I dunno—I'd have to think about it." He mused for a moment and toyed with his cigar. With a shrug, he said, "If I had to guess, I'd say at least sixty grand—you understand that's just a guess."

"I'm pretty sure I can get it."

Mac shook his head. "Now where you gonna get money like that?"

"Need-to-know only, Mac. Right now just believe that I can get it. All I want in return is to go on the mission—I've got to do this. Next, you said this place was on some kind of an island. Well, I know where I can get a boat too. Not just a boat: a cigarette boat with one hell of an engine."

All three men fell silent for a moment. Each realized they had just taken a gigantic step. Tim finally spoke up. "Are we really going to do this?" His companions nodded. "OK, so when?"

Mac responded quickly, "Look, in this unit everybody's always got more damn leave built up than they can never take. We pick guys who have time coming. Now, when is it that 10th Group don't do shit?"

Tim and Frank answered simultaneously, "Summer—nothing but details all summer."

"That's right, and the deadest month is August. This mission's goin' down in August." He let this statement dangle for a second, then continued. "Tim, you're going to be in the area of operations a long time before us, so you'll have to lay the ground work. . . . Wait a minute, forget that. If somebody makes you, you're history."

"Mac, I may have somebody on site who would love to help."

"OK, good. You lay low somewhere until we're ready to start moving in July. Frank, you'll have to get hold of this mystery money man of yours and be sure we got financing."

"Done, Mac. I'll let you know as soon as I can."

He grinned. "I can't believe this shit. So now what about the people? Before we even think about it, we gotta keep certain things in mind. Without even seein' the target or the situation, I figure we need six—maybe nine or ten guys, good guys, we gotta get the best—security prohibits makin' it any bigger, so we only take as many as we have to, no more. Next we figure who we want and make a list in order of preference. We're not going to get all the people we like, so we gotta be careful who we feel out, and we might have to figure on twenty different guys to get our six or ten."

Tim said, "The best thing to do is find out who, on our list, can actually be there and might go for it. We also should only use guys at least one of us has worked with in the past. Don't pick anyone by reputation alone. It can only be people we trust absolutely."

Frank blurted, "Here's what we do! Once we find out who we're going to take, we feel them out. You know, ask them if they're going on leave soon. They'll probably say 'no' because they can't get the time to do it. They'll most likely tell you how much leave they have. If they don't, ask them. We need to set a minimum of thirty days. If they have less than that, pass them by. If they have enough, feel them out on the drug issue. If it's something they care about, let the other two of us know, and we'll approach them together so they know we're for real."

Mac smiled approval. "I like it. The thirty-day minimum is smart. As far as the guys we feel out, I think anybody we pick is ninety-percent sure to want to go anyway. All these guys're just sittin' around prayin' for war. It's what they fuckin' live for. You give 'em real bad guys like these, they'll eat this shit up. I really think we can do this."

Tim stretched. His legs felt stiff. He said, "I like everything I've heard so far, but I think it would be good if we all slept on it. I'd feel better hearing this stuff from guys who are completely sober and have had a night to chew it over. Take a look at your wives and kids and make damn sure you want to get involved. If it really happens, we might not all come back. Hell, none of us might come back."

Mac agreed and suggested that, since his German wife Renate was visiting her family that week, they all meet at his place around noon for lunch the next day. Everyone said they could be there, so they left it at that. Frank headed home to his wife for dinner, Mac went over to the bar to talk to some of his friends, and Tim tried dinner in the back dining room.

The steak tasted good. After a week of bad humor he finally felt better, so after dinner he went back to his room, cleaned up, and went downtown with two of his friends, but he could not relax and enjoy himself. No matter what he did, his mind came back to the letters. If he hadn't done what he had with Lisa, she would probably still be alive. Sometime soon, he would have to tell Andrea, and he was not looking forward to that. Finally, there was the contract. Was somebody on the way to Germany to fulfill it?

Wednesday, April 5, 1989—Bad Toelz

By twelve o'clock the three men were seated around Mac's kitchen table. It was typical of most kitchens in married N.C.O. quarters in Toelz: high ceilings, white painted wooden cabinets, a small wood table, and a serving window facing the living room.

Mac opened the conversation. "Well, I don't know how you two feel about it, but I like this mission. We're takin' all kinds of risks, but it's a chance to do somethin' right. There's enough money in it to make it worthwhile, and Tim needs help."

Frank agreed. "Tim, I'm in—no matter what."

Tim shrugged. "Then I guess it's going to happen."

Mac frowned and said, "There's just one thing I wanna get straight with everyone here and now. We're not the bad guys. That means we can't kill any cops, kids either. We have to work this so the police don't get involved. If we get in a position where we have to take on cops, then we all lay down our weapons. That's the only way this can be done."

Frank and Tim agreed.

"Next," Mac said, "we have to do a good enough job so that it looks like a gangland hit when it's over and we fade away. We've got one big advantage here. These people don't know who we are, and they don't know anything is coming. If we're gonna pull this off, then it has to stay that way."

Again, the others agreed.

Once they began talking about potential team members, the work went fast. Within an hour, they had a list of friends and associates to check on. They agreed to use men from various bases around the world so that when everything was over, they could all fade into different directions.

Tim left the meeting with mixed emotions. The plan was in motion, but his common sense told him that a lot could go wrong before August. It might never come off—though his sixth sense told him it would. He just hoped that when it was all over, he would be able to live with the consequences.

CHAPTER SIXTEEN

Thursday, April 6, 1989—Bad Toelz

Tim's next move was to contact Andrea. She lived near the source of his troubles, she was motivated, and for now, she was all he had.

Letters could be lost and read by the wrong people, but German telephone records would be difficult to trace, so he decided to call her. About 9 P.M. German time, 3 P.M. American time, he dialed her number. She answered on the third ring. "Hello."

"Hello, Andrea?"

"Yes, who is this?"

"Tim Reardon. Are you alone? Can you talk?"

"Oh, Tim, did you get my letter? And yes, I can talk."

"Yeah." Tim paused; he wanted to move ahead carefully. "So, how are you feeling? I mean is everything OK?"

"Right now I'm not really sure how I'm doing, but you probably think I'm crazy after that letter."

"No, I don't think you're crazy, but I'd be lying if I didn't say I'm a little worried about you."

"Don't worry, I'll get over it. It will just take some time. You should know I meant what I said. I know Lisa didn't kill herself, and I can't just let this thing die with no answers."

She sounded sincere, so Tim went on. "Look, maybe I can help. I'm kind of working on something now, but it may or may not come together. I'm coming back to the States, and we'll talk then. I'll contact you. Just take it easy until I get there. . . . There is one favor you can do me in the meantime—if you would?"

"Sure, I mean, what is it?"

"You know anything about a guy named Michael Pyne?"

The line remained silent.

He asked, "Andrea?"

She blurted, "Why did you ask me that?"

"I can't say right now."

"I hate him! Everyone in Branford knows who he is. He lives on a goddamn island in a mansion I sold him. You understand, Tim? I knew what the hell he was, but I still sold it to him! Now Lisa's dead."

In Germany, Tim Reardon smiled. "OK, I understand how you feel. Now calm down. Look, maybe I can help you, but I need to know more about Pyne. Since you sold him the place, would you have the floor plans on file?"

"Of course. In fact I've got diagrams of the whole island as well as the house."

"Could you get those diagrams to me—and any other information about where Pyne lives?"

"What are you going to do, Tim?"

"I can't say right now, but I hope you'll trust me."

"I don't know, Tim. This sounds a little strange."

"I know it does, but you must believe me when I say that it may lead to answers about Lisa—and Heather."

A short silence came over the line, then she said, "OK, I guess it's not a big deal. I'll mail it either this week or next."

"Thanks. Now be careful until I see you. And please don't tell Marian anything about me coming back. In fact, don't even mention my name around her—or anyone else, especially Larry. You don't know me, OK?"

"No problem, I won't say anything to anyone. Besides, I hardly ever see them."

"Thanks, Andrea. Look, I won't be writing any letters, but I'll call you as soon as I know exactly what is happening. Meantime, do you have my phone number?"

"Yes, Marian gave it to me."

"If you ever want to talk, just call. If I'm here, I'll answer. If not, keep trying. Maybe something will happen in the future that will make things better than they seem now."

"Thank you, Tim."

"Andrea, one last thing: make sure nobody knows you're taking any diagrams of Pyne's house. In fact, don't show any interest in Pyne at all."

"Don't worry, I'll be careful."

"Thanks, I'll call you."

"Bye, Tim." They both hung up.

Tim sat on his bunk and considered what he had just done. When he had placed the call, he hadn't been sure where it would go. Now he had his answer: he had involved someone he didn't know very well in something that, if it worked out the way he wanted it to, could only end in destruction.

Saturday, April 15, 1989—Bad Toelz, West Germany

True to her word, Andrea had sent Tim what he had requested, and he gave Frank and Mac the material in Mac's kitchen—though he kept her identity a secret for the time being.

She had sent them Robin Island in-depth, and it proved invaluable for their planning. There were floor plans, interior and exterior photographs, and nautical charts. They indicated an English country house mansion atop a hill on an island that was heavily treed and contained several other structures, including a large guest cottage. The size of the target bothered them all, but three hours after beginning his study of the material, Mac had a rough plan and told his friends, "OK, now we got an idea what we're up against, but I need to know how many men this asshole's got out there, and I still need to know a hell of a lot more about the terrain. These real-estate photos just don't cut it. Anyway, I think nine guys ought to be enough. For now, I estimate we need two, maybe three, demo men—and they've got to be able to blow a safe; two good weapons guys; at least one top-flight medic to back up Frank. Tim, commo isn't that important on this, but electronic surveillance is. You can handle the surveillance before the mission, so we probably don't need an extra commo man to go in."

Each agreed with Mac's assessment, so they made final decisions about which of the available men best fit the operation. When contacted, each of the soldiers was interested in the raid. By the next evening, they had a team.

* * *

Back in his home, Frank locked himself in the bedroom, then dialed a number in Rhode Island. It rang twice, then a female voice answered, "Whitworth residence. May I help you?"

"I hope so, ma'am. My name is Tim Franklin, and I would like to speak with Mr. Sean Whitworth, if that is possible."

"I'm sorry, Mr. Whitworth is extremely busy this afternoon. Perhaps there is something I could help you with. I'm Jean Lockery, Mr. Whitworth's personal assistant."

"Thank you for the offer, Ms. Lockery, but I think it would be better if I spoke directly with Mr. Whitworth."

"Mr. Franklin, I can assure you I am privy to all of Mr. Whitworth's affairs."

"Ms. Lockery, I have no doubt you are a superior and capable assistant, but if you'll just bear with me on this, I'm *absolutely* certain that if you'll just tell your boss that Sergeant Franklin's on the phone, he'll want to speak to me. I am also just as positive that if you do not, he will be highly displeased. Believe me, this is one bit of business with which you are unfamiliar."

Ms. Lockery fell silent for a moment. As the personal assistant to the largest retailing giant in America, she was unaccustomed to anyone addressing her as this man had. Nevertheless, he did sound sincere, and she was just cautious enough to take him at his word. "All right, Mr. Franklin, please hold, and I will see if Mr. Whitworth is available."

Frank heard a clicking noise as he went on hold. A minute later an energetic, husky voice that belied the age of its owner came on. "Sean Whitworth here. Is that really you, Sergeant Franklin?"

"Yes it is."

"Hah! I knew you'd call someday. How can I help?"

"Can you talk, sir? I mean, is anyone there with you?"

"Don't worry, I can talk."

"Well, sir . . ."

"I told you years ago to cut out that 'sir' stuff. To you, my name is Sean."

"Yes . . . Sean. You remember you once told me that if ever I needed anything, money or anything else, I should come see you? Well, I need something, if the offer is still good."

"Sergeant, I am a man who hates unfinished affairs. As old and sick as I am, I have made it my business to conclude just about everything. The exception is you. When you saved my nephew and his wife in that automobile accident, you saved the only family I have. Hell, yes, the offer is still good! I owe you, and you will be repaid. What I wonder is, what happened that you changed your mind? You in money trouble?"

"No, nothing like that. But before we go any farther, there are a couple of things I should tell you. It wouldn't be right if I took your money and you didn't know what it'd be used for. I've got a friend who lost his sister to a drug overdose. Anyway, he tried to find out what happened, got some people mad, and now they're trying to kill him. He doesn't deserve this. He's a good man, and some of us want to help him. We'll need money to do it, and we'll probably have to break a few laws along the way—you should know that. But you have my word—if anything goes wrong, I'll be the only one who knows who you are, and I won't tell anyone. You'll get the money back when it's all over."

"Enough bullshit. How much?"

"Right now we figure sixty thousand."

"Sergeant, you're no businessman. Everything always goes over budget. I'll give you eighty."

"Sean, thank you. Uh, there is one other thing."

"What do you need?"

"A fast boat, preferably a cigarette boat."

"Done. Just tell me when and where you want it. Anything else?"

"No, that should do it."

"When and where do you want the funds?"

"Initially, we're going to have to send thousand-dollar increments to several places, so I guess we'll need ten thousand here in Germany next month, and the rest in a bank in the States within a month of that. When I see you in person, I can tell you where and when we want the rest."

"All right, now here're my conditions. You can have whatever you need, but I want to meet your friend personally. After that, I will distance myself from this project completely and never admit to having associated with you. All our transactions will be in cash for that reason. However, I do not like surprises, so I want you to keep my personal assistant, Ms. Lockery, apprised of the situation through separate channels. She will deliver the first installment that you requested to you in person on safe and neutral ground. Where are you in Germany?"

"At a place called Bad Toelz, near Munich."

"When can you and your friend meet Ms. Lockery in Munich?"

"We've got a major field problem coming up, but we should be back by Monday, May twenty-second."

"Fine, Ms. Lockery will be in Munich on May twenty-second."

"Thank you, Sean."

"Sarge, I'm doing this because you are who you are, and you want to help a friend. As far as your methods go, they sound wrong. There are official channels you should try first."

"We've done that."

"Well, then, I know some powerful people. I'd rather help you through them."

"I think we're out of choices like that now, Sean."

"All right, do as you wish. I wouldn't be where I am now if I didn't understand how to be ruthless, but remember: violence usually brings more of the same. I hope you succeed, but think again about my other offers."

"Thank you, Sean."

"Here's a number in Munich: 08-049-9786. Call that on the twenty-second; Ms. Lockery will be waiting. Don't talk to anyone but her."

"I understand. Good-bye, Sean."

"Good-bye, Sarge, and good luck."

That night, Frank told his friends about the money and the conditions that went with it. Mac was already uneasy about Tim bringing in someone in New Haven, and the idea of including even more civilians bothered him a great deal. However, they could not move forward without the money, so he accepted the situation, reluctantly.

CHAPTER SEVENTEEN

May 1, 1989—Munich, West Germany

When the call had first come in from the United States, Jean-Michel Thibaut had still been in the process of fulfilling another contract, but now that his last target had "accidentally" drowned in his swimming pool, Thibaut was ready to give the American his full attention. Munich was far larger than Bad Toelz, so he took a room at one of its larger hotels to remain as anonymous as possible.

Since he had no pictures, target identification was his first problem. To solve it, he placed a call to Flint Kaserne from a pay phone amidst the hustle of the Munich train station. A tall, slender, clean-shaven man with blue eyes and brown hair, he wore a dark green suit with a type of woolen overcoat favored in that part of Germany. To any passersby he looked every bit the local lost in conversation with an old friend.

It was 7:30 P.M. when a bored voice answered, "Bad Toelz Staff Duty N.C.O., Sergeant First Class Ryan speaking. This line is unsecure. May I help you sir?"

"Oui, this is Captain Francois LeClerk of the French Army. I am calling from the Munich train station. I am here in Germany on vacation, and I have an old friend in Bad Toelz, a Sergeant Reardon? I was hoping to—how do you say it—surprise? Yes, surprise him. Could you locate him for me?" He did his best to make his tone cordial—a brother-in-arms looking for an old friend.

"Well, sir, can you tell me what unit he's in?"

"No, I am sorry. I am not sure. He telephoned me recently

and told me he was in Bad Toelz, but he did not mention his unit. I do not think he was expecting to see me."

"No problem, sir, I'll look him up on the roster. What was the name again?"

"Timothy Reardon." Thibaut smiled.

"OK, Reardon, Reardon." There was the sound of papers shuffling. "Here we go. . . . Staff Sergeant Timothy Reardon . . . Bravo Company 1st Battalion, 10th S.F. You want his home number, address, or what?"

"*Oui*, his home number and address would be excellent. I was hoping to reach him tonight so we could have dinner tomorrow."

"Oh, I doubt you'll get to see him tomorrow, sir. There aren't many Green Beanies around here right now. Mostly, they're all gone on an exercise."

"Pardon? Green Beanies? I am afraid I do not understand this term."

"Green Berets, sir. Reardon is a Green Beret, and most of them are gone on an exercise. . . . Wait a minute, the Staff Duty Officer is in Special Forces. He'll probably know if Reardon's gone and when he'll be back. Could you hold a minute, sir?"

"*Oui*, of course."

Jean-Michel heard the sounds of muted conversation as the sergeant conferred with his officer, then Ryan came back on the line. "Yes, sir, Reardon's gone on the exercise. He'll probably be back around May twentieth." In an effort to be of further assistance, the N.C.O. went on to give the Frenchman Tim's address and phone number.

After he hung up, Thibaut felt pleased with the information he had gained, but also alarmed. He picked up the phone once more and dialed a number in the United States. A woman answered, "Mr. Pyne's office."

"This is the Frenchman. I need to speak with Monsieur Salka, *s'il vous plait.*"

A male voice came on the line. "Salka."

"There are some problems on my end you did not warn me of."

"What?" Salka sounded suspicious.

"You did not tell me who your friend was. Green Berets are not routine business."

"Reardon is a Green Beret?"

"*Oui*, if you want this done, the price will be double—one hundred thousand U.S."

"Hold." The line began clicking, and a minute passed before Salka's voice came back on. "You got a deal, Frenchman, but it better be good. We want results soon."

"You will get your results by the end of the month, provided the money is received in Marseilles."

"You'll get it. Just do the job." The Frenchman had already hung up.

CHAPTER EIGHTEEN

Monday, May 22, 1989—Munich

Parked at a small rest stop next to the most likely route to the Munich Autobahn from Bad Toelz was a light green Mercedes 190 common to the area. It was driven by a tall, thin, gray-haired gentleman in a tan overcoat who remained seated on a park bench from noon until shortly after two. To passersby, he seemed to be enjoying the afternoon sunlight and the view of the scenic German meadows and the Alps in the distance on the opposite side of the road.

Freshly returned from a rigorous month in the field, Tim and his friends now turned their full attention on their mission in Connecticut. Ms. Lockery awaited Tim and Frank in Munich.

When they started for Munich that afternoon, Tim was cautious but not overly so. His concern for his own safety had lessened somewhat. Even with the large sum being offered for his death, the time he had spent in the woods on the exercise had given the whole idea of a contract an air of unreality. Still, while his location remained fixed by the army, he took to carrying a .380 Walther PPk in an inside pocket of his coat anytime he went out—just in case. Choosing concealability over killing power, he knew the weapon was somewhat underpowered; but as a professional, he knew how to "double tap"—to fire two bullets in rapid succession—in the event he used it. As a backup to the Walther, he also carried a small Gerber fighting knife on the inside of his left leg when he and Frank left for their 3:00 Munich meeting with Ms. Lockery that day.

Wanting to be early so they would have time to check for anything suspicious, they left Bad Toelz in Tim's old blue BMW shortly after 1:00. And they had a terrific day for the trip to the city, one unlike most normally soggy spring days in Germany. The skies were clear, the sun bright, and the vivid, contrasting greens of the Bavarian countryside exploded by them as air pungent with freshly tilled soil came through the open windows of the BMW. For the thousandth time Tim found himself marveling at the beauty of Germany. Unlike American towns and cities, the German communities he knew had grown up largely before the advent of the automobile, so they were concentrated tightly. Town limits were obvious, and most arable land was put to good use. The long-standing European timber shortage resulted in tasteful, high-roofed concrete structures, built to last, white-walled, and magnificent against the contrasting greens of the fields and forests. Also, as opposed to the States, here his eyes were struck by no neon signs, prefabricated structures, or garbage littering the highways. With scenery such as he viewed that day, he enjoyed driving.

Tim's BMW was in excellent condition, and when he reached the Munich autobahn, it powered easily to over 120 mph. As they approached Munich, an alarm went off in the back of his mind. He was at first unsure why, but he listened to it anyway. Years of training had formed an uncanny extrasensory apparatus in him, and it now told him that something was wrong. He scanned the traffic around him. Nothing.

Frank noticed Tim's face. "What's up?"

"I don't know. Soon as I figure it out, I'll let you know. For now it's just a feeling."

In response, Frank produced the .45 Colt he had concealed in a leather shoulder rig under his windbreaker. "If somebody wants to play, we'll play."

Tim carefully studied the traffic in his rearview mirror. "Where have I seen a green 190 before?"

"Rest stop just before Holzkirchen. He pulled out behind us. That green was a sick color. That's why I noticed it."

"That's it. . . . Well, now he's cruising along behind us about four cars back. Let's slow down and see what he does."

Tim moved into the slower traffic lane and decreased speed—so did the Mercedes. "OK, this guy wants to play. What do you say we go to Munich and have a talk with our friend there?"

Frank smiled.

"One thing—remember that the pistols are absolutely a last resort. If it comes down to using them, we'll probably end up in jail. If possible, use the knife or hands and take him alive. I want to know what's going on. I've got to know what the hell I'm up against!"

Frank nodded his agreement.

Jean-Michel, too, had grown worried. Why had the American slowed down? Had he been seen? He already regretted his decision to kill the soldier in Munich. Grimly, he decided that it would have been far simpler to have placed some explosive in the BMW back in Toelz—but then there would have been a greater chance of getting caught by a nosy gate guard. Besides, it wasn't Jean-Michel's way. Thibaut was a city man. He preferred to do his work in crowds and fade away. It was cleaner that way, and then he had no problems with verification. He'd get the Green Beret in Munich. Minutes later, he relaxed. The BMW had gained speed, and soon the American exited onto a road leading into Munich. The Frenchman felt certain he remained undetected.

Once in Munich, the tailing grew far more difficult. Facing busy streets clogged with traffic, he had to take chances and close on the BMW. Still, Sergeant Reardon showed no sign of concern as he neared Marienplatz.

Suddenly, an old Citroën swerved out from a parking space

and forced the Frenchman to lock his brakes. Jean-Michel cursed as he helplessly watched the Americans turn at the next corner into a narrow side street. Marienplatz was an ornate tourist trap where foreigners by the thousands flocked to see the Glockenspiel, and its streets were narrow. If there was a worse place in the world to try to tail someone, he hadn't found it. The American must be long gone by now, he reasoned. Still, perhaps he could get lucky. If he could make it work, the afternoon crowds would be an ideal cloak for the hit. While waiting for the light he checked his silenced 9mm Czech CZ-75 pistol one last time. It was ready. As he slid the menacing weapon back under his jacket, the light turned green and the Citroën turned left. Thibaut accelerated straight past him and, with squealing tires, powered toward the next corner into the tight right turn. *Merde!* The American's blue BMW sat empty in the middle of the street, just meters down the block. In a panic, he locked his brakes once more. The Mercedes swerved to a halt within a foot of the American's back bumper.

Milliseconds later, the passenger door was jerked open and a tall, blond man leapt across the seat, pistol-first. Jean-Michel reacted like the professional he was. With no time to get the CZ, he instead popped the clutch and lurched hard into the back of the BMW. The jerk and snap of the car tossed the blond man, still with his body only half in the car, forward onto the floor; for a second, his pistol lost its orientation. Thibaut threw open the door and sprinted back toward the rear of the Mercedes.

Tim had positioned himself behind Frank and could have shot Thibaut, but he knew that firing in Munich next to his own car with the conspicuously American plates was certain to get him jail time. As a result, when he saw the tall man in the tan coat spring from the car and dash down the street, he yelled for Frank to move the car and ran after him.

Tim closed the distance fast. Within half a block, the man's thirty-foot lead turned to twenty. Tim heard Frank behind him in the racing car, but so did their quarry. Reacting to the engine noise, the killer threw open a door to his left and leapt in. Tim lowered his head and pumped his legs harder. He had to catch him. As Frank disappeared around the next corner with the car,

Tim reached the door and jerked it open. No bullets came, so he moved inside quickly.

He found himself in the back of a clothing store among about twenty dressing cubicles, and the assassin was nowhere in sight. Moving past the cubicles, he surveyed the retailing area out front but did not find his target there either. He paused to think. He had been too close to his quarry for the man to have made it through the store before he arrived. The man must be in a dressing cubicle. Frank arrived outside and waved to Tim through the front-door window. Good, he thought, if their man came out that way, he would have him. Tim retraced his steps for the cubicles.

He took up a station by the back door, hoping he looked like a patron waiting for a friend. A minute dragged by, and three customers emerged. First came a young man in leather with two pairs of jeans over his arm. The next was a tall, brown-haired man with a dark suit and glasses, and the third was a bearded blond business type with two sweaters on his arm. Where was he? Others came and went. Then Tim realized he had not actually had a clear look at the driver of the Mercedes. All he had seen was gray hair and a tan overcoat. The tall man! Where were the clothes he was supposed to have been trying on? Tim moved and checked the cubicle from which the man had emerged: on a hook hung a gray wig and a tan overcoat. He cursed. Walking as fast as he could without attracting unwanted attention, he checked the retailing area again. It was high and cavernous, but it was all on one floor, and the racks were low enough that he could see the faces of most of the patrons, but the tall man was gone.

Exiting via the front, he found Frank leaning against the wall to his right. "You see a tall, brown-haired guy in a dark suit come out? He's our man!"

Frank pointed towards the Glockenspiel. "He's only got a half-a-minute lead! Let's go!" The two fanned out and moved into the dense crowds at a distance that guaranteed they covered the maximum area possible while securing each other. Both scanned faces. Both saw nothing. Tourists took pictures. Germans in lederhosen drank beer at outdoor cafes. People young and old thronged by with shopping bags. Over it all towered the reason for the abundance of tourists: the ancient cathedrals, the strong-boned but graceful architecture, and the festive, neat atmosphere Germans worked so hard to preserve.

Tim reasoned that if their man was a professional, he would stay within the comfortable folds of the thickest crowds. On the opposite corner, among the abundant sidewalk performers and musicians ubiquitous to Marienplatz at all hours, was a street-corner juggler surrounded by onlookers. His man was there—he was sure of it. Swiftly, Tim moved. In the corner of his eye, he saw Frank follow his lead.

Starting on opposite sides of the crowd, they scanned more faces and saw nothing but smiles and tourists. Perhaps he was wrong, he thought. He wished he hadn't been so quick to check this crowd. Then Tim saw Frank wave towards a side street beyond the performers. His eyes followed the gesture. A Mercedes taxi moved away from the curb, and Frank sprinted after it. Tim knew the street. It was one-way and L-shaped. If he could get behind the church on the corner fast enough, he could cut the man off. Managing his best speed, he sprinted around the corner cathedral, down narrow, traffic-worn stairs beside it, and out onto the back street.

Then several things happened at once. To his left, he saw a truck unloading its cargo into a small café, and behind the truck sat the cab—unable to move because the truck blocked the street. Seeing Frank approaching the rear of the taxi fast, Tim closed on the front. As he did, the taxi door flew open, and their man leapt from the vehicle, a silenced automatic in his right hand. Seeing the Green Berets closing from either side, he hesitated a moment, then squatted at the edge of the taxi door and took up a firing position with Tim in his sights. Tim dove for the ground and rolled toward the beer truck. As he did, the cab driver saw the man with the gun at his back door. He panicked and slammed the car into reverse. Tim heard the soft *pfft* of the silenced pistol simultaneously with the noise of the racing taxi engine. Then he felt hot air rushing past as the bullet whizzed by. Reaching the safety of the truck, he heard a scream. As he sprang to his feet, he saw that the bullet meant for him had hit an older man seated at the sidewalk café.

What had been tranquil turned to pandemonium. The patrons saw arterial blood spurting from the injured man's chest, and an overweight gray-haired woman fainted while people jumped from chairs and milled in confusion. Quickly Tim pulled his pistol and spun around the truck.

The scene in front of the truck was also chaos. The racing taxi had backed into a clothes rack on the sidewalk. A Japanese man furiously photographed the halted taxi, and the enraged store owner and recently menaced shoppers joined in the screaming. To compound problems, a speeding Volkswagen squealed around the corner and hit the motionless taxi. What he could not see was his quarry. Where was he?

The sudden confusion worked against them, but not being able to see the assassin, Tim knew, did not mean that the man was gone. Cautiously, he placed his pistol back beneath his overcoat and moved forward. Then Frank sprinted up and waved toward an alley running next to the store.

Tim met him on the opposite side of the alley entrance. Frank said, "I saw the taxi door hit him in the leg. When he moved down this alley, he was hurt." Both redrew their pistols and carefully checked the entrance. It was clear as far as they could see.

With Tim leading, they charged and found that the alley quickly narrowed to little more than shoulder-width; about fifty feet down, it broadened into a truck-delivery area. They paused and scanned it. Nothing. The alley was vacant except for a row of wheeled garbage receptacles and a pile of neatly stacked cardboard boxes. He cursed, then cautiously moved forward. Frank followed his lead, and they took opposite sides of the alley. When he reached the row of garbage cans, he looked for Frank. There was a wooden door on Frank's side, and he tried it but found it locked. He moved past it a yard, and raised his weapon to cover Tim as he checked behind the first dumpster.

Tim turned to clear the dumpster, then heard a crashing sound to his rear. Spinning, he knelt with his pistol ready. The wooden door hung open with Frank pinned behind it, and the dark-suited man stood in the open entryway, his pistol raised. Hearing a soft *pfft* sound, Tim felt brick splinters shower down from the wall to his rear as the first bullet slammed into a spot just above his shoulder. He returned fire, the thunderous sound of the PPk barking twice in quick succession echoing in the alley. The assassin spun against the outside wall next to the door, and his pistol fell to the ground as Frank kicked the door off of himself. Tim put away his pistol fast and ran to his unknown enemy, now sliding down the wall. Blood trickled down the front of his chest from two small holes an inch apart. As a medic, Frank instinctively squatted to see if anything could be done for the victim. Nearly too late, Tim noticed the man's left hand emerging from his coat pocket with an open switchblade. Tim lunged and kicked at the hand with the knife. The kick landed true, and the weapon fell into a growing pool of blood on the ground. Frank pulled his .45 from its shoulder holster and rammed it into the man's mouth in a shower of smashed lips, blood, and broken teeth.

"Motherfucker! I ought to blow your goddamn brains out right now! Who the fuck are you?"

The man's eyes were glazed with pain, and he was losing consciousness quickly. He mumbled, his dying eyes settling on Tim Reardon as police sirens wailed in the distance, *"Vous êtes mort. Si ce n'est pas aujourd'hui, puis dans l'avenir. Vous êtes mort!"*

Tim felt Frank's hand on his shoulder. "Hey, man, the cops are coming. He's finished. Let's get the fuck out of here!"

Tim nodded. They stood and retraced their steps down the narrow alley. Back on the street, they stopped and joined the murmuring throng now gathered about the dead café patron—as any Americans out for a day on the town would if confronted by sudden death on an otherwise quiet street. A minute later they heard the sound of sirens in the alley they had just left; and they slowly moved in the direction of their car. As they passed the street where the accident had occurred, they saw a tow truck arriving to remove the abandoned green Mercedes. It was blocking traffic.

Finding that no one was unduly interested in their BMW, Tim and Frank were back sparring with the Munich traffic seconds later. Tim checked his watch and realized they would be late for their meeting with Ms. Lockery. They remained silent as they crossed Munich to their rendezvous, sobered by the incident in Marienplatz. Finally, Frank asked Tim what the Frenchman had said as he died.

Softly, Tim replied, "He said, 'You are dead. If not today, in the future, you are dead.' "

The medic let out a long sigh. "Timmy, if they're coming to Europe to try to do you, you're in deep shit. You know that?"

"Yeah, I know it. I also wonder how many more they'll

send, and how long this thing's gonna drag on. Frank, all I wanted to do was find out what happened to Heather. I never imagined it would come to this."

Frank sighed. "Can't look back now, Tim. These people started this war. We're going to surprise them and finish it."

Tim hoped he was right.

CHAPTER NINETEEN

Monday, May 22, 1989—Munich

When Frank first told Tim that their meeting was planned for the Munich Hofbräuhaus, Tim had laughed. Of all the places Ms. Lockery could have selected for a discreet rendezvous, this one was without a doubt the most ridiculous. Far from being a local meeting place for Munich residents, the Hofbräuhaus is nearly exclusively a tourist stop, a place Americans visiting Munich invariably frequent, and exactly the sort of place an executive secretary who had watched one too many spy movies might visualize as the ideal spot to conduct clandestine business.

As they entered the heavy wood front doors and dove into the crowds amidst the structure's cavernous off-white and wood-trimmed environs, a smirking Frank asked, "What d'ya wanna bet she's wearing sunglasses?"

Tim smiled.

Frank was wrong. Jean Lockery was sitting alone at one of the rough-hewn tables beneath an elegant stone archway, and she was not wearing sunglasses. Moreover, she did not fit the image they had created of her at all. Rather than being dark-haired and prim, the executive assistant was blond, in her late thirties, tanned, tall, slender, high-cheekboned, and casually dressed; she appeared very much the fashion model on vacation. The tip-off, though, was her eyes. They were brown, intelligent, and penetrating, leaving little doubt that this woman expected to be taken seriously indeed. Around her neck hung a gold chain from which was suspended a very large ruby bordered in more gold. She fondled the ruby with her left hand, and held a two-thirds–empty liter mug of very fine Bavarian beer in her right. On the table before her was a partially eaten half of a roast chicken.

Frank made the initial approach. "Ms. Lockery?"

"Yes, you must be Mr. Franklin. . . . And you're twenty minutes late."

Choosing to ignore her remark, he said, "Most people call me Frank." He motioned to Tim. "This is Tim Reardon—the man you came all this way to meet."

"Good afternoon, Mr. Reardon."

"Tim," he corrected.

She nodded. "Gentlemen, please sit down."

They did so, on the opposite side of the table, and she continued, "First of all, you should know that as Mr. Whitworth's personal assistant, I am privy to all, and I do mean *all*, of his interests—including your project. Don't worry—whatever you have to say to me will go no farther than Mr. Whitworth himself. Unfortunately, his present physical state, and his wish to distance himself from your project, prohibits him from meeting with you; therefore, you will have to deal with me."

A beer maid arrived with an armload of liter mugs, and Tim purchased drinks for himself and Frank. Ms. Lockery, he saw, was still working diligently on hers while toying with the jewel suspended from the chain about her neck.

As soon as the waitress departed, Ms. Lockery continued, "As my employer has already told you, he is prepared to invest in your enterprise, but he has some concerns and conditions. The first concern is the nature of the work you intend to perform. Would you give me some more details, please?"

Tim leaned forward across the table and made eye contact, but found her cool gaze unwavering. "We're going to take on the largest drug dealer in New England, run him out of business, and finance the job with money he provides."

Frank jumped in. "By doing this, we'll be able to put an end to a contract on Tim's life, and we might just add a new highlight film to the president's war on drugs. As a bonus, we may also get some retirement money."

"Then what you will be doing will be illegal."

Tim saw Frank smile. "Totally."

"And there may be people killed."

Tim leaned forward and said quietly, "Yes, Ms. Lockery, there will be people killed, but they started it. They started it when they destroyed my sister, the only person in this world I thought of as family. And then they tried to murder me for standing up to them. If you want to know what these people are like, check tonight's Munich papers."

"What do you mean?"

"On the way here, we came across a gentleman sent to fulfill the terms of my contract, but we killed him first. He was good, so I'd bet he's got a reputation. By the time the evening news gets out, they'll have an ID on him—I can't wait to read it."

"Couldn't you go to the police?"

"I did," Tim responded. "They said they couldn't help and suggested I spend the rest of my life in hiding. Ms. Lockery, we've told you what's going on. Could we get to the point here? Are you going to give us the money or not?"

The executive assistant clearly did not like his tone, and her color returned. As if to indicate her displeasure with Tim's directness, she took her hand from the ruby and placed it down on the table. "My employer has made it clear to me that this project is important to him, so I will provide all the help I can. I am to give you the money and to make arrangements for Mr. Reardon to meet Mr. Whitworth. However, there is one more condition—and believe me, gentlemen, I like this even less than you. Before I am to release this money to you, you must agree to consult with me throughout the course of this project so that I may keep him abreast of your progress. A special telephone has been installed for just that purpose."

The soldiers answered simultaneously, "What?"

"That is correct, gentlemen. I am to be kept informed of all aspects of the project so that I can report back directly to my employer. Mr. Whitworth wants to be prepared for any potential disasters."

An incredulous Tim asked, "And what if we refuse?"

"If you refuse, Mr. Whitworth will not provide your funding."

Tim looked at Frank. Frank shrugged. Tim responded, "OK. We'll do what you want."

"Good." She passed them an envelope. "Ten thousand U.S. in cash. Mr. Whitworth wants Mr. Reardon to be at his home on the morning of Monday, July third. Our business is concluded." She rose as if to go; then she paused and leaned on the table. "Gentlemen, I understand your predicament, and I sympathize. Mr. Reardon, I'm very sorry that your sister died, and I understand your anger. I just wanted you to know that as my employer's closest advisor, I had to oppose this thing because of the potential damage to his reputation and his business should something go wrong. But Mr. Whitworth believes in keeping his word and so do I; therefore, I will do everything I can to make this venture successful. You can count on that."

Frank said, "I understand, and thank you."

Tim gazed once again at the gemstone she habitually played with and said, "Ms. Lockery, that is a beautiful necklace you are wearing."

Surprised by his comment, she moved her hand reflexively toward the ruby. She cocked her head, smiled a small smile, and said, "Thank you. Mr. Whitworth gave it to me as a birthday present. I wear it always. . . . If there is nothing further?"

Tim shook his head.

"Good day, gentlemen, and good luck," she said. Pivoting on her heel, she strode off through the crowds towards the front exit. As if on cue, a Bavarian brass band began playing a traditional drinking song in her wake.

Tim and Frank both stared after her. Finally, the medic broke the silence. "Mac's gonna love this. Now we got a damn civilian on our back."

"Frank, I've had a long day. Let's get out of this place and get back to Toelz. Hopefully, that French son of a bitch is the last guy who will try to kill me today. Maybe tonight I can get some sleep."

"I don't know if that Frenchman will be the last or not, but I do know you can't sleep in your room anymore. Until you leave, we're going to keep you moving from place to place so they can't get a fix on you. The only time you'll really be in trouble is when you go to work, then we'll keep an eye on you both to and from and while you're there. Tonight you're sleeping at my house. Tomorrow night we'll figure out something else."

"Sounds good to me. Now let's get out of here."

When medical help reached the unconscious assassin, he was nearly dead. Only prompt attention by an extremely competent ambulance attendant saved him.

Authorities who found him were instantly suspicious with the discovery of the silenced handgun next to the body, but Frank and Tim had far overestimated the efficiency of the local police. It was not until the next morning that enough information had been pieced together by the German police to issue a statement. When they did, it caught the attention of a large portion of Europe's law-enforcement community. Considered one of the best in his profession, Jean-Michel Thibaut was wanted for murder and drug trafficking throughout the continent. How he had come to be lying in a Munich alley with two bullets in his chest was then only a matter of conjecture; however, German authorities suspected that either an attempted hit had gone bad, or he had finally angered someone powerful enough to take action. Meanwhile, Thibaut himself remained mute on the subject.

CHAPTER TWENTY

June 26, 1989—Fort Dix, New Jersey

Tim had a quiet month following the incident in Munich. He and his friends had expected more reprisals and maintained the appropriate security; however, the anticipated attack never materialized, and he processed out of the army uneventfully. His final act as a soldier was to turn in his official file to a busy and indifferent personnel clerk at the Fort Dix, New Jersey, outprocessing center amidst a sea of dissatisfied GIs impatient to rejoin civilian life. In return for his file, the clerk handed him a plane ticket to Vermont, thereby fulfilling the government's obligation to return him to his "place of origin." Tim did not need the ticket, so immediately after receipt he cashed it. Yet, unlike most of the other GIs that day, Tim felt no hurry to leave Fort Dix. He had other concerns.

Tim assumed that whatever Larry knew about him, Pyne knew as well. Therefore, he reasoned, Pyne had to know he was leaving the army. If he did, then he would probably have also figured out that all residents of the northeastern United States who leave the army from Europe do it at Fort Dix. If he did know that, then that would explain why his last month in Germany had been so quiet. They were going to do it now.

For that reason, Tim spent his first morning in civilian life zigzagging about the post, watching for anyone showing too much interest in his activities. He detected no one, so he moved off post by bus and rented a car. Shortly thereafter, he took a motel room. Then he found a vacant phone booth and placed a call to Connecticut. There was no answer. Deciding his business would have to wait for later, he returned to the motel room to plan his next moves. But before he could do anything, he had to get through to Connecticut. Like it or not, he needed Andrea. She was the only contact he had in the New Haven area who he thought might be trustworthy. He knew this amounted to little more than manipulation; however, he still believed he could keep her role limited enough to ensure her safety—if he could convince her to go along. Whether he would reveal his plans to her or not, he had not yet decided. He would meet her first, then decide how far he could go.

New Haven

Andrea's depression over Lisa's death had not lessened. Those who had known her before Lisa's death barely recognized her now. She had little appetite, and though she was well aware that she had become emaciated, she felt powerless to help herself. Even her old career ambitions were on hold now because of her obsession with Lisa. When not at work, she spent long hours watching old movies but not seeing them as she puzzled over what she knew about the murder. Nearly every night she sipped her wine and drank herself into fitful sleep. She now wore a silver bracelet she had once given her sister so she would not forget. Her guilt over her ignorance of her sister's drug problem was severe, and suicide occasionally entered her thoughts. But her resolve saved her, her resolve to prove that her sister had been murdered, and her resolve to find the murderer. That was now her consuming obsession.

At work, her career was in jeopardy, but she cared little about it. She was always distracted and she chain smoked. Her client base, drawn largely from an educated Connecticut upper middle class, no longer found smoking fashionable. It was also causing problems at the office. Her boss permitted absolutely no smoking in the office, so Andrea now spent far too much time smoking outside. She was there when her boss, Sam Reynolds, came looking for her to discuss a new account. Angry, he opened the back door and said, "Andrea, would you please come into my office. We need to talk."

She took a last drag and, cigarettes still in her hand, followed him to his large plush office. A short, permanent-press sort of man with immaculate thick dark hair, Sam appeared far younger than his forty years, and she knew he achieved it by spending much of his free time working out or tanning.

Seated behind his desk, he said, "Andrea, you look terrible." He gestured at her cigarettes. "You know, you can't live off those things."

He paused and looked out his window at the immaculate grounds outside. "Andrea, I know things have been hard for you the last couple of months; but dammit, I need agents who can sell. Until this . . . unfortunate death in your family, you were my top agent. For the last two months, you've been the worst. You call in sick; you come in late. When you actually work, to say your performance has been poor would be a gross understatement. . . ."

Andrea interrupted. "Sir, if you are trying to say I'm fired, I understand. I'll clean out my desk."

"Andrea, don't think I haven't considered it; but no, you're not fired—unless you want to quit. No, I'd like you to take some time off. We'll call it a leave. You won't be paid, but you can have two months. When you come back, we'll see how things go. If the old Andrea returns, she'll be welcome."

"Thank you, sir." She turned and left the office. As she walked past her desk, she collected her shoulder bag and car keys, and without a word to anyone, went out to her car.

Shortly after dinner time, her phone rang. She poured her second glass of wine and let it ring. Finally her answering machine picked up. After the beep, Tim Reardon's voice came on. "Hello, Andrea, this is my second try today. If you're there, I hope you'll pick up."

She did. "Hello, Tim. I'm here. Don't hang up."

"Hi, Andrea. How are you?"

"OK, I guess."

"Look, I'm at a pay phone, and I don't have much change. This will have to be quick."

"I understand."

"Can you travel?"

"Travel? What do you mean?"

"To New Jersey. It concerns what we discussed."

"Yes, for that, I guess I can."

"Can you take off tomorrow?"

"Yes, no problem."

"Good. Tomorrow morning get on 95 South at 11 A.M. and head to the New Jersey Turnpike. Once there, get off at the Metuchen exit. Find Main Street in Metuchen. In the center of the town there is a Mobil station. Park there and wait in your car. Someone will meet you. Now repeat those directions back to me."

She read the directions back. He said, "Excellent. Do you still have the red Firebird?"

"Yes, that's what I'll be driving tomorrow."

"Fine, don't worry about time. Trust me. Someone will meet you there sometime after you show up. We'll talk then."

"I trust you, Tim. Do you have any news for me?"

"Not over this phone. We'll talk later. . . . I do have lots to tell you though."

"I'll see you tomorrow."

"Yeah, take care."

Andrea hung up slowly. She felt odd. Her curiosity was aroused over why this soldier wanted her to go to New Jersey, but she also felt better than she had just minutes ago. Hearing Tim's voice was a tonic for her. Something about his voice made her feel as though he could handle just about anything. As she fondled the silver bracelet on her wrist, she thought about his deep blue eyes.

Tim Reardon fell into a light sleep that night in New Jersey. He still could not shake the idea that something was planned for him soon.

He was right; something was.

The man doing the planning was named Johnny Barton ("Johnny B" to his friends), and he was one of the very best. Now overweight and middle-aged, his education on how to end human lives spanned more than twenty years. Over that time, he had varied his techniques to include everything from shotguns to cyanide, and he had worked for nearly every crime organization in the East. On the surface, he was a devout family man, and most people, like the clerk in the motel where Reardon and Johnny B were staying, took him for a less-than-successful traveling salesman. In his early years in the trade, Johnny B had planned all his killings carefully; however, that had become boring. Now he valued the ad-lib above all else. He simply picked a day and shadowed his victim, then selected an implement from the black leather bag he carried and did it. Tim Reardon's day was tomorrow. He wanted to give the soldier time to relax first—in case he was looking for it. Figuring Reardon would have trouble sleeping due to jet lag, he left a wake-up call for 4:00 A.M. He would be ready when the target came out of his room if the situation looked right.

CHAPTER TWENTY-ONE

10:00 A.M., June 27, 1989—New Haven

When Detective Pulcinella entered the office of the chief of police, he found the large, gray-haired man smiling. He also saw Brown, Foster, and a well-dressed man he did not recognize. The chief, out from behind his desk, sat in an easy chair with the others clustered about him in a conference area by the windows. Tony liked the chief. The old man handled the tremendous stress of his position well and could be an adroit politician when he needed to be. But his greatest asset was that, in a city eaten by decay, his solid figure never failed to reassure both press and population that all was being handled as it should.

As Tony approached him, the chief smiled and extended a large, rough hand in greeting, and they shook.

The chief motioned toward the two vice cops. "Officers Brown and Foster, I assume you know Detective Sergeant Pulcinella and vice versa."

They nodded.

"Good, now grab a seat on my couch and let's have a talk, Tony."

After Tony sat, the chief turned to the stranger. "Tony, I would like you to meet Special Agent Oscar Bonning of the Drug Enforcement Agency. For the next few months you'll be working with Special Agent Bonning and Officers Brown and Foster." He paused to let that sink in, then continued. "Let me fill you in. Over the last few months, organized crime has been tightening its control in Connecticut. Under the leadership of the new Godfather, DeFrancesco, they've gone after the drug rackets in particular. They don't want to run them all, but they do want their cut. Through our surveillance of DeFrancesco, we have learned a great deal more about Michael Pyne, and we had no idea how big he was—until now. He is the main cocaine source for this region, with direct connections to the Quintero cartel in Colombia. Agents on DeFrancesco in New York led us to Pyne, and these three men here have been part of a secret task force we organized to follow Pyne—so were Officers Ferucci and Mongelo, who died on Shelton Avenue. What I suspect is that somehow Pyne found out about them, and that's why they're dead now. Tony, you're going to work with these gentlemen and take over where Mongelo and Ferucci left off. I want that yuppie drug dealer on Robin Island finished."

Stunned, Pulcinella popped a candy into his mouth. When his captain had told him that the chief wanted to see him, he had been under the impression that it was for something routine. He'd had no idea it would be anything this big.

The chief continued. "Meanwhile, this assignment is to be kept in the strictest of confidence. You may tell your friends and fellow officers that you are on special assignment, but not what that assignment entails. Any questions?"

Tony asked, "Yes, chief, if you don't mind my asking, why me?"

"I picked you personally and based on recommendations from Officers Brown and Foster and your captain. Tony, you're one of the best cops on the force, and that big drug haul you came up with last spring was a fine piece of work."

"But Chief, I'm Homicide—not Vice."

"Yes, Tony, but most of all, you're a good cop, and when it's all over, you can go back to Homicide again. Meanwhile consider this one a vacation." He stood, and Tony realized it signaled the meeting was over. "I'm going to turn you over to your new partners now." Nodding his head he said, "Gentlemen, I'd like to thank you all for coming."

All shook hands with the chief on the way out. Tony was last, and as their palms met, he caught Pulcinella by the elbow with his other hand. Using the detective's squadroom nickname, he said, "This is an important one, Pooch. Get the bastard and make it stick."

Tony smiled, "I'll do my best, Chief." Then he began turning toward the door, but the chief still held his elbow.

In a low voice, he said, "Hold it, Detective. I need one more thing."

"Yes, Chief?"

"One of the reasons I liked you for this is that you are Homicide. Whoever took down Ferucci and Mongelo is still walking around. Nobody wastes my detectives for free. You'll be covering some of the same ground they did. Find out what happened and give me somebody I can barbecue." He reached back on his desk and pulled an envelope from his in box. "Here's the file, Tony, look at it good. I want whoever did this even more than I want Pyne."

"I'll do my best, Chief."

"I know you will. Good hunting and good luck."

Once free of the chief, he found the DEA man waiting for him in the reception area. Bonning, too, had a file for him. He told Tony to take the rest of the day off and familiarize himself with the material enclosed. Tony thanked him and headed home. He had a lot of reading to do.

Metuchen, New Jersey

After an uncomfortable, traffic-stalled trip, Andrea parked at the Mobil station Tim had described at around 2 P.M. It was in a quiet downtown area lined with small neighborhood stores and towering elm trees. A boring hour passed, and she took to counting patrons coming and going at a liquor store on the opposite corner. Several cigarettes later, she had counted forty-two patrons, her patience was gone, and the excitement she had felt the previous evening was turning into that lethargic feeling she had come to know since Lisa's death.

She felt confused again, just as she had that night on Shelton Avenue. She had waited for Tim Reardon for a long time, but now that the time had come, what did she expect Tim to do, murder Pyne for her? Then she thought back to that somber day last spring when he had stood amongst the throngs of mourners at the funeral, proud, towering, and handsome, a powerful symbol for her to grab onto. What did she want from him now? She admitted that she didn't really know. Well, maybe she did. Perhaps she just wanted to feel his strength.

Now, after having waited an hour, she was sure he would not come. If he was going to meet her, it would already have happened.

She put her head down on the steering wheel, and suddenly the passenger door opened. Surprised, she looked up and discovered a smiling Tim seated next to her. "Hi, Andrea. Are you hungry? Let's grab a late lunch. There's a mall nearby, and I need to do some shopping."

Unable to speak, she put the car in gear and followed his directions.

The sign at the mall proudly proclaimed it to be the largest in the New York area. Whether or not it really was, Tim had no idea, but it was, with its two endless levels of glittering shops, unarguably the largest he had ever seen. Having been there previously he knew exactly where, out of the thirty or so restaurants in the place, he wanted to eat. But first he had some shopping to do.

Johnny B was right behind Tim, but he had his problems. This target scared him a little. Though it wasn't conspicuous, Johnny B could tell that Reardon remained alert no matter where he was, and there was a worrisome feeling about this guy, almost as if he was waiting for it. Approaching him directly, he knew, would be difficult. Frustrated, the hit man decided he no longer had a choice. If he tailed the guy much longer, he'd be noticed. He had to do it in the mall, and since the girl was with him, he had to take her too. All he needed was for Reardon to settle somewhere so he could plan something. And it had to be soon—this guy was too good to fool with.

But Reardon, at first, didn't seem interested in staying in one place. He and the woman stopped at cutlery, sporting goods, and clothing stores. All the while, Johnny B had to keep his distance, so he could not tell what the soldier was buying and he didn't like that either. Finally, Reardon and the girl entered a restaurant, and the killer cracked his first smile of the day. He had him now.

Tucked away neatly on the second level, the restaurant was small, but it had a comfortable bar and high-backed booths that guaranteed Andrea and Tim privacy. Multicolored bar lamps and a profusion of hanging plants created a dim but congenial atmosphere, and the menu offered a diverse array of international fare. The food had been excellent Tim's last time there. He hoped it still was.

The hostess greeted them warmly. He requested a secluded booth, and she gave it to them.

Andrea had been quiet while they shopped, and he had kept the conversation superficial all the while to try to relax her. She was still, to Tim's eye, a fantastically beautiful woman, with her long, shining dark hair and blue summer dress, but now, seeing her seated across from him, he noticed how worn she looked.

The waitress came, Andrea lit her third cigarette since Tim had joined her three-quarters of an hour before, and he ordered chicken teriyaki and sodas for both of them. She departed, and he began the conversation. "How's it been, Andrea?"

"Good and bad, I guess." Her face remained a mask of makeup and imperturbability. Yet he could feel her desperation and yearned to break through it.

"What does that mean? Your letter sounded like it came from someone with some anger."

"Well, I guess it did."

"Why did you send it to me?"

"I'm not altogether sure."

"Then let me help you. You said that Lisa was dead and you thought somebody had killed her. Do you still think that?"

Like a roof collapsing under the weight of too much snow, she broke down. Tears came with the strain. "I don't know, Tim! God! It's been awful. I've felt so damned terrible, and so responsible. Lisa was special. I loved her so much. It was my greed. . . . I thought I knew her, but I was too damn busy making money. Now my sister's dead. If I hadn't been so busy, I might have noticed her long enough to have seen what was happening! You know, families are supposed to be caring. I always thought I was caring. . . . How could I not have seen it?"

"What do your parents say about it?"

"They don't talk about Lisa—ever."

Tim extended his hand. Shaking, she took it. "Andrea, I understand your guilt—God knows I felt that way too. But it won't change anything. Lisa's dead. Drug dealers still sell drugs. You must know that."

Her eyes met his, and he could see that she was listening intently.

He continued. "Now let's get back to why you wrote me."

She nodded. "I guess I wrote you because I thought you were the only person in the world who could understand or help."

"Good, then you do want help. That means that you still have hope. Lisa is gone, but you are still here and you need help. I think you understand that. Why else did you write me?"

She extinguished her cigarette and reached for another. Once it was lit, she closed her eyes for a moment, then she opened them as if surprised and said, "Because I still can't believe the police reports."

"Why?"

"Because they make no sense. Look, there is no doubt that Lisa did coke, but that's not how she died. She died from a massive dose of heroin. But Tim, there was only one needle mark on her whole body, just like Heather. Oh, yes, then there's the suicide note: it was in this weird handwriting. I've seen it, and it just wasn't her writing. Then, I found the address of a house in a bad neighborhood in New Haven in her room. I went there, and a guy pulled a gun and threatened to kill me if I asked questions. I've got nothing concrete, but I've found too many coincidences. You see what I mean?"

The question remained hanging because the waitress arrived with their chicken. Once she departed, Tim asked, "OK, now what exactly do you want me to do?"

She said, "I don't know. I guess I thought that you would somehow know. I asked the police for help, but they just think I'm a nut. It was a long shot, but you once said you could do something about Heather's death, and you offered to help me if I ever needed it. I need it."

Tim didn't know where to go from here, so he took a bite of chicken, chewed it slowly, then said, "Hey, this is good." He motioned her to try some.

Almost absentmindedly, she did as he suggested.

He asked, "Well, do you want to find who did it yourself or get the police to do it?"

"I'm not sure. I just want whoever is responsible to be punished."

Tim nodded. "What you've said so far makes good sense. Look, something is going on. Heather and Lisa both died the same way—and just a few days apart. Neither of the deaths makes sense." In a gentler tone, he continued, "Look, I went through the same guilt trip after Heather died. It's not real. It's just a luxury bereaved people like you and me take to justify the death. Sometimes I think we do it just because we're so angry we want someone else to suffer. Only we can't find anyone else, so we hurt ourselves. So you didn't know about your sister's drug problems; that just means she hid it well. But justice is something else. Justice is right. And what you're calling for is justice. You want Lisa's killers caught?"

She nodded slowly.

"Good, they should be, and I will help."

Tim felt the conversation was going his way. Now he had to make decisions about how to move it farther in the right direction. He needed to think it over, and the bathroom offered a good excuse for him to take some time to collect his thoughts. He excused himself and moved off towards the men's room in the rear of the restaurant. With him, he took the bags from the cutlery shop and the sporting goods store. In the bathroom he positioned a new Gerber in the small of his back, and concealed a larger knife on his right calf beneath his pant leg. He was not certain he needed them, but their weight felt reassuring. Meanwhile, he pondered what he would next say to Andrea. He would need her help in New Haven.

Tim froze as he left the bathroom. Andrea, seated facing away from him, was no longer alone. Beside her, he saw the top of a large, balding gray head. Tim was uncertain. It might have been nothing. The man could be an old client or friend who had simply happened by—or he might be the guest Tim had feared would come.

Scanning the rest of the restaurant for other signs of danger, Tim approached them slowly while sliding the Gerber up into his shirt sleeve. He called out, "Andrea?"

Andrea remained facing forward, but the gray head turned and Tim saw a kindly broad face gazing his way. However, as he drew next to the table, he saw that the man held a small revolver firmly against Andrea's side—with the hammer already pulled back. Tim sat down and said, "OK, your move, man."

The man stopped smiling and said, "OK, soldier, put some money on the table, then the three of us are going to get up and walk quietly out of here. You got that?"

Tim nodded.

"And don't be a hero. If I pull this trigger, your date's going to be dead—though not soon. The bullet'll rip her kidneys and lungs so she'll have time to enjoy the pain. Ever hear them gurgle when their lungs are ripped up?"

Tim looked down at the table. This man was going to die, of that he was certain, and Tim did not care what it cost him. But he answered, "Just don't hurt her. I'll do whatever you want."

Tim threw a twenty on the table, and they slid out of the booth. The man kept his revolver expertly concealed under his coat but still pressed into Andrea's side. Tim felt proud of her. Fear showed in her eyes, but her face remained calm—even after the killer put his arm around her waist to hold her tightly against his gun. He nodded for Tim to get in front of them. He did, and they all moved out from the restaurant and onto the main concourse.

The killer told Tim which way to go and he followed the directions. First, they descended the stairs to the lower level; then they headed for the main entrance. Still Tim's mind searched desperately for options. What he wanted was for the man to take his gun off Andrea so he could do something, but the killer was a professional, and Tim figured he would know that it would be stupid to move the gun because as long as it was there, there was nothing Tim could do. Now, when would he do it? Most likely, not in the mall. It would be far too messy here, and it would attract attention. Suddenly Tim knew: it would be in her car! He would take them outside to her car, then he would make Tim get in front and keep her in back with him. Then he would either do it in the parking lot with the doors closed, or have him drive somewhere and kill them there. He had to make a move before they left the mall. That only gave him about a minute, but first he needed an opportunity. It came.

As they passed a toy store near the bottom of the stairs, a small child pulled a large plastic ball out from the bottom of a basket full of balls, and several followed it. In one fluid motion, Tim spun and picked up a ball rolling behind him with his left hand, launched his coiled body at the killer and threw the ball in his face while he reached for the revolver with his other hand. If he could just get his hand between the pulled-back hammer and the firing pin, the gun couldn't go off.

Johnny B for once acted the amateur. The ball coming at his face made him flinch, and Tim's hand covered the revolver as the hammer fell against his thumb. Andrea reacted too and spun hard away from the arm about her waist.

Tim wrenched at the gun but it did not come free. This man was strong, and before Tim could react, he felt a well-placed knee land in his crotch. The pain was fierce, but he knew it wasn't fatal and ignored it. His Gerber was still up his right sleeve. That hand couldn't release the gun, so it was worthless—and there was no way to get the other knife from beneath his pant leg in time. He would have to do this with his hands—and fast, before security came.

He jerked at the gun again without success. Then, from the corner of his eye he saw his adversary reach his free hand into a pocket. Tim knew he couldn't let that hand get out either. A railing protecting an indoor garden was behind his assailant, and Tim, like a linebacker fighting a block, slammed him back and into it, then jammed two fingers of his free hand into the killer's eyes. Using his adversary's blindness for a cover, he released the gun, spun to his left, and dove to the floor while fighting to free the Gerber from his sleeve.

Johnny B shrieked in rage, flopped forward from the rail, and fired his revolver blindly. A millisecond later, his other hand, now with another gun, came out of his coat pocket, and he fired that one too. Both bullets went harmlessly into the ceiling.

Finally, Tim freed the Gerber and threw it at the assassin's chest. It hit squarely and buried itself to the hilt. Johnny B, his mouth open in a silent scream, dropped both guns and groped for the knife, but Tim was already there. Using a circular motion to make certain as much internal damage was done as possible, he jerked the knife hard before removing it. Then he let the assassin's heavy body fall to the floor, where it came to a rest in a sitting position against the railing.

Tim wiped his blade on the killer's pant leg, slid it back up his sleeve, turned, and moved towards Andrea. A voice behind him yelled, "Stop!"

Grabbing Andrea's wrist, Tim said, "They'll kill us if we stay here! C'mon!" She did, and they ran for the doors—all the while waiting for shots to come from the rear. None came, and they burst outside where a husband was just dropping off his wife from his Ford. Tim dove past the emerging woman through the open passenger door and yelled, "Get out!"

Frightened, the man who had been driving did as he was told. Andrea slid in next to Tim, and he squealed the tires as she shut the door. Tim fishtailed to the light at the exit, caught it while it was still green, and joined the traffic at a more sedate pace.

Ten minutes later, he parked the car on a secluded side street in a development just a few miles from the mall. With the engine off, he spoke to Andrea for the first time since the fight. "OK, now we have to go back and get your Firebird."

Andrea's eyes widened, and she turned and faced him. "Tim, what the hell is going on? You just killed a man!"

"If I hadn't we'd both be dead now."

"No way! I'm not leaving this car until you tell me what is happening here. Look, I came here to meet you for lunch and conversation. Now I'm part of a murder and a stolen car. Forgive me if I have a question or two, but my sense of humor has limits."

He looked away and down the street. "There's no time now."

"Make time—or I'm getting out of this car, going to that house over there, and calling the police."

"All right, that man came here to kill me—not you. But now you've been seen with me, and if the cops pick you up, the same people who sent him for me will send others to find you. The only way to make sure you're safe is to get you and any sign you were here—and that means the Firebird—the hell away from it while they're still sorting this out inside."

"Christ," she said, "you're awfully goddamned good at this! You kill somebody on every first date?"

He turned and studied her. The makeup had smudged a bit, but her face's smooth angular lines were no less powerfully captivating. Her bright green eyes stared at him in consternation and anger. Aware that those same eyes might soon flash hatred, he began, "No, Andrea, this is a first for me too. All right, I guess you deserve some answers. When you get them, I hope you don't hate me. In at least some way, I'm the one responsible for your sister's death."

She straightened, and her voice filled with suspicion. "What do you mean?"

He sighed and told her about Lisa, the cocaine he had taken away, and the hit the next day. He finished with, "I don't know if what I did triggered her murder, but I hope to God it didn't."

Andrea exhaled a thick plume of smoke and then said, "No, I won't hold that against you—though you should have told me this sooner. You were trying to help. Do you really think your problems and her death are related?"

"I don't know for sure, but there's lots more." He told her of the drug shipment he had broken up and the contract out on his life as a result. "Maybe it's because she was seen with me that she's dead. Andrea, I just don't know."

She shook her head. "No," she said, "I won't pin Lisa's death on you, but something is definitely wrong back in Branford. God, I thought stuff like this only happened in movies." She shook her head. "Now, what are you going to do about this contract? These people are never going to give up!"

"I know. They sent a pro to do me in Germany. It didn't work, but he gave it a hell of a try. The police suggested I go into hiding. Forget it. But I'm sorry you saw what you did, and sorrier that you might have been hurt."

"Next time, let's have some warning. Though I can say one thing, Reardon: you do have some serious moves. So what happens now?"

"First, we've got to get the hell out of this car before somebody spots it. Then, since they'll be looking for a man and a woman, go over to that stand of trees and wait there. I'm going to take a bus to the mall, get the Firebird, and come back for you."

She gave him her keys and did as he said. He retrieved the car, and they returned his rental. Then, he had her point her car north towards Vermont. He had already arranged to use a friend's cabin there as a hideaway—though when he had arranged it, he had not expected to need it quite so urgently.

Gradually, Andrea relaxed as she drove. She felt some of the old energy racing through her. Also, she felt very safe with the man in the passenger seat. She suddenly realized, as they crossed the border into Massachusetts, that she had not thought of Lisa for several hours.

The sun was setting, and as it did, she glanced over at his face. It was handsome in an angular way, and the colored light bathing it accentuated its best points.

She asked, "Well, what do we do tomorrow?"

"Right now I'm not really sure. To tell the truth, I'm sort of making this up as I go along."

"Great, that's reassuring. Why did you need me in New Jersey today?"

He sighed. "The truth is that I wanted your help."

"So that's why you had me dig out that file for you."

His tone defensive, he exclaimed, "Andrea, I don't have a lot of options right now. Michael Pyne declared war on me—he is going to learn he is dealing with someone who can fight back. I'm taking the war to him, and some of the most talented warriors in the world are going to help me. We've already put together the team, and we're going to do it in August. When it's over, one of us—me or Pyne—is going to be dead. I came to you because I need help making some connections in New Haven, and . . . well, I liked you. Damn, I was worried about you!"

Andrea smiled and said, "All right Tim, for now, let's just get to Vermont, then we'll figure it out—though, if you want to know the truth, and I'm sure I'll regret this later, I'm inclined to help you. You're a dangerous man, Tim Reardon, and I know just how dangerous now. But I'm going to help you—to a point, anyway—because somebody killed one of mine, and dammit, I want to know who it was, and then I want them punished—if you'll promise that's part of the deal, then I'm in for now. And, man, you sure have a lot stacked against you. Maybe it's time you had something going for you. But hey, Agent 007, just don't expect me to be Agent 008. I sell real estate, remember?"

"Are you certain? I mean you've got to be sure of what you're saying. Some people will die in this thing. You might be one of them. You've got to know it could get really ugly."

"Tim, I can't stand someone telling me 'no.' I've made my

decision. Besides, my boss kicked me out of the office. I've been acting real weird since Lisa died, and he gave me two months to get my act together or to find a new line of work. I think when I wrote you that letter, I was sort of hoping for something like this—though I couldn't have seen it clearly at the time. Well, what happened today cleared my vision."

Tim was quiet for a moment, then said, "I had hoped that you would say something like this. But there's something else. You were incredible today, but if you're going to be part of this, you need real training. Mistakes can cost lives, so you're going to have to learn how to survive."

"All right. Is this going to be like basic training?"

He laughed. "Well, not exactly. Do you know why I had you wait in that gas station?"

"No, I don't, but I bet it'll be entertaining."

"I did it to make sure you weren't followed. Apparently, I should have checked my own rear better. You're going to have to learn to do everything very carefully. Ever handle a weapon?"

"Yes, I used to go shooting with my dad—only, you've got to understand that I'll only use one in self-defense, and then reluctantly."

"Understood. In Vermont we'll begin your training, work out some of the mission details, and I can grow a beard."

"Well, I had no plans for the next couple of months." They fell silent. Andrea thought about what she had just done. Part of her could not believe what she was volunteering to do. The other part relished it. And she wondered what, if anything, she could refuse the man seated next to her.

CHAPTER TWENTY-TWO

June 27, 1989—Robin Island

On a fine New England summer afternoon Salka and Pyne sat in Pyne's blue-and-white cigarette boat just off the island. Its powerful engine burbled threateningly in the stern, but Salka, who was at the helm, kept the throttle just above idle. He looked at his boss and half smiled. Predictably, Pyne wore white shorts, a navy blue shirt, and a captain's hat—he even had the boating shoes. Salka himself had on only a bathing suit, so his bronzed, muscular body could soak up the sun as he piloted them through the calm sea. Under the dash in front of him was a waterproofed container for his submachine gun and pistol; it opened with the push of a button.

Since Pyne seemed to be in a good mood, Salka decided to tell him what their contact inside the police department had relayed. As he did, he slowed the boat so Pyne could wave to friends on other islands.

Pyne responded, "Julian, you are sure of this news?"

"No doubt about it. The DEA and the New Haven Police have set up a special task force to put us out of business."

"I am truly flattered by their interest. How many agents do you think they will devote to the project?"

"Right now it's too early to tell, but whatever they do, it'll be no fucking problem."

"Why do you say that?"

Salka laughed. "Simple, we own a cop inside the fucking project."

As Salka steered around a small obstruction, he could hear

Pyne laughing. "Julian, who said there is no justice in America? This gives us a wonderful opportunity to reinforce the notion that I am a legitimate businessman. The most important thing now is for me to remain as visible as possible around the community. I understand the Committee to Save the Long Island Sound is planning to hold a large fund-raiser in Branford. Don't you think Robin Island would be an ideal spot for their event? I shall have my secretary contact them tomorrow morning. In fact, not only should we host the party, I think a sizable donation is in order as well."

"Good idea, but there are some other precautions we should take, too."

"Such as?"

"If our phones ain't already tapped, they will be. That means we'll have to remind people in the pipeline not to contact us on the phone. Also, you and I are going to have to be real careful not to say anything important over the phone."

"Good thought, Julian. Yes, we must take precautions immediately."

"Next, there's the money. Maybe it's not a good idea to be bringing all the cash out here anymore."

"I'm afraid I disagree with you there, Julian. The counting room is the only place I want my money—I simply would not feel correct with it anywhere else. Perhaps you could just do a better job of hiding it as it comes and goes?"

"We could try to camouflage it with food and other stuff, but it won't be easy."

"Please do, Julian. I'm sure you will handle it well."

"What about these DeFrancesco people? They want thirty percent now."

"Perhaps we can negotiate. We just have to stall them for now. Don DeFrancesco is paying us a visit next month. Perhaps he will listen to reason."

"Whatever you want, sir."

"Julian." Pyne's smile broadened. "I think it would be a wonderful idea if we gave our law-enforcement friend a raise in pay. He has been doing truly exemplary work and should be rewarded immediately. I do so sympathize with the economic plight of our hard-working police force. They risk so much every day for all of us."

Salka laughed. "I couldn't have said it better myself, sir."

Pyne was silent for a moment. Salka looked over and saw that his boss's face had grown pensive. Then Pyne asked, "Do we have any further word on Sergeant Reardon?"

"I'm afraid I have some bad news on that, sir. We have another mess in New Jersey."

"What? I thought you said this Johnny B was the best."

"He is, but Reardon took him. Apparently, there was some sort of a shoot-out in a mall, and our man got the worst end of it. The cops haven't ID'ed Reardon yet, but they're looking for someone that fits his description. Now he has fucking disappeared. After this and the mess that fucking Frenchman left behind, we're gonna have to take this bastard a lot more seriously next time."

"You think you will be able to locate him?"

"Yeah, we'll find the bastard. We got his picture from his stepbrother in Branford, and we've got copies out to our people all over town. If he comes to Connecticut, we'll find him. He can't hide forever."

"Julian, I am concerned about what happened in Munich and in New Jersey. This Reardon seems to be supremely well skilled—I fear he will not be easy to dispatch. Perhaps when we locate him, we should consider probing for his weaknesses first, then moving in. Every man has his weaknesses, Julian."

"However you'd like it done, sir. I'll keep you informed."

Pyne smiled again. "Julian, today is a glorious day. Let's see what this wonderful product of American capitalism can really do." With that, Salka pushed ahead the throttles, and the powerful engine roared to life like an angry bear. The stern dug in instantly, the bow rose, and they surged forward across the ocean.

CHAPTER TWENTY-THREE

June 28, 1989—Northfield Mountains, Vermont

It was after midnight when Tim and Andrea finally made it to Vermont. The cabin was in the Northfield Mountains, an isolated area just south of the state's capital. As they drove up a long dirt road to the isolated house, Tim decided the rough-hewn structure looked perfect; when they entered the front door, he was even happier. The central room was comfortably rustic with a cathedral ceiling and a large fireplace—the epitome of the secluded hideaway. On further inspection, he found a small kitchen and a bathroom at the rear of the first floor and a half-loft with two generous sleeping areas on the second. Overall, it was an excellent place to hide while he trained Andrea and finalized the arrangements for the mission.

On the way to the cabin, they had stopped at a grocery store and purchased food and two bottles of Tim's favorite wine; but on their arrival, he found that the house was already exceedingly well stocked. The kitchen cabinets were full of canned goods, the beds were already made, and there was wood in the fireplace waiting for a match.

At first, Tim felt tired from the long trip, but the calm of his surroundings reenergized him. There was a slight chill in the air, so he lit the wood in the fireplace. Once the fire was blazing, he went to the kitchen and prepared sandwiches. Andrea was in the loft, and he assumed she was going straight to sleep, but he made two sandwiches in case she came down. With the food ready, he grabbed a bottle of wine and two glasses and settled on the rug in front of the fire to eat.

He had just gotten comfortable when he heard steps on the loft stairs—he turned and caught his breath. Andrea stood poised on the bottom step, fresh from a shower, wearing a short green cotton bathrobe, her long hair wrapped in a towel. But it was her face, scrubbed clean of makeup, that caught his attention. Tim now saw the real Andrea in the dancing light of the fire: her slender neck, her small smile, and glistening emerald green eyes—and at that moment, he found her truly beautiful.

As he watched, she surveyed the wine and the fire and smiled. Batting her lashes playfully, she said, "I see you have wine and food for two. Are you a confident man, Sergeant Reardon?"

"It's Mr. Reardon now," he corrected. "And no, I'm not confident, just optimistic." He flashed her his most inviting smile. "Might I recommend a sandwich, Mademoiselle? I know the chef personally, and he is the best."

She gracefully sat next to him, and Tim felt electricity move down his spine. He poured her a glass of wine, and then she said, "Monsieur, my mother always warned me about servicemen, but since you are no longer in the military and you do know the chef, I suppose I can make an exception just this once." She quietly cleared her throat.

"Oh!" Tim said. Sitting up fast, he dropped his own sandwich, seized the second plate and passed it.

Andrea laughed.

"What?" he asked.

She pointed to the carpet. Looking down, he saw his own sandwich in a jumble on the carpet between them.

"Well," he said ruefully, "you know how hard it is to find decent help." Then he laughed and cleaned up the mess.

She bit into her sandwich, then picked up her wine glass and studied it thoughtfully.

"Something wrong?"

"No, Tim, well . . . yes, it's a couple of things. I've been drinking a little too much lately. Actually, I've been getting loaded nearly every night. But, this is OK. For the past two months I've been drinking to get drunk. Tonight, I'm drinking to enjoy the wine. There's a big difference."

He looked at the fire. "You're over that now?"

"Yes, things changed today."

"What about your smoking?"

She laughed. "That will never change."

"You smoke an awful lot."

"Everybody says that, but if you knew me, you wouldn't bother to ask. Tim, everybody enjoys something about life. With me it's tobacco. It's legal and I feel better doing it than not doing it. Without my cigarettes, I would feel almost undressed. That's just me: Andrea."

"It's not fashionable anymore."

"Neither are violent men. Plus I've seen you smoke one or two."

"True, but only when I'm stressed. You said something else bothered you?"

"Yes, you, and in a way me. What I saw you do today—it was incredibly violent and in a way, revolting. All my instincts tell me you're trouble, but here I am. That's because there's something really decent and gentle about you too. Yes, that's it. You're a gentleman. Besides, amidst all this craziness, I feel really alive for the first time in months—almost powerful. Maybe tomorrow morning I'll wake up sane again and get the hell out of here."

There was an awkward pause. He was conscious of the wine, the fire, the quiet, and above all the woman next to him.

Andrea finally broke the silence. "Tim, I haven't felt well for a long time. I was beginning to feel like I had lost complete control of both the world and myself, but today changed that. You changed that."

"I'm glad, Andrea. That night you saw me in the bar getting plastered, you did something for me, too. I almost never go drinking to get drunk. That night I did. Anyway, I've been thinking about you a long time."

She smiled at him and stretched out on the rug. The flickering patterns the fire created on her dark features accentuated her beauty, and he badly wanted to reach out and touch her face. Then he felt himself blushing in embarrassment and hoped that in the dimness she couldn't see it. Yet he feared what the consequences of reaching out for her might be. He had involved her in something that could kill her, and for that, he hated himself.

If Andrea was aware of the turmoil churning inside him, her features gave no sign of it. Eating her sandwich serenely, she gazed at the fire with a tranquil smile. Finally, her food finished, she turned and met his gaze. Her eyes were warm and wide, and even in the dimness, he again felt lost in their green depths. The tension between his fears and his desires reached a peak, and he felt nearly paralyzed. Then she reached over and touched his hand. Squeezing it gently, she whispered, "Tim, thank you for being there for me."

He opened his mouth to respond but no words came. As if she could read his mind, she lowered her gaze and rose to her knees. She placed her index finger across his mouth and shook her head slowly. She leaned close to his face, and brought her two hands up to his head. Her long fingers intertwined with his hair. He smelled her perfume, discreet, with the faint scent of roses. She kissed him softly on his forehead. He remained frozen. She said, "Good night, Tim," and seconds later, he heard her pad softly up the stairs to the loft above.

Once he was sure she was gone, he expelled a deep breath, reached for his glass of wine, gulped its contents, and collapsed backwards onto the carpet. He poured himself another glass of wine, and gazed once more at the hot coals and blue flames. But though his eyes had settled upon the fire, in his mind he saw nothing but Andrea's soft green eyes. Thirty minutes later, the bottle of wine empty, he too made his way to the loft. As he passed her closed door, he paused for a moment and wondered a last time about the woman behind it. Then suddenly, as if to remind him of the dangers reality can bring when it enters the realm of the mythical, images of Heather and Lisa invaded his consciousness. Sadly, he turned away from Andrea's door and entered his room.

Tim had difficulty falling asleep that night, and when he finally did, he dreamed that he heard Heather's voice shout a warning to him through a dense forest full of dark menacing trees. All through the night, he fought a frenzied quest through the trees to reach her, but he found himself blocked by dark shadowy creatures. When he awoke at dawn, covered in sweat, he had still not found Heather.

Unable to go back to sleep, Tim showered, dressed, and went down to the main level to cook breakfast. Before long, he had eggs frying, and Andrea came down the stairs still in her bathrobe. When she came into the kitchen, Tim had just put the finishing touches on a cheese omelet. She tossed a sleepy smile his way and sat on a stool near the breakfast counter adjacent to the kitchen. Tim felt the same excitement he had felt the night before creeping up his spine again, but he shrugged it off and said, "Morning. Hope you like cheese omelets and Canadian bacon."

Her smile grew brighter, and she said, "The smell brought me here."

With a reciprocal smile and a flourish, he served up her breakfast, but found he could not meet her eyes. They ate side by side at the counter, and remained quiet throughout.

After breakfast, Tim explained to her what they needed to accomplish that day. They were in the Firebird and headed for town by 9 A.M.

Tim had only six short days to train his new associate, so he had to make every moment count. First, he needed firepower. His personal weapons were being shipped over from Germany and would not arrive until September. As a result, except for his knives, he was defenseless. In town they found a well-equipped sporting goods store that catered primarily to hunters. It presented him with exactly what he needed, and when the proprietor saw the size of the purchase his customer intended, he seemed delighted Tim had come. After wading through the store's large selection of new and used rifles and pistols, Tim departed well prepared for future trouble. Among his purchases were a bolt action .30 Remington hunting rifle, a used Ithaca 12-gauge pump shotgun, two stainless-steel Walther PPk's, and a .223 semi-automatic Ruger rifle that bore a striking resemblance to its larger-calibered military cousin, the M-14. He also procured ample spare magazines, day packs, ammunition bandoliers, ammunition, targets, and two compasses. Training was about to begin.

As soon as they returned to the cabin, Tim set up some targets outside, and put a pistol in Andrea's hand. She had never fired a pistol before, her father having been an avid shotgun shooter, but she proved a quick study. She possessed a talent for tasks involving manual dexterity only found in the most natural of athletes. Before long she showed signs of developing into a fine marksman with both rifle and pistol, and her experience with shotguns showed as she confidently hit target after target from the hip. When not shooting, Tim taught her the basics: tailing, communicating with clandestine methods, taking photographs, recognizing fields of fire, employing cover and concealment, and recognizing and employing the principles of electronic surveillance.

Tim also began getting her into shape. Each morning began with an hour of exercise including a twenty-minute run and calisthenics. Tim enjoyed the exercise, and it surprised him to see that Andrea seemed to like it as well—though he swiftly concluded that she had a long way to go. Nevertheless, she did her best. During high school she had been the captain of her track team; although she had not run seriously since then, she still possessed natural stamina and a graceful stride. They would have a great deal more work to do before their departure on July 3, but he knew she would be in better shape then and far more knowledgeable about how to survive in the dangerous days ahead.

When they were not working, they spent long hours talking. He told her about Heather, and she told him about Lisa. He told her about his years on A-Teams, and she laughingly told him of the absurdities of the real-estate business. Each night, they talked past midnight, but Tim did not dare break the distance barrier that remained between them, and Andrea seemed comfortable with the situation just as it was.

On their last full day at the cabin, Tim decided they had spent enough time training, and they deserved a day to enjoy the forest outside their cabin. That morning they left at dawn with day packs and rifles for what he hoped would be a twelve-mile hike over rough terrain; however, unsure of Andrea's stamina, he planned an alternate shorter route without telling her. By noon, he felt embarrassed that he had ever doubted her. Her bright cheeks and eyes shining with appreciation for the magnificence of the Green Mountains, she almost danced along the rough trails and logging roads he had selected. Though she was not in the best running condition, her lithe body was every bit as healthy as it appeared, and she was absolutely tireless.

Tim selected a spot atop a series of granite ledges, and they stopped for lunch. Andrea had made what she called "a gourmet lunch" that morning and had been very mysterious about it, saying only that he would love it. Seated on a rock near the ledge, Tim asked her, "Well, where's this fantastic mystery lunch?"

Smiling mischieviously, she reached into her day pack, pulled out a paper bag, and held it up for his inspection. She asked, "Are you sure you're hungry?"

"Ravenous."

Like a pitcher's fastball, the bag came hurtling in his direction. Tim caught it deftly, ripped it open, and pulled out its contents. Holding the sandwich up before his face, he gaped at it with a half-smile. "Oh, it's very gourmet—peanut butter and jelly?"

She bounded over, plopped herself next to him on the rock, and said, "Yes, but you do love peanut butter and jelly sandwiches—don't you?"

Laughing, he said, "OK, I admit it. How'd you know?"

She tossed her head, pulled a handful of hair into her lap, and looked directly into his eyes. "There's a lot of things I know about you, Mr. Reardon."

Tim felt unable to break her gaze. Slowly, he asked, "And how do you know all these things?"

Her grin turned into a subtle smile. "I just do. Now eat your sandwich before it gets stale."

He did.

After they finished eating, Tim said, "Andrea, I've been dying to ask you one question."

"Go for it."

"How did you get that scar on your chin?"

Andrea laughed. "I was the original wild child. My paratrooper dad wanted a boy but got me, and I mostly played army with boys in the neighborhood. I got the scar jumping on the bed. I fell off and went face-first into the bedframe. I remember my mom asked me after they stitched it up if I wanted to be a nurse and help people someday. I told her, 'I don't want to be a nurse! I want to be a paratrooper.' "

Tim chuckled, and Andrea rose and walked over to the edge of the massive rock. Tim followed and stood by her side. From where they stood, he could see far into a valley below them where a stream ran over rocks and an old pickup truck made its way down a dirt road.

Andrea lit a cigarette and sighed. She said, "You know, Tim, from here, you can see so far that if the future were in the distance, we'd be able to see it."

"You want to see into the future?"

She took a drag on her cigarette, then her breast heaved with the force of her answer. "Yes, I do."

Surprised at the conviction in her voice, Tim asked, "What would you like to know?"

She didn't answer immediately. Instead, she turned toward him and looked once more into his eyes for a long time. Finally, she said, "I want to know what's going to happen to Tim and Andrea. Yet . . . " She lowered her eyes from his.

Tim placed his hands on her shoulders and asked, "Yet what?"

Her response did not come right away. In its place came the sound of distant birds and the whisper of the wind on the rocks below them. His hands felt her shoulders tense.

Almost reflexively, he pulled her tightly against him and said, "Whatever it is, we'll get you through it."

Almost violently, she jerked her head up and looked once more into his face. "What did you say, Tim?"

"I said that whatever it is, we'll get you through it."

"You said 'we.' Don't you see, Tim! That's it! All of this is so nuts. Just days ago, I didn't even know you—and I did this crazy thing and ran off into the mountains with you—but I wanted to. I wanted to because you were the only person I knew who might know a way to get even for Lisa, to get retribution for what those animals did to my sister. But that's not all. . . ." Her voice trailed off.

Tim held her tighter. "I know, Andie. You don't have to say it. I felt it too that first night in the bar, and it's been between us since we came here, and it's almost driven me crazy since."

"Tim, I don't just want retribution, I want you, too!"

Unable to restrain himself any longer, he kissed her, and she kissed him back with force.

Pausing for a breath, she said, "My emotions are going crazy now, but it feels good to be in your arms."

"It feels great having you there, but this makes me so nervous. Andrea, I never met anyone like you—never. But it's just not the right time now. This is happening all wrong."

"I don't care, Tim. I don't care! Tim, there are certain things we can't change. Look, I can't live with myself until I find who destroyed Lisa! And you: my God, they've taken your whole life from you! We have to do what we're planning or we'll both end up with nothing. What other choice do we have? But none of that seems to matter right now. I haven't felt happy for a long time—not until you showed up. Today, right now, this mountain we're standing on is all ours, and this day belongs to us too. Dammit, I'm not going to be cheated again. Let's use it together."

They kissed again, long and searchingly. The pull he felt was so powerful that he thought he couldn't let her go, but he realized he had to, so he pulled back and said, "Whatever you put in that peanut butter was potent stuff. If we could market it, maybe we could run Pyne out of business."

Laughing, Andrea slithered out of his arms and grabbed her day pack off the ground at a run. She headed down the trail, calling back, "You stand around up there much longer, you're going to grow roots. Bet you can't beat me back to the cabin."

"Bet I can," he yelled and, scooping up his day pack, he quickly followed her rapidly distancing form.

Tim cooked their final dinner in Vermont that night. Afterwards, she helped him do the dishes. Then they took their wine and settled on the floor before the fire. This time, they did little talking. When they headed upstairs to go to the loft, the fire was out and the wine remained untouched.

By the next morning, he knew a lot more about the new woman in his life, enough to know she loved him as he did her—though they had not yet said it aloud.

CHAPTER TWENTY-FOUR

9:00 A.M., July 2, 1989—New Haven

Tony Pulcinella waited for Oscar Bonning outside an innocuous camper situated in a quiet neighborhood near the town dock in Branford. When Bonning arrived, he looked much as he always did—immaculate.

Though Bonning had not worn a suit since Pulcinella met him in the chief's office, even in casual shorts and a T-shirt he managed to stay in character. No wrinkles, every hair carefully placed, trim and athletic, and his whole outfit carefully color-coordinated. He wondered if the man had once worked as a model for clothing catalogues. He looked down at his own scuffed shoes and stained slacks and sighed.

With a quick but friendly gesture, Bonning motioned Tony to follow him into the camper; when he entered, Tony was impressed with what he saw. From the outside the camper looked exactly like all the other recreational vehicles parked about the neighborhood's driveways. Inside, its floor was covered with a thick brown shag with matching plush seats and sleeping quarters, but every space not used for living was given over to electronic surveillance devices now targeted on Michael Pyne.

A tall man sat at a built-in folding table. He had a cup of coffee before him and gestured for them to sit down. "Hey, Oscar, how's it going?"

"Not too bad," Bonning replied as he sat and waved at Pulcinella. "Bill, I want you to meet Tony. He's one of the New Haven guys on this one."

Bill reached over and shook Pulcinella's hand. "Have a seat. You want some coffee? It's fresh."

"No, not now, but thanks for the offer." Tony sat next to Bonning.

Bonning said, "The reason I brought Tony out here was to show him what you've got. You know, give him the same tour you gave the other New Haven guys."

"Sure," Bill replied. "Well, as you probably already guessed, this is where we monitor Pyne. We got taps on all his lines and each tap is its own transmitter, so we can park this thing anywhere within about a three-mile radius of the circuits we're monitoring. We're hoping to put some mikes out on the island too, but as of yet, we haven't figured out how to get 'em there. All the shit's voice-activated, so all we have to do is let it tape, then check every few hours to find out what's been said. The whole thing's automated, so there really doesn't have to be anyone here, but two of us hang around as per administration policy to make certain everything is working and nobody bothers it. For security, we sleep in shifts. My partner, Dennis, is in the rack even as we speak."

Bonning asked, "How's it been going? You got anything new?"

Bill shook his head. "No, and I'll tell you one thing, I don't like it. When we first set up, we were getting some useful stuff, but about forty-eight hours after the first tap went in, we started getting bullshit. It's like this guy has started being careful with every word. I gotta wonder if he knows we're listening—or it could be that he's just a cautious guy. I don't know."

Pulcinella felt Bonning's eyes on him. "That's the problem we've had throughout. Everything Pyne does seems to be staged for our benefit—it's been going on like that since the whole damn thing started. So what is it? Has he figured us out?"

Pulcinella shrugged. He didn't know, but he decided he would find out.

CHAPTER TWENTY-FIVE

July 3, 1989—Newport, Rhode Island

As they left their Vermont hideaway, Tim Reardon—a man who had always maintained a strong sense of inner-direction—felt off-balance for the first time in his life. The cause of his discomfort sat to his left behind the wheel of her Firebird. He had always yearned to find that special woman who could complement him as he could complement her. Andrea was that dream made real. For the thousandth time, he surveyed her beautiful face and sighed. What they wanted for each other—passion, caring, comfort, and happiness—could never be, would never be, until they exorcised the ghosts of Heather and Lisa. But what he feared even more was that they would have no future after she saw how savage this war would make him. Preoccupied with these thoughts, Tim remained silent for most of the drive to Newport, where he would set the mission in motion by meeting a man named Whitworth.

As they approached Newport, he went over last-minute arrangements with Andrea. "After we leave here, I need you to do something in New Haven for me."

"Well, depends what it is."

"We need a base of operations. That means we have to rent someplace."

"That's right up my line. What do you want, an apartment or a house? And where do you want it?"

"We want neither. If anyone is looking for us, they'll check hotels and apartments first. No, what we need is office space.

As a cover, we'll be international art dealers. That way, anyone watching will not be suspicious when they see boxes of equipment moving in and out. We'll need a reception area and good storage space. Also, a room we can use for sleeping, and it would be good if we had a separate room for planning. Next, we'll need another place on the coastline off the Thimbles—preferably a beachfront rental. We'll need it soon, so the area residents can grow accustomed to seeing us. To them, we'll just be young men on vacation having a good time in our boats, but we'll really be gathering intelligence for the mission. In fact, the more obvious we are, the more we'll become a part of the scenery and the less we'll be noticed."

"So you want something high-profile for the beach but something discreet for the office?"

"Yes indeed."

"Both should be easy. I'll have something by tomorrow, and you can rent under false names. Nobody but me will ever know."

"Good. While you're at it, I need a good rental car. Tell them your car has been involved in an accident, so you'll need the rental for an extended time. I'd do it myself, but it would be dumb to advertise my presence right now. We'll also need to buy or rent a van or a truck, the more decrepit the better."

"No problem, boss."

He smiled at her and continued, "The first of the men will come in tomorrow, and we've got to have someplace to put them. Meanwhile, I want you to keep that PPk in your pocketbook. I doubt you'll need it, but you stay alive by being ready for anything. The rifle and shotgun are hidden in a box in the trunk. For now, we'll have to store them at your house. I'll keep the Mini 14 in my bag in case I need it, and I have the other PPk here." He patted a place beneath the light, tan windbreaker he wore over his T-shirt and jeans. "From now on we have to be ready for anything."

She smiled, and he noticed how well she filled her green halter top and shorts. She said, "Don't worry, Dad," and then, in her best Cagney imitation, "they'll never take me alive."

He returned her smile, but the fear of losing her tugged at his heart. "Just be careful, OK?"

* * *

When they reached the gates of the Whitworth estate, Tim saw that Sean Whitworth obviously knew how to live. He gazed up the long driveway and admired the sweeping roofs, graceful architecture, and opulent trimmings. The grounds were immaculate—even the pine needles in the treed areas seemed to have been groomed. There was a buzzer at the front gate, and he pushed it. A voice from a steel box admitted him, and they drove up the long drive to the massive oak front door, where Ms. Lockery greeted him. She wore nothing but a bikini top, shorts, and her ruby. Tim wondered if she had a tan line under the shorts. He doubted it. She was far too thorough for that. She smiled and said, "Mr. Reardon, I hope you had a nice trip."

With exaggerated civility, he responded, "Why, certainly, Ms. Lockery."

She turned her attention to Andrea.

Tim said, "This is my associate, Andrea."

She nodded as a tall, gray-haired butler, in actual livery, swept past her.

"Robert will show your friend to the kitchen where I'm certain he can find something for her lunch. Please follow me. Mr. Whitworth is waiting for you by the pool."

Before he could reply, she disappeared down the entry foyer. Tim turned to Andrea. "Well, see you in a few minutes." Then he hustled off after Ms. Lockery.

Seated next to the pool was a heavy-set gray-haired man in a wheelchair. He had a large nose and a weather-beaten face that belonged more on an old fisherman than on a corporate genius. It was an honest and direct countenance, and Tim decided if it was an accurate indicator of the man, he would like him. The old man heard him coming and waved him over. Ms. Lockery was already seated next to the octogenarian.

The old man's smile and handshake turned out to be as strong and honest as his face. Whitworth began, "Mr. Reardon, I've waited a long damn time for this meeting. Frank spoke well of you."

Robert magically appeared at Mr. Whitworth's shoulder, and the old man gestured at Tim. "Can Robert get you anything? He's an excellent bartender."

"Nothing with alcohol, sir."

Whitworth looked up at the butler. "I believe we have some fresh lemonade somewhere. Do we not, Robert?"

"Of course, sir."

"Well, get some for our guest, a Scotch on the rocks for me, and I imagine Ms. Lockery would like some of that designer water she's so fond of."

Robert nodded and disappeared as quickly as he had arrived.

"Well, Mr. Reardon, I prefer to be called Sean. Do you have a first name? I hate keeping things formal."

"Tim."

"Tim, I realize you probably find my wanting to meet you somewhat irregular, but you understand that I am investing a considerable sum in a venture that I find as unusual as anything I've ever seen. Since I'm a curious man by nature—and you seem to be the one who has instigated all this—I thought it would only be proper to meet you in person. If you would be willing to indulge an old man, I wonder if you could please tell me the whole story?"

Tim liked Whitworth's directness, so he launched straight in. He told them about Lisa and Heather, about Ronny and Michael Pyne. He told them of the contract and what had happened in Marienplatz and New Jersey. Then he told them what he planned to do.

Sean Whitworth heard him out without a question. The only interruption came when Robert returned with the drinks. When the story was over, Sean leaned back in his wheelchair with eyes closed and lips pursed, deep in thought. It suddenly grew quiet by the pool, except for the sound made by the warm summer breeze from the ocean blowing across the carefully manicured grounds. While he waited, Tim sipped the lemonade. It was excellent. He imagined that Sean accepted nothing less.

After what seemed an interminable period, Whitworth opened his eyes and gazed directly at Tim. "Young man, you appear to be in one hell of a tight spot. This team you have put together, are these men truly the best?"

"They are the best commandos on earth."

"Have you considered all other options? As I told Frank, there are legal actions you could take. I know a couple of senators I could telephone. If I called, they would listen."

"Sean, at this point, I have to handle it my way. I've already tried working with the authorities and nearly got killed for it. Twice. Forgive me if I'm reluctant to give them the opportunity."

"I thought as much, and you're probably right anyway. I learned something from my father a long time ago, and it has stuck with me throughout my life. He cautioned me that if a man threatened me directly with destruction, I should take the threat seriously. So seriously, in fact, that I should destroy him first. If I tried to do it any other way, my enemy would never have enough respect for me to quit. In practice, I have discovered that premise to be valid. Frankly, Tim, you probably should have killed that son of a bitch when you had him in the woods. If you had, this thing might be over already."

Tim responded, "At the time, I thought I might already have gone too far. I underestimated my enemy. I won't do that again."

Whitworth nodded. "I am certain you will not." The old man paused and stared out over the ocean with eyes that had seen much in their day. Turning his gaze slowly back to Tim, he said, "All right, Mr. Reardon, you can have your money."

Ms. Lockery finally spoke up. "Sean, as one of your advisors, I have to tell you that I don't like what I'm hearing here. What this man is saying is that we can't win without going down to the drug dealer's primeval level. There must be another way, and I think Mr. Reardon should try to find it."

Whitworth regarded Ms. Lockery carefully. "You know I have always respected your morality and integrity. I cannot dispute that what you're saying is important, nor can I say that I disagree with you. However, as far as descending to their level goes: if a man points a gun at you and says he's going to pull the trigger, I would say it's rather necessary to do the same in return—and faster than he does it. It is how I have survived in business all these years."

She began to answer, but Whitworth raised his hand. He continued. "There is another factor at work here as well. I owe Frank Franklin a family. What I am doing is paying that debt. How he chooses to spend the money is his business. All I ask, Tim, is that my name is never mentioned outside your inner circle. If it is, I will naturally deny I have ever met you. You understand that?"

"I understand."

"Finally, Tim, I would like you to stay in contact with Ms. Lockery, but keep her at a safe arm's length while she monitors your progress. She'll serve as a conduit should Frank need additional help; plus I like to know if and when trouble is coming. You are to contact her within three days. After that, you are to check in with her periodically. A special telephone number has been assigned for just that purpose."

"Do you have any news on that boat we requested?"

"Yes, it's already been taken care of. Ms. Lockery has the details, so you can coordinate that with her."

"Mr. Whitworth, I would like to thank you for your help up to this point."

"Young man, I wish you the best of luck." He passed Tim an oversized briefcase from next to his wheelchair. "The additional seventy thousand dollars is here in cash. Due to the nature of your work, we assumed you would want no denominations larger than hundred-dollar bills. I hope you understand that this interview never took place."

"Thank you, sir."

Whitworth nodded and gazed once more out to the distant ocean.

Ms. Lockery showed Tim to the front door where Andrea was waiting. On the way, she passed him a card with a telephone number and simply said, "Good luck, Mr. Reardon."

New Haven

As they left Newport, the traffic was heavy, but Tim found himself relishing the sights and sounds of a New England he had missed while overseas, as well as the excitement the woman sitting next to him made him feel, so the ride passed quietly.

The gas light came on as they reached the outskirts of New Haven, so Andrea pulled off at an exit immediately before the Quinnipiac Bridge. She drove into a busy self-service Shell station in front of a shopping plaza and parked next to a pump behind a white Continental. Tim hopped out and grabbed the nozzle while Andrea trotted into the office to pay the cashier. He saw them just as they spotted him.

Tim felt eyes upon him and glanced at the Continental. The driver sat in the car behind heavily tinted glass; but another man, tall and bearded in a white shirt and black pants, stood pumping—and his eyes bored into Tim.

Casually, the tall man looked away, finished pumping, and headed back to his car.

Tim looked for Andrea and saw her approaching the rear of the Firebird. When he returned his attention to the Continental, he saw the bearded man climb into the car, but Tim felt certain that he had been recognized.

He heard Andrea's light step behind him, and she asked, "So, where would you like lunch?"

He turned toward her as casually as he could and said, "Up to you," but he motioned with his eyes for her to get in the Firebird quickly.

Concern flashed across her face, but she did as his eyes had instructed.

As he replaced the nozzle, the Continental suddenly moved forward and parked next to the curb by the exit.

Tim slid into the Firebird and said, "One of the men in that white Continental recognized me—I'm sure of it. They're either not sure it's really me, or they want to make their move somewhere else. Let's get out of here and see if they follow."

Andrea, starting the engine, asked, "Where should I go?"

"I don't know the area, but stay off the freeway. We need room to maneuver. This car as fast as it looks?"

"Faster. I've got every performance option they make."

"OK, drive out of here normally, and let's see what they do."

Andrea released the clutch and pulled out of the Shell station onto a two-lane cut-off that forked, offering a way back onto the freeway, or an entrance to Route 1 leading to Branford. Tim watched out the back window for the Continental as he slid his PPk out of his jacket and clicked off the safety catch.

In the rearview mirror, he saw the Continental pull out several blocks back. Andrea turned left toward Branford. Tim watched the white car to their rear and saw it turn the same way. Tim said, "Head somewhere you can let this car loose, someplace where you've got lots of options. Keep us out of traffic."

"All right, I know where to go, but we've got to make it through a couple of congested lights to get there."

"That's OK. Drive normally until we clear the lights, then punch it."

As Andrea had predicted, a line of cars stretched back at the first light, but the white car remained two cars back as they waited. She turned left and accelerated, but as she approached the second light, it turned red. They were forced to stop and the Continental pulled in directly behind them. The Firebird was first in line, but two dense lines of traffic streamed through the intersection in front of them.

Suddenly, Tim saw the bearded man lean out of the passenger window to their rear, with a revolver in his hand.

Tim spun in his seat with the PPk ready and hissed, "Go! Now! And keep your head down!"

The engine roared, Andrea popped the clutch, the back tires squealed, and Tim felt the car simultaneously leaping forward and fishtailing, and the sudden acceleration compressed him into his seat. He heard a gunshot and horns blaring and out of the corner of his eye saw a car spinning in the intersection, but the Firebird gained speed and powered through untouched.

As Andrea flung the Firebird around a sharp bend, the Continental disappeared from sight for the moment, so Tim faced forward and said, "Keep pouring it on. He's just got a pistol, so distance'll keep us alive right now."

Ahead of them he saw a slow-moving Plymouth nearing another blind bend. Andrea never hesitated—she threw the car into a lower gear and twisted the Firebird across the yellow line to pass the Plymouth. A truck coming around the curve suddenly loomed before them, but Andrea coolly twisted the wheel right. They made it, just inches from the Plymouth, and she worked the gear box and continued to accelerate.

They were racing down a long, tree-lined straightaway when Tim spotted the Continental, rapidly closing on the Plymouth. He glanced ahead and saw a slow-moving fuel truck with a line of cars behind it. He cursed.

A small side street approached fast on their right. He urged, "Turn right. We'll never get past that line of cars fast enough."

Andrea downshifted abruptly and pulled the hand brake, and Tim felt the back end of the Firebird sliding left. She threw off the hand brake, tossed the gear lever, and gunned the straining engine. The tires caught and the car shot down the side street.

Pointing at a sign, she exclaimed, "Tim, this is a dead end."

"I know, just keep going."

Looking for options, Tim studied the street. Neatly groomed houses lined each side. A baseball field flew by in a blur. He saw that the road ended a quarter of a mile ahead in a large circular turnaround area at the base of a steep, heavily forested hill.

Calmly, he said, "We'll have to make a stand. Park at the back edge of the turnaround and let's make a run for those trees. I hope we've gained enough time to get under cover before they see us."

"Whatever you say."

He slid the PPk back beneath his jacket, reached into the small back seat where he had left his duffel bag, opened it, and pulled out his Mini 14 and two full magazines. He inserted one and cocked the rifle. The other he placed in a pocket of his windbreaker. He looked to his rear, but the Firebird had crested a small hill that blocked his view. Tim glanced at the assault rifle in his lap and thought of taking a shot at the Continental as it crested the hill, but dismissed the idea. Gunshots would bring cops, and they might end up arrested with a briefcase full of cash and a trunk full of weapons. Plus he wanted to interrogate his pursuers. He had to know how they had found him. Had they followed him all along or were they just lucky? Then he felt the bulk of the fighting knife on his ankle and found the solution there—just as the car squealed to a halt in the turnaround. To make it work, he would need the knife.

They flung the doors open and sprinted forward to a six-foot chain-link fence just beyond the road.

Tim said, "I'm going to help you over. Jump and grab the top." With his help, she deftly swung over and dropped to the other side. He followed, just as he heard the sound of the racing Continental approaching fast. They sprinted for the safety of the trees. Tires squealed behind him; then they passed the first tree and foliage closed in.

They charged toward the hill, but Tim saw the trees were thinning, the slope was steep, and the soil was muddy. They would be too easy to follow, and too vulnerable to bullets in the back. His ambush needed thick undergrowth, and he saw a perfect spot just yards to his right beside a muddy trail that ran along the base of the hill. Grabbing Andrea's hand, he pulled her parallel with the trail toward a thick clump of saplings with a large fallen tree limb, well-covered with pine needles, in their center.

He jumped a bush and spotted a triangular boulder surrounded by undergrowth some ten yards ahead. He motioned for Andrea to crouch behind it and noticed she already had her PPk out. He whispered, "Look, for now lay low. Keep your head down behind the rock and don't put it up until I tell you it's safe." He motioned at her pistol. "Only use the gun as a last resort, but if you have to shoot, make damn sure you take them before they take you. Remember what I taught you: no movement! As long as you're stationary, you'll see them first."

"And you?"

"I'll be fine. Now get going."

She nodded, sprinted for the rock, and disappeared behind it.

Tim faced back down the trail and saw no one, but he could hear someone climbing the chain-link fence. He yanked his fighting knife from its ankle sheath and hacked some branches from the saplings to his rear. Then he slid under the fallen branch, scraped pine needles from beneath his body and sprinkled them over his back. He placed the boughs over the needles and slid his mini M-14 under the pine-needle carpet near his right hand. It was there, concealed, if he needed it. Quickly, he scanned the area about him for visual clues of his labors and saw none. He reached under his chest, filled his hand with dirt, and smeared it on his face. He curled the finger of his right hand onto the trigger of his rifle and held the knife with his left. If they spotted him, he felt confident he could take them with two shots. Then he concentrated on the trail to his front, hoping he had camouflaged himself well enough, and that his pursuers would do the logical thing and come up the trail.

Seconds later, he saw them. The tall, bearded man and a bald, stocky companion of average height walked up the trail warily. Both carried large stainless-steel revolvers. Unaware, they stopped just ten feet away from the waiting Green Beret and gazed uncertainly up the muddy hill.

The bald man murmured, "I dunno, you think he's up there?"

The tall one answered, "Where else could he go? But I don't like this shit. If what I heard from Salka's true, this guy knows what he's doing."

"Yeah, that's what I hear. But I know he's the one in the picture Salka passed around, and we gotta shot at a whole lotta money."

The tall man glanced in Tim's direction and said, "Shit, let's try the trail. They can't be far, but we don't find them, we just tell Salka about the car, and maybe we get some cash for that."

The bald man shrugged and followed close behind his companion, already heading up the trail. Neither showed any indication they had spotted Tim.

Tim tensed. There were two targets, so his timing had to be perfect. A millisecond off, and they would have time to shoot. He decided to take the bald one from behind and drive him forward into the back of his companion.

He waited, coiling his muscles and keeping his head low, his eyes glued to the trail. Then he saw their feet pass. Driving himself up and forward, he released his rifle, and tossed the knife from his left to his right hand. The bald man stopped, and Tim hit him hard, reaching around and thrusting so that his knife sliced into the base of his assailant's throat, traveling downward through the jugular vein and into his chest cavity. Tim knew the first man was finished, but drove him forward like a tackling dummy into the back of the second while jerking out his knife.

All three hit the ground hard. Tim rolled off the now dead bald man, fluidly sprang to his feet, and saw the bearded assailant, pistol still in hand, struggling beneath the corpse. Tim leapt across the dead man and heard a muffled shot. The panicked man on the ground had pointed the gun up and fired blindly into his dead friend, then pushed the bloody body away. The Green Beret leapt onto the back of the rolling man as he came clear and thrust his knife up and into the side of his stomach cavity. The man released the pistol convulsively, and when Tim rolled him over, he found himself staring into lifeless eyes.

Tim cursed, then heard a sound behind him. He twisted at the waist and saw Andrea, pistol raised.

She lowered her pistol and said, "My God! I heard the gun and thought he had you. Are you all right?"

"Yes, but I blew our shot at finding out how they found us. They're past that now."

She glanced at the bodies for the first time and drew in a

breath. Tim followed her eyes. The bald man lay with sightless eyes staring skyward. Blood that had spurted from the arteries in his neck and chest covered the side of his face. His companion lay in a frozen fetal position, still clutching his crimson abdomen. Andrea grimaced and looked away.

Tim rose and said, "We've got to hide the bodies. The longer they stay lost, the less likely someone will be to remember the red Firebird that flew in here. We've also got to move their car."

Andrea nodded.

Tim continued, "I could use your help moving and hiding them, but if you don't want to . . ."

"No, I'll help."

They took their assailants' pistols and wallets to slow down identification and hid the bodies in shallow graves beneath the saplings. Then Tim drove the Continental and left it parked on a street in New Haven, certain it would be towed that night. Andrea picked him up, and they were in her townhouse and watching the evening news by six. The program gave no indication that the two bodies had been found.

Finding ground beef in her freezer, Tim offered to make dinner, and she let him. He had a meatloaf ready by seven, but he noticed Andrea ate little.

He said, "I know what happened today is difficult for you."

She shook her head and said, "No, it's not what you think. After what I saw in the mall, this time it didn't shock me. They gave you no choice. But when I heard that gun go off, I thought . . . God, I thought I lost you. Will it always be like this?"

"I hope not, Andrea—not after we finish with Pyne. But what really bothers me is how they found us. Was it luck? Or does Pyne somehow have people watching the roads? I heard them say something about a picture, so maybe it was just luck. Pyne's got enough men to cover a lot of territory."

"You think they were looking for my car?"

"No. If I thought that were true, we'd have already ditched the Firebird and not come here—because if they know your car, then they know your house, and they would already be here. It just isn't possible. Nobody's seen your car, and we're clear because they had no phone or radio in their car to call anyone. All I can figure is we just came to the wrong gas station at the wrong time." Rubbing the stubble on his chin, he added, "I wish this beard would come in faster."

Andrea was exhausted, but she had one more job for the night. Armed with rolls of quarters and a list of phone numbers, she went to a pay phone on the corner. While Tim, armed with a rifle, watched from the window, she called the men and finalized their travel arrangements. She came back inside and reported that all of the Green Berets would be there. Then she turned in early.

He remained in her living room and watched several movies, remaining awake with his rifle in his hand until the morning sun's rays poked through her curtains.

CHAPTER TWENTY-SIX

July 4, 1989—New Haven

Andrea went to her office early and found her boss already there, ready to take advantage of the holiday customers. Surprised, he asked if she was ready to come back to work, but she explained that she still needed time and was just doing a favor for a friend. It took her little time to find the two properties Tim wanted. By noon, she had cleared it with the owners, had his signature on the leases, and had given him the keys to each property.

4:22 P.M.—J.F.K. International Airport

Shortly after the plane arrived from Panama, Joe Gonda emerged from the arrival gate amidst a large crowd of passengers. A hulking man, he appeared at first glance to be in poor physical condition, but the confidence and strength of his gait belied that notion. Somehow, in spite of his bulk, he was the only passenger in the crowd not to be jostled.

The thousand dollars he had received by telex from Germany had paid for the flight, and he had enough left over to get him to New Haven. As per his instructions, once he had retrieved his baggage, he telephoned a prearranged number in New Haven and received directions on which train to take and the time it departed from Grand Central. Alert for anyone taking an inordinate interest in his activities, he detected no watchers as he entered a taxi bound for the train station in Manhattan. Though his impassive demeanor did not reveal it, he was in very high spirits indeed. There was a mission to be done. This was what Joe Gonda lived for, and he was anxious to get started.

The Yankee Clipper Amtrak Train

Originally from Wyoming, Wayne Murphy was tall and thin with light red hair, gray eyes, and a rancher's lean, weatherbeaten face. He preferred flying to riding trains because his long legs were always cramped and planes travel faster, but his instructions dictated otherwise, and he didn't question them. Still, as always, he had difficulty sleeping in the small seat, and being a man who favored activity over idleness, he finally pulled out his guitar, and began to play it in the quiet way he favored. By the time the train had pulled into New Haven, several people on his end of the car had joined him in singing old songs. If Wayne himself was the least bit worried that he was embarking on a mission that could get him killed, it didn't show in his demeanor and in the firm, deliberate way he put away his guitar, fitted on his cowboy hat, and debarked onto the platform.

New Haven

As Joe Gonda had been told, an attractive dark-haired woman was waiting for him in a red Firebird at the New Haven train station. She dropped him off outside an apartment, where he found Tim reclined on a couch with a growing beard. About a half hour later, she returned with Wayne Murphy, who was surprised to see Gonda and greeted both him and Tim with bear hugs. Andrea left the reunion to handle some business for Tim.

Tim produced some bread and cold cuts, and the three had dinner while they talked about old times and who else was coming. After eating, they moved to the living room and the briefing began.

Joe asked the first question. "Wayne, I don't know what the hell you know, but these guys told me shit, just that it was a chance to waste some drug dealers, get rich, and get this shithead here outta some kinda trouble."

Wayne shook his head. "Same here. Tim, what the hell's up?"

Tim briefed them on all the developments up to this point. Gonda made the appropriate comment about the first trip to Vermont. He thought Tim should have killed Ronny. Joe would have killed him without a second thought.

Tim concluded the briefing by telling them about the beach house and the office and showing them the pictures he had of the island. As was his custom, Murphy remained quiet throughout the briefing, but Gonda, typically, had lots to say. He didn't like the lack of intelligence they had, and he worried that Tim might get spotted in New Haven. Finally, he asked, "You got any weapons yet? I couldn't carry shit on that damn airplane from Panama. You bring anything, Wayne?"

In reply, Murphy patted a shoulder holster hidden under his windbreaker.

Tim nodded in acknowledgment. "Good, every extra weapon helps right now. Joe, we'll get you armed as soon as we can. . . . OK, here's what we got going for now. The rest of the guys'll be here by tomorrow afternoon. Meanwhile, Andrea's renting us a truck. First thing tomorrow morning, you and she are going on a buying spree."

The big man asked, "What we gonna buy?"

Tim replied, "Office furniture, all the stuff we'll need for the planning area we're going to set up, and everything you'll need for a sleeping area. When the rest get here tomorrow, they'll have to live somewhere."

Gonda was curious. "Hey, if we're using a business as a cover, what business we in?"

"Joe, consistent with your love of culture, we have elected to call ourselves brokers of fine art."

The big man snorted. Fine art was not among his top interests. "No shit."

Wayne liked it even more, and spoke for the first time. "I can see it now—a new business for you: Joe Gonda, fine-art commando."

Tim laughed and said, "All right, you two are going to have to help Andrea get the office set up tomorrow. We'll make decisions about what we're going to do next once the others get here."

Joe asked, "Tim, how much money we got, and where the hell'd we get it?"

"Right now we've got seventy thousand dollars and a cigarette boat. Where it's from doesn't matter, but it's not stolen." With that, their conversation turned once again to past exploits.

Going to bed late that night, Tim slept with Andrea, while Gonda and Murphy found accommodations in her living room. He had been planning to get some sleep, but he found she had very different ideas on what to do with their time.

CHAPTER TWENTY-SEVEN

Wednesday, July 5, 1989—North Haven

The office Andrea had found for their base of operations was above an apothecary in an old three-story red brick building on Main Street in an area that had long since been taken over by shopping malls. In the place of the old stores, doctors and attorneys now owned tasteful businesses in keeping with their visions of how an Old New England town should appear.

Their building had a good-sized loading area that was relatively private except for some apartments that overlooked it from an adjacent brownstone. The neighborhood was quiet and secure, and the locals were pleased to learn that an art agent had entered their community.

That morning, Andrea's business savvy proved invaluable. With almost amazing speed, she located and purchased everything they needed to set up the office. To pick it up, Gonda and Murphy had to make three trips in the predented white generic van she had rented the previous day.

The last shipment contained, among other things, bunk beds. A friendly pharmacist taking a break on the loading dock asked about the beds. Andrea rapidly explained that because of the international nature of their enterprise, they had clients in several time zones, so there would often be people working extremely late in the evenings, possibly the whole night. Additionally, the valuable merchandise they had to store required that twenty-four-hour armed security be present. The druggist liked hearing that. Armed security upstairs meant a lower likelihood that his store downstairs would be robbed during the quiet hours of the morning.

While the unloading continued, Tim remained in Andrea's apartment both to stay out of sight and to guard the cash in her living room. He had loaned Joe Gonda the PPk, so he spent most of the afternoon sitting beside the shotgun. Around three, the phone rang. Frank was in New York and would be in New Haven by six. Immediately before four, Paul Curtis telephoned. He was at the New Haven bus station, so Andrea went to pick him up. Following these two, the others arrived in quick succession by bus, train, or air. Finally, the entire team had assembled, and Tim and Andrea joined them at the office.

When they got to North Haven with the money, Tim found that his friends had been busy. The sign painter had already finished, and the smoked-glass front door read "Northeast Art Imports Ltd." Inside, the reception area had been outfitted with a generous finished-wood desk, a reclining swivel chair, and Andrea's own personal computer on a side table. To the right of the entrance, a generously stuffed Naugahyde couch sat amidst easy chairs and matching wood-grained coffee and end tables. Andrea had also purchased paintings from an authentic art dealer downtown, and in the corners were the types of potted plants found in offices the world over. She had even gotten the little things right—the receptionist's desk had a Rolodex, a cup for pens, a telephone/intercom system, and an in box. On a small table next to the desk was a television with a built-in VCR and a stack of her old movie tapes. The carpet was a tasteful pastel green color, and the walls were white. And, she informed Tim, business cards with four different fictitious names were being printed even as they spoke.

He asked, "Andrea, what's with the television?"

She smiled, "Where would I be without Bogart, Stewart, Bette Davis?"

He laughed, and they continued on to the next room, another large office with a double window facing the rear and a single window holding an air conditioner facing the alley on their left. On the right was a long room with one window. Also with an air conditioner, it overlooked the loading dock below. This last space would serve as their equipment storage space and sleeping quarters, while the back office would serve as the planning area.

In the back room Gonda and Murphy had already set up small desks around the periphery. In the center stood a large sand table they could use to fashion an accurate representation of Robin Island using dirt, models, and other materials. Sheets of soundproofing leaned against a wall, ready to be installed.

He found the eight other members of the team in the sleeping area. Each of them was helping to set up, and they were almost finished. There was a sectional sofa with easy chairs, assorted tables, and lamps in one corner. Against the wall were pre-cut sheets of plywood to be crafted into storage bins, which each team member would need for his personal equipment. Four bunk beds were already out of their boxes and put together, giving them a total of eight beds. There was also a refrigerator, a small microwave, a television, a radio/tape player, and a hot plate. In the front end of the unit was a bathroom complete with a shower that could be accessed from both the storage area and the reception room.

After another round of greetings, Gonda spoke to Tim. "Tim, before you got here, we all talked and everybody kind of knows the score about Pyne and your sister and everything.

We want you to know we're all with you on this one. Somebody's gotta stop these people, and it might as well be us."

"Thanks, I hope you feel that way a month from now." Tim called the new team into the planning room. The men took seats around the room, Andrea stood in the reception-area door, and Tim walked up to the portable chalkboard set up opposite the windows, which were covered with shades. He could smell the odor of Mac's cigars already permeating the room. "OK, first of all, thanks to all of you for being here. Each of you already knows Mac, Frank, and me; but not all of you know each other, and it's time you did, so first I'll introduce you and then tell you why you're here."

He looked at Joe Gonda. He had barely squeezed his giant frame into one of the desks, and he was smoking a cigarette impassively. The dark eyes set within his swarthy face were a cold void beneath his short, jet black hair. Tim knew that the big man was relaxed, but even so he had the look about him of a bear about to strike. Tim waved in his direction. "Gentlemen, I'd like you to meet Joe Gonda. Joe comes to us from Panama. He's one of the best weapons men I've ever known. Aside from his knowledge of just about every kind of military small arms, he is also adept with the crossbow and a master of silent-kill techniques and the martial arts. But his absolute best quality? If you ever need anything heavy picked up, he's the best man for it." He turned to Andrea. "And he's single, so watch out."

The team laughed. Even Gonda cracked a miniscule grin. Tim moved to Wayne Murphy. The redhead sat next to Gonda with his guitar leaning against his chin and a large chaw of chewing tobacco in his cheek. Tim continued: "Now the man seated next to Joe is Wayne Murphy, and he's up from Fort Bragg. He don't talk much, but don't let that worry you. He's from a ranch in Wyoming, so the only thing he knows how to talk about is herding cattle anyway." Tim paused for another round of laughter, then went on, "Wayne's our second weapons man, and he's also scuba-qualified. That means he's our expert on all things maritime—and we're going to have plenty of those. As you can all see, his hobbies include playing the guitar."

Joe said, "That's fine as long as he don't play the fuckin' thing while I'm trying to sleep."

Wayne smiled and, in his slow, careful way, replied, "Shit, then that's the only time I'll play."

Tim said, "I worked with Wayne in Lebanon, and I can tell you he's one of the best."

He turned and regarded Pete Sayers. Seated next to Mac, he was kind-looking, over forty, short, round-bellied, and also had red hair, but his was streaked with gray. "Our second redhead, the man next to Mac, is Pete Sayers. Don't let his gut and age fool you. The gut is a legacy from a belly wound in Vietnam. I worked with Pete in Beirut, and Mac was with him in 'Nam. He's as hard as woodpecker lips. He's been to all those secret demolitions schools, so when it comes to making things go bang in the night, he's the best. He's got one hell of a lot of planning sense, and when he and Mac get together, they're a good team. He's based at Fort Lewis in Washington, and his wife thinks he's come East to visit with some friends on Long Island. Whether or not he ever tells her what he's really doing here is up to him."

Stan Radawicz sat by the door. Also short, he was black-haired, extremely thin and wiry, and wore glasses. Tim knew that Stan's slender appearance had little to do with his strength and endurance. He was absolutely tireless. Tim began: "The other little guy is Stanislaus Radawicz, but we all better just call him Stan or we'll never get past the name. He's another Panama guy, and one of the best damn medics I've ever worked with. There'll be no doctors on this one, so he and Frank will have to be good if any of us gets hit. He's divorced, so if anybody calls claiming to be his wife, it means he's up to something we don't know about." That brought another round of laughter. "He talks a lot, but don't pay it much attention. For as long as we've known him, he's never been serious."

Tim then turned to the young black man next to Stan. Unlike Joe, he looked as powerful as he was. "Next, I'd like those of you who don't know him to meet Art Simpson. Art hasn't been in S.F. as long as the rest of us, but he's a super demolitions man. As you might be able to guess, his main hobby is weightlifting. He's also scuba-qualified, so he'll be working closely with Wayne, and they'll make a hell of a team, even though neither one of them talks enough to fill a cassette tape in a year's time."

The final soldier sat next to the chalkboard. Blond, blue-eyed, of average height, and average in appearance, this man would go unnoticed in a crowd, but he was one of the toughest soldiers Tim had ever seen. "Last but not least, I'd like you to meet Paul Curtis. Paul spent a lot of time in the Ranger battalions before he came to S.F. We also worked together in Lebanon. I can tell you, he'll do whatever needs to be done and do it well. He's our third demo man, and he's stationed just two hours away at Fort Devens. That'll be handy when we need some favors. Oh, and he's our third scuba-trained member, so when Wayne and Art get tired of listening to each other not saying anything, Paul can help them along."

Tim glanced at Andrea, who still stood in the door, slowly revolving Lisa's silver bracelet around her wrist. "Gentlemen, I want you to meet Andrea. She and I are kind of friends. So far, she's made a lot of what we've gotten done possible. Like me, she already lost family in this thing, so it's personal for her too. We've been together through some bad shit lately, and she knows how to handle herself. She's local, so if you want to know anything about New Haven, ask her."

Andrea held up a hand and Tim nodded. She said, "I want you to know that I appreciate each one of you being here. Anything I can do to help make this mission work, just let me know what you need."

There was a general nod and Gonda spoke up. "Yeah, you got a sister?"

Andrea gave him a hard smile. "I used to, Joe. That's why I'm here."

Gonda's dark eyes bored into her green ones. She met his gaze impassively. Then he nodded. "Yeah, I understand. Glad to have you, Andrea."

"Glad to have you, Joe."

Tim continued, "OK, now let me give you an idea on how things will work from here on out. Tonight, we'll make some decisions on what weapons we need, and tomorrow Joe and Wayne are going to Fayetteville, North Carolina, to go shopping. Frank, since you know our money man, you and Stan can go pick up the cigarette boat. I'll talk with you later on how you're going to get there."

They nodded and Tim continued, "For those of you who haven't heard yet, we've got another house rented in Branford.

It's near our target, and I haven't seen it, but Andie says it's nice: some kind of a furnished two-bedroom with a small beach and a shared dock where we can park the boat. Anyway, Frank and Stan are moving in there tomorrow. Their job is to look like party guys out for a fun summer, so every day they've got good weather, they should be cruising around the Thimbles in that boat raising hell and having a good time. What we need them to do most of all is to recon both the island and the waters around it. The Thimbles are a bad place to try and navigate, and we don't want to sink our boats while we're trying to pull off the mission. For that reason, all of us are going to get ample time visiting our wild buddies on the beach so we can learn the waters. They've also got to be as social as possible and get to know the neighbors—especially anyone in the drug scene. They will throw lots of parties, and we'll come as guests. It would be good if the neighbors got used to seeing our faces coming and going."

Gonda cut in, "Then I assume if Frank and Stan are living at the house, the rest of us are gonna park it here."

"For now, yes. This area consists mostly of business property. That means there will be a lot less questions asked about what we're doing than if we were in a residential area."

Wayne rubbed his hands. "No parties, but at least we got air conditioning. If those two cocksuckers got it too, I'll kill them myself. We gotta spread out the perks."

Everyone laughed, and Tim continued, "Next, we've got to go over the organization of this thing. I went over it with Joe last night so he'll brief you."

Gonda stood up and addressed the group. "As is already obvious, Tim's the team leader. That gives him the final word on most things. He's also gonna handle commo and electronic surveillance. Mac's our S-3 operations guy, and you can consider him the team sergeant. He's done just about everything, so I guess he's qualified enough to plan this thing. Pete, you're gonna be in charge of demo and S-2—Andrea, S-2 means intelligence—also, you can help Mac out with the S-3. He's been around a lot too, so we'll use that experience to our advantage. Art Simpson and Paul'll work with Pete on the demo part. Wayne and I'll handle the S-4—that's supply—and the weapons part. Art can do some running for us there too. Tim and Paul have worked together a lot before, so Paul, you can help out Tim with the electronic bullshit. When Wayne and me're out running to Fayetteville or some other damn place, Art and Paul can fill in as S-4's. Andrea, you're what we call an S-1. That means you handle all the administrative shit like you've been doin' already. Keep track of money. Take care of rental payments. Basically keep everything working that we need to keep ourselves going. Since according to Tim you got a little more class than some of the rest of us, during working hours you're gonna have to act like our secretary out front. That means nine to five every day, you're gonna have to be out front."

She nodded and said, "Just don't expect me to take dictation or get you coffee."

Gonda smiled. "Now Frank and Stan are goin' to be pretty busy with boats, fast cars, women, and shit like that; but when they get a little spare time, they're also our team medics. You guys figure out what the hell you need for the job, and we'll see what we can do to get it. Basically, we're gonna have no military support, so the medics gotta be ready for anything. That about cover it, Tim?"

"Good, Joe. Now here's some of the rules for this operation. While we're here, we've got to be extra careful of civilian authorities. We don't want any traces of our work here left behind, so don't get caught speeding. Don't get into bar fights. Don't drive drunk. Don't even get parking tickets. Be real courteous to our neighbors both here and at the beach. We don't want to attract any of the wrong kind of interest.

"In public, never use your real name or anyone else's. If you have to make calls, use pay phones. Only call this number in an emergency. If you want to go out and have a dinner, see a flick, have a couple of drinks, or whatever, never do it alone. We have to get used to moving in pairs. Remember, this is for real.

"As soon as Wayne and Joe get back from down South, we should have some weapons to issue. Until they do, you'll have to pack your own weapons, but try not to use them if they are registered and can be traced. Personally, I don't think this thing will heat up too much until they get back anyway, so you shouldn't need to do any shooting for a while. The money, plans, and equipment are all going to be here. For that reason, it should always be guarded by at least two people. If it's compromised, we'll have to go down fighting. Remember that.

"Now that this thing is rolling, we're going to keep all vehicles under Andrea's name to limit our own exposure as much as possible. And anytime you're driving somewhere, always check for tails when you come back. If you feel anything even remotely suspicious, deal with it in whatever way you have to. Just don't bring anybody here. A lot of shit is going to start happening at once. When it does, each of you is going to have to let the rest know what's going on. That's the only way we can stay ahead of things as they develop.

"Finally, everybody cleans up after themselves in this place. We all have to live here, so let's have some courtesy for everyone else. I'm sure most of you will do it automatically. Anybody got any questions?"

No one did.

"OK, to date, no one has fully stated exactly what the mission of this team is. I will do so now. The mission of this detachment, which came about for reasons you've all already been told, is multifaceted. First, we will infiltrate Robin Island by any sound and appropriate means to interrupt Pyne's drug operations there in such a manner as to render his network completely useless. Our second goal is to bring about the termination of Michael Pyne and all other key members of his organization. Our next objective is what makes this thing possible—it is to blow Mr. Pyne's safe and make off with every penny he has. The final portion of the mission is probably the most difficult—when it's all over, we want to fade away like we never existed.

"The bottom line here is that when we go in, it will have to be with maximum effect. We'll only get one shot, so we're going to pack a lot of firepower. This thing is going to be fast and bloody, but we want no civilians killed, and we want to bring the whole team back. No one gets left behind. The clock is running, gentlemen, and we've only got thirty days from now to finish this operation."

The room remained silent for a minute. Joe Gonda smiled. Andrea stood wide-eyed. Frank and Paul both looked thoughtful. Mac lit a fresh cigar. Wayne leaned back in his chair and asked, "That's all fine, but I still want to know why Frank and Stan get the fancy beach-front house and we don't."

Stan piped up, "Because we're sophisticated, and we don't want the locals to get bad ideas about Green Berets. That's what we studied in medic school, how to be high-class and shit."

All the soldiers laughed, then Stan asked Andrea, "Hey, Andrea, this town is supposed to be famous for its Italian food. You know any good pizza take-outs?"

"As a matter of fact, I do. Why don't you come with me, and I'll show you where one is."

They left, and Tim stood up once more. "OK, a couple of last details. We'll fill Stan in later." He pulled out the briefcase with the money and laid it on the large table in the center of the room. When he opened it, the others caught their breath. He said, "This is our entire bankroll. If it gets lost, we're finished, so we'll guard it carefully. Also, Andrea is in charge of it, so nobody takes any money without asking her."

Before closing the briefcase, he reached under the money and slid out a manila folder. Holding it up, he said, "This is our file on Robin Island. Frank, Mac, Wayne, Joe, and myself have already seen it. The rest of you need to get to know it. Don't worry, you'll all get to be experts on Robin Island real soon. Anyway, here's the layout: the place is about twelve acres in size, and we can expect that it'll be heavily guarded. Let's talk about what kind of firepower we need to go in and pull this thing off. Mac had some ideas on this." He looked at Mac. "Why don't you go over what you've got so far."

Mac nodded and without removing his cigar from his mouth said, "OK, first of all, I'd like to keep the weapons as standard as possible, and since we're going to be working mostly in close quarters—the island is only twelve and a half acres square in area, and some of that work will be indoors; .45s and MAC 10s seem good to me."

Gonda agreed. "Yeah, the Ingram Model 10. It's light, small, damn near more pistol than submachine gun, and has a cyclic rate of fire of 1145 rounds per minute. We could get it in nine millimeter and forty-five, but forty-five would be better. It don't penetrate for shit, so we won't be shootin' each other by accident through walls, but it packs a load. You hit a guy, he'll go down. Using MAC 10s we got both submachine guns and pistols in forty-five caliber. What's really good about a MAC

10 is that it comes with a suppressor, so we can keep it quiet. How about it, Wayne?"

"Yeah, I like the Ingram too."

Gonda was still thinking. "Now, I'm a believer in peace through superior firepower, so I'd also like to see everyone packin' shotguns. Nothing discourages a target from puttin' his piece up at the wrong time like a blast from a twelve-gauge. Also, buckshot don't penetrate, so it's good indoors."

Tim smiled, "Joe, I knew you'd have some ideas. So we need nine .45s, nine Ingrams with suppressors, and nine twelve-gauge shotguns."

"Yeah," Gonda concurred, "and if you want, we could get extended barrels and I could suppress the .45s too. Also, I'd like to have some heavy firepower to back us up, just in case. M-234 SAW's would be perfect. They're light, twenty-two pounds, a good weapon, and the 223-caliber ammo comes in two-hundred–round boxes and is compact enough so we can carry a lot of it. You get a cyclic rate of fire of 750 rounds a minute and a range of 3600 meters. Best of all, one guy can man it himself and fire from a tripod or moving. Since we don't need to take in any food, cold-weather gear, or any other heavy shit, we can go in weapon-heavy. I say it's better to have it than not."

Tim liked the idea. "Good. Put it on the list. What about explosives?"

Pete Sayers spoke up. "An XM-122 would be nice to have, too. It's got a radio-controlled electrical firing system, and it's got several receivers so we can place multiple charges and activate each one remotely. The nice thing is that we'll be working around salt water. That should give the XM-122 a range of up to a mile. You just match whatever transmitter code you pick with the receiver, push a button, and a big bang happens a mile away. Nifty. We'll also need an M-32 blasting machine for setting off charges on command electrically. Naturally, we need any explosives we can get. M-27 fragmentation grenades would be great, and if we can get hold of some white phosphorus for starting fires, that would be great too."

Tim looked around the room and asked, "Anybody got any more ideas or suggestions?" When no one indicated that they did, he continued, "OK, Joe, you got that? Mac knows somebody in Fayetteville for you to see. Talk to him as soon as we're done here.

"One more thing. I'd like to say thank you all for being here. This is a tough one, and you're all taking big chances just by knowing what we're doing. I appreciate it."

Simpson spoke up. "Tim, you're family."

Just then, Andrea and Stan entered with the pizza and the meeting broke up. After eating, Andrea left and the men went to their new bunks. It had been a long day for each of them, and the coming weeks would not be easy. Tim slept in a bunk with the rest of the team, but his mind was filled with thoughts of the girl who had left. He had difficulty falling asleep.

CHAPTER TWENTY-EIGHT

Thursday, July 6, 1989—New Haven

Pulcinella sat alone with a file in his hand in the airy commercial space the DEA had rented for its headquarters. He popped a candy in his mouth and smiled. For the first time since joining the team, he felt excited. The day before, they had gotten their first real break through a tap on a secondary dealer. A three-kilo shipment of cocaine was coming in from New York via the Metro-North commuter train. The mule was a high-school kid named Bonnie Murry. Agents on the train had intercepted the drugs and the girl, but the kid knew what she was doing. Young and innocent-looking, she wore shorts and a T-shirt; she carried an athletic bag and looked like a suburban teen fresh from an afternoon of tennis in the city. Spotting the police closing in, the girl had quickly tried to hide the dope in the bathroom. She hadn't made it, but her ploy had warned Tony that they were dealing with someone far more streetwise than they had anticipated.

In return for not going to jail, the kid and her lawyer had cut a deal, and she had given them all she knew about her contacts on both ends. Given this windfall, Tony and Bonning planned a sting operation. Tony figured that if these small dealers could be broken, the task force might be able to work their way up to higher levels of the organization. He was thinking about some final recommendations he wanted to make to Bonning when the phone rang.

He picked it up quickly and heard Bonning's voice. The news was bad. Bonnie's confession was all they were going to get. The dealer in New Haven had been found slumped over the steering wheel of his car with a single bullet through his brain. The supplier in New York was also dead—in his case, by shotgun. Bonnie, whose lawyer had arranged for her release, had turned up too—the Branford police had found her disemboweled in a ditch next to Route 1.

After he hung up, Tony leaned back and steepled his fingers on his chest deep in thought.

He had had doubts before, but they were gone—somebody within the task force was working for the wrong people.

North Haven, Connecticut

The Green Berets rose early that morning. At 9 A.M. Andrea counted out $30,000 to Joe Gonda for weapons-shopping. Then, he and Wayne took their beat-up van to I-95 and headed south for North Carolina. As soon as they had departed, she contacted Ms. Lockery to coordinate the pickup of the boat; then she took Frank and Stan to a rent-a-car office to pick up a car they could use to get to Newport. Shortly after that, they headed north toward Rhode Island on I-95. Of the four, only Tim Franklin was unarmed. Stan and Wayne Murphy both had their own .45s, and Gonda had Tim's PPk and Mini 14.

Andrea and Paul spent the morning shopping for more materials for their planning center and laying the groundwork for the arrival of the men at the beach house. Tim worked at soundproofing the work area, then installed a buzzer at the front door. Anyone interested in visiting would have to buzz the secretary to gain entrance. He also placed an intercom in the living area and one by the secretary's desk.

Pete Sayers and Mac helped Tim put up the soundproof panels. They talked of the mission while they worked and all felt upbeat. The plan was starting to come together.

After dropping off their rental car, Frank and Stan had no trouble picking up the boat. Long and sleek with a large V-8 engine, it was a marvel of maritime technology capable of almost suicidal speeds. Skimming lightly across the blue-gray swells, they headed south from Newport, and reached the Thimble Islands in less than two hours. With a nautical chart, they easily found the beach house and dock Andrea had specified; as they pulled in, she was waiting on the dock with the keys. The two medics loved the house—a raised ranch with a full-length deck overlooking the beach, sliding doors, skylights, and a fireplace. It was completely furnished and even had fresh sheets and blankets. Stan looked at Frank. "If I got to put up with too many hardships like this, I'm quitting."

Andrea laughed and pointed out the window. In a deep announcer's voice she said, "But wait, there's more!" Peering outside, the men saw a fifty-thousand-dollar Cadillac convertible parked out front.

Amazed, Stan asked, "Ours?"

"Well, technically it's mine, so take good care of it. It's leased in my name, and it has to be returned in good condition."

"Think we'll get noticed living like this?"

She shrugged. "In this neighborhood, you'd get noticed if you didn't."

"Well, if we work hard, I bet we can establish a reputation as party animals somehow."

"Whatever you want to do. I'm sure you two will survive."

Stan rolled his eyes heavenward, and whispered, "Yes, there is a God."

Andrea gave the men $3,000, and they dropped her off at the office by late afternoon. That evening, after rectifying the empty bar problem, the two Green Berets toured the local night spots.

* * *

By the time Andrea returned to the office, the other men had finished their work. The planning room was soundproofed, the windows were covered, the desks were installed, a chalkboard and bulletin board hung on the wall, and the supply cabinet was stocked with paper, pencils, and other office supplies.

The living area was also now soundproofed down to the storage end, the bunk beds were installed, the cooking area neatly set up, and the refrigerator well stocked. Pete was pan-frying some steak and onions for dinner, and the smell of the food challenged Mac's cigars for supremacy as the men watched the evening news.

After dinner, they moved to the planning room and got to work. Andrea sat at a desk smoking cigarettes and watched Mac move to the chalkboard. As the others settled in, he said, "OK, let's get started. I see certain potential problems already. The first is you, Andrea."

Surprised, she asked, "Why do you say that?"

"You've left a paper trail of car rentals strewn all over New Haven. That's fine as long as these vehicles aren't used for anything noticeable, but we've gotta be real careful with them. Frankly, I don't see how the hell we could have avoided the situation anyway. It wouldn't have been good for any of us to leave paper behind to verify that we were here, and stolen cars are far too chancy. But let's be careful. Now to my biggest worry: Ms. Lockery. Tim, I know we needed this woman to keep the money, but damn—I don't like an outsider knowing too much."

"Doesn't really matter, Mac. She's involved, so if anything happens to us it happens to her. Our money man vouches for her, and that's good enough for me. Besides, she wants as little to do with us as possible, so she only has general concepts, not specifics."

Mac chewed his cigar and said, "Good, let's try to keep things that way. The only points of contact she has with us are Frank, Tim, and Andrea. I think our best bet is to let Andrea do all the talkin'." He regarded her thoughtfully. "Just to be safe, best thing for you to do is to give her as little as possible. You have a schedule of when you're to contact her, right?"

Andrea nodded.

"Good. Before you make those contacts, we'll brief you on exactly what you can tell her. If she wants anything more, say you have to ask Tim—only Tim is never gonna be available. You just keep makin' excuses."

Tim replied, "Mac, relax. The old man trusts her, and he just wants her to monitor the situation. I see no problem."

Andrea added, "Don't worry, guys. I'm an old pro at the runaround."

Mac smiled and puffed his cigar.

They spent the rest of the meeting finishing the organization of the unit itself. When Mac emphasized that physical conditioning would be important and Tim proposed a running regimen, Andrea felt some satisfaction. The runs in Vermont had been agony, but she was glad she was getting back into shape. For safety, they decided to run in two-man teams. Mac reminded Tim about the men at the gas station and urged him to be careful, but Tim asserted that he would have to be in shape for the raid, so they would have to chance it. Mac made up a conditioning schedule and posted it on the bulletin board.

Next, Pete moved to the front of the room and called their attention to an enlarged photo of the island. Robin Island was shaped somewhat like a short-legged buffalo, with a rocky coastline about its entire circumference. Pyne's large brick-and-stucco mansion stood facing south at the highest point on the north corner, and a 290-foot granite pier jutted into the sea behind the house. In the center of the island on the north side, a 200-foot L-shaped pier had been built for smaller vessels. A large pool with a gazebo overlooking the rocks sat in the southern corner. A two-story wooden guest house with a long deck overhanging the water was located on the western shore, and tennis courts were laid out in the center of the island. A system of paved walkways wove through the entire complex. Though the southern end of the island was barren, the northern half was well treed.

"At this point," Pete said, "we aren't ready to plan the entire operation, but we do know a few things from the intel we do have."

Mac asked, "You got some ideas?"

"Of course I got ideas. I always got ideas. OK, problem one: our objective is on an island. That means we come in by air or water, right?"

Tim and Mac grunted.

Pete asked, "Anybody know how to fly a plane or a chopper? No? OK, let's look at this thing. First, no matter how many people they've got on that island, they definitely have more than we do. Also, they've probably got more firepower. Even if they don't, we've got to plan worst-case, so we'll expect a hundred guys armed with everything short of tanks and howitzers. Given that, we can't come in hard, guns blazing, and we can't come in on a noisy goddam helicopter. Plus if we use any aircraft, we need somebody else to fly it, and aircraft are highly regulated and have annoying things like flight plans, tail markings, and other traceable shit like that. No, we've got to come in quiet and by water. The problem is that we're going to have to blow a damn safe, and as soon as we do shooting's going to start. But at least if we come in quiet, we can already be set up and moving before things heat up. The bottom line is that without surprise, we can't pull this off."

Mac rose and stood by the chalkboard again. An avid freefall parachutist, he argued, "I see freefall as the way. It's quiet, and they won't be watching the air."

Pete shook his head. "No way, look at all the problems you've got. First, not all of us are freefall-qualified. That means you're going to have to train a lot of people and we don't have that kind of time. Next, when you land, you're going to be coming down in the middle of the island in the open where the whole damn world can see you. If that isn't enough, what if the winds are bad, or some guy does a lousy job flying the chute? Then you've got part of the team in the sea. Then there's the weather. We can come in by water no matter what—rain, snow, fog—so we can just set a date and go whenever we want."

Mac held up his hand. "OK, I get the idea. Now exactly how're we goin' to do it?"

"Scout swim. We get dry suits—there's a new Gore-Tex model on the market made by D.U.I. I've used it, and it's light, comfortable, and it blends in well at night. We infil in black dry suits and pull the whole mission that way. They're not the old rubber pieces of shit, so we won't die of heat exhaustion."

Tim's face mirrored his approval. "It makes sense. In fact, if we're lucky, we'll get a night when the weather sucks. Then the guards who are supposed to be protecting Mr. Pyne while he sleeps will be hiding from the rain instead. Even if the weather's good, at least we'll be able to see what the hell is in front of us. It's the best way."

Pete nodded and continued, "Now, it's good we're getting silenced pieces. Who knows, if we're lucky maybe we'll never have to make any noise until we blow the safe. But if we're realistic, we know we probably will, and as soon as the shooting starts, the police'll be called. We have to figure that the police, Pyne's people, or both will be in hot pursuit after the hit. Given that, we'll never make it to shore in a boat. Scout swim is fine if they're not making a concerted effort to find us, but it's not worth a shit if they know we're there somewhere. That leaves scuba. Tentatively, I think we should plan it like this. We get a boat, preferably stolen, have it get us to within five hundred yards, scout swim from there, then clear the beach and bring the boat in behind us. We leave our tanks in the boat, then on exfiltration, we have the boat get us a little out from the island and dive. We swim back to the beach from there. If we've got to leave hot, we can just strap the tanks on and dive from the shore. Sound good, Mac?"

"It's got some holes, but I like it. At least it gives us a place to start. If we can't get in or out, then we can't do the job. Anyway, we should at least plan for both scuba and scout-swim capabilities and procure the equipment. Art, Paul, and Wayne're the only scuba guys here. Paul, do you think it's any problem to train the rest of us enough to pull this off?"

Paul said, "Nothing to it."

Mac leaned back against the wall and chewed slowly on his cigar. "Good, I like the sound of this so far." He straightened. "But we have to be realistic about a couple of other things. We're facing an enemy we don't know. Hell, we wouldn't even be trying this crazy mission if we didn't think we were better than them. That's an idea we need to get out of everyone's heads right now. For all we know, these guys train constantly, are combat vets, and will be a hundred percent ready when we come in. That's what we need to count on—nothing less. We're good, we're going to be ready for anything, and we're going in with a hell of a lot of firepower if Joe and Wayne can come through for us; but the only way we're going to pull this off is if we train. Anybody know somewhere we can rehearse?"

Tim nodded. "Mac, I've already got a place in Vermont

where we can try out the weapons and set up something make-shift for some practice runs. Paul has a friend with a cabin, and we can use it all we want."

"Beautiful. Paul, you sure we can use it?"

"Yeah, long as we keep it clean."

"Good, then why don't we plan on using it in a week if we can get all the intel we need."

Tim nodded.

Mac continued, "All right, next point. We're going to have to do a safe, and we won't know what kind it is until we see it. That means you demo guys," he motioned at Pete, "are going to have to bring everything you might need to blow anything they could have; it wouldn't hurt to try a couple of test shots."

Pete agreed. "That would be *real* nice. Anyone else think of anything we can work out now?"

"Commo, electronic surveillance, and intel collection," Tim answered. "When we do get to the objective, we'll need some type of walkie-talkie—hopefully something water-resistant. I suggest that we plan on each man carrying one. That way, if some of them don't work, we'll have back ups. Nearly any electronics store should have exactly what we need. I'll go shopping tomorrow. Damn! I hate trying to work blind. We need more pictures of that damn island."

Mac said, "Already thought of that, Tim. Andrea chartered a plane for me the day after tomorrow, and I'll tell the pilot I want to get some aerial promotion shots of the Thimbles. A few flyovers should be all we need. Also, it's time for the boys in the boat to get busy and start feeding us pictures. I'll set up a darkroom, and we'll need to get cameras for Frank and Stan. I'll go shopping tomorrow."

Tim said, "Here's some bad news. It would be no trick at all to tap Pyne's phone, but somebody would have to sit around the town dock to monitor the tap. How do we do that without being caught?"

"Shit," Mac responded. "I guess we'll have to find another way. Tim, I got one last question for you. If we're going to do this Pyne guy, do we have any pictures of the bastard?"

"Sorry, Mac. You know, the son of a bitch is willing to spend thousands of dollars to have me killed, and I have no idea what he looks like!"

Andrea stirred. "I know how we can fix that. About two months ago he was on television when he got off on tax-evasion charges. We can get the broadcast on videotape. He was in the papers, too, and I saved the clippings. I'll get it all together tomorrow, and we can use my VCR."

Tim smiled at her. "Sounds good, Andrea."

She continued, "I also might know a way you can find out more about what goes on in the New Haven drug world, maybe even on Robin Island." She told them about the address she had found in Lisa's room, what she had discovered there, and her run-in with the Axeman. Tim agreed to let her return there with Wayne and Joe after they picked up weapons. Then he said, "If you all don't mind, we've got a long day coming up, so I'm going to turn in."

The meeting broke up, and Tim walked Andrea out to the receptionist's area. They held each other for a long time by the front door. She badly wanted him to come with her to her apartment, but she knew it was too risky. With soft good-byes, they parted for the night.

CHAPTER TWENTY-NINE

July 7, 1989—Fayetteville, North Carolina

Wayne Murphy and Joe Gonda cruised into town without incident and took a room at a cheap motel on Bragg Boulevard, one of several roads that lead into the giant military reservation of Fort Bragg. Running directly from the base to the local "red-light" district downtown on Hay Street, the road was a sea of neon signs, pawnshops, seedy motels, laundromats, bible stores, bars, and used-car dealers—

everything a young soldier needs to get himself in debt and trouble.

The two soldiers quickly found a seedy gun-and-sporting-goods store belonging to a gray and overweight retired Special Forces soldier named Stubby Aikens. Because he knew so many Green Berets, and Green Berets love owning their own weapons for training and pleasure, he did a brisk business. In 1968, Mac had saved Stubby from a Viet Cong sniper, so he was willing to help them get whatever they needed.

Stubby himself did not have the automatic weapons they wanted, but he did know people who did, plus he offered to let Wayne and Joe have whatever was in his shop. As the older man made his calls, Gonda and Murphy went through his inventory carefully. In fifteen minutes, they put together a pile that included web belts, Israeli assault vests, Gerber Mark II knives, lightweight black nylon day packs, bandoliers, waterproof compasses, ammo pouches, camouflage sticks, first-aid kits, chemlights, belt and breakaway concealable pistol holsters, shotgun bandoliers, ropes, heavyweight waterproof bags, extended barrels for .45 pistols, and other items. In case of breakage, they purchased eleven of each item. They were placing the last of it on the counter when Stubby emerged from his office.

"Here's the deal," Stubby said. "You guys ever come across a guy in 5th Group named Jim Singer?"

They hadn't.

"Singer got out about five years ago. He's kind of a nut case and got into a lot of trouble in the peacetime army. Finally, he dropped out of sight and went merc. Turned out there weren't many jobs for him—except in Libya, working for that crazy motherfucker. Now, he's turned up working for an Arab arms dealer. He's the guy's stateside rep. He's in town, and I connected you. Go to the Holiday Hotel downtown, and somebody'll meet you in the lobby. Be there 1300 sharp."

"No problem."

"Hey, Singer can be a wacko, so watch out. I mean, don't tell the guy you're S.F. It won't do you no good. Most of his business is with drug people, so you gotta watch yourself. Thing is, this guy can get you a howitzer if you want it. I told them your name was Al Smith, and described you, so just go in the lobby and they'll find you." He looked at the pile of equipment on the counter. "OK, let's get the stuff counted and boxed."

A half hour and nearly $2,000 later, everything was boxed anonymously and devoid of any written records.

Stubby saw them to the door. "Hey, you guys tell Mac hi for me, huh? And good luck with whatever the fuck you're doing."

Joe grunted.

As instructed, they strode into the lobby at precisely 1300. Two men in suits approached, and the taller one asked Joe if he was Al Smith. Gonda nodded, and the men led the two Green Berets to the elevator. After a silent ride, they all got off at the sixth floor and were ushered down the hall with the tall man in front and his shorter, muscular partner to the rear. The tall man stopped at suite 614 and unlocked the door. As soon as they entered, the short one produced a revolver. "Save us lots of bullshit and give up whatever the fuck you're packing right here."

As instructed, Wayne removed his .45 from its shoulder rig, and Joe untaped the PPk from his left calf. The short man frisked them and told them to wait. About a minute later, he returned and had them follow him into the permanent press suite. A tall, slender man with thin blond hair sat in a recliner near the window. Examining him carefully, Gonda thought he had the wild gray eyes of a man constantly fighting for control. He extended his hand, and as Joe shook it, he said, "I'm Singer. You must be Mr. Smith. I assume your associate is Mr. Jones. And I bet you're both fucking gun collectors, right?"

Joe nodded.

"Good, now that we're all chums, what the fuck do you want?"

Joe said, "We need some serious hardware, and we heard you can produce."

"That might be true, but it depends on the kind of cash involved. First, you gotta tell me what kind of hardware you want and in what quantity. We don't deal in anything but quantity. You want a single piece, you're wasting my time. See a fucking street dealer."

"OK, we need seven Ingram Model 10s in forty-five caliber complete with suppressors, nine forty-five–caliber model

M-1911A1 pistols, two M-234 SAW's, one XM-122 electric demolitions firing system, six M-118 Claymore antipersonnel mines, thirty-six M-27 fragmentation grenades, nine white phosphorous grenades, seven Remington or Ithaca twelve-gauge shotguns, sixty pounds of C-4 plastic explosive, fifty pounds of dynamite, twelve M-60 fuse ignitors, twenty electric blasting caps, twenty non-electric blasting caps, fifty feet of time fuse, fifty feet of det cord, one M-58 blasting machine, and large quantities of ammunition. No less than three thousand rounds of 5.56 for the SAW's, five hundred rounds of number one buck for the shotguns, and five thousand rounds of forty-five caliber for the Mac 10s and pistols. And it all has to be in top condition."

Singer waved the tall man over. "Did you get all that?" He handed over the list.

"All right, you two go downstairs to the bar and make yourself at home. I'll check it out." He stared at Joe for a moment. "Hey, fat boy, if you got any ideas on fucking with me, or if you're a cop, I'll splatter your goddamn brains all over North Carolina. When I want you, somebody'll come down and get you. Your pieces stay here."

With no other option, the Green Berets headed for the elevator.

Two hours later, upon reentering the suite, Gonda and Murphy were again frisked, and then led to where Singer waited. "Here's the deal: you get the weapons just like you want. They're all U.S.-made. You got lucky, even the Ingrams are the real thing—not some cheap foreign rip-offs. We got the XM-122 and Claymores too. But the rest, explosives and everything else, is foreign. That includes all the rounds except for the SAW rounds, they're American. Bottom line is you got everything you want, thirty-six thousand."

Joe shook his head. "Thirty's high as we go. We give you half today and half on delivery."

Singer stood up and stared. "You fuckin' crazy? You come in here and wanna argue! You think I'm running some kind of open-air fucking market?"

"We got cash. You got a product you wanna move. It don't make no money collecting dust."

Singer's face relaxed. "All right, fat boy. You got it for thirty-two. I want sixteen today."

"No problem, but we ain't gonna come up here to give it to you. You come down to the lobby in one half hour, and my associate will hand you the cash in a rolled-up newspaper. When and where do we pick up the shipment?"

"New York. There's a warehouse on West Eighteenth Street. Number is 519. Be there three days from now with the cash at eight P.M. In case you can't count, that's the tenth. You got that, fat boy? You want bargain-basement prices, you got to travel. We don't fuckin' deliver. You turn out to be a cop or play any games, you're fuckin' dead."

That was too much for Gonda, and he snapped, "You fuck with me, asshole, and my people gonna find you."

Singer laughed. "Glad we understand each other. Now stop stinking up my suite and go back under whatever rock you crawled out from under."

The tall man returned the guns at the door, and Joe and Wayne went to retrieve the money.

Thirty minutes later, the newspaper changed hands without a snag.

CHAPTER THIRTY

Saturday, July 8, 1989—New Haven

Oscar Bonning had problems. His investigation was going nowhere, and at a meeting that morning, the desk commandos in charge in New York had asked if he had a single lead. He had admitted that he didn't, and they had given him one more week to come up with something solid or he was out. Even worse, as soon as he had returned to New Haven, Tony Pulcinella called. The detective told him that something was seriously wrong, but he wouldn't talk about it on the phone or at headquarters. So now Bonning sat on a park bench on the Green in the center of town, waiting for Tony. Depressed, he gazed at a homeless man asleep on a bench under a tree.

Looking like a man on a day off, Pulcinella showed up in blue jeans and T-shirt and sat down casually next to Bonning. The DEA man asked, "All right, what's the newsflash?"

He was still watching the homeless man, but he felt Pulcinella's eyes studying him. "Had a bad day?"

Bonning sighed and looked at the New Haven detective. "Oh, it's been great so far. If I don't make some progress in one week, New York says I'm out. Other than that, everything's fine."

"Well, what I tell you might be good news, it might be bad—depends on your point of view. Look, a lot of things about this investigation don't make sense. Your people tapped Pyne, and everything's cool for a while; then it's like he just shuts up. You know, it's like now they use that phone to entertain us. So what's up? I got nothing to prove this, but I think they know exactly what we're doing. The one break we got turned into a massacre, and twenty-four hours later we got nothing. Even the crack houses on the street are out of business and moved before we even start looking."

"So you think they have somebody inside?"

"Yeah."

"I've been thinking the same thing. The question is who?"

"Maybe I know that too. I've been checking. The tap went bad within forty-eight hours of Brown and Foster hearing about it. Your guys busted that kid. When our guys got in on it, less than a day later, all the leads we got are dead. I think our leak is Brown or Foster—maybe both. I also think there's a way to prove it."

Bonning was intrigued. "Tell me about it."

"Now, nothing is sure; I mean, I'm guessing all this. But if we are compromised, how could I find the leak and whom could I trust? I figure your career is on the line here, so you're clear, and I know it isn't me. Beyond that, if we tell any of your people, I'm sure they'll try not to show it, but we both know their suspicion will show. Whoever it is'll hide until they think it's safe again. No, if it's a bad New Haven cop, I want to find him—not scare him off. Then, I want to put him in jail."

"So do I. If you're right, and it is one of your people, then we're going to have to keep this to ourselves and check it out carefully. For starters, I'd like to know a little more about our two detectives. If they're getting paid off, the money's going somewhere. If they've got it, we can find it."

Bonning sighed. An elderly man walked a pair of large dogs up a path in their direction. As frail as the man appeared, Bonning wondered how he controlled the animals so easily. He had just bought a collie for his kids, and the dog pretty much walked him. He looked at Pulcinella and Tony said, "It's bad when you suspect dirty cops. The problem is that God made cops human too. Then when you catch them, the press goes to town. It's the same old shit every time. If this cop's bad, then how deep does the rot go? They assume at least half the department must be bad."

"Oscar, give me three days, and I'll get the information on Brown and Foster. If one of 'em's bad, we'll bring him down. Meanwhile, let's keep it between ourselves. If they're not bad, I'll be damned if I'll start rumors that they are."

"Detective Pulcinella, we have a deal." The two stood and faced each other. "Thanks."

Pulcinella studied his face. "We'll get Pyne, too."

"I never doubted it."

CHAPTER THIRTY-ONE

July 9, 1989—North Haven

Soon after Gonda and Murphy returned, they divided the equipment from Stubby's into nine bundles and issued them. The black nylon Israeli assault vests with the equipment pouches were the most popular items.

Much progress had been made. Mac had rigged up a darkroom and taken his aerial photographs of the island, and Paul and Art had begun searching for the needed scuba gear. Because bubble trails would betray them, they wanted gear equipped with rebreathers, like the Draeger Lar V that Special Forces uses, but they had been unable to find any yet.

Now all that remained for them to do was to collect their weapons. Dealing with Singer worried everyone, so they took precautions.

Monday, July 10, 1989—New York City

Thanks to a row of thunderstorms that had moved in and stalled over New York, the day dawned with high winds and hard rain. Still, as Tim reviewed the progress the team had made so far, he liked what he found.

Andrea had purchased a decrepit Chevrolet Impala for general team use, and Tim laughed when he saw it. It was the perfect car for the city. What had once been a blue body was now a sea of rust and multicolored primer, but under the hood sat an engine to which someone had devoted a great deal of time and attention. With an oversized carburetor and high-performance components throughout, it was extremely powerful. Ugly, fast, and dependable, the Impala was the perfect surveillance and pursuit car. Meanwhile, with Mac's pictures, plus the photos provided by Frank and Stan, the team now had some images of the island they could use, and Pete had the sand table coming along nicely.

Joe Gonda and Tim had finalized the plans for their work in New York the night before. Joe and Wayne would go in with the same armament they had carried in North Carolina; Tim had a borrowed .45 and the shotgun. In addition, Art had the Mini 14 and Andrea's PPk, and Paul, a sniper, had his .45 along with the bolt-action rifle and a scope he had bought the day before. He had sighted in the rifle as best he could from the boat at sea with floating cans.

Their plan hinged upon a phone signal. As Joe explained to the others, "Wayne and I will call you within five minutes of going in that door. You'll have the money. If the gear is there, and everything looks straight, then we'll say, 'The stuff is here, and it sucks, but we'll take it.' If something is wrong, it'll be, 'Everything is great. C'mon in.' If we say the first thing, Tim and Art'll come in soft, bring the money, and we'll finish the deal. If it's the second way, you guys better come in hard. Either way, Paul's going to stay outside in the car and cover the front. When our van comes out, one of our people will be guiding it. If it comes out any other way, something has gone bad. In that case, Paul, do whatever you can. Unfortunately, we can't bring any mikes or radios in—if we did, they'd think we were cops. Tim will carry the money in a day pack so his hands are free. Any questions?"

They were in New York around 4 P.M. Joe and Wayne rode in the van, and the other three took the Chevy. Once in the neighborhood, Joe and Wayne left the van in a parking space with a fine view of the front of the warehouse and piled into the Impala with their friends. The four-story brick warehouse was long and narrow, had a high, roll-up metal door, and a side alley with an entry door. After making several passes with the car, they knew how they would approach the buy. A small bar with an Irish motif was located around the corner. Dim and crowded enough for the Green Berets to avoid detection, it had a functioning pay phone, a decent lamb stew, and was the perfect spot for the back-up team to wait for Joe's call. If they were noticed by the other patrons, in their blue jeans, casual shirts, and windbreakers, they would be taken for blue-collar workers out for a beer after work, even if their beers remained virtually untouched.

Not long after they arrived, a group of longshoremen sat down at the table next to them. They were loud, but Tim didn't mind that. The rowdy group drew most of the attention, which meant less for his team.

At eight o'clock Paul, with a good field of fire, concealed himself in the Impala covering the door. Gonda beeped his horn at the warehouse, the metal door rolled up, and the van pulled inside, out of the sniper's field of vision.

In the bar, Art Simpson walked over to the phone located in a cramped hallway leading to the restrooms. Three minutes later, a burly, bearded longshoreman in a plaid shirt tramped down the hall in the direction of the phone. Simpson placed himself between the man and the phone and said, "Excuse me, buddy, I'm waiting for a call."

The big man sneered, "It's a public fuckin' phone. Now get the fuck out of my way."

Tim saw the trouble coming, so he maneuvered himself to the longshoreman's rear.

Art smiled and motioned for the guy to go by. "No trouble, huh, buddy?"

The fat man grunted and started to push his way by as Art's wave accelerated and turned into a swift jab to the solar plexus. As the air left him, the longshoreman staggered into Tim, who caught him and kept him upright. Swiftly, like they were helping a sick friend, they propelled the gasping man into the bathroom just as the phone rang.

Tim hurried back and answered on the second ring. "Mr. Brown here."

"This is Mr. Smith. The stuff is here, and it sucks, but we'll take it."

"Got it." He hung up and turned to Art. "It looks good. Let's move before that asshole gets his wind back." Seconds later they were out the door. To let Paul know there were no problems yet, they did not stop by the Impala to pick up the Mini 14 and the shotgun. Instead, they headed straight from the corner bar to the side entrance in the alley. It was locked, so they had to knock. A muscular man in a suit opened it up and asked, "You Mr. Brown?"

"Yeah."

"You got something for us?"

"Yeah." He motioned them in.

They found themselves in a large, well-lit delivery bay. Wayne leaned against the van, and Joe waited in a small glassed-in area off to the side that served as an office. Boxes of all types were stacked throughout the warehouse. Two men Tim did not know flanked Gonda in the office, and two more stood by the van. An open wood crate outside the office revealed several Ingram Model 10 submachine guns wrapped in oily plastic. Art joined Wayne, and Tim entered the office. As he did, Gonda motioned at a tough-looking man with blond hair and cold blue eyes seated with his feet up on a gray desk. "Mr. Brown, meet Mr. Singer. He says he wants some money."

"Did you check everything out?"

"Haven't had time yet."

Tim peeled his pack off and handed it to Singer. "You can count while we look at your merchandise."

Singer nodded. "Look away. It's the pile right outside the door."

Tim and Joe motioned to the other two, and they removed the lids from the crates. In short order, they knew exactly what they had. Some of the equipment was foreign, but it was all there and in excellent shape—even the XM-122 and the two SAW's.

Tim called out to Singer, "You got any way we can test fire one of these MACs?"

The arms dealer pointed to a line of 55-gallon drums to the rear of the warehouse. "That's what they're there for. They're full of sawdust. Fire away."

Joe picked up a Model 10, loaded a magazine, and moved towards the drums; then he hosed them effectively with several short bursts. Wayne loaded a SAW with a two-hundred-round box and repeated the process Joe had just completed. The SAW was brand new and also performed as it should.

Tim looked at Joe, who nodded. "Let's load it up."

Art opened the rear of the van, and the Green Berets formed a human chain passing the crates from hand to hand.

When it was loaded, Singer came out of his office and motioned to Tim. "Mr. Brown, I assume you're the chief gun collector here, since you control the money."

Tim shrugged. "Maybe."

"Let's get one thing clear, asshole. It's all new shit that can't be traced. Whatever you plan to do with your fuckin' collection, you get in trouble with the law, and tell anyone where this shit came from, you're a fuckin' corpse. And we'll know it was you 'cause that's the only way the cops can find out. You got that?"

"Yeah, I got that, but the same goes for you. You never seen us. Understood?"

"Glad we understand each other. Now I got a business to run, and you're wastin' my fuckin' time."

The metal door opened, and Tim guided the van out to signal Paul. Once on the street, he and Art rejoined Paul in the Impala. Forming a small convoy, the van followed them back to North Haven.

CHAPTER THIRTY-TWO

Tuesday, July 11, 1989—New Haven

Early that morning, Michael Pyne, having been contacted at home by a business associate, returned the call from a safe pay telephone. After the greetings, Pyne launched into an explanation. "Sorry I couldn't talk yesterday, but the police are presently taking an inordinate interest in my affairs, and I understand they have tapped my phone. Naturally, because they are watching me so closely, I will not be able to get anything to you until the situation here quiets down. However, you should be prepared for a rather large money shipment in a couple of months."

"I'll help in any way I can," the financier replied. "Now, I've got a spot of news for you. At some point, did you display some interest in locating a Mr. Reardon?"

"Actually, I am still very much interested in the whereabouts of that young man."

"Then you should know that one of my sources says he's in the New Haven area."

"You're not serious?"

"Oh, I'm afraid I am. In fact, not only is he in the New Haven area, I understand he plans to visit you fairly soon."

"Pay *me* a visit?"

"Yes, he has assembled a group of army friends, and from the sounds of things, they are planning to kill you. My informant believes these men to be particularly capable, so you might want to take the information I'm giving you seriously."

"Well, where is he? How many friends does he have? When is he planning this visit?"

"I do not now know any of the details. However, if I hear any more, I'll pass it along. In the meantime, if I can assist you in any way at all, please do not hesitate to ask."

"Thank you for the information. I shall prepare a reception for our friends in the event he arrives before I can locate him. Thank you again, and good-bye."

Pyne hung up the phone, returned to his limo, and had a lengthy discussion with Salka. They decided to install some formidable security on the island. The financier was a good source, and they would take the threat seriously indeed.

North Haven

The morning after the gun buy, each of the specialists sorted through his new equipment. The weapons men now had everything they wanted, but the demo men were not quite as happy. Their explosive was largely of French manufacture, so some test shots were needed to establish its reliability. Fortunately, most of the firing devices were American.

Meanwhile, Gonda, with parts procured from a local gun shop and a hardware store, modified each of the .45s with elongated barrels he had threaded himself. Then he fitted a homemade silencer onto each barrel. That evening, the medics took him far out to sea in the cigarette boat, where he test fired the silenced .45s and the Model 10s at floating plastic jugs. Each weapon functioned perfectly.

The news from the beach house was positive, too. Paul and Frank watched Pyne while establishing themselves as part of the local scenery. At the bars, they had already discussed their plans for some skin diving with some local hands who knew the waters well.

When Stan was not in the boat, he visited the local surgical stores; soon, between his own purchases and controlled drugs supplied through a contact at Fort Devens, he had everything they would need to treat the type of trauma and infection that combat might bring. Since he now had an ample supply of surgical gloves, everyone agreed that whenever they handled one of their new weapons, they would wear gloves. In this way, they would leave no fingerprints and they would be accustomed to the feel of the gloves. The only exceptions to this were the Gerber knives and .45s, which would be the detachment's standard concealed defense weapons.

Scuba gear, though, remained a problem. To avoid raising local curiosity, they used a wholesaler in New Jersey for their order, claiming to be young businessmen opening a new diving service. The wholesaler was happy to be of assistance, since their order was rather large. The D.U.I. dry suits were easy to obtain, as was everything else—except the recirculating Draegers. They were simply not available in the United States to anyone not under government employ. After a long discussion, Tim and the S-3 men decided to go with conventional diving equipment. They would just have to try to launch the mission when the sea was a little choppy to camouflage their bubbles. Paul telephoned the wholesaler a last time and placed the orders. Everything was in stock, and they could pick it all up the next day.

Tim and Pete took a trip to a local electronics store and purchased nine Motorola walkie-talkies. Simple to operate and lightweight, they had a range of a mile (two over salt water), and casings of durable plastic. Each battery was supposed to last for three hours of continuous operation, but only about ten minutes would be required for the actual mission. Most importantly, they included a small ear mike.

As they'd feared, tapping Pyne's phone line at the busy dock was impossible. However, the druglord sometimes used a cordless phone and Tim did manage to modify a receiver that worked on those frequencies so it could be powered by the cigarette boat's battery. He also fashioned a battery box that could supply power to the receiver unit should it be necessary to remove it from the boat. Unfortunately, the cordless telephone produced signals of limited range, so they had to be very close to the island to pick it up. They could get close enough if they acted like they were fishing, but only for limited periods. Nevertheless, Tim decided it was better than having someone risk the crowds of people on the dock.

The intelligence thus far collected on the island gave Mac some definite ideas on how to take the objective, but getting out caused him the most worry. Consulting Tim and Pete intermittently throughout the day, he continued to work on the problem, but he was no closer to solid answers by day's end. Meanwhile, as various terrain features became clearer, they updated the sand table to make it as accurate as possible.

Now that the various problems of the mission were moving rapidly towards resolution, Andrea became the busiest member of the team, and she relished it. The same energy and savvy that had helped her become one of the best real-estate agents in New Haven now made her one of the best detachment S-1s the men had ever seen. She was indispensable in organizing information as it came in, she handled all monetary disbursements, and she did all the work necessary to ensure that all the logistical requirements were met. Occasionally, a salesman or someone who had heard of their art business would come to the door and push the buzzer. At times like these, Andrea's sales experience was vital. With practiced ease, she would entertain the visitor politely and quickly end the visits with one of several standard excuses. Her competence had already earned her a place among the men in terms of the mission; and her enthusiasm, energy, and ready smile had earned her a place in all their hearts. She made many things possible that would not otherwise have been so.

Andrea had not stopped by her real-estate office for several days, so she used her lunch hour the day after the weapons buy to see her associates and pick up her mail. Art Simpson escorted her but remained in the Firebird while she went inside.

When she returned to the car, she was excited—by a stroke of luck, a critically important opportunity had come her way.

Mac and Tim were puzzling over the sand table, trying to figure out how to accurately determine what some of the structures on the island's grounds might be when Tim heard a crash. Instinctively, he reached for his .45 in its shoulder harness. Then he saw Andrea, face radiant, standing in front of the door she had just thrown open.

Mac relaxed, scratched his chin, and asked Tim, "What d'ya think? The girl won the lottery?"

Andrea blurted, "Gentlemen, you will not believe what I found in my mailbox at work."

Tim groaned. "Andie, you can tell us any time you're ready."

Face shining like that of a schoolgirl with a fantastic secret, she playfully tossed her long hair and said, "Mr. Michael Pyne has decided to become a pillar of the community. He is holding a charity reception on his island to benefit the drive to preserve Long Island Sound, and guess who he invited? His favorite real-estate salesperson, me."

"Darlin', I needed this! When the hell is it and can you bring a friend?" Mac queried.

Hugging Tim, she said, "It's this Sunday, and I can bring a friend. Now where do you think I might find a man interested in attending a formal function at the Pyne residence?"

Tim kissed her. "I have no idea."

Branford Point

After a busy day, the team had its usual after-dinner meeting, then broke up for a night off. Mac and Pete agreed to keep watch over the office, with loaded MAC 10s at the ready. The others left to find a place where they could relax. Joe Gonda was their designated guard and driver.

Andrea and Tim waited until the sun went down and then went for a drive. In the car, she asked him if he would like to see her favorite place. He said he would, and she twisted her Firebird through the back streets of Branford until they reached Branford Point. Tim had never been there before, but as she pulled in, he understood why it was special. A steep, rocky hill, covered with trees and winding paths, it sloped steeply down to the water. In the protection of a natural bowl hollowed out from its side was a small children's park that bordered a parking area overlooking the ocean. After Andrea parked, they exited the car and walked to an old wooden rail overlooking the water. It was a sultry evening, but the ocean breeze felt cool on his cheek. He looked skyward. Dark rain clouds raced across the sky. Perhaps because there was a threat of rain, they were almost totally alone. He turned his eyes from the sky and sea and regarded her. She wore a long, white, almost transparent summer dress that the setting sun colored fantastic shades of orange and pink, and the breeze blew it in graceful folds about her legs. No matter how often he looked at her, he could not believe her loveliness. Looking down at his old blue jeans and T-shirt, he wondered what she saw in him. Her eyes met his, and he put his arm about her lithe waist.

She ran her fingers through his hair and softly said, "I love the way the wind ruffles your hair."

Embarrassed, he did not answer.

Changing the subject, she said, "When I was small, my dad used to take me here to play after he came home from work. We often stayed until dark, and he told me stories. I was a tomboy, the wild child, and often the son he never had, but when he took me here, I was always his 'fairy princess.' He used to promise me that someday I would work my magical powers and be famous. I always believed him and stayed up late at night dreaming of all the things I could do with my future."

He touched his lips to the side of her neck and felt her body press tightly against him in response. "What kind of things did you dream?"

She smiled an introspective smile. "Of being president, of being the first person on Mars, of putting an end to world hunger—I always wanted to be someone everyone would remember."

"Andrea, your wish is coming true. You are someone special, and everyone knows it. You could still be president."

"Tim, I fantasized about something else too. There would be a man for me. Strong and handsome, but most of all, he would stand next to me and work for what we both believed. Together, we would be something we couldn't be apart."

She turned and looked into his eyes. "They say a girl should never say things like this because she might chase her man away; but I love you, and I'm scared because of it."

"Why are you scared, Andrea?"

"Because you might not love me back, because you are exactly what I wanted; but most of all, I'm frightened because I know you but I can't fathom you at the same time."

"What does that mean?"

"It means that from the time I first saw you at Heather's funeral, I wanted you. Then Lisa was killed, and I was left with this horrible void nothing could fill. Then you came back—and just like when I first saw you—you were tangible and steady. You were sure. You stood for something. But you came back wrapped in violence. Now, I don't know what to do. Tim, what we're doing is crazy. Your world is unreal to me. And your friends—they're so nice, it seems almost like a play that we're all acting out. Yet, when it's all over, real people are really going to die. I detest Pyne and all he stands for, and I hate the people he has around him. But Tim, one of those dead bodies might be yours, and if I lost you too, I would die this time. You see, I've heard you and your friends talk about how you believe in what you're doing, but it's not that way with me. I care most about things and people I can touch."

He pulled her close. Standing in the soft ocean wind they blended together into a single form. Softly, he whispered, "I love you too, Andrea, and I won't go anywhere." Stroking her hair, he asked, "Do you want us to stop this thing? Do you want us to end the mission?"

She pushed him away. Nervous, she pulled out a cigarette with trembling fingers. She couldn't light it herself, so he did it for her. Her eyes turned towards the sea. Silence hung between them, but he decided to give her time. Finally, she said, "Tim, it's more than that! It's your damned dark side. Look, I hate Michael Pyne—I want to see that bastard destroyed. But not at any price! I don't want to see you destroyed doing it. And what you're doing—what we're doing—is it so different from what he does? Deep in you, Tim—my Tim, my love—there is this violent animal capable of doing anything, and I'm not sure how to cope with that. You're what I always wanted and everything I never wanted at the same time."

Tim's gaze was still upon her. The sun had set, and in its place came darkness punctuated only by distant street lamps.

Only the red glow of her cigarette illuminated her face. Slowly, he said, "Andrea, when I was small, I had dreams, too. I wanted to be a soldier. My dreams were of battlefields, and in them good triumphed over evil. I wanted to fight for what was right. Then, I became a Green Beret—a political soldier, at the service of my government, whoever happened to be in charge. Nothing was right or wrong anymore, it was only the mission and how well it was done. Well, Andrea, this time there is a bad guy. He's destroyed someone close to me and a lot of other people along the way. I didn't go looking for this fight, but it's my kind of war, and I'm going to win it because I have to if I ever want to live a normal life again. As far as the killing goes, this time I'm doing it for me. I know that sounds cold, but it's what I am."

Andrea's hands closed around his waist, and he embraced her. She whispered, "I don't know what you are, Tim. I don't know what I think. I just want us to have a life. But remember this—I'm with you now, but deep down, all I want is for it to be over."

Joe Gonda brought the revelers back just after midnight. They had found just the right bar where they could all relax, except Gonda, who had remained at the ready. As soon as they returned, Mac told Joe that Tim had checked in and that he and Andrea were at a small motel down the shoreline. Gonda shook his head. He knew Andrea was important to the mission, and he knew how much his friend cared for her, but to him, the professional avoided the kind of intimacy that could get him killed and the mission compromised. That was why Gonda was still single himself—he always put the mission first. He looked at Mac and asked, "Maybe they need a guardian angel tonight?"

Mac nodded.

Joe slid a Model 10 under his overcoat, and went out to the Impala. The motel was easy to find, and he parked where he could see their room and their car. Tim had been through enough, he decided. They weren't going to off him at this stage. He would make sure of that, he thought, as he settled in to await the dawn.

CHAPTER THIRTY-THREE

July 12–15, 1989—New Haven Area

On Wednesday, Tim met with Mac and Pete to discuss the status of team equipment, and they found they were close to being ready. The scuba gear was now in, and the men were training every day. The last of the medical supplies had also arrived ahead of schedule the previous day. The medics, Frank and Stan, had put together individual first-aid packets for each man to carry. Meanwhile, Joe Gonda and Wayne Murphy had finished the homemade silencers and tested them and all their other weapons, but each man would have to familiarize himself with his personal weapons, practice room clearing, and rehearse team standard operating procedures. That would be the priority now, and they would have to move faster. By the end of the month, their leaves would begin expiring. The way it looked now, Tim concluded, they needed three more weeks to get all the training done—and they only had two at the most.

Pete Sayers pulled a new file he had made off his desk and held it resting on his stomach. His red brows were furrowed and he said, "I've got some bad news. Things are changing on Robin Island."

Spreading a series of photographs across his desk, he said, "Tim, these were taken by Frank and Stan. Look carefully." He passed the pictures to Tim, who examined each one closely. Each showed an image of an armed guard. Some had shotguns, and some had poorly concealed submachine guns, but each one was armed.

Tim asked, "More guards?"

"Yeah, suddenly they're all over the place. And not only has the number of people on that island increased, so has their armament. There's no doubt about it, Tim; these guys are ready for something heavy."

"Could be extra security for the party this weekend."

Mac spoke up. "Why would you need security for a charity ball?"

"What are we saying here? We saying they know we're coming?"

Pete shrugged. "I don't know what it says. Maybe they know we're coming. Maybe it's something else. Whatever it is, this place is a damn armed camp and it wasn't a week ago."

Mac said, "The good news is that they work in shifts, and we know their rotations and sectors. Plus they haven't come here. If they know about us, why haven't they hit us?"

Pete stood, leaned over the table, and placed his palms flat. "Tim, we just don't know what's going on over there. Never in my life have I seen a mission with this little intel, and I don't like it."

Tim looked at him hard. "You think we should pull out."

"Nope, I'm in it all the way, but I knew you'd want my opinion."

"Thanks, Pete. . . . Sorry I snapped."

Sayers sat back slowly. "No problem. Now to law enforcement: Stan was in a bar where he met a local cop. Here's what he found out: the Branford police department has six speedboats, and at least one of them is in the water all the time. They also own a helicopter and sometimes hire out fixed-wing aircraft. My estimate is that a boat will be at Robin Island within ten minutes of the first shots. Since we'll be making the hit at night, and they'll have to get the pilot out of bed, the chopper will take about half an hour."

Tim sighed and looked at Pete. "You got any good news?"

"Yeah, we've been hearing the name Julian Salka a lot over the cordless phone. Yesterday, Frank was fooling around with the receiver while our man Mr. Pyne was talking in his gazebo. During the conversation, he told the party on the line that he was going to pass the phone to Julian. Stan got some wonderful pictures of the guy he passed the receiver to, and the enlargements Mac made are fantastic. Tim, we've IDed our man's top lieutenant, number two on our list." He passed the photos to Tim.

It was the first time he had seen Julian Salka, and he was astounded. Standing shirtless next to Pyne, his height and massive bulk made him almost superhuman. Yet there was something about the man in the picture that struck him as even stranger. Salka was smiling, and there were laugh lines about his eyes.

Dressed in a red business dress, Andrea came in, and he passed the picture to her. "You ever seen this guy or know anything about him?"

She studied the picture intently and pursed her lips. "Yes, I met him once at my office. Pyne never goes anywhere without Salka nearby. Other than that, I don't know very much, but I can tell you the guy is disgusting."

"Why do you say that?" Tim asked.

She shrugged and pulled a cigarette from her pocket. Mac lit it for her and she said, "It's kind of hard to describe, but Salka always smiles this stupid smile. When he looked at me, it was like he could see right through my dress and that's why he was smiling. At the same time, I had the sense that this guy was just looking for an excuse to do something nasty to me." She shivered and continued, "I remember that I was relieved when he left."

She passed the picture back to Tim. He glanced at it again, then, satisfied that he had memorized Salka's face, he turned his attention to the man he considered to be his true tormentor: Michael Pyne. In the photograph, he looked much as he had in the newsreel footage Andrea had provided: well-tanned, successful, healthy, and immaculate in his boating shoes, slacks, and deliberately loose-fitting shirt. Tim shook his head. Pyne appeared every inch the young rising executive. Tim asked Andrea, "What's Pyne like in the flesh?"

She shrugged. "He's kind of strange. I mean he goes out of his way to cultivate this high-class investment banker demeanor. He speaks in a soft voice with an educated accent, and he keeps his appearance impeccable, but it just doesn't ring true. When you look underneath the bullshit and think about it for a minute, you get the feeling that you've just met a lizard all dressed up in a tuxedo. I think he's capable of anything, and Julian Salka is the force that makes him possible. Salka's not smart enough to handle things on his own and Pyne doesn't have the spine or the balls for it."

Tim remained silent after she finished and stared at Pyne's picture. Then he passed the photos back to Pete, turned to his friends, and said, "Post these. Every man in the detachment's got to know these faces, every man—and don't forget the shots of Rembard we got from the news footage."

Andrea asked, "Tim, should I take Joe and Wayne to that house in New Haven tomorrow?"

"Yeah, I don't know what it'll get us, but you never know. Any intel is better than the crap we got. We've got to know what's happening on that damn island. But hey, you just show Joe and Wayne where to go. Believe it or not, I'm kind of getting used to you."

The team now had a routine. At varying times each day, detachment members went for runs in pairs—Tim and Andrea included. As protection during these forays, one of the joggers generally concealed a stainless-steel PPk in his pocket.

Meantime, the three scuba men, Art, Paul, and Wayne, trained the rest of the team in what they needed to know to dive successfully by bringing each man in turn out on the boat for dives off the Thimbles.

Daily surveillance of the island continued as well. What they got from the cordless phone told them that Salka was definitely Pyne's lieutenant, and they also learned a great deal about Rembard. Most importantly, he never came to the island without first confirming his visit by phone. Tim liked that. If Rembard was there, so was Pyne, and Julian Salka never strayed far from his master. If they planned it carefully, they could get all three. That was important because, from all they had learned so far, the Pyne organization was nothing without them. If even one lived, he felt certain his contract would never disappear.

Photographic reconnaissance also turned up other invaluable pieces of information. In one frame, Mac's expert eye picked out a camera, and closer inspection revealed that the entire island was ringed with remote-control video cameras. Since there were cameras, there could also be alarm sensors. They might need to knock out the electricity to disable them.

Tim was also bothered by several other unanswered questions. How did Pyne move drugs and money on and off of Robin Island? Was there a way to detect when the maximum amount of money would be present to make the hit the most lucrative? What was the size and skill level of the force of armed defenders?

Though at this point, a full-scale rehearsal was not possible, some type of rehearsal was necessary, so Tim decided that the detachment would split into two groups and rotate up to Vermont for training.

New Haven

On Thursday night, Andrea took Joe and Wayne in the beat-up Impala to Shelton Avenue. Driving down the block slowly, she pointed out the house, and the gang members on the same corner.

Joe told her to circle the block and park, and asked, "Last time the guy came over to you about an hour after you parked?"

"Yes, the Axeman."

"Well, that's it, then. There's no way we can move around in this neighborhood without being seen and remembered, so let's park and wait for them to get interested. Andrea, you're gonna have to lay down in the back seat and get out that PPk. You're kind of unforgettable looking and this Axeman knows you."

As instructed, Andrea parked in a spot even nearer to the corner than she'd parked the last time, slid into the back seat, and waited. Joe sat behind the wheel, rolled down the window, and lit a cigarette to be as obvious as possible. Wayne, too, rolled down his window. Gonda thought for a few minutes; then he smiled. He had a plan, and when Murphy heard it, he smiled too. If what Gonda had in mind worked, they would not only learn something about Pyne, they might solve Andrea's problem too.

Over an hour and a half passed, and Gonda witnessed numerous drug buys and counted seven different gang members wandering on and off the corner. Finally, a large youth separated from the group and moved down the block past their Impala on the opposite side of the street. Joe asked Andrea if he was the Axeman, but she indicated that he wasn't. True to

Gonda's expectations, the gang member doubled back and approached from the rear, trying to appear casual, a heavy-set teen with a street-tough face. He stopped about five feet from Wayne Murphy's open window.

Murphy asked, "Hey, you know where I can get high?"

The kid replied, "No, officer, I don't know nothin' 'bout that."

"Hey, I'm no cop, I just want to get high."

"Lemme see some money; maybe we talk."

"Come here, and I'll show you some real money."

The drug dealer pulled back his unbuttoned shirt to reveal a stainless-steel nine millimeter in his belt; then he shuffled to within arm's reach of Wayne, with his pistol still exposed. He bent at the waist and peered into the car. In one fluid motion, Wayne jammed the barrel of his silencer under the drug dealer's chin with his right hand and grabbed the man's hair with his left. He jerked the dealer's head into the car saying, "Don't even think about reaching for that nine millimeter. Now, I'm going to open this door and you're going to get in."

Wayne released his hostage's hair and eased the door open. Joe cocked the MAC 10 in his lap and pointed it at the dealer. Wayne lowered his .45, deftly removed the nine millimeter from the man's belt, tossed it into the back seat, and pulled the drug dealer into the seat next to him.

Hoping to get moving before the group on the corner could react, Joe started the engine and drove toward them.

Wayne pressed his .45 into the street tough's side and said, "Wave real happy-like to your friends as we go by."

The tough swallowed but waved energetically.

Gonda drove quietly for several blocks until they reached a garbage-filled vacant lot and parked.

In a high-pitched voice, the gang member asked, "What you want, home? You fuck with me, my boys gonna toast your ass."

Leaving his MAC 10 on the seat, Joe Gonda, .45 in hand, wordlessly got out of the car, walked around the front, opened the passenger door and said, "Get out."

The drug dealer did as instructed, and Murphy followed him. Gonda motioned to Andrea in the back, and she followed as well.

They marched the drug dealer between a stripped car and a pile of broken furniture and Gonda said, "Stop."

The tough, uncertainty showing on his face, turned and faced the big Green Beret. Murphy maneuvered his way to the man's rear, and Andrea stood behind Gonda.

Joe said, "Julian Salka says hello."

The drug dealer stiffened, and his confusion gave way to fear. He said, "Why Salka interested in me?"

"You tell me. Word is you and your friends have been talking too much."

"Talkin' too much? Who we talkin' to?"

"Cops."

"Shit, we ain't . . ." Gonda fired the silenced pistol, and a bullet struck the ground next to the drug dealer's feet.

"The cops have been in our faces lately, and somebody's telling them something."

"Wait, man! Maybe that's between you and DeFrancesco. Word is he tryin' to move on you from New York. Maybe he's your problem."

"Why you think we got trouble with DeFrancesco?"

"Shit, man, you don't got no trouble, then how come you been hirin' so many boys to watch that island? How come DeFrancesco's comin' to visit you? My friend workin' out there say you don't even bring the cash off no more. You must be 'fraida somethin'."

Gonda smiled internally. It was almost too easy. "You know way too much. When does your friend say DeFrancesco's coming?"

"Monday, soon as that big party's over. They say Mr. Pyne and him gonna try to cut a deal."

Gonda looked at Murphy. "You were right; these assholes are too damn stupid to be the source. We tell Salka he got the wrong people."

Murphy responded, "Whatever you say."

The tough piped up, "I told you we didn't do nothin'."

Gonda turned to face him, and responded, "Not so fast, dirt bag. I got a message for the Axeman." He motioned toward Andrea. "You see that woman? Remember her? She's a friend of Mr. Salka. He heard the Axeman was bothering her. Your friend needs to forget he ever heard the name Andrea. You got that?"

The tough nodded.

"You better get it right, or we'll be back to see the Axeman and you, and Mr. Salka will be with us. Now get the fuck out of here."

The drug dealer took off at a run. The Green Berets and Andrea walked toward their car. Gonda smiled at Murphy and said, "See what you can do if you drop the right name?"

Murphy responded, "Joe, that was a beautiful thing."

As they reached the Impala, Gonda asked, "Andrea, you know who DeFrancesco is?"

Andrea shrugged. "Who doesn't? The papers say he's the Godfather who killed his way to the top in New York, and now he's moving on New England."

Gonda let out a low whistle as he got in the car. As he pointed the Impala back toward North Haven, he looked at Andrea and said, "Man, you and your boyfriend sure know how to get in the shit. This thing keeps getting bigger and bigger."

North Haven

After Gonda, Murphy, and Andrea returned, Tim, Mac, and Pete debriefed them thoroughly, then convened to discuss what they now knew. They sat in a small circle next to the sand table.

Tim said, "The clock's ticking now. From the sound of things, Pyne's got a lot of cash out there right now. Who knows what's going to happen after he meets with DeFrancesco. I think we got to go Sunday."

Mac stared at the floor and chewed his cigar for several seconds, then said, "No, I say Monday."

Pete started in his chair. "You both crazy? Nobody's had time to train, and to get to the money we got to get past cameras and a company of armed assholes."

Mac responded, "Look, the money's nice, but we all know it's not why we're really here. We're here because each one of us likes the idea of doing a son of a bitch like Pyne, and we're not going to let Tim down. So Monday's perfect. We get Pyne and DeFrancesco both—and we get the money! Besides, we heard Pyne's been recruiting on the street, so how good can his troops be? I think we can do it."

Tim interjected, "This is big. For now, I say we look at it tonight and plan it both ways. Tomorrow, we ask the team. It's their necks too, so they ought to have a say."

Pete and Mac nodded. Mac said, "I think that's the way it's got to be."

With that they set to work; but when they finally went to bed, they had a good idea how they were getting on the island, but they still couldn't see how to get off of it.

The next morning, Tim called the entire team together in the planning room. It was just before lunch when all arrived, even the medics. Standing before the chalkboard, Tim began by letting Mac and Pete both state their cases for when the assault should be carried out. The vote was easy and nearly unanimous. They wanted DeFrancesco, so they would go Monday.

Tim shook his head as the men put their hands down. "You realize this makes you the most certifiable bunch in Special Forces history."

Stan said softly, "You know how it is, Tim. 'Cry havoc and let slip the dogs of war.' Hell, when you get old you get arthritis and shit. Might as well get it over with now."

Gonda rasped, "I don't know about that 'old' shit. I'll have to consult Pete and Mac."

The two veteran soldiers chuckled.

Tim said, "OK, it's Monday night. That gives us two days, just enough time to send half the team to Vermont for at least some weapons familiarization." He paused, then continued, "There's something else that needs to be decided. As you know, we need an up-close look at the island before we go. Mr. Pyne is throwing a party tomorrow, and much to our delight, he has chosen Andrea to be one of his honored guests. Someone has to go with Andrea and that someone will have two purposes. The first is obvious: to recon everything they can. The second purpose is far more dangerous, and perhaps even more important. We all know that Pyne has cameras positioned around the entire perimeter of Robin Island, and that will make any infiltration damn near impossible. So Pete, with his flair for nasty tricks, has devised a way around it. We learned from the real-estate files that all the electricity on the island is provided by one big generator, and wires run from that generator to the house. Here's what Pete has devised."

Tim held up a small contraption that consisted of a bottle taped to an XM-122 receiver and said, "First, during the party we plant this baby next to a wire. When the time comes for the attack, we activate the receiver, and it pops a squib that breaks the bottle containing acid, which eats through the wire. Out go the cameras, with no mess and not much noise."

A murmur went about the room. The irrepressible Gonda smiled and said, "I like it."

Pete bowed his head in recognition for the praise.

"Now," Tim continued, "what remains to be discussed is who is going to accompany Andrea. But I have already made that decision and it is irreversible. I will be Andrea's date for tomorrow."

Suddenly, the room became absolutely quiet. It remained that way for nearly a minute, until finally Mac spoke. "Tim, nobody here seems to have the courage or the sense to say something, so I will. You're fuckin' nuts! The bastard has a contract out on your life, you got spotted and damn near killed the minute you came back to this town, we've had to hide you since Europe, and now you wanna go to his fuckin' party? If you do, the mission is blown and you're dead all in one smooth sweet move."

Tim shook his head. "No, I don't think so. First, my beard has come in, and I've got longer hair now. Also, I'm going to wear contact lenses that will make my eyes green, and I'll dye my hair black. None of them have ever seen me in the flesh, so there's no way they'll recognize me—I'm sure of it."

Tim could see that several of his friends were fighting back comments. Finally, Gonda spoke. "Why you wanna go?"

"Look, that son of a bitch out there on his island paradise has made my life miserable in ways I never dreamed were possible, and I've never even met the bastard! I want to meet Pyne up close."

Mac said, "Bullshit. You know it's fuckin' nuts. Hell, we all know." He shook his head. "But I can see why you'd wanna go. And you know," Tim saw him raise his head, and their eyes met, "you're just crazy enough to pull it off. Hell, if it works, it's a nice touch. You'd be right under the slimeball's nose and he'd never know it!"

Mac's grudging assent won over the rest of the team, and the issue was settled. Tim was going.

CHAPTER THIRTY-FOUR

Sunday, July 16, 1989—Robin Island

The morning of Michael Pyne's gala charity affair was sunny and cloudless, and Tim and Andrea were ready well in advance of the time stated on their invitation. Tim wore a rented black tuxedo, and the rest of the team had to admit that with the beard, dyed hair, and contact lenses, he was much changed from the Tim Reardon of two months before. When Andrea showed up at the office that morning, she was greeted by admiring glances from all. While some women favor clothes that glorify them, she glorified her clothes. Not that her full-length green summer dress looked unattractive, but it was the woman who filled it, the woman with the long dark hair and the radiant smile who did it all. As they left with the device that would cut Pyne's electricity tucked in Andrea's pocketbook, Tim found himself feeling glad he had found her.

When Tim and Andrea arrived at the town dock to board Pyne's launch, they found over fifty formally attired couples like themselves waiting to ride across to the party. Tim could not help being impressed by Pyne's organizational abilities. In spite of the large numbers of passengers, boats ferrying the guests in and out were extremely efficient, so their wait was short. Fifteen minutes later, he and Andrea arrived on Robin Island.

Once on the island, Tim found that Pyne had spared no expense to make his soirée memorable. The groomed walk from the shore wound gracefully through a sea of flowers and manicured trees; colored ribbons guided them along its entire length; and pictures of species of fish found in the Long Island Sound hung from each tree they passed. All the while, their noses filled with the scent of the sea and the flowers, and strains of classical music floated down from the mansion above. Much to his delight, the path led directly past the humming generator shack, and his eyes registered every detail about the small building as they passed it.

At the end of the path, they entered a receiving line, along with most of the notable members of the Branford community—including the mayor. As Tim waited, he used the time to survey his surroundings casually. To his left lay the tennis courts, behind which he could make out the guest cottage. To his right he could now see Pyne's home, a huge mansion in fine English country style. All of the grounds were impeccably groomed and designed so that each element coexisted in harmony with its neighbors.

Finally, they reached the front of the line, and Michael Pyne stood before him. Calmly, as if he were combat-bound, Tim scanned Pyne's eyes. In them he saw no flicker of recognition. A servant behind Pyne was reading from a list of name cards, and he introduced them as Mark Rohrback and Andrea Volente. Every bit the immaculate young banker in his white dinner jacket and black pants, he shook Tim's hand without meeting his direct gaze. Then he turned to Andrea and stylishly bowed and kissed her hand. Erect again, he said, "Ms. Volente, I am honored you have chosen to attend. I cannot tell you how much I have enjoyed living on the island you sold me. I hope your business is still going well?"

Tim marveled at her composure. Smiling, she responded, "Why, thank you, Mr. Pyne. And yes, my business is doing extremely well. Please feel free to recommend me to your friends."

Returning her smile with the oily sincerity of a practiced politician, he said, "I will do that. Now please, won't you and your friend enjoy our hospitality—and please help us save the Sound!" Still smiling, he turned to his next guest.

Tim led Andrea to the banquet table on the front lawn of the mansion. Once there, he murmured, "Our man seems to remember you."

Still smiling, she responded, "Stay calm, Tim. I'll have to wash my hand fifty times to get that snake's drool off."

"Who's calm?" he laughed. A waiter came by with goblets of wine. Taking two, he led her about the grounds.

Pyne had restricted the movement of his guests severely. A system of carefully placed colored ribbons marked the limits of the party, but they were still able to check all the information they already had, plus learn some new details. Tim visually located the electrical wire in the trees some twenty feet outside of the tape. Undaunted, he checked the angles of the surveillance cameras until he found a dead zone on an open knoll behind the generator house where the wire lay partially buried. Taking Andrea by the hand, he led her there slowly; seated on a rock in her embrace, they looked like lovers seeking privacy. Carefully positioning his body between the power line and the other revelers, he slowly dug a hole right next to the wire with the heel of his shoe. When it was large enough, he placed the squib device in the ground, pushed the loose soil back over the top, broke off their embrace, and taking her hand, led Andrea back to the affair. Two hours and several glasses of champagne later, the Green Beret and the realtor were in her Firebird en route back to the planning room, laughing with joy and relief at their successful penetration of Robin Island's surveillance system.

New Haven

Michael Pyne was not the only one using surveillance cameras at the party. Oscar Bonning's task force also took pictures that afternoon. If Pyne had invited any new connections to the party, the police wanted to know about them. As a result, they too had appreciated Mr. Pyne's efforts to organize his guests on the dock. It made snapping the picture of each guest far easier than it might have been; by that evening, Detective Sergeant Pulcinella had all the photographs sitting upon his desk and divided into two piles: "knowns" and "unknowns." Amidst the unknowns he placed a snapshot of a tall, elegant dark-haired woman who sold real estate and a bearded man in a black tuxedo.

By midnight, Pulcinella had identified most of his subjects, but the realtor's date still eluded him. He knew he recognized that face, yet maddeningly, the name would not come to him. Partly out of pride, and partly because of his unshakable faith in his ability to remember faces, he had no intention of leaving the office until he had identified the mystery man. Once again, he scrutinized the picture. Besides the beard, the man in the photo had medium-length black hair and was dressed in a well-fitted tuxedo. Pulcinella decided he looked almost Mediterranean—except the features were all wrong. The photo showed his face turned towards the camera. He looked relaxed yet alert—it was almost as if he knew he was being watched. It was the eyes; Pooch knew them. Where? Where had he seen them before?

Suddenly, he knew, but it was too absurd to believe, so he studied the picture once again. Reardon. The soldier had grown a beard and dyed his hair, but the man in the photo was Tim Reardon. Tony sat up in his chair. What was Reardon doing there? Men who have contracts out on their lives did not usually attend parties thrown by the people who wanted them dead. What the hell was Reardon doing there?

Pulling out the slim file he had kept on Reardon, he rose slowly from his chair and headed for Bonning's office.

Monday, July 16, 1989—New Haven

Brown and Foster had watched a suspected dealer in the Hill Section for most of the morning, but shortly after 11 A.M. they checked in and told the dispatcher they were going to lunch.

As was their habit, they went to a Greek restaurant on Whalley Avenue. The Olympia was really more of a diner, but the place had been on their beat long before they had received their gold shields. They knew the owner, were never charged, and actually enjoyed the food. In fact, several times Foster had tried to suggest different places, but Brown would hear none of it. The Olympia was their ritual, and Foster had to agree it was bad luck to break a ritual.

Sitting in a cramped car all morning had been hard on both their bladders, so as soon as they entered the door, Foster went to the bathroom while Brown held his seat. When he returned, they switched roles and Brown went into the bathroom.

Knowing Foster would be busy ordering, Brown felt no need to watch his back when he entered the multistalled gray facility. Instead, he checked each stall in turn for occupants. There was someone in the fourth and last one, so he casually walked over to use the urinal and waited.

Seconds later, the fourth door opened, and a short, unpleasant young man named Enrico Fabrucci, under investigation by the police for narcotics trafficking, stepped out.

Surprised, Brown zipped his pants, turned to face the man, and said, "You ain't supposed to be here. You're just supposed to leave the envelope in the trash. Don't you fuckheads know I'm taking a big chance doing this?"

Ignoring the big man's scowl, Fabrucci passed him an envelope and said, "I got a message for you from someone real important."

At the lunch bar, Foster had just ordered a sandwich when he realized he had left his sunglasses by the sink. Motioning for the waitress to hold their seats, he stood and headed back to the bathroom.

Brown, still waiting for the message, had his back to the door when it opened and Foster came in fast. Turning, he saw confusion on his partner's face. Then he realized that Foster both saw the envelope in his hand and recognized the dealer. What he saw next seemed to happen almost in slow motion; his body refused to move until it was too late. First, Foster reached uncertainly toward his service revolver. Sensing movement from the dealer, he turned his attention back to Enrico. Fabrucci had an impressive 9mm automatic out and pointed at Foster. He snapped off three bullets in quick succession. His first shot missed the big black cop altogether, hitting the doorjamb instead; but the second struck Foster's left shoulder, and the third hit the left side of his skull—and as Brown looked helplessly on, his friend of many years went down like a duck caught in the hunt.

The dealer had advanced on Foster as he fired. Now Brown found himself standing behind Fabrucci's right shoulder. His shocked reverie over, he reacted quickly as he saw the dealer's head turning back in his direction. Brown slid his small automatic from its holster and fired, hitting the dealer in the center of the forehead.

Before the deafening sound of the shots had died in his ears, he saw the arm of a uniformed policeman trying to push the door open, but Foster's body lay in his way. Brown stooped and pulled his partner clear so the others could enter—and enter they did. Yet at first, he did not look at the uniforms. Instead, he stared at his partner's blood spreading across the tile floor until he felt a hand on his shoulder. Holstering his pistol, he turned and found one of the uniforms staring at him. His name was Pelligreno, and like Brown and Foster, he and his partner often had lunch at the diner. Brown suddenly realized that his left hand still held the envelope. Quickly sliding it into his pocket, he wondered if the beat cop had seen it. Slowly, he lowered himself to the bathroom floor and sat next to Foster. The uniform took charge. As time passed, he dimly heard the ambulance attendant proclaiming Fabrucci dead but Foster still alive. Brown looked up and absently told Pelligreno to call Pulcinella, as they had been working with him on a special assignment. Then, he placed his head in his hands and began crying. He kept asking himself why his partner hadn't just stayed out of the damn bathroom.

Pulcinella pulled his car up to the restaurant twenty minutes after he got the call. Inside, he found Brown still sitting on the bathroom floor, and he listened to the detective's story intently. According to Brown, he had been in a stall, came out, and found Foster trying to arrest the dealer for drug use. The dealer had shot Foster, and Brown had tried to defend his partner.

Cocaine found in Fabrucci's pocket lent some credence to the story, but when taken as a whole, Pulcinella decided, it had a lot of flaws. First, Foster, an experienced cop, was on a special assignment and would have ignored a simple user. Next, witnesses stated that Foster had just gone in the bathroom when they had heard shots, so there was no time for him to have tried to make an arrest. Then, there was the question of the envelope the uniform swore he had seen in Brown's hand. What was in it, and where did it go? Tony would have loved a look at the inner pocket of Brown's jacket. It sounded like a payoff gone bad, but Tony elected to pretend he was convinced and let the whole thing go by—for now. Brown would have to face an immediate Internal Affairs interrogation routine to every police discharge, and he told him to take the day off when he was finished.

After Brown left, Tony looked around the bathroom one more time. Blood still stained the walls and floors, and tape marks showed where the bodies had been. He was sure of it—Ralph Brown was the turned cop he wanted. And he planned to prove it.

On the way to the I.A.D. hearing, Brown stopped at a pay phone and placed a call. He knew he was in serious trouble already, but if Foster ever regained consciousness, it would get worse. He would need help, he knew, to fix this one. The party he spoke with was happy to oblige, but wanted any and all information the police had on Tim Reardon as payment.

As soon as Pulcinella arrived back at the office, he sat quietly at his desk for several minutes. He needed time to think, and his mind mulled over several things at once. What was Reardon doing? This kid was a top-flight fighter capable of doing a lot of damage, and Tony knew that something was going on. Disguised or not, why had the kid gone to the party? Could it have been a reconnaissance trip? He scratched his head. The idea of Reardon taking on Pyne directly seemed absurd, but it still nagged at him. Searchingly, he gazed at the official photo of Reardon once more. Well, maybe he couldn't locate the soldier, but he did know where the girl was. That evening, he would find her.

After discussing Brown with Bonning, they agreed that one of the two of them would follow Brown twenty-four hours a day from now on. Since he had to be panicked now, they were sure he would make a mistake soon, and they were right.

Late that afternoon, Pulcinella and Bonning tailed Brown as he left the Internal Affairs hearing. Using two different cars, they alternately closed in on him in traffic so he wouldn't make his tails. They used hand-held radios to communicate, and the first sign that they had a problem came almost immediately when Brown made straight for the task force office. Feeling foolish as they sat outside for some minutes wondering what their quarry was doing, Tony finally asked for and got permission to go inside. After all, it was a place Brown would expect to find him.

After sprinting from his car, Pulcinella opened the door as

casually as he could, and found Brown standing next to Pulcinella's desk with a large tan envelope in his hand. Tony asked, "You OK, Ralph?"

"Well, other than seeing the shit shot out of my partner, and facing a firing squad at I.A.D., I guess I'm doing fine. Pooch, I'd have given anything not to have been in that stall when Art walked in. Jesus, I hope he pulls through. You hear anything yet?"

"Yeah, the docs say that he's lost a lot of blood. He's still unconscious, and he might stay that way forever. The bullet to the head caused some swelling to his brain. For now, we just gotta wait and see. . . . Hey, take a seat. At least you got the scumbag, right?"

"Yeah. . . . And thanks for the talk, but I've got to go. I need some time."

"OK, you take it easy now."

As soon as Brown had left, Tony checked his desk and knew right away what Brown had been doing. A meticulous organizer, Tony found that the Reardon file had been moved to the corner of the desk where Brown had been standing. An old cop, Brown was too smart to take it, so Tony figured he must have made copies and ran to the copy machine. Trying to reduce its tremendous budget deficit, the City of New Haven now demanded that every copy be logged, and Pulcinella grabbed their log book. The Reardon file was eighteen pages long, and according to the log, the last time the copy machine was used, the counter read 4868. Now it read 4886. Brown must have copied that file. Pulcinella had left his radio in his car, but he remembered that Bonning had a car phone, so moving at a run, he hurried back to his desk and dialed Bonning's phone number.

As soon as he answered, Tony exclaimed, "I think we've got him. He has a copy of the Reardon file in his hand."

"Good, I've got his car in sight. Hurry down to the corner of Chapel Street. He's parked on a one-way, and has to pass that corner, so I'll pick you up there. It'll be faster than getting your car."

As Pulcinella and Bonning followed, Brown drove a short distance, parked on a side street, and headed for a nearby pay phone.

Next to the phone booth was a trash can. Reaching in, Brown removed a package, then he replaced it with the tan folder he had taken from the office. Next, he made a phone call.

Back in Bonning's car, the two policemen made a quick decision. Bonning would stay to see what happened to the envelope, and Tony would take the car and follow Brown while calling the office to send someone to pick up Bonning.

Tony found following Brown difficult, and luck turned against him. Nervous that he would be spotted, Tony took a side street that should have placed him on a path to intercept his quarry just before the hospital, but it did not work out that way. A delivery truck pulled out just as he came down the street, and it had to make several short swings to get out. As he waited, the phone rang.

It was Bonning. "Pick him up, Tony, the man who came for the envelope turned out to be a local pharmacist. He looked more like a civilian than a soldier, so on a hunch, I decided to pop him, and he talked. He was instructed to leave a needle and a lethal dose of potassium in that trash can and pick up an envelope later. He had already passed the envelope on by the time we got here, and I got a man tracing it, but he did look at the contents. It was the stuff on Reardon. Tony, you've got to get that bastard now. He's going to kill Foster!"

"I'll make it, Oscar. See you when I get back."

By the time Pulcinella reached the street Brown should have been on, he knew he was far too late. Wishing he had a blue light to turn on, he squealed his tires and fishtailed the car into the traffic. One intersection to go, he thought, and he would be there. Then the light turned red and a slow-moving Honda stopped in front of him.

Brown was indeed already at the hospital. He had seen several wheelchair patients in the lobby, and he had paused to watch them. A paraplegic had a chair with an electric toggle switch before his face. Brown saw that he manipulated his speed and direction with his nose. The man looked at Brown, and the detective looked away. In a strange sense, the wheelchair victim made him feel better. Maybe that would be Foster's fate, he reasoned, and if it was, well, then he would be doing his partner a favor. After all, he didn't want to do it—he really liked Art—but if Foster lived to talk before he could get out of the country, Brown was finished. He considered all of this as he rode the elevator up to Art Foster's floor.

Still, when he turned the corner of the corridor leading to the room, he stopped short, backed up, and leaned against the wall. A uniform stood outside the door, and he needed time to get up his nerve. This was bad. According to Salka, the potassium would be untraceable, but it wouldn't do to have Foster die while he was known to be in the room—not while I.A.D. was interested.

He toyed with the package in his pocket. His fingers were slick with sweat, and for the first time, he noticed how they were shaking. Thumping the back of his head against the wall in frustration, he thought once more, "If only he hadn't walked into that bathroom. . . . Aw, shit, Art, I got no choice." Then thinking again of the paraplegic, he steeled himself, turned the corner, and strode off in the direction of Foster's private room.

Pulcinella cursed the Honda. Desperate now, he swerved over the curb onto the sidewalk and powered in front of an approaching semi. Seconds later, he slid Bonning's car into a maternity slot at the main entrance, threw open his door, and ran through the lobby for the room-pass desk. There he flashed his badge and asked if a Detective Brown had come to see Art Foster. The gray-haired woman working there had no record of it, but Pulcinella knew he had to check the room itself. It was possible that Brown had not come to the hospital, but he doubted it. The detective felt sure he was there someplace.

Arriving at the room at a dead run, Tony found a young uniform outside, obviously a recent academy graduate. He hoped the kid was good.

Tony asked, "Anyone in there?"

"Yeah, Detective, another detective just went in a minute ago."

Leaning close, Pulcinella said, "Now listen to me carefully. Everything may be fine in that room or it may not. When I go in, I want you to follow me. Be casual but ready for anything. You got it?"

Somewhat uncertainly, the officer nodded.

Pulcinella opened the door briskly, but not excessively so.

Brown, face full of surprise, turned about with one hand behind his back. He looked nervous. The tube from the intravenous in Foster's arm was swinging as though just released.

Uncertainty suddenly filled Pulcinella—what if he was wrong about the whole thing? No! His instincts told him otherwise! He pulled out his pistol and pointed it at Brown's chest. "I'm sorry it has to be this way, but put your hands in front of you, Ralph."

Brown looked perplexed. "What the fuck, Tony?"

Yelling now, he bellowed, "Step away from that bed, and put your hands in front of you!"

Brown moved to the foot of the bed. "OK, Tony, whatever you want. . . ." Once clear, he spun and dove backwards to place the bed between himself and Pulcinella. A small glass vial fell and shattered on the floor. Then a deafening shot rang out from under the bed, and out of the corner of his eye, Tony saw the young policeman next to him fall backwards out the door. He himself leapt from the room to place the wall between himself and Brown. Kneeling, he saw Brown under the bed with his gun pointed at the downed officer in the doorway. Behind him, he heard screaming in the hallway. Somewhere, he heard the sound of breaking glass and running footsteps. Tony yelled, "Police! Everyone clear the hallway!"

He turned his concentration back to the room. Brown still had his gun pointed at the pale-faced police officer on the floor. Still intently sighting his pistol on Brown, Tony asked the kid, "Where'd you get it?"

"In the leg . . . God, it hurts."

The kid needed treatment—and needed it fast. Eyes riveted across his gun sights to a point just above Brown's nose, Tony asked, "Isn't it time you gave it up? This kid's had it if you don't let him go. How many more cops you going to kill before you quit, Ralph?"

"Just the one laying in front of you if you don't get me the fuck out of here."

"You were one of us until tonight, Brownie. Now I'm going to move this kid. Won't do any good to kill me. You know there's lots of help on the way. This kid dies or not, you're not leaving here on your own." Slowly and carefully, keeping his pistol pointed at Brown with his right hand, he reached across to the kid's body with his left and began pulling him out of the door.

In an anguished voice Brown yelled, "Don't touch him!"

With his peripheral vision, Tony saw two uniforms arrive to back him up. Pulling back his hand, he used it to motion one of them over, and the man squatted next to him. Softly, he said, "Tell your partner to keep all the civilians back, then come here, squat behind me, and get your gun pointed at the man in the prone position under the bed. He's got a gun on the officer down lying next to me."

While the uniform did as he was told, Brown spoke. "Pooch, I've got two hostages here. You're going to get me the fuck out of this place or they're going to die."

"I just got one question. We know about the potassium. Did you shoot up Art yet?"

"That's for me to know, Tony."

The uniform took up position behind Pulcinella with his gun aimed at Brown. In a whisper the detective told him, "Take him if you get an opening." Then in a louder voice, he said, "Well, Brown, you're going to have to kill another cop, because I'm putting away my gun, and I'm gonna pull this kid you plugged the hell out of it. If he don't get medical attention, he's going to die. Sorry, buddy, I can't let that happen."

Pulcinella holstered his pistol and reached out for the prostrate cop. Blood was pooled about his leg, but he was still conscious. His chest now exposed to Brown's fire, Pulcinella waited for the impact of the bullet. It didn't come, so, slowly, trying not to kill the kid by moving him, he inched him to safety. Finally, with an intense feeling of relief, he realized that he had the body out of the door and had judged Brown correctly. He was not a natural killer, just a desperate man. Waiting attendants grabbed the policeman and rushed him down the hallway.

Pulcinella began positioning himself behind the uniform when a pistol discharge filled his ears. The uniform had fired his weapon. Tony swung out into the center of the door and fell to a prostrate firing position. The bullet had struck Brown in the left shoulder, and the force of the impact had jarred his aim away from the door, but as Tony watched, the wounded man tried to swing his weapon back on line.

Tony yelled, "No! It's over! Put the gun down!"

But the pistol was almost on line and still swinging, so Tony fired; milliseconds later, the bullet entered Brown's eye socket, snapping his head back against a metal bar beneath the bed. Mesmerized, Tony watched as the body came to rest on the floor.

Scrambling to his feet, he cried, "Get a doctor here! Now!"

Doctors confirmed that Brown was dead, and that he had either not had the chance or had lacked the resolve to inject the potassium into Foster. The uniformed officer was easily stabilized and would be fine, and though Foster was still borderline, he was alive.

The I.A.D. people wanted Tony to report, but when they reached the hospital, he had already left. The other officer who had discharged his weapon informed them that the detective had not left word on where he was going.

CHAPTER THIRTY-FIVE

Sunday, July 16, 1989—Robin Island

In all their years together, Salka had never seen Michael Pyne this angry. The folder he had on his desk hadn't just infuriated him, it had made him crazy. "All the money I pay!" he screamed at Salka. "All the illiterate punks I have walking around with guns! Are you trying to tell me you can't stop problems like this?"

With his eyes ablaze, Pyne stared at Reardon's file. Salka detected that behind Pyne's anger, there was also a measure of fear. Sometimes, he thought, the Wall Street prig disgusted him. Salka remained mute.

Waving the police photo of Reardon on the town dock, Pyne continued, "Let us go over all this one more time. First, that son of a bitch Reardon is not only here, he came to my damn party and shook my hand! Next, my source tells me that this stupid soldier is planning to hit me. Then the same bastard cop who busted my shipment last spring kills my detective. To compound this wonderful mess, DeFrancesco is visiting us on his yacht tomorrow so I can pay my respects! Well, Julian," Pyne actually hissed. "I want Reardon dead. You will accomplish that by tomorrow. I told you before that there is a way to get anyone, and the way to get Reardon is through the girl, so tonight you will pick up that girl—alive. Oh, we'll kill her too, but first she's going to give us her boyfriend. Twenty-four hours, Julian, I want him dead in twenty-four hours. And I want that detective out of the way. Nothing is going to aggravate this DeFrancesco deal—nothing! Do you understand me, Julian?"

He nodded and left the room quietly. The last thing he saw was Pyne swiveling in his chair and looking out the window.

New Haven

Andrea reached her condominium around nine that evening. Half the team was in Vermont training, so there was not much to be done that day. As she placed her key in the lock, and wished Tim were with her, she noticed a man approaching from across the street. Nervous, she reached into her pocketbook and gripped her PPk. Now unlocked, her door swung open, and she heard the sound of a foot on the front step behind her. She lunged through the door, spun behind its thick oak for cover, and pointed her pistol at the man's head.

Her gun immediately wavered. The man held a badge before him. Calmly he said, "Ma'am, I'm a police officer—Detective Sergeant Anthony Pulcinella—and I mean you no harm. I just want to talk."

Something about the man convinced her he was sincere. Slowly, she lowered the pistol and hoped she wasn't making a serious mistake. In the dim light afforded by the streetlights, he appeared somewhat tired—even dazed. Short in stature, he was wearing an impossibly rumpled suit, and his shoulders sagged.

After taking a deep breath, she nodded and motioned for him to precede her inside.

As they moved down her foyer and into her living room, she replaced the PPk into her pocketbook; but, reassured by its weight, she kept the purse close by her side. Motioning the detective into an easy chair, she asked him, "Are you sure you're in the right place, Officer?"

"Please call me Tony. You are, I hope, Miss Andrea Volente?"

She squeezed her pocketbook. The reassuring hardness of the pistol was still there for her fingers to feel. "I am."

"Miss Volente, I'm not even going to ask if you have a permit for that firearm you're fondling, but I wish the hell you'd leave it alone. All I want to do is talk."

In response, she sat on an opposing couch and set her shoulder bag next to her. "Fair enough, what do you want to talk about?"

Pulcinella looked down at the floor, took a breath, then returned his gaze to Andrea. "Are you the Andrea Volente who attended a benefit affair on Robin Island hosted by Mr. Michael Pyne?"

"I am. Was that against the law?"

"No, not at all, ma'am." She saw he was back to studying the floor once again. His hand went into his jacket pocket and he pulled out a red hard candy. After popping it into his mouth, he continued, "If I am not mistaken, a sister of yours died of a drug overdose in Branford some months ago."

She nodded.

"I find that interesting, Miss Volente. You see, I know someone else who lost a sister about a week before you did. What I find even more curious is that you and that particular someone attended a function sponsored by a man everyone knows is part of a drug cartel. You do know a man named Tim Reardon?"

"I've never heard the name."

"Then perhaps this will be helpful." From an inside pocket, he produced the surveillance photo taken of the two of them standing arm in arm on the Branford town dock.

She studied the photo in silence for a moment, then looked straight into Pulcinella's eyes. "What do you want, Detective?"

"I want to save some decent people from getting involved in

a very messy thing. I want to save your life." He paused. It was almost as if he was waiting for her to flinch. She didn't. He continued, "Ms. Volente, I know something is going on. Frankly, I think you and your boyfriend are planning a surprise for Pyne. I have come here to talk you out of doing a stupid thing before it's too late, so I want you to put me in contact with Tim. That way I can talk to him directly. Why don't you place the call?"

"Why can't you just talk to me?"

"With all due respect, ma'am, you seem very nice—competent, too—but to carry off the type of operation I believe you have in mind, Tim would have to be the primary figure here. He's the one with the knowhow."

Andrea remained quiet for a moment. If the police knew about the mission, what would that mean to the team? Deciding she would have to let Tim handle this one personally, she shrugged and said, "Why not? I'd feel better if we used a pay phone—just in case you want to tape what you say to Tim."

"Whatever you want." They stood, and she led him from her condo. As they left, she noticed the street was quiet. With Yale out of session, this end of town seemed virtually deserted. She turned her mind back to the detective. What did he really want? Preoccupied, she never noticed that four men seated in a car up the street were watching their departure carefully.

Andrea led Tony around the corner to a bar in the basement of what had once been a textile mill. It had neon beer signs in the windows, and a brass rail on a long, poorly lit bar. It did sparse business, so she figured its phone would be unoccupied. It was.

She dialed while his back was turned. Gonda answered, and he hustled up Tim. "What's up, Andie?"

"Tim, I've got a cop here named Detective Pulcinella who wants to talk to you. He says you know him."

"Are you in any kind of trouble?"

"No, this is strictly voluntary on my part."

"OK, put him on."

Pulcinella took the receiver. "Sergeant Reardon?"

"Yeah, what can I do for you?"

"I don't know, that depends on what you're up to."

"Well, Detective, I'm taking your advice and hiding so the drug dealers don't get me."

"For a man in hiding, you have odd tastes in social events—you're lucky you didn't end up as Pyne's guest of honor—permanently."

"You liked that, huh? I just wanted to meet the source of my discomfort personally."

"Listen to me, Reardon! I know something's going down, and whatever it is, forget it!"

"Hey, Detective, you can prove what you're saying, come arrest me."

Choosing to disregard Tim's challenge, Pulcinella continued, "When I first met you, you seemed like a decent guy. That information you gave me resulted in one of the largest drug hauls we've ever made. For that I thank you, but what you're trying to do now won't work. Michael Pyne has left a trail of bodies behind him wherever he's gone, and, believe me, if you go after him, you're going to be his next victim. If he doesn't kill you, I'll end up busting you. If you know something, give it to me. Maybe I won't get him this week, but sooner or later I will. You have my word on that. If you come clean with me now, you can still leave town with no questions asked and maybe start a life somewhere else. My way you got a chance. Your way, you end up with nothing."

"Detective, I might be up to something—I might not; but one thing I can tell you: your way won't work. How many years has this guy been going about his business? How long have the police been after Pyne? What you're offering me sucks. It's not an answer to my problems. Even if you put the bastard in jail, my trouble won't go away. You know that."

"Dammit, my way is the right way. It has to work, or we don't have anything. According to your personnel jacket, you believed in it enough to risk your life for it."

"I don't see the point to this conversation."

"The point is this: if you are thinking about taking on Pyne, forget it. If the reasons I already gave you aren't enough, then let me give you one more. Pyne knows exactly who you are and he knows you're coming."

"How?"

"We had a bad cop. He got hold of your file and the pictures we took of you and your girlfriend at the party, made copies, and sent it off to Pyne. He isn't stupid. You can't win, Tim. Believe me. You just can't. Come talk to me."

"Thanks for the phone call. Want to put Andrea back on?"

Andrea saw Pulcinella slump inside his coat. Slowly, he took the receiver away from his ear and passed it back to her.

"Hello."

"Andrea! Don't go home! Pyne knows you're involved with me, and I'm sending Art to pick you up. He'll be waiting on the corner of Grove and Church. Don't stop or talk to anybody! Just go to that corner and wait! He'll be in the Impala."

"I got it. Thanks, Tim." She hung up.

She smiled cordially at Pulcinella. His brows were furrowed and he chewed on another candy. Extending her hand she said, "Good evening, Detective."

Ignoring the hand, he shook his head and walked away through the near-empty bar, up the stairs, and out the open door.

Andrea decided she would be better off ordering a soda to make sure Pulcinella was gone before she went out to meet Simpson. When five minutes had passed, she could wait no longer and went up the stairs. As she came out, she could see the corner just a half a block away.

While listening to Pulcinella, Tim put his hand over the phone to give instructions to Simpson. He did not need to tell his comrade that the situation was serious.

Pete Sayers joined Art and they ran out to the Impala. Pete drove.

After weaving through freeway traffic and pushing several yellow lights, they arrived on Grove Street in record time, but they slowed considerably about two blocks short of Church. As they moved toward the corner, the four-lane street narrowed to two and passed by several tall office buildings, empty now that the work day was done. Scanning the area, Simpson spotted four men stationed on the right-hand side of the street, in a loose box fifty feet up from the corner where they were supposed to meet Andrea. Simpson recognized Julian Salka among them. As he glanced at Pete the other man's eyes met his—he had seen the trap too.

There were a great many apartments above the stores, so there were no parking spaces—except in front of a fire hydrant on the left. Pete pulled in, and from there Art had an excellent view of Salka and his men. There was an open newsstand, just past the pub entrance Andrea had to come out of. Art left the car and casually walked past the men to the stand.

Then things started to go wrong. A police cruiser pulled up next to the Impala. Art couldn't hear the words, but the cop's gestures told the whole story. Pete was obstructing a fire hydrant, and the policeman wanted the car moved. With the cop watching, Pete had to comply. Seconds later, both the Impala and the police cruiser disappeared around the corner just as Andrea emerged from the pub.

The four men waiting outside never gave her a chance to react. One man ripped her bag off her shoulder, two others roughly grabbed an arm apiece, and they began forcing her down the street towards their car. Andrea stiffened. Then she kicked one of her assailants' legs hard. The man slapped her, and, smiling and whistling, Salka pushed her violently forward.

Though Art knew he would need a lot of luck to take all four, he had to try. Sauntering out of the newsstand as casually as he could, he had a newspaper over one arm and he tried to affect a look of boredom. Reasoning that they were after information, he figured he would have some advantage because they wouldn't want to kill her. He again wished Pete was there to back him up.

With the .45 concealed under the newspaper, he made his way to within arm's reach of the man with Andrea's purse. He squeezed the trigger, and the man staggered backwards into Salka. Simultaneously dropping to one knee and shedding the paper, he fired two more quick shots at the men holding her arms. Both dropped directly to the sidewalk and fell still.

Art swung his pistol toward Salka, but the giant's reflexes were too quick. His pistol was out, and he had seized Andrea as a shield. Art knew he had to shoot anyway, but before he could bring the weapon on line, Salka fired twice. Shocked, Art felt a hard jab in his gut and found himself sinking. He fought the downward slide, but felt his strength leaving him fast. He struck the pavement, but curiously, he felt no pain from the impact.

Somewhere in the distance, he heard the sound of running feet and a woman screaming. At first, he couldn't understand the significance of the sounds; then his mind began working, and an image of Salka came into focus. He had to do something. Feeling as if it all moved in slow motion, he sat up and saw blood streaming from his abdomen and shoulder.

He shook his head and tried to concentrate. Looking across the street, he saw Salka push Andrea into a car, and begin to climb in. Simpson had hung on to his pistol, and he raised it now. As the door closed, he pulled the trigger and Salka's massive form staggered.

Simpson struggled to his feet with the sounds of a running car motor filling his ears. In spite of being hit, Salka was steering his vehicle away from the curb. Simpson ran a few steps, then felt himself start to slow down. He tried to shake it off—he had to stop Salka—but the world started to spin and he fell to the concrete. This time, he didn't get up.

When Pete Sayers rounded the corner, he was on foot. He had found a spot for the Impala on the back side of the block. Hearing gunfire as he left the car, he had run toward the sound as fast as he could. There he found Simpson with three dead thugs lying spread-eagled before him.

He knelt over Art as a crowd formed. Hoping most of the spectators would be paralyzed by the bloody scene, he took charge. His first priority was to get Simpson out before the police arrived. "I'm a doctor," he said. "Everyone stand back."

He knelt over Simpson, who was unconscious but still breathing. The bullet had ripped the side of Art's abdomen wide open. He had another wound in the shoulder, bleeding heavily and steadily, but less severe than the abdomen.

Glancing back at the onlookers, he saw that a man in a service-station shirt and blue jeans was nearest. He pointed at him and ordered, "You, go call an ambulance. This man is bad. I'm taking him to the hospital myself. Maybe the ambulance can help the others."

The man nodded dumbly and left at a run, anxious to be a good Samaritan.

Meanwhile, Pete picked his friend up and slung him over his shoulders in a fireman's carry. Then he spotted Andrea's shoulder bag in the hands of one of the dead men. He squatted fast and grabbed the purse and Simpson's pistol. That accomplished, he ran toward the corner as fast as he could. In the distance, he heard loud sirens getting closer. Softly, even though he knew Simpson could not hear him, he said, "Hang on, Art. We'll get you back to base and give the docs a chance to work. You'll be fine."

After they rounded the corner, Pete ran even faster until he reached the car. Once they were in the vehicle, he whipped off his shirt, tore it into strips, and made pressure bandages for Art's wounds. They would have to do for now. Then he drove like hell.

Several hours and several witnesses later, the New Haven Police roughly reconstructed the events on Church Street that night; however, the abducted woman was never officially identified, and the police never officially found any of the parties involved.

Exhausted, Pulcinella returned to his office for a last talk with Bonning. I.A.D. was still looking for him, but he would get to that tomorrow.

Bypassing his own desk, he headed into Bonning's office and collapsed in a comfortable chair. Tony knew he was near the threshold of his stress limitations, but there was business to conduct, and he was glad Bonning was there. The DEA man began, "I got some good news, Pooch."

"I could use some."

"We followed the papers Brown dropped off to a catcring service in Branford. Turned out that Pyne owns it, and it appears that the place serves as his main conduit for getting money out to the island. Now we know where the money is, and it'll lead us to the drugs."

Suddenly, Pulcinella felt his energy returning. "Oscar, that's great! How's Foster?"

"Still unconscious, but the doctors are getting more optimistic."

"That's the best thing I've heard all day."

Tony noted that Bonning's face was full of concern. He said, "You probably know it already, but I.A.D. wants to talk to you. The shoot was fine, but they got their papers to fill out. Anyway, don't worry about it tonight. Go home and be with your family."

Pulcinella closed his eyes and spoke in slow, soft tones. "You know, I hate bad cops. You take an oath, you ought to live by it. . . . I had to shoot a guy I drank beer with. I know his wife. . . . Damn, he was bad, but why'd he make me kill him?"

The DEA man sounded uncomfortable when he spoke. "Pooch, you've been a cop a long time. You know things don't always turn out like we plan, so we just have to take what we get. Now why don't you and I go out and have a beer? I'll bring you home afterwards."

"Sounds good to me."

Bonning grabbed his coat and the two men headed out the door.

Bonning's car was in a large parking garage near Yale–New Haven Hospital. It was a gray, concrete edifice with twisted mazes of spiraled access lanes and low-slung ceilings. As they approached the car, Tony thought about going up to check on Foster, but gave up on the idea fast. He'd seen enough of the hospital for one day.

The traffic in the garage was heavy because of a shift change at the hospital, so Tony paid little attention to the passing cars; but when they walked up to Bonning's car, the machine gun opened fire. Instinctively, Pulcinella dropped flat and pulled out his pistol. He felt shattered glass from Bonning's car showering him. To their rear, he saw muzzle flashes coming from the window of a station wagon. A shard of glass embedded itself in his forehead. He winced and felt blood filling his left eye. He aimed, and his revolver roared its defiance at the windows of the station wagon. Between his shots, he heard Bonning's automatic doing the same. Seconds later, the submachine gun fell silent and car tires squealed. Tony jumped to his feet and saw their attackers' car speeding down the exit ramp toward freedom.

Hoping there was a line of cars at the exit, Pulcinella took off in pursuit on foot with Bonning right behind him. Tony's depression had given way to anger; reloading as he went, he ran like a world championship was at stake. Second later, the decision to go on foot paid off. The station wagon was parked and empty at the end of the line by the exit. Hearing Bonning on his heels, he used a large pillar on the exit ramp for cover and peered into the station wagon. A dead man was slumped in the passenger seat with a bullet in his head, but otherwise it was empty. Looking towards the exit, he spotted another man limping, blood streaming down his leg. Two others, one with a sawed-off shotgun, were helping him hop over the ramp railing that they had to hurdle to get out of the garage and the line of fire. Almost academically, Tony noticed that his assailants had the look of street punks from the Hill Section. He pointed his gun at the three of them and yelled, "Give it up! Police!"

The man with the bad leg raised a magnum. Tony dropped to one knee and he and the man fired simultaneously. Through the smoke from his pistol, Tony saw his target take two in his chest and fall, but felt no damage to himself. The next man tried bringing his shotgun to bear, but before he could take aim, Bonning's automatic cut loose. The shotgunner spun around in a grisly pirouette, then fell sprawled upon the cement floor. The fourth member of the killing team had seen enough. Throwing his hands in the air, he screamed, "Don't shoot, man! Christ, don't shoot me!"

Tony already had the man in his sights and was tightening on the trigger. Then a hand slammed against the pistol, knocking it away from his intended target, and Bonning's voice rang firm in his ear saying, "It's over, Tony."

Pulcinella turned and gazed into Bonning's fiery eyes, then smiled and said, "Yeah, I guess it is."

Tony checked the two men on the floor and the gunner in the station wagon. All three were already dead. Bonning handcuffed the survivor while Tony walked to the parking attendant's booth to call for assistance. The man told him he had already made the call.

BOOK THREE

RETRIBUTION

Cry 'Havoc,' and let slip the dogs of war.

William Shakespeare

CHAPTER THIRTY-SIX

Monday, July 17, 1989—North Haven

For Tim, the night had become a nightmare. He had just finished helping Pete and Joe carry Art's battered body up from the Impala when Pete handed him Andrea's shoulder bag. Art regained consciousness briefly after they got him up the stairs, and with his feeble recounting and Pete's less than complete summarization, Tim now knew what had happened. But that didn't help. When Art lapsed back into unconsciousness, Tim staggered into the planning room and collapsed in his chair. Above all else, he had not wanted Andrea hurt, but now he knew she would be.

His mind stopped functioning. Images of Heather, Lisa, and Andrea swirled around in his head. The images intermingled and pointed accusing fingers that struck like spears at his soul. He thought back to the spring, when he had been getting ready to leave Germany and the army for college and a new life. He had had a future then, and he had been happy. Then the disaster had come. Forces had pushed him, and he had responded. He had fought back because he had wanted his future back, but he was losing all that mattered. The loss of Heather had destroyed his past, his roots, and his family; now the loss of Andrea threatened to take away his future.

Lost in these thoughts, he rested his head atop his arms upon the work desk. Suddenly, he felt strong hands pulling at his shoulders. Erect in the chair, he opened his eyes, spun around, and saw Pete Sayers's face just inches from his nose.

Pete's piercing gray eyes demanded that Tim focus and get himself back to the realities of the present. Slowly, he blinked and shook his head as Pete said, "Tim, I know it hurts. But dammit, listen to me. The last round hasn't been fought yet—unless you've given up! Whatever you're thinking, stop thinking it. Right now, we need calm. I know it's in you. Just look for it."

He heard Pete stop speaking, and, concentrating hard, made out the familiar shapes of the planning room. He was a professional. It had been tough before and he hadn't broken. Peter was right, he thought, this thing is not over—not while he still breathed. He focused on Pete Sayers's familiar form: the red hair, the big stomach, the calm, gray eyes that had seen nearly everything. In the familiarity, he found reassurance.

"OK, Pete," he said, "tell me what's happening."

Pete nodded. "Glad you're with us again. You've been sitting there for half an hour. Now here's what's going on: Stan's working on Art in a makeshift surgical area. I've called Wayne, Mac, Frank, and Paul in Vermont, and they should be here by midnight. As far as everything else goes, you already know the problems. There's a cop out there who knows we're up to something. . . ."

Tim interjected, "My read on that is that he's just guessing."

"Well, either way, Pyne definitely knows something's going on—and that's a big problem. But there is some good news. He doesn't know where this office is. If he did, his men would already be here. Good thing, too, since we have to stay here until morning—Stan says there's no way we can move Art before then. The question is: how long can Andrea hold out before she tells them?"

Tim's mind worked fast. He had a solution to that. "Pete, how soon could we be ready to move on the island?"

"I'd like to say tonight, but to be honest, there's no way we can be ready to move until tomorrow."

"OK, then we'll have to stall Pyne. If we don't, Andrea's going to be in bad shape, and they'll hit us here before we're ready. It's time we started turning this thing around." Standing up, he motioned in the direction of the front office and said, "Let's make a phone call."

* * *

Tim made himself comfortable at Andrea's desk. From their phone surveillance, he knew Pyne's number, and he dialed it. A woman's voice answered on the second ring: "Hello."

"I would like to speak to Michael Pyne, please."

"Might I ask who's calling?"

"Tell him it's an old soldier friend of his. I think he'll want to talk to me."

"Please hold." Moments later, she came back, "Mr. Pyne says you should call 555-7943 in ten minutes." Then the line went dead.

As instructed, Tim dialed the number ten minutes later, and Pyne's smooth liquid voice answered. "I thought I might hear from you."

"Is she OK?"

"She is quite well, but it is you I would really like to meet. I have no quarrel with her."

"Let me talk to her."

"Certainly. . . ."

Almost immediately, Andrea's voice came on the line. "Is it really you?"

"Yes," he said, "are you OK?"

"So far."

"Don't worry about anything. You'll be fine."

Pyne's voice came back on the line. "Of course she will. Now when can we meet? I've been looking forward to seeing you for some time."

"You can meet me only if I'm satisfied that she remains in good health."

"To be frank, I do not think you are in a position to bargain right now. You have until midnight tomorrow—that deadline applies to both of you."

"All right, I have some personal things to take care of. I'll call you. I'm warning you: whether or not we do business depends completely upon my associate's continued well-being."

The sound of laughter distorted Pyne's voice when he replied, "Don't wait too long."

Tim hung up. It wasn't good, he thought, but at least he had bought some time.

One hour after Tim's call, the men arrived from Vermont and Stan finished with his labors. The report on Art was positive—none of his vital organs had been hit and he would be fine, though he would be sore for a long time. With that news, Tim assembled all the men in the planning room, and standing before the chalkboard, he began. "The situation's changed and Pyne knows we're coming, so if anybody wants to back out now, feel free. Pyne gave me twenty-four hours from midnight to give myself up or he's doing Andrea. Now, I have to go after her, but that doesn't mean any of you men have to jeopardize yourselves further by staying in this thing. You all have fine careers and lives to go back to. I started this mess, and I'll finish it. . . ."

Interrupting, Wayne Murphy said, "Great speech, Tim." He paused as if to collect his thoughts. "But it's all bullshit. First of all, you can't do it by yourself. Second, I know I'm speaking for all these other crazy bastards when I say that none of us are going to leave Andrea on that island with assholes like Salka and Pyne—none of us. It's personal now."

Gonda began in a low voice, "Damn, I keep looking at the fucking door to the reception area. I keep expecting to see her." Gonda shook his head. Then he looked up at Tim, his eyes pools of black ice. Images of tombstones flashed briefly through Tim's mind. Gonda continued, "It ain't official yet, but Mike Pyne and Julie Salka are both dead men. Nothin's gonna change that."

Mac gazed absently at an unlit half-smoked cigar in his hands. "There's no decision to make, Tim. Pyne made it already. We're going." He turned to Gonda. "Damn, Joe, just like you I keep lookin' at that door and expectin' that damn woman to burst in to bum a light for another of her cigarettes. Hell, I can still smell her perfume in the place."

No one else said anything for a moment. No one had to.

Mac finally broke the silence: "Prepared or not, we're going in tomorrow night. Let's move on to the next problem. Without Art and Andrea, we're short a man on the island and a boat driver. We can live without the driver, but it would damn sure be nice to have another man on the ground."

Frank spoke up. "Nobody's going to like this, but I know where we can get somebody. It'll just depend on how much you want another guy. Bill Massey's in Massachusetts on vacation even as we speak, and I know he'd go for this."

Gonda laughed, "If you're talkin' about the same Bill Massey I know, you're fuckin' crazy. Massey'd mess up tyin' his own damn shoelaces. How the sonofabitch ever made it through Special Forces School, I'll never fuckin' know."

"Unfortunately," Frank responded, "I am, but he's pretty good with demo, and as long as we don't give him too much responsibility, he'll be all right."

Tim shrugged. "Anybody know anybody else?"

No one did, so he said, "Good, let's put it up for a vote."

Massey won the vote by a narrow margin. Frank and Joe left for a pay phone to call him in Massachusetts.

Mac stood, pulled out a fresh cigar, and said, "Gentlemen, if we're going to make our appointment, then we'd better get on it. We were going in tomorrow anyway, and just a few things have changed. It would be nice to have a finished plan."

The whole team worked at a frantic pace. In their favor, they already had a fair picture of what went on within Pyne's sanctuary. Photos suggested that there were between twenty-five and thirty men on the island who could be considered combatants. Known armaments ranged from pistols and shotguns to a collection of submachine guns. The guards themselves did not appear military-trained, but they were organized somewhat along those lines—within their ranks were supervisors who served as sergeants and lieutenants. Most of them were local "tough guys" brought in from the streets of New York or New Haven. Men like that were undisciplined and fought for money, not for each other. How they would react to a direct assault was, in Tim's mind, difficult to predict, but it was far better than going against disciplined, trained men who fought with conviction.

Still, there were some major negatives about the mission. They had done little with their weapons, and that bothered Tim. But he knew they were all Special Forces soldiers, and somewhere along the way, they had all already used the weapons. They would just have to go as they were. He was also worried about the Ingrams. Though fine weapons, they had one serious drawback—the barrel was extremely short. This made the gun more concealable, but when used on the range, it often proved to be more machine pistol than machine gun. Not an insurmountable problem, he thought, but some training time to work on accuracy would have been nice. The .45s, on the other hand, were weapons the detachment members used all the time, so he felt certain there would be no problems there. The SAWs would also probably be fine: Wayne and Joe were the designated SAW gunners and both had lots of experience.

He next checked with Paul on the demolitions. They had a case of C-4 plastic explosive in its 2½-pound block raw form. Tim picked up a block and looked it over. Years of training had made him very familiar with it. Though this batch was of French manufacture, it was identical to the American-made variety: white in color, sweet-smelling, and extremely stable. Paul had taken out nine blocks and was fashioning each into sliding charges complete with eight-second fuses and nonelectric firing systems. This way, he explained to Tim, each man would have a charge he could place anywhere the situation might warrant. To make them explode, he needed only to pull a pin on the fuse igniter and run a reasonable distance. But the safe might be a problem. They knew Pyne had to have one, but what kind it was remained a mystery; since Paul had no idea what model they might have to blow, they had to be ready for anything, so the demo expert planned to go in with twenty pounds of C-4. Once there, he and Pete would have to improvise. Most likely, Paul indicated to Tim, a circular-shaped charge of C-4 known as a donut charge positioned about the dial would suffice. Once he was finished with the C-4, he would turn to the dynamite, and for that they had a special purpose. Nothing extravagant was needed; they could simply set the detonator and load it on the boat in its case.

Tim asked him about the generator, and Paul smiled. Holding up a device so Tim could see it, he practically beamed with pride. Using two pounds of C-4, Paul had made a shape charge that would easily punch directly through several inches of armor, let alone the block of a generator. The device was as simple to manufacture as it was devastating. Paul had used an old soup can, filled it with explosive, and pressed a funnel into its one open end. Then he had punched a small hole into the steel at the back of the can so a blasting cap could be inserted to ignite the charge. What they had produced, Tim knew, was actually identical to the charge inside armor-piercing shells that tanks fired. When ignited, the funnel would be liquified into a narrow molten mass that would punch through the engine block and into the internal components. While the demo men might have had some doubts about the safe, they were confident that they would totally destroy the generator.

At 3:30 A.M., Tim called the entire team (minus Art, who rested) in for a briefing. Using the standard NATO operations order format familiar to them all, he began the briefing himself. Each of them had their weapons at the ready in case they were interrupted, and everyone sat around the sand table except Tim, who stood by the chalkboard. "OK, it's show time. You all basically know the mission, so I'll let Pete, our venerable S-2, get into the details of the revised situation." He motioned to Sayers.

Pete assumed Tim's place next to the chalkboard. His face looked calm, but Tim noticed that his heavy eyebrows were furrowed beneath his red hair. Beginning with what they knew, he filled the whole team in on the suspected strength and firepower of the enemy forces and finished with a summary of local police capabilities. "The Branford Police Department will most likely have two radio-equipped speedboats on patrol tonight. Four more will be standing by and will ferry additional officers if required. There is also a helicopter available, and it's on standby for rescue missions or if the weather is too foul for the boats. We now estimate that that chopper can be on our tails in about twenty minutes while the boats can be there in five. Coast Guard assistance is on call from New London. Any questions?" No one indicated that they had any, so Pete sat and Mac stood.

He had a yardstick, which he used as a pointer, in his right hand. "In case you don't know, I'll be giving the execution portion of the briefing. Now, we've split the group up into two teams. As a reminder I have put a list of what each of you have to bring in, and what your special duties will be once we get there. OK, here's how it's all going to work. Team A consists of Tim, Pete, Stan, Paul, Joe, and myself. Team B will be Wayne, Frank, and Bill Massey. We have split you for several reasons. First, we have two sites suitable for a landing." He indicated them both on the sand-table model of Robin Island.

Mac continued, "The first is on the north end next to the house, and the coastline there is both rocky and treed right to the water. It's patrolled lightly by a roving patrol. The primary guards are located as follows: two are in the gazebo on the southwestern corner where they can easily survey both the southern and eastern shores. There's one on each dock, and from there they have a great view of the north shore; another one sits on the back porch of the guest house—along with other bored off-duty guards—where he surveys the west shore. Meanwhile, there are another four or five guards walking on roving patrol. Much to our advantage, the east coast curves in in such a way that our boys in the gazebo and on the docks won't be able to see us land there. The same is true of the west shore on the northwest corner. This should allow us to hit both sides simultaneously—which is important, because the reaction forces are split between two locations: the guest cottage and the mansion. Team A lands next to the mansion with more men because they have the bigger job—they go after Pyne and the money, while Team B takes out the guest cottage. Because the success of the entire mission depends on Team A, they land first. The boat'll drop them off about five hundred meters out, circle the island, and drop Team B. Tim and Joe, because they have the most experience with scout swimming, will then swim to the landing site, clear it, and signal by placing a green light between their fins when they're satisfied it's safe. Once the rest of the team has landed, they will radio B to come in on their side, and Stan, who'll be driving the boat, will bring it in. While they're waiting for the call, B should be hiding in the shelter of the Pine Islands near the guest cottage. Let me get back to A now. Once everyone is ashore, Joe and I will head for the mansion and clear the immediate exterior of guards. Stan, you're responsible for Joe's SAW while he's in there."

Stan nodded and Mac went on. "Once the exterior's clear, the rest of us'll move in on the house. Because the woods behind the house are dense, and there's only one path that gives it access from the docks, we have no one field of fire we can use to keep it secure. To get around that we put Stan on the back with claymores and trip wires. While the rest of us are inside, Stan'll set up his boobytraps. Now, the house has three floors. Pyne's bedroom and the safe are on the second floor—according to the real-estate brochure. Paul, Joe, and I will come in through a rear door in the basement and clear the first floor. Because the front of the house offers us a great field of fire for the SAW—half the island can be covered from right there—Joe will set up his SAW in one of the front windows as soon as the downstairs area is clear."

Frank asked, "Why not use all five guys to clear the downstairs? I mean, what're Pete and Tim supposed to be doing while all this is going on?"

"We don't want more than three guys working the downstairs. Any more than that and they'd get in each other's way. Tim and Pete will wait on the basement stairs. Soon as it's all clear, they'll move up. Joe then sets up the SAW, and the remaining four split up into two teams: Tim with me and Paul with Pete. They'll go up the stairs, and split up. Tim and I'll take the third floor, and Pete and Paul'll take the second. As soon as everything is clear, Pete and Paul'll go to work on the safe and Tim and I'll secure 'em. Pyne should be dead in bed by then, so demo takes priority. Speaking of Pyne, whoever has the pleasure of doing the bastard let everyone else know. The same holds true for Salka and Rembard, who we heard on the phone telling Pyne he'd be there. That's what the radios are for. We can't leave that fuckin' island until we know those three bastards are toasted."

He stopped motioning with his pointer and looked directly at the men surrounding the sand table. "I want everybody to notice something—and it's important. If everything goes right, up to this point no damn noise has been made. Everything's been done using silenced weapons. No alarms ought to be sounding, and we've gone in soft. If it works out like that, then we should have just about won the battle before anybody knows we're there. If it don't work out like that, then we'll probably be in deep shit tryin' to fight about fifty angry armed assholes. Remember that and don't fuck up!"

Stan asked, "It seems like you've forgotten one big thing. What about the TV cameras? They're all over the damn island, and what if they found the squib?"

"If the XM-122 fails, then we'll just have to shoot them out from the boat, and hope for the best. I just hope they haven't found it.

"Now to Team B. As soon as we call on the radio and tell you we're in, you move to your landing site. Once you're in, Wayne moves with his SAW and plants it here." Mac pointed at a rock formation backed with trees next to the generator near the center of the island. "From there, the machine gun should have a field of fire wide enough to cover the main route from the docks and the guest cottage to the mansion. Then, once he has his site selected, he'll place the shape charge on the generator, run the det cord back to his position, and wait. One way or another, Team B, remember that you *must* take out that generator.

"Meanwhile, Massey and Frank'll move up to these trees next to the cottage, place a claymore facing the front door, and wait with a white phosphorous grenade and a frag ready to go.

"OK, here's the deal. The first serious noise ought to happen when that safe blows. After that, the bad guys are gonna start movin' in a hurry. As soon as they hear any explosions or shootin' from the direction of the house—or anywhere else on that goddamn island—Massey and Tim waste any guards outside the cottage, run up to the front, check to see if Andrea's in there, and throw grenades through the windows—one frag and one willie pete each. If that doesn't take care of everyone in there, it'll at least start a hell of a fire; that's what the white phosphorous grenades are for. As soon as you guys toss those grenades, haul ass back to the treeline. Simultaneously with Massey and Frank doin' their thing, Wayne blows the generator, then turns his SAW on the boats at the dock, and hoses them down. That ought to prevent anyone from leavin' too soon. Also at this time, Joe is free to cut loose and engage any targets in his field of fire.

"OK, now that the shit's flyin', as soon as Frank and Massey reach the trees, they wait until whoever is left in the cottage tries to leave, and they finish them with the claymore. Then, with all due haste, they run to Wayne's A.O. Now when they reach the path that runs past the generator to the docks, they'll be in Wayne's field of fire, so they'll have to use a password to get through. Wayne, you're gonna see all hell break loose around that guest cottage. As soon as you do, be alert to your buddies comin' through."

Wayne nodded.

Mac continued, "Once Frank and Massey get past Wayne, Frank'll stay with him and pull security, since we don't need Wayne gettin' popped from behind. Massey'll continue on to the house and back up Stan—who might well be in a whole world of hurt by the time Bill gets there. There's not much cover behind that house, and we don't know how many he'll have to take on."

Joe asked, "Why not have him set up in a back window?"

"Simple—no one window can cover the whole back. No, he'll just have to stay there and do his thing fast and mobile. It's the best way.

"OK, now up to this point—if everything's gone right—we've come in quiet, got set up, then all of a sudden shit flies from everywhere. The bad guys ought to be confused, 'cause it'll seem like there's a lot of us, and we're everywhere with a lot of firepower. They're gonna be looking for something to fix on, and it'll be the SAW's. They make a lotta noise and flash, so they'll attract the serious attention. That's fine, because it'll keep them busy with bullshit while we go on about what we're really there to do."

He took his pointer and pointed to the rear seaward corner of the house. "As soon as we have all the money bagged in waterproof bags, we'll toss them down from the second floor to this back corner. By radio, we'll call in Wayne and Frank. Now, if you haven't noticed it yet, the way this thing is set up, we start out all spread around; but at this point it's designed so we all collapse inward toward the house where we meet at that corner. That's our final rally point. From there, we go silent again and stick to the quiet Model 10s so whoever the hell is left to chase us doesn't know which direction we're going. Anyway, once we're together and everything's done, we go down to where the boat is waitin' at the same spot Team A came in. Movin' real fast, we then get on our tanks and fins and go through the exfil plan, which I'll brief you on later. For now, concentrate on actions at the objective. Know your job and everybody else's and be ready to put any necessary contingencies into effect. Among ourselves, we'll discuss contingency plans for as many things as we can think of that can go wrong." He paused for a moment and looked at the men seated in the room. "For now, D-Day is planned for tonight at midnight. That gives us about twenty hours to work out the final details. Now to our last problem—and this is a big one. Presently we have no idea where they're keeping Andrea, and I doubt if that'll change by tonight. That means that while our basic plan is fine, everyone has to remember that wherever she is, we have to find her, so look before you blast. As soon as somebody does find her, tell the rest of us on the radio. If you need help, we can redeploy to give you whatever you need. Gentlemen, we ain't leavin' the island without the girl. One last thing: if we ain't found Andrea and we find Pyne or Salka before her, sweat 'em before ya waste 'em. They'll know where the fuck she is even if nobody else does. Any questions?" Everyone remained silent. "Good, let me turn you over to Joe for the S-4 briefing."

Before he could resume his seat, Wayne Murphy spoke up. "Hold it, Mac, what about the police?"

Mac paused and regarded Murphy with a thoughtful look. "We think we've got something for that. You get filled in later. Meanwhile, concentrate on the actions at the objective."

Joe Gonda stood and replaced Mac by the chalkboard with the satisfied look of a man who was truly in his element. "OK, each man is goin' in heavy with firepower, light on everything else. We're going in to kick ass, not party—that comes later. The demo men already know what they're takin', and you know what we've got for individual equipment. All equipment gets wiped for fingerprints before we go, we all wear black-dyed surgical gloves, and everybody's absolutely sterile on infil. That means no wallets, no pictures of the wife and kids, and no jewelry. You're all already dive-trained, and your dive equipment's ready to go. Any problems or questions? Write your congressman. Next, Tim'll tell ya about commo."

Tim stood and replaced Joe. "Each radio has been tested, and they all work—for now. That doesn't guarantee they won't break exactly when you need them most. So each man's going in with a radio to provide lots of backups. Now they are 'water resistant.' That does not mean 'waterproof.' For that reason, we've made up special watertight bags for each man, and they'll all be double-bagged by infil. Also, so anybody listening can't tell what we're talking about, we've drawn up a code list made up of words you can use to mean certain things. See me after the meeting, and I'll give you yours. Get to work and start memorizing it tonight. By infil, it's got to be second nature or we'll get blown on the radio.

"Now to chain of command: I'm in overall command, next come Mac and Pete, and below that, we'll go by rank. On the B-Team, Wayne is in overall command until we link up. Any problems beyond that?"

He stood and looked at the men arrayed before him. "We've already drawn blood on this mission, and we're about to draw a lot more. There are a couple of points I'd like for you to keep in mind. First, we've said this before, but I'll point it out one last time: there will be no dead policemen on this. Everyone agrees with that?"

Almost in unison, the team nodded.

Tim continued, "If it comes to fighting cops, we lay down our weapons. Next, most everyone we find on that island will be combatants; however, Andie's there somewhere, and I'd appreciate it if you didn't shoot her. We'll all be wearing ski masks, so no one left alive will be able to ID us. That means if you're clearly dealing with a maid or a kid, or any kind of noncombatant, you can leave them alone. Finally, if any of us are wasted, the body has to come out. We leave anything behind, and we're all blown. I know this thing is difficult enough without conditions, but they're there anyway. Failure to follow them means we're just thieves, and frankly, I think we're a hell of a lot better than that. Good luck and thanks. Now get some rest."

CHAPTER THIRTY-SEVEN

Monday, July 17, 1989—New Haven

Marvin Dokes, known to his friends as the Axeman, was the sole survivor from the attempted Pulcinella hit. A street-level New Haven enforcer, he had a long record and a reputation for being "the baddest." More than anything else, though, the Axeman knew how to manipulate his way to safety no matter what the threat. That was why, Tony concluded, the Axeman, sitting tall, black, and serene next to his lawyer, looked like a man without a care. Even as Tony explained to him that being an accomplice to the attempted murder of two law-enforcement officials was a serious charge, Marvin simply studied the soundproofing on the walls. His face said that it was all irrelevant to him.

In frustration, Tony finally asked, "Do you hear what I'm trying to tell you?"

Unmoved, the Axeman continued studying the soundproofing for some moments while the detective's question lay unanswered. Finally, Dokes's head turned slowly toward his lawyer. "Man, they wastin' my mothafuckin' time. I ain't goin' to no jail."

Pulcinella saw furrows form on the public defender's forehead, and he repeated, "Mr. Dokes, you have committed a serious crime. . . ."

The Axeman slammed his fist on the table. "Man . . . don't say I committed no fuckin' crime, 'cause I ain't. Man say he want a cop dead. It's business. Ain't no crime. We don't fuck it up, we don't get caught. It's like a penalty in sports. Like holdin' in football. See, the man, I know he want somebody bigger than me. I ain't nobody . . . but I can give them somebody. Oh, yeah, a real major somebody—Mr. Michael Pyne himself. Then I don't go to no jail. Police gonna give me a medal, take me to the airport, and help me get a shiny new life someplace else."

Pulcinella was intrigued. The attorneys stepped in, and a deal was made. Then Tony listened intently to Dokes. And when he heard what Dokes knew, he smiled. Marvin was right. He would not go to jail.

Pulcinella hated allowing a man who tried to kill him to go free, but he had to admit it was worthwhile. Dokes had a friend, working as security on Robin Island, who said that Michael Pyne had just received a major drug shipment from South America and the whole thing was still sitting on the island, along with several months' worth of accumulated cash. As a bonus, Don DeFrancesco was scheduled to visit Pyne in his yacht that very afternoon; so Pulcinella figured he could implicate two of the East Coast drug network's leaders in one big bust. In Pulcinella's eyes, the trade was more than equitable. They placed the island under observation, so that, if the yacht did arrive, they could raid the place that night. If it came off, Tony figured it might well be the most spectacular headline in a long time.

Robin Island

Michael Pyne paced a small room in his dank basement with great frustration. In spite of all the men he had combing the city, the damned soldier was not dead yet. That, most likely, meant trouble with DeFrancesco coming, and Salka had gotten nothing from the Volente girl. They had to find Reardon, and she would have to tell them where he was because he doubted very much that the soldier would come to Robin Island of his own accord.

He gazed down at the girl. She looked bad. Unconscious now after a night-long beating, she lay prostrate upon the filthy cement. Yet, up to the very moment of her collapse, the defiance in her eyes had lived on. It was now nearly noon, and they knew nothing more than they had when they had brought her to the island; indeed, the only progress they had made was in the destruction of her body, now swollen and bruised to the point of the grotesque, except for her lovely face. That, he had told his men, had to be left alone in case it needed to be showcased for Reardon.

Salka, in a Hawaiian shirt, leaned against a wall. With his left arm in a sling and a sleepless night behind him, he looked both exhausted and uncomfortable.

Pyne wondered about the girl's endurance. Most people would have given up hours before, and the fact that she had not angered him even more. Where did the bitch get her strength? He reached down with his right hand, grabbed her long, matted hair, and slammed her head against the stone foundation, then watched impassively as a renewed flow of blood oozed from her already shattered shoulder. He did not comprehend such resistance. Somewhere inside her, he speculated, there must be hope. What was her hope? He wished he knew what Reardon was doing.

Softly, Pyne said, "Julian, we do not wish her dead yet. No, we need her alive, but obviously this woman's threshold for pain is higher than we planned. We must continue with our present treatment. I know she will break."

Salka's smile returned, and new vigor showed on his face. He nodded, then he asked, "Mr. Pyne, is there any way to stop DeFrancesco from coming? I mean, the timing don't seem right."

Pyne shook his head gravely. "That would be stupid. I will not have him criticizing the way I run my business. He wants to come tonight, and so he shall. We will just have to keep our security measures adequate. My concern is Reardon. Do you think it's really possible that he might attempt to rescue his sweetheart?"

"If he does, it'll be exactly what we've hoped for. Last count, I've got nearly fifty armed men on this island plus what DeFrancesco brings with him."

Pyne nodded.

Salka walked over to the prostrate girl, scooped her into his arms, and tossed her on a filthy bed against the wall. Pyne noticed Salka's limp again and wondered momentarily what had caused it. Internally, he shrugged. It did not matter, he decided. Limp or not, Salka was not one of the brightest men he had ever met, but he was fiercely loyal and utterly ruthless. "Julian," he said, "I want you to wait until the girl wakes, then I would like you to to finish this."

Salka smiled and whistled quietly to himself. For a moment, Pyne felt a modicum of sympathy for the girl.

New Haven

The plan was set. To prevent further security leaks, Bonning and Pulcinella would hold off until there was a report of a yacht pulling alongside the dock at Robin Island. Even then, once that report came in, they would wait until just before midnight to alert the men they needed for the arrests; if all went as planned, they would be on the island by 1 A.M.

Robin Island

When she awoke, Andrea had no idea what time it was, or sensation of anything except the most awful pain she had ever known. She tried to sit up, then felt powerful hands clamped on her naked shoulders lifting her. She opened her eyes. Julian Salka's face swam before her. Then she remembered where she was. She screamed. He laughed and tossed her back onto the floor. She looked at the face once again. He was huge and studied her with solemn eyes. He licked his lips and said ominously, "Where's Reardon?" She stared back at him and resolutely shook her head. His features tightened with rage and he lifted his hand. Looking up reflexively, she saw the leather sap in his hand. Andrea closed her eyes before the first blow crashed into her ribcage—she fell back into darkness after the tenth.

Branford

Round-faced, dark-haired, of average height, and awkward in his movements, Bill Massey arrived at the bus station that morning on time. He had a reputation for making stupid mistakes, but he was on the team now, so he was grudgingly accepted. Still, he made the others nervous, and they showed their distrust by briefing him again and again on the plan and asking him to repeat it. Tim wondered if they should have taken him at all. He was an element of uncertainty no one needed now, but they had to have the extra gun.

By early afternoon, the North Haven office was sterilized and the team had settled into the Branford beach house. They spent the remainder of the afternoon going over last-minute details and drilling Bill. The good news was that Art Simpson was vastly improved. He was over the shock, and his wounds had not been nearly as serious as they looked. Seeing him walking about, greeting the other men, Tim felt grateful. He knew Art was in no condition to go on the island, but he did have a special job for him that would only take forty-five minutes and not be at all strenuous.

Near the town dock, there was a small boat-rental service. Their selection largely consisted of rowboats, but the flagship of the fleet was a ten-foot-long sailboat with a small outboard. With a phone call, Frank reserved the ten-footer, and Wayne Murphy picked it up that afternoon. He and the boat arrived at the beach house at three. Now, Tim decided, everything was ready with the exception of a single detail, and he made sure that one was taken care of shortly after nine that evening.

Robin Island

Michael Pyne finally lost his temper when he arrived in the basement and saw Andrea. The shocking condition of the girl was one thing; however, though her pitiful appearance and her discomfort were not of concern to him, the fact that she now seemed useless as an information source was.

Outwardly, Pyne found that Andrea still looked very much as she had that morning. However, though she seemed conscious, her blank eyes simply stared sightlessly at the floor. To Pyne, it seemed that she now was mindless and spiritless, of no use at all. Huddled in the corner of her room as if for protection, her eyes remained open and her chest moved rhythmically as she breathed. Yet the picture as a whole was somehow vacant. He leaned over her, grabbed a handful of hair, and tilted her head upwards so he could look into her eyes. Red-rimmed and blank, they only stared without life at a point that did not exist. He reached out for her hand. It felt lifeless, and when he released it, it flopped as if dead onto the floor. Frustrated, he spat on the girl. Andrea Volente had never told them anything, but in the process, Pyne concluded, they had destroyed her. That brought him some satisfaction, but he would rather have had information. Staring at her face once more, he felt certain that hope and defiance would never again fill the green of her eyes.

He turned to Salka and found him examining his pointed shoes. Cautiously, and with a twinge of what was as close as Julian Salka could come to a conscience, he said, "I dunno, Mr. Pyne, uh . . . it's like she suddenly went blank. I used my sap on her and she just stared like she is now. Maybe I ought to just off the bitch." He looked furtively at his master for a response.

Pyne tensed and shook his head. Somewhere, he felt a band tightening about him. He looked once more at the girl huddled in the corner. "Damn," he said, "keep a guard on her. Maybe she'll come around. Don't kill her yet. We still might need her for Reardon. We can always get rid of her tomorrow. Meanwhile, dress her in something."

Salka nodded and Pyne left. He did not want to see the woman anymore. The sight of her made him ask himself things he would rather not have thought about.

* * *

Earlier that week, Frank had noticed a vacant, secluded house down the coast towards New Haven. A new outboard-equipped speedboat sat on sawhorses behind the house, and Wayne and Bill got there just after nine that night in the cigarette boat with a can of extra fuel. Their mission was to steal the speedboat.

At first, the engine proved difficult to start, but somehow Massey made it work, and they had the boat back by 10 P.M. On their way, they had to fight a fair swell, and the wind blew dark clouds swiftly past the moon.

Though Tim planned for the actual assault to take place just before midnight, movement to the target would commence at eleven. The scout-swim portion of the infiltration required more caution than speed, so they allowed extra time for it.

While Massey and Murphy were procuring the speedboat, they noticed that a large yacht had docked at Robin Island's long stone quay. Mac agreed with Tim that it must belong to Don DeFrancesco, and it meant there would be more guards on the island than they had expected. But Andrea was there, and whatever might face them, they were going in and nothing could change that. All the yacht caused Tim to do was to make a slight adjustment of the plan, which he did easily.

Tim stood before a window in the living room overlooking the ocean and glanced at his watch. It was already after ten P.M. There was little to do now, so he thought back over all the events that had brought him to this point. While doing this, he tried not to think of Andrea. He also tried to tell himself that they could not have moved any quicker. He even tried to believe that she was not in serious danger. In all these endeavors, he failed. The mission would go, but his instincts said that it was probably too late—and if it was, he knew it would also be too late for everything he had ever believed in and fought for. When things had gone well, when she was at his side, he had expected to feel an exultation as they went in for the hit. He was doing something in which he had an unshakable faith, but now that the climax was near, he felt only remorse. Then he realized that the time for making decisions had passed when Andrea was dragged into Salka's car. Maybe it had left him even earlier than that. The consequences, the morality, and the feasibility of it all had suddenly disappeared completely. By tomorrow morning, he thought, the mission would be done, and more people would be dead—and maybe he would be one of them. As he called the men into the living room, he just hoped that it was not too late for Andrea.

A small fire danced in the fireplace, and Tim moved to it and faced the men, their darkened faces illuminated by flickering flames. They now wore their dry suits. All the accoutrements of impending battle hung about them, and they looked fantastically unreal among the plush furniture.

Standing before his friends, he wondered momentarily what had brought them all there that night. Then he realized he already knew—they were there because their own code said they should be there. As men who hated peace and lived for combat, they survived through each other, and no matter what, they helped their own. Tim was one of their own, and he knew their bond was for life, and death.

He called for and got their attention, and they went over the plan one last time; after they were done, they moved toward the stolen speedboat waiting outside.

After wishing his friends luck, Art took to the sea first in the little rented sailboat with his carefully waterproofed bundle and radio. There was no lack of wind, but as soon as he left the beach, he realized he was in for a less than comfortable ride as the small boat bucked the rapidly growing swells in the dark waters. His wounds gave him intense pain, but he forced himself to ignore them. He had far more important things to consider, and he was glad for the chance to be part of the mission.

CHAPTER THIRTY-EIGHT

Tuesday, July 18, 1989—Robin Island

Fate favored the Green Berets with perfect weather that night. By the time they got into their boat, the full moon was long gone, the sky was pitch black, and the wind gusted at nearly twenty m.p.h. Scanning his surroundings, Tim could barely see the eight other men hooded in their black dry suits and polyester masks. As instructed, they pressed themselves against the deck of the small speedboat, clutching their carefully waterproofed bundles. Stan took the wheel, and the soft growl of the engine and the bucking of the deck indicated that they were on their way.

Every human being faces the thought that his or her own death may be near differently. Some find that their fear and emotions rise to tumultuous peaks they cannot control, and their panic becomes larger than themselves. These men usually die swiftly in combat. Others, though, are warriors who meet danger with calm. At the critical moment, their minds dismiss all thoughts of destiny and replace everyday concerns with total concentration on the task at hand. Common sensations are heightened and a clarity of concentration is achieved that makes them the most dangerous of all foes. It was the mindset ancient Sparta developed its entire culture to foster; it was the state the greatest of samurai warriors strove lifetimes to achieve, and it was the condition Tim Reardon entered aboard that pitching boat bound for Robin Island.

As the boat lurched ahead, Tim's thoughts of his past and his future dimmed. He was aware of the aquatic odor of the sea, the feel of the buffeting wind upon his body, and the taste of the salt spray cascading over the boat's gunwales. The night wrapped him like a blanket, and he became one of its creatures. He believed each man has a destiny that he must fulfill, but he no longer agonized over his own. His answers, he knew, would come before dawn.

Finally, he saw the dim outline of the island in the distance, so he peered over the side and watched Stan's course carefully. As instructed, Stan followed a circuitous route. Once they reached a carefully selected area devoid of silhouetting shoreside lights due east of Robin Island, he slowed the pitching boat. Nodding to Team B, Tim and four others slid over the side into the dark sea.

Gliding along silently, he found the water to be warm as he watched the boat whisper off into the darkness to the other side of the island where Stan would drop off Team B.

New Haven

Just before eleven, Bonning and Pulcinella sent out the alerts from their office. This time, Pulcinella was certain they had Michael Pyne, and, since the yacht had arrived earlier, hopefully he had Don DeFrancesco as well. He fingered the warrants in his coat pocket. They felt reassuring, and he was certain that on the island he would find not just Pyne and his cocaine, but records that would yield even more charges and arrests. They would go in at 1 A.M., and Robin Island would be covered with law-enforcement officials within minutes. He could already see the impressive headlines the morning papers would carry.

Robin Island

Art Simpson checked his watch, and at precisely one minute past midnight, he entered a code into the transmitter in his lap, then pressed the SEND switch. Seconds later, a mile away, powerful acid ate through an electric wire and darkness descended on the western half of Robin Island.

When the lights went out, Michael Pyne was reclining comfortably in the after stateroom of Don DeFrancesco's yacht, sipping a glass of the Don's specially blended Scotch malt. Loud and overweight, DeFrancesco had large eyes and larger jowls, and he seldom smiled. Earlier, DeFrancesco's middle-aged wife had been in the room serving clams and white wine, but once talk turned to business, she had departed at a flick of his hand. At the same time, DeFrancesco had sent Salka and his own messenger boy Nicotra out on deck as well.

But Jean Lockery, beautiful in a tight red dress with her ruby dangling between her breasts, remained. She and Pyne had been lovers in college and business associates ever since. Without Sean Whitworth's knowledge, she had been using the tycoon's financial empire to launder Pyne's dirty money for years. Because of the Reardon threat and the police surveillance, Ms. Lockery, a cautious woman, had refused to accept shipments of Pyne's money for several months. He had not argued because her financial genius was as vital to the continued success of his drug empire as was the violent strength of Julian Salka. Of course, he had not paid her during the period of inactivity. That was why she had taken a chance and come for the DeFrancesco meeting.

They had barely begun the meeting when a knock at the door interrupted them, and Salka burst in without waiting for an answer. "Mr. Pyne, the lights have gone out on the mansion side of the island, and our surveillance cameras are down."

Angered, Pyne said, "Julian, we are discussing something important. Just find out what the problem is and handle it." Then he had another thought. Just in case, he should take some precautions. "Hold it, Julian. Bring the girl down here to me."

Wordlessly, Salka shut the door.

Once back out on deck Salka moved quickly down the gangway, up the dock, and onto the shore below the mansion. Peering into the darkness to his right, he saw two figures he recognized as the two roving guards he had stationed on the desolate northwest corner of the island. Why are they here and not where they should be, he wondered? Then, looking to his left, he saw their reliefs approaching and understood. The first two had inched over because their relief was late. Angry, Salka motioned all four men to him, and after letting them know the extent of his displeasure, he took one guard with him and sent the other three back with instructions to keep a good watch.

The man who had thought his shift was over did not dare take his anger out on Salka, so he expressed it in another way. As he preceded the two replacements through the trees, he kicked and swore at the undergrowth as he stalked along the shore.

As soon as he saw the electricity go off, Tim motioned, and he and Joe left their equipment bundles with the other three men in the water and finned rapidly but smoothly to shore. Only their blackened faces broke the surface. Once in the shallows, Tim removed his fins in unison with Joe, and they slung them over their left wrists. Next, he pulled his silenced .45 from a waterproof bag attached to his weight belt, then lay half in and half out of the water next to Joe amidst the breakers and waited.

He heard the cursing and crashing before he actually spotted the guards, so he was ready when they came into view. With arms supported by a handy rock, Tim aimed carefully and sighted on the leader; he hoped Gonda could see which one he was aiming for. When he squeezed the trigger gently and deliberately, the soft *pfft* of the pistol nearly surprised him. The man dropped straight to the ground. Almost as if it was choreographed, the next guard went down simultaneously. Then he put his sights on the last sentry, but the efficient Gonda killed him before Tim could squeeze the trigger.

As Gonda covered him from the water, Tim quickly and silently checked each guard for signs of life. Finding none, he signaled his partner and the big man slid out of the water on amazingly light feet.

Scurrying up the bank, Tim moved stealthily through the trees and scouted his portion of the landing site. It was clear, so he made his way back to the shore. When he got there, he found Gonda already back and shooting out the lens of the camera overlooking their portion of the coast in case the electrical power returned. Tim set his fins on their side with heels joined and tips open in a ninety-degree angle on a strip of sand just above the waterline. Then he placed a glowing green chemlight between them to signal his companions waiting amidst the swells. Two minutes later, they too had arrived ashore and fanned out for further security. Tim keyed the mike on his radio and said, "The door is open, Bravo. The door is open, Bravo."

Wayne Murphy's voice came back, "Roger, Alpha." Team B was now headed in.

Tim then rapidly covered and uncovered the chemlight between the fins three times to let Stan know to bring in the boat. The noise of the wind made the engine inaudible, and the boat glided in uneventfully.

Tim helped Stan to beach the boat, and Stan reported that everything had looked fine when he had dropped off Team B. Then they concealed their scuba equipment and the dead guards in the bushes and joined the others securing the perimeter.

Stan took Joe's SAW. Tim gave the signal, and Mac and Joe moved up the hill to clear the exterior of the mansion. They reappeared almost immediately, and using a waving motion, signaled that it was clear.

Tim assembled the team at the rear of the mansion near a worn door they planned to use to gain entry. It was unlocked. According to their floor plan, the door led to some storage rooms and a staircase that would bring them up to the kitchen. He hoped no one was in the basement inside the door.

Salka cleaned up Andrea and took her down to his boss. She could walk, but she still seemed in shock and spiritless. He wished his boss would just get it over with and let him kill the bitch.

With the girl delivered, he and the guard slowly traced the electrical wire from the generator toward the house. He found the break behind the generator house where the wire left the protection of the tangled undergrowth and entered the ground. Salka did not need to use his flashlight, because the live wire was still sparking dangerously. But that did not bother him—the broken glass and scorched grass near the line did. Carefully avoiding the live wire, he dug in the dirt around the separation. There, partially damaged from the acid, he found a small green device with which he was not familiar. Nevertheless, he could tell it was military in appearance, proof enough that the lights had not gone out by accident. Shouting for the guard, he ran for the guest house to sound the alarm.

Wayne had patiently waited with Team B behind the Pine Islands for the signal to move, and when it finally came over his radio, he responded and led the others to the landing site. Detecting no guards—though earlier reconnaissance had indicated that patrols sometimes did pass through the area—they quickly slithered from the water and into the safety of the undergrowth. En route to the shore, Wayne had heard loud music and seen several off-duty guards lounging on the back porch of the guest cottage. Since there were far more men awake and enjoying themselves on that porch than he had in his team, he kept stealth uppermost in his mind as he positioned Bill and Frank in the treeline at the edge of the cottage. When he left, Bill was already aiming his claymore from the treeline, so it would devastate anyone coming out the front door.

Wayne's trip to his firing position proved easy, and the rock formation next to the generator was exactly as they had envisioned it. He set up his SAW quickly, then moved to the generator, placed the shaped charge, and unreeled the firing wire. Then he heard the sound of fast-moving feet to his rear, and fell prone. Lying motionless, he saw two men, one a giant, running recklessly in the direction of the cottage. That, he concluded, was an ominous sign. Still, he heard no shooting, so rather than stopping them, he quietly continued the wire-laying process. Less than a minute later, he had connected the wires to the blasting machine, so he settled behind the SAW and surveyed his field of fire. To his right, he dominated the entire area from the cottage through the tennis courts to the center of the island. To his left, he controlled the whole length of the path that led to the shore and the three boats at Pyne's small boat dock. His only worry was the trees to his rear. He hoped Frank got there fast to cover his backside. If they didn't, he knew it might not be long before it got shot off. Satisfied he had done all he could to get ready, he settled in to wait. He just hoped Bill and Frank stayed alert to whatever the hell was going on.

Tim cringed when the door opened with a squeak that sounded loud enough to wake the whole island, but he waved Joe, Mac, and Paul on anyway. He and Pete followed hard behind and covered their backs as they moved up the stairs and into the kitchen.

They made it without incident, so Tim signaled Pete and

they set about carefully checking the remainder of the basement. They found nothing in the cellar except a storage area and the monitors for the surveillance cameras outside. No one was manning the monitors, so he destroyed them without incident. That finished, he joined Pete, but they found nothing else remarkable, although one room made him curious. A moldy cubicle, it contained a chair, ropes, and a filthy, bloodstained bed. He couldn't help but wonder if it had been used as an interrogation room. And how recently.

Clearing those thoughts from his head, he joined Pete on the back stairs to wait for their signal to move up.

CHAPTER THIRTY-NINE

Tuesday, July 18, 1989—Robin Island

Frank was well concealed in high grass next to Massey when he saw Salka running towards the cottage. Unsure of what to do, he glanced at his fellow Green Beret, but found no guidance there. Darkness and the mask obscured Bill's face completely. Frank shook his head; his orders had been to wait until he heard firing. They had peered through the windows and seen no sign of Andrea, so they were ready but would wait.

He watched as Salka threw the front door open and charged inside; in his wake, activity erupted. The music abruptly stopped and shouting began. Seconds later, guards began to spill out the door, and Frank's doubts evaporated. Something was very wrong. He turned to Massey and passed his grenades hissing, "Shit! You throw the frags and I'll cover! Here's mine." Massey nodded. Frank took careful aim with his Model

10, and squeezed the trigger. Quiet muzzle flashes streaked out before him.

Three guards in his field of fire fell immediately, and the others milled in confusion. Panicked, they fired their pistols, rifles, and submachine guns wildly, blindly, and randomly. Then, one after another, Frank saw Bill Massey's four grenades arrive with brutal blasts and heard the generator explode viciously far to his right. The effect of the blasts was tremendous as the scene before the cottage became a tangle of terror and death. The guards Frank hadn't hit in front of the cottage were now an obscene pile of human parts, their remains splattered across the front of the building.

The shooting stopped, but Frank still heard cries from inside the cottage. Clearly, there were more men in there, but he surmised that the fate of their quicker friends had warned them of the potential consequences of venturing out. Frank decided it was time to show them it could get even worse. He squeezed the claymore clacker briskly, heard an explosion, and saw the side of the house shake as though struck by a flaming tornado. Now, the shouts from inside turned to screams.

Turning to Massey, he said, "Let's finish 'em, and get the hell out of here." He did not have to tell him how. Getting to their knees, each popped the pins on their white phosphorous grenades and threw them at the house. Not waiting to see the result, he grabbed Bill by the shoulder and, crouching low, they weaved in the direction of Wayne's SAW, which was singing its vicious ripping song in the distance. Midway there, Frank heard the blasts behind him, and, turning for just a second, he smiled. The wooden guest cottage was an inferno.

Reaching the path Wayne was covering, he shouted the password, heard an acknowledgment, and charged across to the safety of the bushes next to the now blazing generator shack with Massey following close behind.

Stan Radawicz heard the gunfire on the other end of the island and realized he had to move faster. He was just positioning the second of two claymores along the trail to the mansion when the firing had started, and he had not had the chance to get in position to deal with the boat. Shaking his head, he finished taping the second claymore tripwire and hurried the intervening fifty feet to the waterfront.

As he had anticipated, the bow of the yacht stretched to within just feet of the shoreline path. Now, he had to make certain that the boat never left.

He removed his sliding charge and two willie pete grenades from his day pack. Surveying the dock as he prepared, he saw people beginning to file off the boat towards the shore. Some were women, but most were armed men.

Using the darkness to cloak his movements, he stepped from the bushes carefully, and tossed the plastique onto the deck behind the bow railing, then dropped back behind a tree with his fingers in his ears. He knew the explosion would be a big one—and he was not disappointed. The blast was gargantuan and nearly ripped the bow off. Looking at the dock, he smiled. Where there had been calm, there was now chaos. Confused men blindly fired weapons at the shore, and people ran aimlessly.

The smoke rising from the bow served as cover, so he stood once more and threw his two willie pete grenades. Then he again ducked safely behind his tree as another fireball, even more devastating than the first, shot up from the bow in a towering pillar of flame. The wooden decks crackled and buckled in the severe heat. Stan smiled again—scratch one yacht.

Still, at least twenty men firing assorted weapons milled on the dock. He decided their forward progress needed to be slowed; so from behind his tree, he engaged them with his Model 10.

Perhaps it was the combination of the bright light from the burning bow and his suppressed weapon, but whatever the reason, his targets had great difficulty locating the precise direction of their attacker, and no bullets came his way. Delighted, he delivered a steady ration of short, well-controlled and well-aimed bursts at the leaders of the dock exodus. Finally, one man screamed and pointed in Stan's vicinity. Suddenly, heavy fire came from the dock toward his position.

Trained professionals know that the only way to engage a target with an automatic weapon is by using controlled bursts of fire, so Stan didn't worry when a hail of the opposition's bullets chewed up the leaves around him. He could see that most of them had some sort of submachine gun, maybe Uzis, but that they employed them like madmen. Instead of suppressing the Green Beret's fire, their wild shooting simply encouraged him to stay a few seconds longer. So, before his magazine was exhausted, he accounted for several more of the opposition. Then, satisfied the enemy was now completely disorganized, he began picking his way back through the woods to the rear of the mansion his friends needed him to secure.

The island was still quiet when Mac, finding the kitchen and dining room clear, halted his team outside the entrance to the living room, where a party was in progress. Joe and Paul positioned themselves at the edge of the door while Mac listened quietly to the laughter of men and women in the next room. Then he heard the gunfire coming from the opposite end of the island, and gave the signal to move. Paul and Joe exploded forward. He followed close behind and found a candle-illuminated room full of intoxicated men and women staring away from their attackers out the windows facing the guest cottage. In unison, the soldiers opened fire with their Model 10s and three men slumped to the carpet. Two other gunmen, seated with their backs to the door, saw their friends fall and scrambled from their chairs. Mac spotted one attempting to raise a pistol, but Joe took him easily, and he landed on the floor and lay silent next to his compatriots. The other guard attempted nothing—he simply stood and stared in intoxicated amazement. Paul, looking directly into his dazed eyes, squeezed the trigger, and saw that Pyne's man died still confused.

One man remained, partially hidden in a comfortable wingback in the center of the room. A very busty young woman in a black dress was squirming to get out of the chair. Upon a coffee table before the two sat a considerable mound of cocaine and a large water pipe. Four other women—all expensively clad and obviously as high as the men who had just died—sat about the room.

Mac pointed and silently waved for the women to exit the front door. The woman in the black dress suddenly raised a pistol Mac had not noticed. Mac fired, and the stream of bullets hammered her to the floor. He told Paul, "Frisk the others while Joe covers. If they're armed, kill them. If not, let them go."

Meanwhile, the form in the wingback tried desperately to

hide behind a large pillow. He yelled, "For Christ's sake, don't shoot. I'm not a part of this. I'm just a visitor."

Mac strode across the room and knocked the cushion aside. He stared at the man, then smiled—it was a face he had hoped for. Calmly, he activated his walkie-talkie and said, "Move one clear."

Receiving the signal, Tim and Pete came in fast. By this time, Paul had found the women unarmed, sent them out the front door, and moved to the base of the stairs where he took up security. Like the professional he was, Joe had jerked open a front-corner window, unslung the SAW he had retrieved from Stan, and was making ready to fire.

When Tim hustled in, Mac said, "Gentlemen, I'd like you to meet Mr. Rembard."

Rembard, his voice a desperate whisper, pleaded, "Look, I can make it worth your while. Just don't kill me—please don't!"

Tim moved slowly towards the attorney. "Stand up!" he said.

With shaking legs, Rembard did as instructed. Mac saw that Tim's blue eyes glowed like hot coals beneath his mask as he cradled his Model 10 almost casually and watched Rembard.

Hearing a noise behind him, Mac spun. He was too late. An armed man had burst down the stairs, but shots from Paul and Pete left him sprawled midway down.

Mac turned his attention back to Tim, who was still staring at the lawyer. Concerned about time, Mac pleaded, "Do him, buddy. We gotta move."

Tim paid him no heed. His eyes remained locked on Rembard's face. He asked, "What were you doing with her?"

"Who?"

"Andrea."

The attorney's hands shook badly. "She was downstairs . . . in the basement. We were up here partying—not hurting anyone."

"She's not there now. Where is she?"

"I don't know. Look, man, I'm sorry."

"What did they do to her?"

"I don't know—really! OK, I know Salka worked her over."

Tim peeled the mask back over his forehead. "Do you know me?"

Rembard's eyes widened. "My God! You're Reardon!"

Those were Rembard's last words—before he could continue, Tim nodded and squeezed the trigger on his Model 10, and the lawyer crumpled to the floor. Tim sauntered to the body, kicked it, then casually reported the lawyer dead on the radio.

Calmly, Tim replaced his mask and the empty magazine and moved toward the stairs. Mac followed him, and Paul and Pete fell in behind. They still had to clear the upper levels.

With the element of surprise long gone, the Green Berets drew instant gunfire when they reached the second floor. Paul slid in front of Mac and checked his corner. As he did, a bullet nicked his leg and he staggered backwards. Bursting in front of him, Mac spotted the gunman in a door down the corridor and returned fire. The man fell dead in the door. Behind him, he heard Tim and Pete handling their end, taking out more targets before they could return fire. Confident all was now well under control there, they began a systematic search of the rooms. They found several more women and herded them into the hallway, but Andrea was not among them. Paul remained to cover all of the women, though he said his leg was OK. Tim and Mac went to the third floor to search for more targets, but found the rooms unoccupied. Cursing the fact that neither Pyne nor Salka was there, Tim declared the house clear. Mac had Paul search and question the women, but they were unarmed and knew nothing of Andrea. Mac personally moved the women downstairs, where he found Gonda happily firing from his window. He let the women go out the front, and Joe told him that he had already taken the two guards on the gazebo. As Mac took up a position to secure Gonda, he hoped Pete worked fast with the explosive—they had already been there way too long.

CHAPTER FORTY

July 19, 1989—Branford

Pulcinella and Bonning got to the Branford Town Dock just in time to see the explosions and gunfire on Robin Island, and Tony gaped at the sight. Fires and flickering muzzle flashes raged across the island, and the spasmodic sounds of automatic weapons fire echoed over the water.

"Christ," Bonning said, "it reminds me of Tet '68. What the hell is that?"

Pulcinella shook his head. "I see it, but I don't believe it."

"How long before we have enough people to move?"

"Jesus, we'd need a battalion of infantry to walk into that. The way it stands now, we can probably have about twenty people ready to go in fifty minutes."

"All right, here's what we do." He turned to his subordinates and ordered, "Radio the Branford people and tell them to keep the fuck away from it. They can circle the island and observe, but they better not go in. Contact the Coast Guard and ask for backup to seal the area. This shit over there can't last forever, so as soon as everyone's together, and they got all the firepower they can find, we move. That should be in fifteen or twenty minutes at the latest. And radio one of those choppers to get in here and pick us up on the dock. Tell them to move it, we don't have time to drive to the airfield like we planned. This shit's a little out of hand right now." He opened up a stick of chewing gum, and with a fatalistic expression, put it in his mouth. Turning back to Tony, he said, "Jesus, I almost feel sorry for that scumbag Pyne."

Tony had reached into their car and had a mike in his hand. He looked quizzically at Bonning. "Really?"

Bonning smiled. "Well, it was only a fleeting thought."

Robin Island

Pandemonium greeted DeFrancesco's lieutenant and enforcer Nicotra on the dock when he emerged from the boat with Pyne and his Don. Forty or so people from the yacht had leapt for the dock to escape the flames—and what flames there were!

The mooring lines on the forward half of the yacht had already burned through, so the boat was gradually drifting seaward with nothing but its stern line to hold it fast. The fire had spread over the entire bow structure and was fast approaching the superstructure. The forward paint locker had already ignited, and as the fire reached the paint cans, they exploded in turn and spectacular sparks engulfed the hulk each time.

Meanwhile, a demoralized band huddled on the dock about Nicotra; and next to the burning bow, several lay dead or wounded. The few survivors did not stand for fear of being gunned down or hit by exploding pieces of the boat. Some had already jumped for the safety of the water.

Nicotra knew he had to get DeFrancesco off the dock immediately. Soon the flames would reach the yacht's fuel tanks, and when they exploded, the dock would become a death trap. He knew his boss could not swim, so he told Pyne and DeFrancesco that they would have to run, but first he had to organize an assault team.

Leaping from man to man and threatening certain death if they failed to cooperate, he soon had a force of fifteen reluctant armed men ready to charge the shore. He ignored the women on the dock, so many followed the others into the water—except for Jean Lockery. She had much to lose if Reardon won, so she armed herself and elected to remain with her associates.

Satisfied with his assault force, Nicotra turned his attention back to his boss. Pyne, he saw, was kneeling with his arm about the sick-looking woman Salka had brought, and the sight of him disgusted Nicotra. Pyne's hands shook, and his eyes were wild. He held a small automatic. Nicotra figured that armed, Pyne would probably be more danger to himself than to an enemy, but the enforcer really didn't care.

Conversely, DeFrancesco displayed no fear. An old enforcer himself, he understood death, and as a Don, he understood power. That gave him confidence, and he strode up and down among his men bellowing for them to fire at the shore.

With a great deal of effort, Nicotra moved his men forward. They began slowly, but when they realized fire was no longer coming from the shore, even the least enthusiastic ran for all he was worth. Soon, the exodus became a stampede. Unfortunately for Nicotra, the charge ended all their organization.

Disoriented, panicked, and trapped in unfamiliar surroundings, most of their so-called soldiers broke and ran in several directions. Some chose the path to the mansion. Others decided on the path leading past the small boat dock and the generators. Still others blindly milled about DeFrancesco hoping for some guidance. Nicotra cursed the night.

Julian Salka had problems of his own. He had been in front of the cottage when the fire and grenades had decimated the ranks of his men; it was only through pure luck that he had survived by leaping back through the doors when the grenades exploded. Once inside, he had attempted to organize those remaining into cohesive resistance, but that had been thwarted by the arrival of the white phosphorous. His shirt had caught fire, and after he had extinguished it, he and the few men he could convince to follow him had jumped from the back porch to the shallow water below.

Once there, he counted six men in good enough shape to do something. Mad with terror, the two other survivors in the house had run out the front door. The heavy thump of the distant machine gun told him their run had ended badly.

He led the remaining six, wading through the shallow water, to a point not far from Team B's infiltration area. From there, they ran through the trees towards the hammering machine gun. Salka already knew one thing—anyone raiding this island would almost certainly hit Pyne's safe. He no longer cared about the fate of his boss, but he did still care for the safe. He would have to swim off the island, but he figured on doing it with a bag of cash to see him through. He was going to get to that mansion, and he had six pawns he could sacrifice to do it.

* * *

In spite of a less-than-successful beginning, Team B fulfilled its function in the later stages of the mission extremely well. Wayne's shape charge had reduced the generator to a worthless mass of twisted metal, and a nearby fuel can had burst and sprayed burning fuel over the shed's wooden roof, which was now burning fiercely. The small boats he had engaged at the dock had settled to the bottom nicely as well. Anyone leaving Robin Island, he thought, would have to do it swimming. The machine gun had also wreaked havoc on the guest cottage, and when the two men had stumbled out the front door, one well-placed burst had put them down amidst the bodies on the front steps. A roving two-man patrol approaching from the south shore exhibited some military knowledge, attempting to fire and maneuver their way towards his gun, but like most of Pyne's staff, they had grossly overestimated the power of their automatic weapons. Their long bursts sounded impressive, but they were way off the mark, and Wayne took them easily by the tennis courts.

Frank and Bill appeared, shouting their running password as planned. Then Frank took up a position to secure the SAW's rear from threats from the dock and the mansion, while Massey moved on to support Stan. After a short lull following the yacht explosion, Wayne's headset came to life and Tim's voice came over with, "Three's complete—two in motion." That transmission indicated that Rembard had been terminated, and they were working on the safe.

Wayne had just sent Frank to his rear to scout for potential threats when he saw several figures on the path from the burning yacht. As he swung the gun to meet them, heavy fire erupted from the cover directly to his front. The attackers on the path joined the shooting. For the first time, Wayne had to put his head down and fire blindly.

The simultaneous assaults seemed like a coordinated attack to Wayne. In fact, they were not. Rather, Julian Salka had been blessed with some luck. The men charging the path were demoralized syndicate men fleeing the nightmare on the dock. Salka's luck came when he and his band just happened to engage the gun at the right moment.

On the opposite side of the island, five of DeFrancesco's men fleeing the dock charged up the mansion path. The two fastest men preceded their cohorts up the path by a good distance, and they were the only two killed when Stan's claymore exploded and hundreds of steel balls ripped them into oblivion. The trailing three retreated and rejoined Nicotra.

By the time the three deserters had returned, Nicotra was already leading the sweating Pyne, his hostage, DeFrancesco, and Jean Lockery to the safest point he could find, a protected spot in the trees just off the walk connecting the concrete dock with the small boat dock. Leaving them there with his most reliable man, Nicotra led the remaining five men diagonally through the trees toward the mansion.

Frank was about five meters to Wayne's rear when the firing erupted. Sensing danger, he turned to help his friend.

Seeing the heavy concentration of fire from the trees, Frank popped off his day pack and removed the sliding charge. He pulled the ring that activated the firing system with a jerk, and the smell of burning time fuse filled his nostrils. For Wayne's benefit, he yelled, "Fire in the hole!", pushed himself off his belly and gave a powerful heave. Seconds later the forest to their front shook with the concussion of the explosion. Wayne swung the gun back to engage the now prone men on the path while Frank, with Model 10 blazing, rose and charged past him to find whatever remained of the band in the foliage to their front.

Wayne had no trouble with the men in the open, and they died fast as they lay on the path.

When he swung his attention and his SAW back to Frank, he saw his friend reach the edge of the treeline and dive in. Suddenly, a pistol discharged, and Frank staggered and went down on his back. Wayne poured fire where he had seen the flash, and a cry told him he had hit his mark.

Frank was down but not finished. The bullet had struck his Model 10 and hammered the weapon into his stomach. In the weird shadows thrown by the burning generator shack, he saw two forms rise quietly from the ground to his front, but because of the intervening trees, he knew Wayne could not get a clear shot at them.

Frank tried to get up, but could not breathe. The MAC 10 had hit his solar plexus and taken his air. He ignored it. Rolling onto his belly, he flipped his shotgun up and pulled the trigger. With a deafening blast, the buckshot slammed the first form against a tree, but before Frank could pump and fire again, he saw a flash and heard a bang from the direction of the second target and felt his body jolt as something hot ripped painfully into his ribs. Resolute on ending the game, he finished jacking the new round in, pointed and fired a second time. To his relief, the man flopped backward and lay still on the ground.

Struggling for air and trying to ignore the pain in his chest, Frank rose to his feet. He knew he had to press on—lying stationary on the ground meant death in place, and retreating over the open area guaranteed bullets in the back—so he charged forward. Beyond the two dead from his shotgun, he found two more splayed in obscene positions from the blast of the sliding charge. From there he turned around and worked his way in the other direction. But as he breathed, he heard the sickening sucking sound that indicated his chest was nearly finished. Still, he stumbled on. Finally, he decided that it was over and the area was clear. Now, he had to get back to Wayne and get attention.

He turned back, but found himself moving slower with each step, and the trees about him began swimming. If he could just make it to Wayne, he knew he would be OK. Nearing the open path, he tried to yell the password but his voice rasped. Suddenly, he saw a hand thrust up from beneath some piled leaves, and a knife entered his stomach. Reflexively, he threw his weight back from the blade and fell to the ground.

The spinning in his head increased, but in the wildly turning panorama he saw a form rising in the darkness. Feeling his strength ebbing fast, he raised his shotgun and squeezed the trigger. He heard the bang and saw the flash; then the gun flew from his hand.

The shotgun landed next to Frank's head. By the time it came to rest on the forest floor, so had Frank's spirit.

In the mansion, Tim anxiously followed the progress of the explosives men and worried about Andrea. Though the situation with the safe still looked under control, no one had reported finding her, and that worried him. Restless, he went down to the first floor to check on Gonda. The big man wore a long smile because he had a terrific field of fire across the mansion's front lawn—the guards who had been on duty on the south side of the island had attempted to reach Pyne's house, but Joe had gunned them down with alacrity. Seeing Tim coming down the stairs, he yelled, "God! This is a beautiful weapon!"

Mac, still covering Gonda's rear, shook his head, and Tim grinned in spite of himself, then moved back upstairs. The safe Pete had to contend with was a full-sized floor-to-ceiling walk-in model. But, with quiet efficiency, Pete and Paul placed their donut charge around the locking mechanism and prepared to give it a try. Shooting Tim a thumbs-up signal, Pete pulled the fuse igniter, and all three men sprinted to the opposite end of the house.

Tim had his hands over his ears, but the powerful roar in the confined space still staggered him and shook the mansion's foundations. Even before the dust settled, Pete took off running to check the safe, with Paul limping right behind him. When Tim caught up, his friends swung the door open. Then they smiled in the satisfied way only explosives men can when their work is successful.

Tim followed Pete into the safe, and what he found there caused him to stop. He had expected a lot of money, but the shelves on the right side contained more bills, neatly counted and organized by denomination, than he had ever seen in any one place. On the left side, in plastic bags sorted for easy measurement, were the drugs—a junkie's dream. Two large bales of marijuana lay stacked like hay in a barn upon the floor. On the shelves sat bags of other substances. Not being of the drug culture, the men couldn't identify most of the chemicals, but Tim stared at the seat of Pyne's power, momentarily mesmerized.

Mac stepped into the safe to help load the money, and they each took large waterproof bags from their day packs for just that purpose. Tim unslung his pack and gave it to Pete, then said, "OK, fill these bags with cash and throw them out back like we planned. After that, let's make a statement. Take all the dope you can carry outside, toss it in a pile and burn it. Good luck, I've got other business."

Before any of them could respond, he was gone.

* * *

Though Julian Salka had positioned his men across from the machine gun, he had not stayed among them. When all the shooting started, he used the commotion and the momentary suppression of the machine gun to work his way across the path and into the cover of the trees. He now had a clear route to the mansion and, he hoped, the money in Pyne's safe. Patiently, he moved in that direction as noiselessly as possible.

Up to this point, Stan and Bill had had an easy time of it. The only sign of trouble had come when the second claymore had erupted. Nevertheless, they both had strong mutually supporting concealed firing positions in the foliage behind the mansion—Stan on the north corner and Bill on the south. Then Nicotra struck from the south.

Massey heard them before he saw them as the cracks and snaps in the undergrowth grew in intensity and volume. Then he got a target. Remaining low, three figures slipped out from the trees to the side of the house and moved in a half crouch along the edge of the building towards the front door.

Several things then happened in rapid succession. Bill engaged the three he could see with two effective bursts, but the third reacted with uncharacteristic effectiveness and dove back safely for cover while his companions absorbed the bullets. Then he heard footsteps to his rear and spun, but as soon as Massey saw the man, he knew it was too late. A stream of 9mm bullets riddled his chest, and he died instantly.

The situation also deteriorated on Stan's corner of the house after he saw Bill go down. Suddenly, accurate fire cut the leaves around him. He attempted to return fire, but his Ingram jammed. Taking the time to clear the malfunction, he knew, guaranteed death, so he broke cover and rolled toward his assailant while attempting to bring his shotgun to bear—but the weapon refused to come free. Looking down, he found its sling hopelessly entangled with that of the Model 10. As he rolled, another man stepped from the bush near where Bill lay, and pistol bullets sprayed dirt in Stan's face. Giving up on the shotgun, he jerked his .45 out of his breakaway shoulder holster and threw an instinctive shot in the direction of the pistol fire. It caught the stationary man's leg and he went down. Stan had now rolled past the corner of the house and the unseen enemy on the path could not observe him. He reholstered the .45, freed the shotgun, and snapped a quick shot around the corner. Jacking a new shell in the chamber as he went, he dove aggressively at the open ground he had just left and fired instinctively again. His first blast caught the man with the leg wound full in the face, but the man on the path had disappeared. Cursing, Stan snapped off a shell in that general direction anyway and jumped for the treeline.

Now in a better concealed position, he heard the other man moving through the undergrowth in his direction. Unfortunately, the dark foliage afforded him no view of his assailant, so he waited, straining his ears. He heard leaves shuffling. Then the sounds came closer. The man, he decided, was trying to be careful, but knew nothing of moving in forests. Finally, Stan judged the target close enough to step on him, and springing to his feet, he pumped two shots at the sound. Stunned, Salvatore Nicotra fell back against a tree and stared in disbelief at what had been his chest as he toppled onto a nearby bush.

Tim arrived downstairs just as the firing outside began. Gonda signalled that he was going to move and help them, but Tim waved him back. They needed him to remain behind his SAW. Tim checked out the side window. At first, he saw and heard nothing. Then scraping noises came from the front porch.

The syndicate man concealed in the dead zone provided by the porch was not brave. Rather, he had paused in a temporary sanctuary against the wall because he was too scared to go on. Previously, most of his acts of violence had been inflicted on the defenseless, but these demons could defend themselves very well. His problem was that he knew that Nicotra lurked somewhere behind him and would kill him if he failed. Slowly, he crawled forward until he reached the front steps. Easing his head up, he saw nothing of the killers he knew surely waited inside, so, hoping for the best, he gathered what fortitude he had and charged.

Tim heard the footsteps and had his MAC 10 raised and ready to fire as the man leapt through the front door. But instead of shooting, when the man stopped and pointed his pistol, Tim laughed, and he heard Gonda join him. Tim watched with a patient smile as DeFrancesco's thug tried to pull his trigger. Nothing happened.

Pointing his Model 10 at him leisurely, Tim approached his former assailant, and said, "Your weapon's empty, shithead. Look at your slide."

Slowly, the man's eyes lowered to the pistol in his wavering hands. His slide was locked back. He realized he had fired all his bullets back at the dock.

Tim stood just out of arm's reach with his submachine gun pointed at his enemy's head. He motioned for him to get down on his knees, and the hired gun did as instructed.

Tim said, "Dumb ass, you got one chance to live through the night. Where is Michael Pyne?"

Seeing the chance to survive, he could not talk fast enough.

When Tim finished questioning his captive, Mac radioed Wayne and told him to move to their final rally point at the rear of the house. Stan indicated that the rear was clear, so the two demo men and Mac threw their heavy bags out of the back window on the north corner of the mansion.

Sitting silently amidst the foliage behind the mansion, Julian Salka had observed Nicotra's abortive attempt to storm the mansion. The rout had been enough to convince him that he would have little chance of getting to the safe alive against men such as these. Still, he had patience, and when he saw the bags tumbling down from the windows, he smiled and awaited his opportunity. It came when a hulking man carrying a heavy machine gun rounded the corner of the house, grabbed some bags, and moved off through the trees toward the shore. Still smiling, Salka cautiously shadowed the large form through the undergrowth. Taking out all of them at once was too much to expect, he thought, but killing just one of the bastards would be easy. He would find the others later.

CHAPTER FORTY-ONE

Branford

As the gunfire grew more sporadic, the crowd gathered on the town dock could tell that the battle was mostly over—though fires still burned across the island. Pulcinella turned to Bonning and asked, "Well, we ready to see what's left?"

Standing transfixed, Bonning still gazed out to sea. Finally, he broke from his reverie, turned to Pulcinella, and said, "Tony, there're going to be headlines about this tomorrow. It's just that they won't be exactly what we'd planned. Fuck it, let's go see what the hell happened out there."

Slowly, the two began walking towards the helicopter waiting at the end of the dock.

Robin Island

It had been quiet in Wayne's sector for at least two minutes—though he had heard the shooting at the back of the mansion. Once that had ceased, a heavy stillness fell. It was as if even the forces of nature had paused all sound and movement—save for those of the wind and the flames—in response to the actions of man.

Relieved when the call came to fall back, he answered quickly. He badly wanted to know what had happened to Frank, but had remained at his firing position as instructed. Now he could find his friend. Carrying the SAW and staying low, he moved quickly across the path, and headed for where he had last seen Frank and heard the shotgun blast. Frank, he knew, must be dead—if he was not, he would have returned—but he hoped that whoever had done it was still there.

The Wyoming rancher was truly at his best in the forest, and he located his friend fast, but what he found made his heart skip a beat. Even from several yards away, he could see that Frank had been disemboweled. Now where was the bastard who had done the cutting? Cautiously, he approached the body in a low but well-balanced crouch. He knew someone had to be there somewhere. There, a pile of leaves—black earth around it. On cat's feet, he glided through the brambles and branches until he stood near the pile, then he kicked.

The pile groaned, then in a flurry of leaves, a figure rolled into the open to avoid a second blow, but it was a feeble gesture. Wayne could see that Frank's shotgun blast had already hurt him badly. His legs were honeycombed with small buckshot wounds. Now the man stopped rolling and attempted to get up into a sitting position. It was to no avail. Before he finished the movement, Wayne killed him quietly with a single .45 caliber bullet through the heart. Still, this was one Wayne wanted to be certain of, so he squatted to feel for a pulse. There was none. Next, he pivoted, reached out for Frank's body, gently hefted it over his shoulder, and set out in the direction of his friends at the rear of the mansion.

When Wayne reached the back corner of the house, he found Mac and Pete waiting next to an immense pile of drugs in plastic bags. Solemnly laying Frank's body on the ground, he asked Mac what the drug pile was about.

Mac looked sadly at Frank's body and said, "Tim's idea—kind of a statement for the police when they get here. Stan went to get some gas, and we're gonna torch this thing."

Wayne nodded and asked, "So where is everyone?"

"Bill's had it. Joe is waitin' down at the boat with some of the money, Paul just left with more money, and Tim's gone to find Pyne and Andrea." He shook his head in exasperation. "We went through these fuckin' assholes like nothin', but all we found was fuckin' Rembard! We still got to find Pyne, Salka, and Andrea. We wanted to go with Tim, but he wouldn't let us. He told us to leave two dive-equipment bundles by the shore and get the hell off the island before the cops got us. It ain't right, but it's what he wanted, so I guess we ought to do it."

Wayne said, "Bullshit, we started this as a team, and we're going to finish it as a team. He's not going to handle this one by himself. Take the SAW and Frank down to the boat, and leave out a third set of dive gear. I'm going to find the silly bastard. Which way'd he go?"

Mac told him what they had found out from their prisoner, and Wayne passed him the SAW.

After pausing, Mac went on to say, "It don't matter now. To make this exfil come off right, we've got to wait for the cops anyway. Timing's everything—but hurry! I bet they're comin' now."

Wayne nodded and silently disappeared into the dark shadows of the foliage. As he did, he heard a helicopter start up in the distance.

Down by the shore, Joe Gonda positioned the two corpses. Mac had brought Frank and Bill's bodies down, then returned to the mansion to build the drug fire, and Joe placed them next to the gunwales of the boat and lashed them in place. Satisfied they were just right, he laid a bag of money in the stern, checked to be sure that the firecrackers were all dry, and checked the fuse on the case of dynamite positioned between the corpses. As a last touch, he pulled two mannequins, each also rigged with explosive, off the deck and placed one in the driver's seat and another in the stern.

Suddenly, he stopped what he was doing. He sensed something. Trying to appear as relaxed as possible, he positioned his SAW across the mannequin's lap and slowly stepped off the boat onto the shore. His eyes surveyed the brush before him, and his ears strained to hear a sound. Then, he spotted it. A navigation light flashing in the distance glinted off something metallic in the foliage to his left. It might be nothing, but instincts and years of conditioning told him otherwise. That left him with a problem. He was in the open, and if he fired wildly into the brush and missed, he would be an easy target. No, he had to get close enough to make sure of his target, and he would have to make the first move. As casually as he could, he sauntered towards a point just to the right of where he had seen the glint of steel.

Just feet from the foliage, like a black jaguar on the attack, he leapt into the brush while pulling his .45 for instant use. Then his luck turned bad. The .45 caught on a tree branch as he was withdrawing it, and he felt it wrench from his fingers. Almost simultaneously, his body slammed into whoever was before him in the brush; and when he landed, a sharp object that felt like a rock sliced brutally into his right shoulder. He had no time then to worry about the injury. The man he had knocked backwards scrambled to get to his feet, and Joe Gonda saw a gun in his right hand. Pivoting on his good arm, Gonda threw a brutal kick at the weapon. The blow landed true, and he heard the weapon fall into the brambles on the forest floor.

Letting the momentum of his kick carry him, Gonda spun to his feet and turned to his assailant. He came face to face with Julian Salka, and his size made even Gonda pause. The giant was smiling, and he held a long double-edged fighting knife. With lightning reflexes, Gonda pulled his own knife out and began circling his enemy.

Still smiling, Salka asked, "So you think you're bad, fat man?"

"Bad enough, cocksucker."

Salka lunged with his knife. Gonda easily side-stepped the lunge and thrust for Salka's exposed stomach, but Salka grabbed Joe's wrist with his free hand. Out of the corner of his eye, Joe could see the blade slicing towards his abdomen. The injury to his shoulder hampered his movement, but he still managed to deflect the thrust with his arm, and the knife point sliced into the radio strapped to his belt.

Since he had just one good arm, Joe knew he had to break free from Salka's grip. To do that, he had to let his knife slide from his fingers. Then, by simultaneously swinging his weight under the giant and jerking his arm back, he tossed Salka over his head and against a tree to his rear. Still on his feet, Gonda followed the toss with a brutal kick to the prostrate man's face. It landed squarely. Gonda felt bones break and heard a cry from the giant. In response, Salka rolled towards Gonda's feet. Joe tried to jump away, but he was still off balance from the kick. He fell backwards and the enforcer rolled on top of him. Salka had lost his knife, but before Joe could react, he felt powerful hands clamped about his neck. Salka hissed, "Who's bad now, motherfucker?"

Joe knew he couldn't break the grip with only one hand. He had flexed the muscles in his neck to try to save his windpipe, but he felt an awful pressure on his throat. He knew he would be dead in seconds. Mustering all his remaining strength, he arched his back violently and drove his knee up into Salka's crotch. As the knee made contact, he felt the grip loosen. Given that opportunity, he drove his good hand hard into Salka's abdomen, and pushed the giant off him.

Rolling to his feet quickly, Gonda spun towards the enforcer and saw that the big man was still on one knee. Instinctively, he went for another kick to the head, but this time, Salka intercepted his foot in mid-flight. Caught with one leg in the air, Gonda threw his weight backwards to break away from the giant and was successful, but he piled violently into the same tree he had thrown the giant against earlier. Looking up, he saw Salka had regained his feet already. To meet the rush Gonda figured must come, he placed his good hand on the ground to lever himself up. Then his luck changed for the better. As his hand touched the ground, he felt Salka's lost knife and grabbed it. Salka charged like a wounded bear. In one motion, Gonda rolled onto his bad shoulder and threw the knife at the giant's midriff. Its flight was true, and the enforcer stopped in mid-stride and looked down at his stomach in shock. The handle of his own fighting knife was protruding from a point just above his navel. Slowly, like an avalanche in slow motion, the giant sank to his knees, then fell onto his side.

Joe moved quickly to the spot in the brush where he had lost his .45, and he recovered it. Once it was securely in his grasp, he walked slowly to where Salka lay. Julian Salka's massive head turned upwards and for a moment, his eyes met Gonda's. In a weak voice, he said, "Help me."

Looking straight into Salka's face, Gonda replied, "I'll help you go to fuckin' hell, asshole."

The soft *pfft* of the silenced .45 did not sound impressive, but when the bullet hit his eye socket, Salka's head jerked back, and a stream of blood darkened the weeds beneath him.

Satisfied, Gonda turned and walked back to the boat just as Stan and Paul appeared with bags of money.

Gonda told them that he had finished Salka, and Stan reported it on his radio. Joe looked back at the boat. Everything on the boat appeared ready, so he motioned for Stan to don his dive equipment and prepare to pilot the boat. Meanwhile, he donned his own equipment and took up a position in the stern with his SAW at the ready. Seconds later, the rest of the team, minus Tim and Wayne, showed up; and Gonda gave the "thumbs-up" signal. Mac answered it, and they put on their scuba equipment. Always the professional, Gonda chose not to tell them then how Salka had died. He knew there would be time for that later when the job was done.

For the first time in his life, Michael Pyne knew true fear. The shooting had stopped, but the silence around him seemed alive with menace. He knew Reardon was somewhere, hunting him. To protect himself, he sat on the forest floor with his back against a tree. He draped Andrea across his lap and pointed his pistol at her head. He noticed her eyes still looked dead. He wished Salka was with him, but he'd have to settle for Nicotra's man. Then he heard the sound of a helicopter and wondered if maybe Reardon was leaving.

Pyne's eyes flicked to DeFrancesco. How could the fat man just sit there next to Jean Lockery and remain so impassive? Pyne finally broke the silence. "The shooting's stopped. Maybe we ought to go see what we can do to help. Could be they left on that chopper we heard."

DeFrancesco's voice floated softly across the clearing. "Shut up, you idiot! That helicopter didn't take off, it landed."

As DeFrancesco's words faded onto the wind, a soft clicking sound replaced it. The guard fired his pistol into the ground and fell dead. A dark figure rose from the forest floor and stepped forward. Pyne shrunk behind the girl in his lap.

The apparition spoke slowly. "Good evening, Mr. Pyne. Nice to see you again, Ms. Lockery." Swinging his weapon towards DeFrancesco, he added, "And as for you, sir, I am afraid we have not been introduced. But first, please let me tell you that I am the man responsible for this evening's festivities, and I hope you enjoyed our affair." He peeled the black mask off his face and let it fall to the forest floor. "My name is Tim Reardon, and I believe you have been expecting me, Mr. Pyne."

Tim watched the responses with amusement. Pyne sucked in

his breath and held it. While he seemed incapable of forming a coherent answer, Ms. Lockery recovered quickly. "Tim! Thank God you came! Somehow these monsters found out I was funneling you money, and kidnapped me. They've been holding me hostage!" She began sliding her back slowly up the tree she had been propped against.

Tim stopped the action short. "Sit!" he commanded.

She sat.

He continued, "I'm not quite sure how, but I know you're part of this. Maybe your friend Mike can fill me in." He pointed his Model 10 at Pyne's forehead. "Mike, you've turned out to be the biggest pain in the ass I've ever had. Believe me, killing you would be a pleasure. In fact, I wish I could do it more than once. Perhaps you can live yet, but you're going to have to do two things. First, release Andrea. Then, tell me the whole deal," he smiled, "and I won't kill you. I understand you read my personnel file. That means you know I won't miss when I pull this trigger. I'm counting to three, asshole! One . . ."

The broken Pyne released Andrea fast, and as she slid to the ground, Tim felt his heart miss a beat. Slowly, she sat up and placed her palms down on the forest floor, but her head drooped, and Tim could not see her face behind the long strands of hair. He knelt next to her; and up close, he could see enough to comprehend her destruction. He looked at Pyne. "Talk! Before I change my mind!"

And talk he did. "Jean does the money. The old man trusts her with everything, and once she got in trouble with a shortfall. You know—bad investments her boss didn't know she made. We knew each other in college, so she contacted me for help, and I fixed her problem. She's been helping us by cleaning our money up ever since. . . ."

A voice behind Tim hissed, "Shut up!" He began turning, but the voice came again. "You don't move, motherfucker!" Tim recognized the voice, and his heart sank. The voice said, "Lose the gun, now!"

Tim tossed his Model 10 in Pyne's direction, where it landed amidst a pile of pine needles.

Emerging from the darkness behind him, he saw a glistening bald pate, and rows of gold necklaces. Ronny. Behind Ronny came another large, dark-haired man he did not know. Both had pistols pointed at him.

The three figures on the ground now stood and Ronny said, "Mr. Pyne, I was just comin' out with my friend Mecro from the shore when I seen what was goin' on, so I parked my boat over by the guest cottage. Why don't we do this guy and get the fuck outta here—the cops're comin'. Uh, you and Mr. DeFrancesco gonna remember who it was got you outta this, right?"

Pyne grinned hysterically. Waving his pistol at Tim, he said, "So, Mr. Reardon, I win in the end. You have cost me much, and you will die painfully."

Tim stared hard into his eyes. Somehow, he would kill Michael Pyne. In preparation, he tensed his legs for the leap.

"No, I will give this pleasure to Mecro. Blow his balls off!"

Mecro stepped before Tim and placed his pistol against Tim's crotch. Tim tensed for a last desperate lunge at Pyne.

He never had to make it. Instead, there was another clicking noise, and Mecro staggered and fell. Tim dove for the ground, whipped his .45 from its holster, and, still rolling, he saw DeFrancesco's pistol pointed at his chest. Tim fired and the big man toppled. Too late, he saw Ms. Lockery's pistol aimed at his head and resigned himself to the bullet he knew must come. But with a fantastic twist, her body spun and she, too, lay dead. Ronny vanished, leaving only the sound of breaking branches as he ran; but Pyne, having lost his pistol, lay prone, his eyes wide with fear.

Tim stood, pointed his .45 at Pyne, and saw Wayne Murphy stepping from the shadows. "Tim, we've got to get the hell out of here. Listen!"

In the distance, racing engines approached from the sea. Tim replied, "Yeah, I hear them. Thanks for doing Mecro before he did me."

Softly, Murphy replied, "Tim, I took the woman, but I got here too late for the other guy. Look."

Tim's eyes followed Murphy's hand motion, and he saw Andrea slumped against the tree where Pyne had been sitting. Her face distorted with hatred and rage, she held Tim's Model 10 pointed at Michael Pyne.

Murphy said, "Tim, I think the chopper that landed was cops, and I'm sure the boats I'm hearing are."

Tim straddled Pyne, pulled him to his feet by his hair, placed the barrel of his .45 under the drug merchant's chin and said, "Last chance for the deal, asshole. Why did you kill Heather?"

Voice strained, he responded, "We bought a cop, two detectives found out, so we executed them. The girl saw it, so she had to die. She would have screwed up everything if she talked. Salka did her."

"What about Lisa?" He twisted his hair harder.

"She told you about the drug shipment, so Ronny took care of her."

"Asshole, she never told me anything! Ronny did. He killed her so you wouldn't find out!"

Tim released his hair, and Pyne staggered back with his hands out before him in defense. Tim leveled his pistol at Pyne.

Pyne pleaded, "You said you wouldn't kill me if I did what you asked!" Tim looked at Andrea, still leaning against the tree to Pyne's rear. Their eyes met, and in them, Tim saw an intense plea that he knew he had to answer. He nodded slowly.

"Well, Mike, it's your lucky day! I said I wouldn't kill you and I won't." Pyne's face relaxed and his hands dropped. Tim smiled, then added, "But she will." Andrea fired a burst into Pyne's legs. The drug dealer dropped straight to the ground. Unsteadily, Andrea staggered next to the prostrate, bleeding Pyne and studied his face. In a hoarse voice, she asked, "You were going to break me, Mr. Pyne? Maybe you should spend some time with Salka, too—in hell!" She squeezed the trigger and held it until her Model 10 was empty. Then she collapsed next to his bullet-riddled body.

Fighting back his emotions, Tim gathered her up in his arms and stood. The death of his tormenter satisfied him, but the exfiltration remained, so he turned his mind to more pressing matters. The sound of the boats was growing louder. He kissed Andrea on the forehead and slung her over his shoulders. Next, he gestured towards Ms. Lockery's body. Murphy understood. Her body might link the mess to the old man who had financed them. Murphy lifted her, and they moved silently through the trees towards their exfiltration point.

Pulcinella and Bonning's chopper had landed on the mansion's front lawn. Out and onto the ground quickly, Pulcinella found Robin Island to be as quiet as the dead who remained. The flames on the yacht had eaten through its mooring lines, and from the air, he had watched it floating free across the bay. Meanwhile, the first sight that greeted him upon landing was the remnants of the guest cottage, still burning fiercely behind a front lawn that had been transformed into a cemetery for the unburied.

Pulcinella realized that they had arrived way in advance of their backup, but since the mansion looked quiet, he decided that they would start anyway. Signaling for the chopper to take off and sweep the grounds with its searchlight, he moved out.

Hoping to catch somebody—anybody—still living, he and Bonning split up so they could cover more ground. Pulcinella closed on the mansion. Then he heard a noise from the trees next to the house. He stopped and drew his pistol, then held his breath to listen. Nothing—momentarily, he was uncertain, but he moved closer to the undergrowth anyway. Though his eyes saw little but the shadows beneath the trees, he still sensed something.

Tim Reardon had just reached the edge of the trees next to the mansion when he spotted Pulcinella. He and Wayne froze, hoping that the detective would not see them. At first he was sure his luck had ended and he was going to be arrested. Then he realized that the cop was not moving in his direction, and motioned to Wayne to keep going.

Carefully, they picked their way forward until they reached the mansion. Pausing to look back at the detective, Tim caught his breath as he spotted a flash of gold. Situated behind a tree where the policeman could not see him, Ronny crouched holding a knife. Suddenly, Tim understood—the bastard was going to kill the policeman, and the detective was headed straight for him.

Tim passed Andrea to Wayne, who dropped Ms. Lockery. "Take her and get the hell out here!" he whispered. "Don't worry. . . . I won't talk."

Wayne nodded, and Tim moved fast on the edge of the treeline towards Ronny.

He wished he could get a clear shot at the bastard, but found he couldn't. The angle through the foliage was all wrong, and he would have to shoot through Pulcinella to hit him. He would have to close to arm's distance.

In his mind, he knew it was all over. If he saved the detective, he would be arrested, but he had no choice. If he ran and left a good cop like Pulcinella to die, he was as bad as Pyne. No, he decided, the detective was not going to die tonight.

Closing fast, he realized that he had not placed a new magazine in his Model 10. Reaching concealment within ten feet of Ronny, he slid out his .45 and searched for the detective. Damn, he was too late. Ronny was just feet away from his target's back. As Tim charged, Ronny lunged, wrapping one arm around the detective's neck and raising the knife with the other. Unable to shoot for fear of hitting Pulcinella, Tim dropped his pistol and leapt forward, then grabbed the knife arm, and felt both dealer and cop fall to the ground beneath him. In the process, he lost his grip on Ronny's arm, but the detective had already rolled free. Jumping to his feet, Tim found Ronny up as well, and out of the corner of his eye, he saw the cop groping on the ground for his gun.

Ronny hissed, "You're fuckin' dead, soldier boy!"

Now minus his .45, Tim reached for the Gerber knife in his vest.

Ronny lunged. Tim slipped the attack but felt a hot slash against his ribs. He moved to his right, and the dealer moved left. They cautiously circled each other. Ronny slashed again and Tim went for his arm, but the dealer changed the direction of his thrust. Tim felt ripping pain in his forearm, his fingers opened spasmodically, and his knife fell quietly into the grass. Reacting quickly, he grabbed Ronny's arm and twisted it down viciously. He felt it separate from its socket and heard a whine of pain. Knowing he had his enemy unbalanced, Tim used his leverage to flip the drug merchant to the ground on his stomach. Tim pounced like a cat, grabbed the dealer's chin in his hands, and snapped his neck with a violent twist. Releasing Ronny's head, he sat back on his haunches and breathed deeply. His adrenaline level fell, and he was aware of a crippling pain in his forearm.

He turned and found himself staring down the wrong end of Pulcinella's gun. In the distance, he heard gunfire coming from the channel and smiled. The exfiltration was on.

His legs stiff, Tim rose and stood before Pulcinella. He said,

"You don't need to point that at me, Detective. I'll come without argument."

Pulcinella considered the bleeding soldier, and asked, "You were free and clear, weren't you? I mean, you could have got away, couldn't you?"

"Yes, but I couldn't let him kill you."

"Did you get the girl back?"

"How did you know they had Andrea?"

"We had their phone tapped, and I heard the tape of your voice last night. I wasn't sure they had her, but I figured they might. Is she safe?"

"Yeah, we got her back."

With a sigh, Pulcinella shook his head and moved out of his firing stance. He stood erect and holstered his revolver. He asked, "Is it over now?"

"Yeah, it's over."

"Good, you got a way off this island, you better take it. Now. In about a minute, every law-enforcement official in the New Haven area's gonna be crawling all over this place."

Tim stared at him.

Waving his arm, Tony said, "Move it before I change my mind."

Tim moved. Stooping to pick up his knife and pistol, he turned toward the mansion, then he stopped and looked back at Pulcinella. "Detective, I know you hate open cases, so here's the deal. Heather died because she saw Julian Salka waste a couple of cops who might have compromised another cop Pyne owned. Ronny killed Andrea's sister, Lisa, because he didn't want Pyne to find out he was the one who had told me about the shipment you busted."

"Thanks, soldier. Now get out of here."

Stopping only to pick up his Model 10 and Ms. Lockery's body, Tim ran for the landing site, where he put on his dive gear and prepared to leave. First, he weighted Ms. Lockery's body, then he put her handbag and the ruby from her neck in his day pack. He entered the water and dove smoothly under the surface. His arm throbbed, but he had no time for it then. Deep under the waters off Robin Island, he released the body and watched it disappear into the murkiness below.

* * *

Art Simpson had been in the boat for what seemed like an eternity. He had watched the fires on the island, and heard the gunfire and explosions, but all he knew for sure was what he had heard on the radio. He had heard that they had gotten Rembard and Salka, but little else.

Frustrated, he looked at his watch. The team had already been in there for a half hour. Then, finally his headset came to life once more—they were coming out!

Art sat upright and checked the settings on his transmitter for the hundredth time. They were accurate, so he picked up his night-vision scope and scanned the shore. He saw something moving, increased the magnification, and spotted the boat pulling slowly away from shore. Behind it, the helicopter swept the island with its searchlight.

Soon machine-gun fire erupted from the boat and the chopper veered away from the island toward the firing. In the darkness, a man jumped off the stern of the boat, just before the engine surged and the craft dug into the water and ran for the open sea.

Art saw the police chopper closing fast on the boat, its powerful spotlight sweeping the waves. When the beam was less than two hundred feet behind the boat, he saw a second man jump and disappear into the water. Seconds later, as the searchlight settled onto the boat, Art activated his transmitter.

What happened next made him smile. A staccato burst of what sounded like machine-gun fire exploded from the boat. The helicopter wavered and skewed back slightly; then officers returned fire out the open side door. Art had already keyed the second code into his transmitter. When more fire came from the helicopter, he depressed the transmit button once again, and the boat exploded. Almost in slow motion, a fireball rose from the boat, and heavy shock waves raced over the seas surrounding it. The helicopter wavered once more, and skewed off to escape the pillar of fire and concussion generated by Gonda's case of dynamite. Marveling at the effect, Simpson remained motionless until the debris settled. Where there had once been a boat, there was now nothing but floating dunnage. Smiling, he weighted the transmitter and dropped it over the side, started his small outboard, and chugged for the beach house. The exfil had been a complete success.

CHAPTER FORTY-TWO

Branford

The surviving members of the team finally assembled in the beach house well after 2 A.M. Even as they packed their equipment for movement to Vermont, Stan remained busy tending to the wounded. Generally, they felt proud of their successful mission; however, they knew two of their own were never coming back and they were sickened at the sight of what Pyne had done to Andrea. As they packed the van, they talked quietly among themselves about what they would do with the money—which looked like more than fifteen million dollars—but too much had happened that night for them to fully understand what it all meant.

Tim remained on the couch with Andrea until the others had finished packing. The medic told him that he could treat her physical symptoms, but the psychological damage could be a lot rougher. After all she had been through, Stan projected that she would sleep for many hours to come. Staring down at her still-striking face, Tim wondered why Pyne had left it unmolested. In her deep sleep, she looked as tranquil as a napping infant, but the sight of her body made him wince. There seemed to be more bruises than skin. She had several broken ribs, and Stan wasn't sure how much damage had been done to her internal organs. He would have X rays taken as soon as they settled in Vermont. Tim wondered at the resolve she must have mustered to remain silent. Stroking her matted hair gently, he whispered, "It doesn't matter what they did to you,

Andie, I'll take you on any terms and in any condition. Just come back."

By 4 A.M., the van was packed. Paul and Wayne would remain in the beach house to continue their cover because Stan had to tend his comrades. The rest of the men boarded the van and headed for Vermont—except for Tim. He took the Impala and pointed it towards Rhode Island.

Newport, Rhode Island

It was still dark when Tim passed through the gates of the Whitworth estate, and he had expected that no one would be awake yet. However, much to his surprise, the butler greeted him at the door and ushered him out to the pool where Sean Whitworth waited in his wheelchair, a blanket across his lap to protect his elderly frame from the early morning chill.

Seeing Tim before him, Whitworth waved toward an adjacent chair, and Tim sat. The old man said, "I have had my people monitoring the radio and television for unusual news from the New Haven area. Judging from the numerous stories the reporters have been filing for the past several hours, it would appear that your business is completed."

"Yes, sir."

"Tim, people have been coming to me with news or demands for a very long time. Judging from your reluctance to speak and the expression you have been trying to suppress since you arrived here, I would say that you have come bearing bad news. . . . Please, begin with that."

Tim looked out over the ocean. The sky was beginning to lighten, and the sun would break the horizon in a matter of minutes. He turned to Sean and saw that the old man, too, studied the horizon. Holding out a closed fist, he said, "Sean, I think this originally belonged to you."

Tim reached out, and the old man took his offering. When his fingers felt the shape of the object, pain clouded his eyes. Slowly, he raised his hand and let the gold and ruby necklace dangle from his fingers. "How?" he asked.

Tim explained what he had learned about Jean Lockery on the island and described how she had died. He concluded, "Sir, even if they find the body, I removed all of her identification, so she will end up as a Jane Doe."

Whitworth remained quiet for some minutes. Tim felt awkward, but he dared not disturb the old gentleman in his thoughts. Finally, Whitworth said, "I once thought she was a good woman, and I still do; however, it seems she gave in to a temptation that ultimately became too big for her to ignore. I know you did not wish this. Thank you for handling it as well as you did. Is there anything else I should know?"

"Yes, Frank didn't make it. But I can tell you that he died honorably—defending a friend."

Sean sighed. "You accomplished your mission, but it carried a considerable cost. Would you indulge me now and give me the details?"

Tim Reardon told him the entire story of the mission from beginning to end. When he finally finished, the sun was up.

Whitworth asked, "Do you think you finished the affair completely?"

"I think so, Sean."

"I'm not sure I agree. You may have destroyed the Pyne organization, but there are many like it still in existence. So what did you really accomplish in the end?"

Tim set his jaw and said softly, "I got my retribution, but now I know that it isn't enough. So there is one more thing I would like to do—one thing that might make it all worth it, somehow."

"Yes."

"Sean, we gave up good men tonight. If you would cooperate with us and contribute to what we have in mind, then perhaps there will be many people who will benefit from what happened on Robin Island." With that, Tim described his idea. When he finished, the old man considered it for just a moment, then nodded. He would help them.

Robin Island

As dawn broke, a massive number of law-enforcement officials from every major investigative body in the country descended on Robin Island. They shared few of their many conclusions with the press, who had chartered helicopters and boats to get close to the island. The official story was that a gangland hit had occurred and that suspects would be apprehended soon. In fact, they *were* looking for suspects, but no one, cop or reporter, really believed this was just a hit.

The most influential report came from Oscar Bonning. It took him three days to write it, but when the document was finished, it was by far the most comprehensive, and it was the one that was forwarded to the director of the Drug Enforcement Agency.

Thursday, July 27, 1989—Washington, D.C.

The director told his secretary to keep the door closed and to hold all calls while he read Bonning's report. Though the first half thoroughly detailed the investigation, it was the summary that particularly interested him. He read:

Summary

1. General
The forensic and laboratory evidence discovered on Robin Island has proved largely inconclusive to this point. We do know that the attackers used uniform weaponry with munitions and demolitions of varied origin, but they did not utilize anything unavailable on the international market. The size of the attacking force has been placed at somewhere between five and twelve personnel, but that too is unclear at this time. No bodies or equipment other than shell casings have been recovered from the attackers, and they seem to have worn gloves, so no fingerprints have been found. As a result, little specific information is available about exactly who invaded Robin Island.

Based on evidence available, certain general assumptions may be made. First, the competency level of the attackers was extraordinary. Clearly, they possessed a considerable amount of professional training. Next, though it is clear that at least one of their motives was robbery, they restricted themselves exclusively to stealing money. Rather than taking the drugs, they set all they could find ablaze. This indicates that whoever infiltrated the island that night were not hit men from a rival organization. They were also not just thieves. Instead, they seem to have been motivated by some sort of a vendetta.

There are also questions pertaining to the whereabouts of the at tackers. Strong evidence exists in the form of eyewitness accounts that whoever attacked Robin Island that night died in a boat explosion while attempting to escape. We must consider, however, whether they just want us to believe that this is what happened.

2. Conclusions and Recommendations.
A. It is the opinion of this special agent that the men or women who executed the assault on Robin Island were highly trained professionals who can only be found in the employ of the Central Intelligence Agency or the Special Operations Branch of the United States Armed Forces in organizations such as the SEALS or Special Forces. If this was the case, and the perpetrators are on active duty, then they might be found simply by tracing personnel who were on leave during the period when the assault occurred. This course might give us some legitimate suspects—if they are still alive—whom we can pursue.

B. To our advantage, the Pyne organization has been completely destroyed and cocaine distribution in New England has been temporarily crippled—though doubtless the void will be quickly filled by other sources.

C. Mafia leader DeFrancesco is also dead, and his organization may be presumed to be in complete disarray because of a power vacuum at its top. This too is of benefit to us.

D. Presently, the press has been informed that the events on Robin Island were the result of a gang feud.

E. While it might be possible to locate the perpetrators of the attack on Robin Island, I question whether or not we should move forward in that direction for several reasons.

a. Whoever did this helped us a great deal.

b. Given the mood of the country at this time, and the press deluge that would result if we were to catch the personnel responsible, they will most likely become national heroes for what they did to the Pyne organization.

c. In that event, further vigilante actions of this type would be encouraged, and that could result in serious loss of life and loss of public respect for the Drug Enforcement Administration and other legitimate law-enforcement agencies.

F. Based on these conclusions, it is my recommendation that we continue to charge the events on Robin Island off to gang rivalry and close the investigation. In fact, the events on the island might in fact have occurred as a result of drug-world infighting. If they did not, the only other explanation is that someone heard the call for a "war on drugs," and that someone took it very seriously. We stand to gain the most from the first explanation.

The director placed Bonning's report down on his desk carefully. Impressed with the agent's reasoning and recommendations, he passed the confidential report on to the president with his approval and endorsement. Police in Connecticut would continue to go through the motions, but the government's Robin Island investigation officially ended there.

Northfield Mountains, Vermont

When Tim pulled the old Chevy up to the door of the Vermont hideaway, he found the ever-vigilant Gonda, his arm ensconced in gauze and a sling, armed and waiting on the front porch in case they had been followed. When Tim asked him if he really thought that anyone was still alive to follow them, Gonda shrugged and admitted that it was doubtful, but just in case . . .

Inside, the rest of the men were asleep, except for Stan. Tim located him upstairs in Andrea's room watching and waiting for when she awakened. As he entered the room, Stan asked, "Whitworth like it?"

"Yes, I think he did. We'll get hold of the attorneys to set it up in a couple of days."

Tim approached Andrea's bed and studied her face. Still in a deep sleep, her features showed the same tranquillity they had displayed in Branford. Without taking his eyes off her, he asked, "So what are we going to have when she wakes up?"

"The truth?"

Tim nodded.

"I don't know. She's a strong woman, but damn, she's been through something that would've killed most people. I've treated the superficial wounds. I had her X-rayed this morning, and they were mainly negative, so I have no reason to suspect that any of her internal organs have been seriously damaged. She does have three cracked ribs. Somebody beat her viciously, and that'll leave scars. I just don't know what effects the last two days may have had on her psychologically."

"Is she sleeping or unconscious?"

"She hasn't awakened since the island, but she's not unconscious. Right now it's just total exhaustion. Her body's trying to defend itself through sleep. Let's just wait and see what happens."

Sleeping fitfully in chairs next to Andrea's bed, Tim and Stan waited the rest of the day and all of the night for Andrea to awaken. It was not until well after the sun came up the next morning that her eyes fluttered open.

Tim was awakened by an elbow in his ribs. Opening his eyes, he saw Andrea sitting up in bed looking about her, attempting to gain orientation. Stan, who had given him the nudge, leaned forward anxiously in his chair. Tim said, "Andrea?"

She looked at him, her large green eyes puzzled.

Tim asked, "How are you feeling?"

She looked around the room again, then back at Tim. "Right now I feel like I just survived a plane crash." She looked down at her sheets. "Tim, is it over?"

He replied, "Yes, Andie, it is definitely over."

"Did . . . God, it seems like a dream. Did I really do what I remember doing?"

"Yes, you saved my life and you killed Pyne."

She nodded her head slowly. "How long are you going to be here, Tim?"

"For the rest of my life."

"Do I look as bad as I feel?"

"I don't care how you look—I only care that you're going to be OK, so we can begin making something for ourselves. Remember that word, 'we'?"

She reached for him. He leapt from his chair and held her close. She said, "Yes, I remember the word 'we.'" Tears streamed down her cheeks. After a minute, she pushed him away.

Alarmed, Tim searched her eyes. He asked, "Are you OK?"

"Tim, my darling, I do love you. You know that, but God, I'm hurting." She looked out the window next to her bed.

Stan asked, "Are you hungry?"

She nodded. "Famished, and I would love a cigarette."

Stan said, "Well, Mac's downstairs, and he thinks he's some kind of a chef. I'll go put the geezer to work, and Gonda, insisting you would want one, bought a carton of your brand of cigarettes yesterday."

She smiled a small smile. "Tell Joe and Mac they're sweet and I love them both."

The medic left, and Tim asked, "You want to be alone?"

"Yes, for now. And please, I'm not ready to see the others yet. . . . Did all the others make it?"

"Everyone except Frank and a man you didn't know."

She nodded and Tim left.

Later that afternoon, Tim rejoined her. Mac had brought and set up the television and VCR she had had in her North Haven office, along with the tapes. She was watching *Going My Way* as Tim entered, but she turned down the volume with her remote. She said, "Tim, you and the guys have been so incredible. You thought of everything, and I appreciate it."

"Well, you're kind of a hero to us now. Are you doing better?"

She regarded him with sad eyes. "Sort of."

He nodded, and she continued, "God, I feel dirty. It all seems so incredible. Oh, hell, I went into this with my eyes open. Maybe I got what I deserved."

"No," his voice sounded raspy, "you didn't deserve this."

She said, "I never hated anyone like that before. It felt so damn good to pull that trigger."

"That means you're human."

She replied, "Tim, you came back for me. You saved me. I have some things to work out. I know that. But it's over now, and I think I'll be OK. Just don't go far while I'm working things out."

"I won't. I'm here and I'll stay."

"I know that."

Bad Toelz, West Germany

Mrs. Rhonda Franklin was not surprised by the news the men had just given her. Authorities at the kaserne had informed her the day before that her husband had been lost in a boating accident with his friend Bill Massey off the Massachusetts coast. Still, she had been waiting to hear what had really happened. She had known Joe Gonda, Tim Reardon, and Pete Sayers for many years, and she was glad they had come in person to give her the news. They had also presented her with a properly folded American flag. After they left, she leaned against the door she had closed behind them with it clutched in her hands for several minutes, caught in emotions so complicated she felt paralyzed.

Was her man really gone? Rhonda had been a Green Beret's wife for a long time and had always known it could happen, but now that it really had, it was still a shock. After a moment she lowered her head and turned back towards her living room. As she did, a thin object slipped from the neat folds of her flag and fell to the floor.

Slowly, Rhonda stooped and picked it up. It was a deposit book from a bank in Switzerland, and it bore her name. Turning to the first page, she found that only one transaction had been recorded: a deposit of 1.7 million U.S. dollars.

The Children's Center—New Haven, Connecticut

After thanking the attorney one last time, Dr. Edward Mendez hung up his phone with a flourish; then he stood and walked over to his window to survey his drug-addiction treatment center. The Children's Center catered to adolescents too poor to afford help elsewhere. Recent cuts in government grants had convinced him that he would have to close soon.

Then that attorney had called. He did not know who was offering the two-million-dollar donation, and the lawyer had informed him that the donors wished to remain anonymous but that they would continue to provide additional funds as he needed them. Anonymous or not, Dr. Mendez felt grateful and pleased to accept it. Before the call, he had been debating how to tell his staff that they would have to close the center's doors. Now he suddenly considered expanding.